ORACLE

RIVER OF ORE

C.W. Trisef

Trisef Book LLC

How to contact the author
Website – OracleSeries.com
Email – trisefbook@gmail.com

Oracle – River of Ore
C.W. Trisef

Other titles by C.W. Trisef
Oracle – Sunken Earth (Book 1 in the Oracle Series)
Oracle – Fire Island (Book 2 in the Oracle Series)
Oracle – Solar Wind (Book 4 in the Oracle Series)
Oracle – Mutant Wood (Book 5 in the Oracle Series)

This book is a work of fiction. Any references to historical events, real people, or real locales are used fictitiously. Other names, characters, places, and incidents are the product of the author's imagination.

Written by – C.W. Trisef
Cover designed by – Giuseppe Lipari
Text designed by – Sheryl Mehary
Back cover photography: "Safsaf Oasis, Egypt" credit NASA
Earth Observatory. Used with permission.

CHAPTER 0

THE DOCTOR'S ORDERS

"Welcome home, Lord Lye," said a cold voice from the dock.

"Thank you, Victor," Lye replied to the doctor, sounding rather weary. "It's good to be back at the Deep."

"How was your trip to Fire Island?" Victor asked.

"Successful," Lye told him.

Dr. Cross extended his hand to help his feeble lord out of the small boat that had ferried him from the large battleship floating in the distance. One by one, the rest of the fleet continued to arrive from Fire Island, anchoring sporadically in the deeper waters around the Deep.

"So you captured the boy then?" Cross said hopefully, walking a slight step behind his superior.

"No," Lye sneered, "but the fire element is now

safely within the Oracle, and, for that reason, it was a success." Lye's words were punctuated by the sharp, rhythmic tapping of his white, spiraled cane. "Fire Island is no more—and the same can be said of Bubba and Carmen."

"He was a necessary loss," Cross concluded. "Too bad about *her* though." They had reached the end of the dock and were now walking on rocky terrain. The sound of crashing waves could be heard nearby. "So the boy got away?"

"His name is Ret, Cross," Lye barked, "and he's not a mere boy anymore—he's getting stronger; he's perfecting his powers. He and the Guardian were not easy on me."

"I should have been there to help you," the doctor apologized. "I mean, given your health—"

"I can take care of myself!" Lye snapped. "I need no physician."

"Yes, my lord."

"Just hurry up with the weapon," Lye ordered. "Is it ready yet?"

"Almost," Cross reported with nervousness.

"I need that device in order to subdue Ret," Lye explained. "It can't take much longer. Time is of the essence. Ret is maturing quickly, and the Oracle is hastening its gathering. It wants its elements back. Things are in full motion now."

"I understand."

"Then why is it taking so long?!" Lye hissed.

"It's complicated, my lord," Cross said softly, his head down. "It will be operational soon."

"Let's hope so, for your sake," Lye threatened. "By the way, you might be interested to know I ran into an old friend on Fire Island: Lionel Zarbock."

"The nuclear physicist?" Cross wondered with eagerness.

"Yes," Lye said with pleasure. "He was taken prisoner on one of the ships and will be here soon. His knowledge should prove valuable to you in perfecting the weapon."

"Do you think he'll cooperate?" Cross asked.

"I doubt it," Lye shrugged, "so feel free to do whatever it takes to get him to talk." Lye cackled. "I'll leave you to handle that. All I ask is that you keep him alive."

"As you wish."

The sun was setting over the south Pacific Ocean, its crimson rays reflected in the many puddles strewn across the ground. These were colorful, vibrant pools of warm water, gurgling and steaming like hot springs. Lye's long, black robes swirled the rising mist as he shuffled along.

"And were you able to secure Argo's relic, my lord?" Cross asked with concern.

"No," Lye answered grumpily. "I searched his robes but found nothing."

"So it is in Ret's possession then?"

"I don't know, Cross," Lye growled, perturbed by the reminder.

"So that means they may now have both the key and—"

"Yes, I know!" Lye shouted angrily.

"Forgive me, my lord."

"Bah!" Lye snorted, mocking his minion's plea for mercy.

The landscape had changed from rocky to riparian, with mature trees rising above thick and low-lying shrubbery. The pair arrived at a door, hidden in the lush vegetation, and waited for it to open. They passed through the entryway and marched onward, entering a large and spacious control room. The underground facility was buzzing with activity.

"Lord Lye," a commander said, approaching his master. "We have been unable to locate the approaching aircraft on our radar."

"Keep trying," Lye told him. "It's mostly invisible, but it's out there. I'm sure of it."

"Yes, sir." The commander hurried off.

"An invisible aircraft, sir?" Cross asked.

"It's Coy's ridiculous balloon," Lye scoffed. "They're headed this way, just as planned."

"Excellent," said Cross.

"Now, if you'll excuse me," said Lye, turning down one of the corridors, "I'd like to spend some time in the dungeon before our guests arrive. I've been gone for many days, and I'm sure our resident prisoners have missed me. You know how much I enjoy the sound of their suffering."

"That I do," Cross grinned.

Lye stepped in front of another door. As soon as it opened, the faint cries of incarcerated souls could be heard, bemoaning their miserable fates and rattling their heavy chains.

"Ah," Lye beamed, "music to my ears." He hobbled into the dungeon. "Now let's see if I can make room for six more prisoners."

CHAPTER 1

OLD WOUNDS, NEW SCARS

It was as though Ana had spoken in a foreign language. For several silent seconds, her words failed to register in the stunned minds of her listeners. Everyone stood so petrified with perplexity that she felt the need to restate her claim, this time with a bit more confidence.

"I think it was—"

"I'm sorry, dear," Pauline said sweetly, like a mother humored by her toddler, "what did you say?" Her tone was a mixture of sugar and spice, as if to dilute a brewing embitterment.

"I said," Ana repeated yet again, "I think I saw Dad back there."

"And what makes you think that?" Pauline asked, still choosing not to believe.

"Because he looked just like him," Ana explained with a seriousness that was very uncharacteristic of her.

"Dirty blonde hair, parted on the left side; really tanned forearms, and calves too big for his skinny ankles." With each evidence, Pauline's pretended incredulity seemed to wane. "Of course, he *was* pretty far away, so I couldn't really see his eyes, and he didn't seem to have his usual smile. But I watched him, Mom. I saw how he helped Lye onto that boat-thing—just like how he used to help you out of the car, remember?" Ana took a step back to reenact the familiar move. "He put his right foot forward, then bent over a little and extended his left hand, helping you up gently and using his right hand to steady your shoulder."

"Yes," Pauline mumbled unwillingly, "I—I remember quite well, thank you."

"But even more than what I saw, Mom, is how I felt," Ana continued. "It's not like I've been looking for opportunities over the years to say Dad's back; you know that. I don't look through a crowd to find people who look like him. And I would never make something up or play a joke on you; I know how much you—and I—miss him." Ana seemed to be breaking down Pauline's guise of guile. "But as I watched them—Dad and whoever the other guy was—it was like someone— something—put the idea in my head. It wasn't my own. I tried to dismiss it as crazy, but it kept coming back."

"Heat and exhaustion can play terrible tricks on the mind, Ana," Pauline suggested, her appearance now more perturbed than playful. "This trip has been tiring, to say nothing of all the—all the lava." She flailed her arms in boiling desperation.

"If this trip has taught me anything," Ana said with maturity, "it's that we can't always get what we want. So if you don't believe me, then that's fine. But I just thought you might want to know."

"Sorry to interrupt your heart-to-heart," Mr. Coy said brightly, entering the conversation, "but the girl's story *is* consistent with one of my theories."

"Oh?" Pauline snuffed defensively.

"Oh yes!" Coy countered. "And my theory is this: Lye captured Jaret." While the others furrowed their brows in bewilderment, Coy raised one side of his in self-satisfaction. "Think about it, folks: the bubbles and the burning, the help of the hurricane, no ship wreckage in the storm surge—Lye was trying to enter Sunken Earth when Jaret came on the scene! How else could Lye have lost the Oracle and Ret have wound up in Jaret's raft had the good Coast Guard Captain not intervened? Of course, it's unclear why Jaret is now presumably *helping* Lye, but I wouldn't be too terribly surprised if the evil lord can toy with minds—" then, glancing at Ret, "—even erase one's memory."

"So you're saying my dad's been brainwashed?" Ana concluded.

"We don't know for certain it was your father,"

Pauline reminded. Ana rolled her eyes.

"But what if it is?" Ana affirmed while still trying to honor her mother's judgment, as jaded as it usually was. "Why can't you just believe, even for a moment? Why not give it a chance? Don't you want him back?"

"Of course I want—"

"Then why won't you believe me?"

"Because I'm scared." Pauline's voice died down as her tears showed up. Ana looked away briefly, then back again, not altogether displeased with herself.

"Scared of what, Mom?" Ana probed gently.

"Scared of…scared of…," she stammered. "Look, it's taken this long for me to get comfortable with what happened. It was impossible at first; a part of me had died—you remember. But, as time passed, I guess I sort of rolled all my sorrows and fears into a hope—a hope for the best, and I could determine what the best ought to be, which might be better than the truth."

"What do you mean 'better than the'—"

"What if it's *not* him, Ana?" Pauline countered emotionally. "What if we get our hopes up and 'just believe,' as you put it, but then it turns out different than we imagined? Or worse, what if it *is* him?" Ana looked puzzled. "If he *is* still alive, why has he never returned to us?—called, written a letter—something, anything?! Does he even remember me—you—us? Wouldn't you hope, then, that he really *has* been 'brainwashed'?" She glared at Coy. "Do you think I've never considered these things? What else keeps a widowed woman up at night?"

Ana wasn't sure how to respond.

"What then?" Pauline pressed on. "What hope can I cling to then?" She buried her sobs in her daughter's shoulder.

For being such a shallow woman, Pauline Cooper's insecurities certainly ran deep. Her plight traced its origin to her incredibly small comfort zone, whose size was exactly according to her personal preference. As tragic as was her sweetheart's disappearance-termed-death, it seemed to have happened for a wise purpose, though she herself would never entertain such a thought. Over the last few years, the whole ordeal had acted like a sort of wild wrecking ball, determined to demolish the walls and sweep the cones that zoned off her comfortable quarters. Imagine her displeasure when another ball, this time the Oracle sphere (though more like Pandora's Box), ran ashore and then amuck in her simple life. Amid all this quaking and shaking, she had thus far elected to buzz about her crumbling safehouse, attempting to take some cover or save the china. But now, in this moment, a profound change was taking root, perhaps because there was, at last, nothing left to hide behind.

As a result of the tense mother-daughter discussion, an acute uneasiness permeated the very strands of the wicker basket as the hot-air balloon bobbed above the clouds. Paige, the great peacemaker, decided to offer a suggestion.

"You know," she said, treading lightly, "we're already following Lye's ships so that we can rescue Lionel. Maybe we'll be able to help Mr. Cooper, too—if it really is him," she added for Pauline's sake, earning a frown from Ana.

"Excellent idea!" Mr. Coy beamed. "That's my girl." Putting his arm around her, they half-embraced, and, for once, it did not look all that awkward. "Ishmael," Coy excitedly addressed his loyal hand, "westward ho!"

"Yes," replied Ishmael from the controls, having already received this same command, "still ho-ing westward, sir."

There was only one person in the floating vessel who had yet to say a word since Ana's disconcerting announcement, and he had no intention of acting to the contrary. This was not because Ret had nothing to say but rather because he was not entirely convinced anyone would understand.

For, of a truth, his muted tongue juxtaposed his swirling mind—swirling almost as tumultuously as the ocean below, where a massive whirlpool made it seem like the Titans had just flushed their personal commode. The whitewater waves had now fully swallowed Fire

Island. The sinking, volcanic islet to their east was wholly unrecognizable, as it had long since fragmented into a thousand lava-strewn pieces before plunging into the underground magma chamber where Ret and the Guardian, Argo, had foiled Lye's attempt to procure the fire element. It had been a heated fight, to say the least. Lye had proved, yet again, to be a very curious opponent. Though clearly at odds with Ret, Lye did not seem to be the most menacing of nemeses. Twice he had tried to prevent Ret from acquiring elements, but all of Lye's other actions appeared to have aided Ret: Miss Carmen with the mark of the moai on her back, Principal Stone's apparently inconsequential loss of the fire-prone and porous rock from his Keep, the fact that Lye had never threatened Ret with death. Of course, on more than one occasion Lye had hinted at some previous alliance between the two of them—that they were once partners working together with a common objective. Could it be that Lye was actually helping Ret to collect the elements, and, if so, was it for a truly unselfish purpose or simply because he needed Ret's scars? Or vice versa: was Ret actually helping Lye to collect the elements? He shuddered at the thought.

Thus Ret's unconquerable hopefulness caused him to wonder if Lye might somehow be an ally—almost akin to a distant relative—on his First Father's side, once-removed, perhaps? Or, though certainly unbecoming of a veteran villain, was it just that Lye had mixed a bit too much friendliness in his fiendishness and was now perpetuating Ret's confusion in order to cover up his own blunder?

Friend or faux pas? Ret wasn't sure, unaided by the flood of emotions washing over him as the smoky specter of Fire Island faded out of sight.

Wait. Where had he seen this before?

Ah yes: on the other side of the globe, in the ocean called Atlantic, where the civilization of Sunken Earth had drunk its demise. Ret was beginning to see a sort of pattern throughout all of this: a world within our world, unknown to the latter except for those who exploited the former; populated by a people who were rich in heart but poor in everything else, victims of a select few with insatiable thirst for power and dominion. And then, one unscheduled day, a random young man showed up—from out of the sea or out of the sky, either way it was out of the blue—and turned everything upside-down from the inside out.

But the thing that impressed Ret more than anything else was the impeccable timing of it all. Thus far, it had proven to be a monumental task just to get to each of the locations where the elements were hidden, greeted by doubt and disbelief at every turn. But as soon as Ret and his unconventional cohorts arrived on stage, everything fell into place like a well-rehearsed play. As if all nature was on his side, Ret was able to procure the earth and fire elements. Yet, despite the gloom and doom that followed—the slaughtered masses; the cascading mountainsides and collapsing ceilings; the swirling, gaping voids left in the earth's crust and oceans' waters—yes, through it all, one solitary thing shined brighter than the sun: the Oracle.

Undimmed by destruction! Untarnished by tyranny! It was the Oracle that was in control; Ret was merely the vehicle who, under the hood, fit the required model to a tee. Indeed, it was Ret's lack of an ulterior agenda that jived so perfectly with the Oracle's decreed yet unhurried schedule.

"You okay, Ret?" Mr. Coy asked, stirring Ret from his endless thoughts, which he hardly ever shared. As if to encourage candid conversation, Coy casually leaned forward to place his arms on the rim of the basket, mimicking Ret's pensive position.

"So what's your plan for rescuing Lionel?" Ret inquired, purposely evading Coy's question.

"I was thinking we'd lower you on deck and let you burn anything that stands in your way," said Coy jokingly. Then, noticing how Ret remained unamused, he added, "Unless you have a better idea?"

"No."

Patting Ret's back caringly, Mr. Coy said, "Don't worry, Ret. We'll make sure we get Lionel back." Then, as if prompted by lingering guilt, he corrected, *"I'll make sure we get Lionel back."*

On the other side of the basket, though seemingly worlds apart, another dialogue was taking place, this one between Ana and her mercurial mother.

"Oh, Ana, dear," Pauline said giddily, "I just can't wait to see—what if it is him? What if my Jaret really is alive, and we're this close? Oh, it's been so long!" She was anxiously combing her hair with her fingers, as if to spruce it up a bit. "Can't this balloon fly any faster?"

"Good grief," Ana mumbled to Paige at her mom's fickle nature. "Maybe I shouldn't have said anything."

"What's that?" Paige wondered, pointing at a strange-looking thing that had just appeared on the horizon. The Cooper women immediately fixed their attention on the faraway object. It lay directly in their path, mostly westward but also a bit to the south, and still well ahead of the fleet of ships that the balloon was pursuing. With each passing second, the unidentified destination grew in width, like an approaching landmass. Given their aerial perspective, the basket riders could see beyond the periphery and a bit inland.

"It looks like..." Ana guessed, squinting, "...almost like a rainbow."

"Yeah, sorta," Paige somewhat agreed, "or like an oil spill or something."

"It certainly is colorful," Pauline added.

"What's all the hubbub about?" Mr. Coy, the adventure lover, chimed in merrily, leaving Ret's side and striding over to where the ladies all stood staring.

"There's something strange up ahead, Dad," Paige instructed, pointing past the ships, "way out there."

Mr. Coy had scarcely laid his eyes on the object in question when his entire face turned white as a ghost. In an instant, it seemed all the life and love had been sucked out of him, leaving him a stone-cold statue. For many moments, he neither blinked nor breathed.

"Dad," Paige pressed, having glanced back to make sure he was looking in the right direction, "are you okay?" No reply. "Dad? DAD!"

Suddenly, Mr. Coy became conscious again, inhaling like a desperate swimmer would gasp for air. He looked at no one, his eyes wide and pupils tiny. He was breathing heavily, almost hyperventilating. A phantom stressor had seized his psyche; a locked-away memory had punctured his heart.

"Turn the balloon around," Mr. Coy demanded in no uncertain terms.

"But, sir—" Ishmael began to protest.

"I said turn around!" Coy barked. "That's an order!"

"Yes, sir," Ishmael obeyed. "Forgive me." Silence prevailed for a second or two as the vessel commenced to turn.

"Is everything alright, Dad?" Paige asked cautiously.

"We're going home," Coy announced coldly, rummaging through his supplies.

"Say what?" Ana balked.

"Going home?" Paige questioned.

"You can't be serious," Pauline put forth.

To everyone's chagrin, Mr. Coy made no answer. Ishmael had nearly completed the turn.

"But, Dad," Paige persevered. "Why are we going home? Are we in danger?"

Pauline joined in, "What are you so worried about all of a sudden?"

"Is there some leprechaun monster up ahead on rainbow land or something?" Ana mocked.

Rather than acknowledge their concerns, Mr. Coy continued to sift through his belongings, as if searching for something.

"What about Lionel?" Paige interrogated.

"The heck with Lionel," Ana interjected, "what about my dad?"

"Yes," Pauline asserted, their tones collectively growing more impatient, "my husband is...er—could be—on one of those ships. I demand an explanation."

Rummaging.

"Ishmael," said Ana, directing her pleading to the person who was literally in charge of the craft, "never mind what crazy Coy said. Turn this baby back around, and let's get this show on the road."

"Ishmael," Coy warned, waltzing to his side with two oxygen masks in hand, "you have your orders." He shoved one of the masks into Ishmael's hands, who promptly put it over his face.

As much as Ret wished to participate in the ongoing protest against Mr. Coy's unfounded decision, he was thoroughly distracted by something much closer at hand: a new scar had quite suddenly illuminated on the palm of his left hand. In fact, he began to feel it light up at precisely the same moment when Paige had pointed out the curious object on the horizon, which is why he never came over to gawk at it with the rest of them, choosing instead to study his new scar. It was on the same hand as the mark of the moai statue, which, now that the fire element had been collected, was still fully visible but not luminescent. Eventually, Ret stood and turned to face his comrades to announce the exciting news.

But the scene before him was one of mutiny, the three females in an uproar. While Ana was trying to tear the controls away from Ishmael, Pauline was following Mr. Coy's every step like a bloodhound, her lips flapping and finger pointing, with Paige unsure of what to do.

At the height of the chaos, Pauline grabbed Mr. Coy's head, ripped off his oxygen mask, and slapped him square across the face. The sound of her smack made the clouds gasp and echoed in the heavens. Everyone abruptly stopped and stood motionless, waiting for Mr. Coy's reaction.

Mr. Coy, who had scarcely winced, closed his eyes for a few seconds, still facing Pauline, who had her white-knuckled hands positioned on her sturdy hips. His assaulted cheek was growing rosy, and a fresh scrape had appeared where Pauline's wedding ring had struck his skin. Opening his eyes slowly, Mr. Coy raised a clenched fist, and, for a moment, it looked like he might retaliate, despite Pauline's unflinching scowl. Instead, he opened his fist and dropped a small canister that, upon hitting the ground, exploded and released a high-pressure gas, which quickly filled the basket and immediately put to sleep every unmasked person.

Mr. Coy, still holding his breath, bent down to retrieve his oxygen mask and remarked, after putting it on, "I can't stand that woman."

"You hide it very well," Ishmael commented through his mask.

Mr. Coy spent the next few minutes tending to the balloon's snoozing passengers. He straightened out each of the bodies that had slumped to the floor, then outfitted them with a blanket and pillow to ensure their comfort for the long journey home. He did so gently, even though the extra-strength gas would ensure their unconsciousness long after they returned home. The group was much more agreeable now that they were asleep.

Instead of chasing a setting sun, they were now fleeing from it, and the sky quickly faded to blackness. Knowing it had been a very long and strenuous day, Mr. Coy offered to relieve Ishmael at the helm, recommending he get some rest. Ishmael gratefully obliged and promptly joined the others in deep slumber.

At last, Mr. Coy was alone with his thoughts—his terrible, dreadful, lonesome thoughts. For miles upon miles, he stared hopelessly into the pitch blackness above, below, and all around him, haunted by bad memories and taunted even more so by the good ones. Warm tears dribbled down his cold, windswept face, the tiny liquids belying the vast volume of grief they represented. His regrets knew no mercy.

Owing to a lesson he had learned long ago to never travel the same route twice when conducting questionable business, Mr. Coy purposely bent the balloon on a return course that was completely different from the one they had taken to get to Fire Island. Rather than heading north and hugging the coastlines of Peru, Ecuador, and Columbia, Mr. Coy steered the airship south around the bottom tip of the South American continent. Still choosing to float a ways off shore, he rounded Cape Horn, then bore north along Argentina, Uruguay, and Brazil. In the darkness of night, the land's great coastal cities sparkled and shined, each as sleepless as was Mr. Coy. Montevideo, Rio de Janeiro, Recife—he had been to them all, which only exacerbated his hemorrhaging heart.

In its constant drift northward, the balloon at length came upon the wide delta where the monstrous Amazon River poured into the Atlantic Ocean. Mr. Coy recognized it quite easily, where large islands sit in a massive mouth fed by sprawling tributaries. He gazed upon it only briefly, however, because a light glowing nearby had caught his attention. It was coming from Ret, who was lying on his back with his hands on his chest. Knowing the effects of the sleeping gas would not wear off for several more hours, Mr. Coy inched closer to investigate, expecting the light to be coming from a neglected wrist watch or ignored cell phone.

Finding Ret still sound asleep, Mr. Coy unfolded his limp hands. They were empty, but the light persisted. And then he saw it: a new scar, shining brightly on the palm of Ret's right hand, just next to the clearly visible scar of the hook and triangle that had led them to Sunken Earth. Coy analyzed the new scar for several moments, but, as usual, it neither rang bells nor jogged memories. In fact, only half of the scar seemed to be lit. Vexed, he replaced Ret's hand and returned to the balloon's control panel, relieved at least to have finally found something to take his mind off other things. A few miles later, the lighted scar faded away completely until it was again indiscernible.

For the remainder of the return trip to Tybee, Mr. Coy's thoughts ran wild, while Ret's dreams did the same, both unaware that they each had seen a different new scar.

CHAPTER 2

A PIECE OF WORK

The Coopers awoke in their own beds the next morning, each incensed to find they hadn't been dreaming.

"That lousy snake!" Ana yelled as soon as she opened her eyes. "He drugged us—he actually *drugged* us. What a big ninny!" She stormed into Ret's room. "Can you believe that guy?"

Ret rolled over, still half-asleep.

"I mean, I'm a reasonable person," Ana continued, starting her usual methodical walk as she thought out loud. "I was willing to talk it out." She straightened a strand of her disheveled hair as she passed the mirror on Ret's dresser. "But he wasn't even willing to discuss it—he didn't say a word. Come on; be a man!"

"He was being coy," Ret mumbled into his pillow, sharing his sister's sentiments. "It's what he does best."

"Well, frankly, I've had quite enough of it," Ana asserted. "I want nothing to do with that man; my nerves can't tolerate any more of his...of his..." then, finding the right term "any more of his shenanigans."

Impressed, Ret remarked, "Nice word choice."

"Yeah, well," Ana steamed, "I can think of a few other choice words that I'd like to—" Just then Pauline appeared in the doorway.

"Good morning," she said pleasantly, untying her cooking apron from behind her back. "If you two can collect yourselves, I'd love for you to join me at the breakfast table."

"Super," Ana cheered, leaving the room. "I'm so hungry I could eat a house."

"You mean *horse?*" Ret corrected, following her downstairs.

"Same diff."

Their modest table accommodated four but always saw three, all of whom sat in their usual seats. As prescribed by propriety, Ret was last to serve himself a stack of waffles, then waited for his turn with the syrup and fruit topping.

Ana picked up where she had left off. "Why do you think Mr. Coy acted so—"

Pauline held up her hand to silence her daughter. "I don't want to hear another word about what happened," she said sternly. "I know you're upset; we all are. But not another word—do you understand, young lady?"

"Yes, ma'am," said Ana, correctly interpreting her mother's tone.

"Now," Pauline continued in a softer voice, "let's talk about something else, shall we? Let's see..." She groped for a new subject—any new subject but the current one. "...School resumes on Monday."

"Lame," Ana responded, her mouth full of waffle.

"The day before that is New Year's," Ret pointed out.

"Of course!" Pauline celebrated. "Let's figure out some New Year's resolutions!"

"Lamer," Ana moaned.

"Ana's birthday is coming up," Ret added.

"Now we're talking!" applauded Ana, suddenly springing forward in her chair. "My sweet sixteen! It's gonna be amazing." While she went to fetch pencil and paper, Ret exchanged humored glances with Pauline.

"This ought to be good," he whispered, Pauline grinning in agreement.

"Don't worry, Mom," said Ana, returning to her seat. "I've already got it all planned out. I figure we can rent out the banquet hall downtown for the night—I mean, come on, we're gonna need lots of space."

"Space for what, I wonder?" Pauline asked sweetly.

"For the dance floor, of course!" Ana explained. "There'll be a mechanical bull, catered food, a mariachi band—the whole twelve yards." Ret snorted at Ana's idiomatic error.

"A mariachi band, hmm?" Pauline asked.

"Yeah," Ana carried on, her excitement building as she added to her list. "The whole school will be invited, so I reckon a mariachi band will span all cultural barriers, you know?"

"Good thinking," Pauline said sarcastically.

"Does that mean there will be a piñata?" Ret teased.

"No," Ana dismissed, "but I *am* working on a design for bilingual invitations: You're invited to my sweet 16! Mi quinceañera!"

"Uh," Ret interrupted, "I think that's when they turn fifteen."

"Close enough," Ana said, undeterred. "I still need to find a dress, make party favors, schedule a manicure—" She scribbled each item on her growing to-do list.

"I admire your ambition, dear," Pauline finally reigned in, "but I have one question." Ana, who thought she had covered every jot and tittle, stared at her mother. Pauline asked, "How are you going to pay for all of it?"

"I knew you were going to ask that," Ana confessed with sudden disappointment.

"I'm sorry, young lady," Pauline apologized without remorse, "but there is no room in the family budget for an extravagant party. We just can't afford it."

"But Mom—" Ana whined.

"If you want this party to happen so badly," Pauline informed lovingly, "then *you* can get a job, and *you* can pay for it."

At the thought of getting a job, Ana fell back in her chair, threw her pencil up on the table, and crossed her arms in defeat. "Then you probably don't want to hear what else I was going to tell you," she pouted.

"Oh?" Pauline said. "There's more?"

Suddenly perking up, Ana declared, "I want to get my driver's license!"

"Watch out, world," Ret snickered. Ana flicked a syrupy waffle crumb on her plate in Ret's direction, and it stuck to his cheek.

"I think that's a terrific idea," Pauline admitted. "I'd be happy to take you down to the DMV next week to get started on the paperwork."

"Great!" Ana clapped. "Then, afterward, we can go car shopping!"

Pauline choked on her orange juice. "Car shopping?"

"Yeah," said Ana coolly. "Once I get my license, I figure we'll need more than one car, considering all the driving I'll be doing."

"And where, may I ask, will you be driving?" Pauline inquired.

"Back and forth to school," then, for emphasis, she added, "every single day; and other places—you know, like the movies, dances, beach days, road trips."

"You can take the bus to school, you can get rides from your friends, and you won't be going on any road trips without *me,*" Pauline insisted.

"But Mom—"

"I'm sorry, dear, but you will not be getting your own car," came Pauline's terms. "You can use the family car."

"That hunk of junk?" Ana protested.

"You could always get a scooter," Ret said as an option. Ana melted in her chair.

"How about a less expensive one?" Ana begged. "I'd settle for a fixer-upper—you know, a cute old VW bug or something?"

Pauline shook her head. "A car is a luxury, and they are not cheap. After you factor in registration fees and insurance costs, not to mention the outrageous price of gas, I'm afraid we just—"

"—Can't afford it," Ana completed the sentence. "You're always saying that, Mom. 'We can't afford this' and 'We can't afford that.' I hate it when you say that!"

"Well, learn to love it, sweetheart," said Pauline without sympathy, "because that's life. If we start saving now, maybe someday we can get you your own car—" then, upon seeing Ana's eyes light up, she added with emphasis, "—a small, *used* one. Until then, there's the family car, and if you'd like to use it, all I ask is that you help pay for gas."

"So I'd need to get a job regardless," Ana surmised unhappily.

"Precisely," Pauline smiled. Then she rose from her seat and went outside to get the mail.

"Too bad about your birthday party," Ret said now that Pauline had stepped out of the room. "It sounded like a lot of fun."

"Oh, Ret, don't be ridiculous," Ana shrugged, her energetic fantasies now subdued by harsh realities. "That was all a big act."

"Really?"

"Of course," she said broadly. "I knew Mom would never go for it. That's why I told her about it *before* I brought up the car idea: I figured she'd feel guilty about not letting me do the party, so she'd be more willing to get me a car."

"Well, that plan failed," Ret observed.

"Yeah," Ana sighed, "but it was worth a shot. Besides, who in their right mind likes mariachi music anyway?" Ret nodded in agreement. "I guess this means I have to get a job."

Ret reached for the stack of scratch paper next to

Ana and wrote the words "Ana's Car Fund" on one of the sheets in big letters. Then he dabbed his finger in the puddle of unused syrup on his plate and wiped a drop on the back of the paper, providing enough adhesive for it to stick to the drained pitcher of orange juice in the center of the table. He found a penny in his pocket and dropped it into the container.

"We're on our way," he laughed as the copper coin bounced at the bottom.

Ana grinned appreciatively and said, with a bit of sarcasm, "Keep it coming, moneybags."

O   O   O

Tybee High had changed little over the course of the winter recess. While girls and boys reported on new clothes and toys, teachers and administrators reminisced of fun vacations and family get-togethers. When asked what he had done over the holidays, Ret dodged the details by simply stating that he had gone—

(—to Machu Picchu, the lost city of the Incas, whose Intihuatana Stone combusted to reveal a pair of cleats, linked to a mystic portal that toyed with time and took them to Lake Titicaca, whose clan of floating-island dwellers led them to the Sacred Rocks that would transport them to the navel of the world, even Easter Island, where Ret jumped inside an active volcano, battled a dark lord, and rightfully claimed a hallowed flame, then escaped an eruption, gave chase to a fleeing fleet, and circumvented the entire South American continent in an invisible hot-air balloon—)

—out of town.

Yes, returning to school on that cold, January day was something of an otherworldly experience. It was like Ret had been to Mars and back without anyone even noticing. No wonder he felt so alienated. Did no one realize what he had experienced? They cheered how elves had stuffed their stockings while he mourned how moai had crushed his rivals; he cared not for video games that were hard to resist but for a real island that now ceased to exist. Ret wished to unload on someone— anyone—but everyone seemed too preoccupied with trivial things—such as, say, eggnog.

Just minutes into the school day's morning announcements, Ret lost interest and started drawing on the palm of his left hand. With little success, he was trying to trace what he could remember of the new scar that had shown up there. Seated beside him in the next aisle over was Paige, who was gazing into Ret's heart as longingly as he was staring into his palm. Ever since returning home, Paige had sensed a wedge growing between her and Ret, no doubt a result of her father's wildly unpopular veto in the hot-air balloon that abruptly ended their westward chase. In yet another effort to mend the hard feelings, Paige quickly sketched a broad smiley face across the palm of her own hand and laid it face-up on Ret's desk. Ret pretended not to notice.

Suddenly, a new voice took command of the announcements.

"Principal Stone here." Ret exchanged anxious looks with Ana, who was seated on his other side. "I regret to inform you that Miss Carmen, our former volleyball coach, will not be returning to our school." Several disappointed groans erupted from the class, all uttered by young men. "She has elected to remain in her native country. I am sure Mrs. Johnson, our assistant coach, will continue the team's tradition of excellence as our new head coach."

"Sounds like you've got a new coach," Ret informed Ana, pretending the news had come as a surprise.

"No," said Paige, inserting herself into the conversation, "Ana and I are planning to quit the team."

"Yep," Ana said satisfactorily, "that ship has sailed. Besides, something has to give if I'm ever going to find time for a job."

"You still going job hunting today after school?" Paige asked.

"Yeah; Ret's coming, too."

"You're looking for work, too, Ret?" Paige wondered curiously, trying to get him to talk to her.

"No," Ana answered for him, "he's just gonna be my bodyguard. Mom has to go into Savannah to run some errands this afternoon, so she said she'd drop me off at the mall and let me look around while she's gone. But only if Ret would come with me."

"Wanna take my place?" Ret offered Paige, not exactly thrilled about his after school plans.

"I can't," she declined. "I have to meet with my academic decathlon team this afternoon."

"I didn't know you were in that," said Ret, impressed.

"Yeah," Paige blushed, "it's just for fun, really."

"Suit yourself," Ana said playfully, "but don't have too much 'fun' with your smarty-pants friends at your automatic decagon meeting—or whatever it's called." Paige chuckled to herself as their teacher got up to begin his lecture.

◯   ◯   ◯

"Now Ana," said Pauline as they backed out of the driveway, "we'll be passing plenty of places along the way. If you'd like to stop at a store or restaurant, just let me know." They entered the main road that would take them north through the heart of Tybee Island, then west toward the large city of Savannah. "What sort of job are you hoping to find?"

"Something nice," Ana described, "and not too dirty. One that pays well, maybe with some benefits. A place with cool people who will recognize my talents."

"How about the Crusty Chicken?" Pauline suggested as they drove by the local fast-food restaurant on the corner.

"You couldn't pay me to work *there*," Ana vowed.

"Funny," Ret reasoned within himself, "I thought that was the point of a job."

It was not a very long drive to their destination. The landscape had quickly transformed from low-lying marshlands and winding waterways to mature trees and plenty of cement. Pauline pulled up to one of the entrances into the mall, where an anxious Ana and a reluctant Ret stepped out.

"I'll pick you up here in two hours," Pauline called out before departing.

"Two hours?" Ana wondered as the car drove off. "How long does it take to find a job?"

"Maybe we'll have time to get a corndog," Ret hoped as they headed indoors.

Unlike all of her previous trips to the mall, on this occasion Ana was not seeking handbags or foot lotions. Instead of looking for signs advertising clearance items and BOGO sales, she was searching for banners bearing "now hiring" or "inquire within." For the first time, she had come with a mind to work, not to shop; to make money, not to spend it.

After several minutes of fruitless walking, Ana said in frustration, "Isn't anybody hiring in this joint?"

"Not in this economy," Ret sighed, repeating a common phrase he had heard on the news and read in the paper over the last several months.

"Well, no one's paying me to walk around and look pretty," said Ana. "I guess I'll just have to take a stab in the dark somewhere." They halted in front of one of Ana's favorite clothing stores. "Wait here," she bade Ret. "This shouldn't take long." With her head held high, she waltzed inside, only to return a few moments later.

"So?" Ret asked.

"The first thing the lady asked me was if I had any retail experience," she explained, "and when I told her I didn't, she thanked me for my interest."

"That's it?"

"Yeah."

"Well, it's a start," Ret said optimistically.

Their next stop was at a shoe outlet. Ana girded up her loins and marched in but was back at Ret's side soon thereafter. Ret waited for an explanation.

"This time," Ana began, with slightly less vim, "they asked if I had any money-handling experience."

"Did you at least say something like you're willing to learn?"

"I told him about the wicked lemonade stand I made in third grade," said Ana, "but apparently that doesn't count as 'experience' in his book."

"At least we're making progress," said Ret. "You were in there about 30 seconds longer than the first." Ana feigned a smile.

In the ensuing fifteen minutes, Ana traipsed into about as many businesses, each bearing no fruit. In addition to questioning the extent of her real-world experience, she was met with a host of other responses and excuses. Several stores only accepted online applications; some only hired applicants of at least eighteen years of age. Many were not looking to add any more new hires to their ranks; others were trying to cut existing employees from their payrolls.

Apparel stores, photography studios, electronics huts, pet shops—at length, they arrived at a place specializing solely in luggage. Ana collected her courage and trudged inside.

"Excuse me," she politely greeted the man behind the counter, "are you hiring?"

"You should ask the manager," said the middle-aged man.

"Okay, may I speak with him or her?"

"You are."

"Oh...good," Ana said awkwardly. "Well then, manager, I was wondering if you might be hiring?"

"That depends," explained the man. "Do you have any experience?"

The odd man's mentioning of the e-word instantly conjured up an internal inferno of annoyance within Ana. However, she swallowed her hot displeasure and persevered, this time employing a different strategy.

"Yes, as a matter of fact, I *do* have experience," she stated proudly. "I am a straight-A student most of the time; I just finished a highly successful volleyball season on the varsity team, of which I was captain, sort of; I always help my mother with her PTA duties; and I was a Girl Scout for a couple of weeks." With dignity, she waited for the man's response to her oral résumé.

"Yes, but do you have any experience with *luggage?*"

Ana exploded. "Who in the world needs experience with luggage?!" she cried, fueling her flailing arms with all the discontent from the day. "I mean, come on— really? All you do is zip it up. How hard can it possibly be to work with luggage?" The strange man was slowly starting to cower behind the counter. "YES! I have plenty of *experience* zipping stuff up—pants and sweaters and boots and backpacks. Oh, and sleeping bags!—those are nice and long, aren't they?" Ana's scene had earned the attention of the few other shoppers in the store. "And how about Ziploc—does that count as *experience?*" The manager had grabbed the phone and asked the operator to get him security. "Want me to zip it, do you? Calling in the big dogs, eh? Well, don't bother; I'll just zip right out of here." She huffed off towards the door, knocking over a large suitcase along the way and shouting "Zip-a-dee-doo-dah!"

Ana stormed out of the luggage shop and plopped herself next to Ret on the bench where he had been waiting for her. He had heard her entire exchange with the manager. She sighed, then slouched in her seat, waiting for Ret to say something.

"Corndog?" he said at last.

Ana's stomach agreed.

After lunch, Ret helped Ana come to the conclusion that there were other employment opportunities beyond the mall, and they decided to continue her job search at other locations in the vicinity. They left the mall and walked to a nearby office complex, whose long directory bore the names of accounting businesses, law firms, and even dental practices.

"Get comfy," she instructed Ret, determined to visit every suite if necessary. She hurried off.

Rather than twiddle his thumbs in the large, marbled lobby, Ret chose to go for a walk. It wasn't very often that he found himself in Savannah, so he thought he'd take a look around. He exited the building, trekked across the parking lot, and headed toward downtown.

Old town Savannah was something of a gem.

Though by no means a metropolis, it had all the common characteristics of a bustling city: hotels and hospitals, buses and bridges, railways and restaurants. And yet, woven throughout all the usualness was an abiding authenticity—a sort of universal uniqueness, or, better still, the pixie dust bestowed by a long, rich history. Ret could see it in the charming eateries and restored storefronts. He could sense it in the mortar between the cobblestones under his feet. He could feel it in the aged air that rustled the broad canopies created by ancient oaks. Ret found it a truly fascinating place, reckoning it would take him just as long to fully appreciate its antiquity as it had taken the city to accomplish it.

Continuing his self-guided tour, Ret observed how the streets had been laid out long ago as one giant grid. Straight avenues frequently intersected perfectly perpendicular ones, creating dozens of short blocks and the need for countless stop signs. As he ventured further away from the river, the shops and cafes gradually gave way to houses and dwellings. A narrow, two-lane road ran down the middle of each block, with a row of a dozen or so homes on either side. The establishments were deeper and taller than they were wide, looking somewhat like they belonged in the crowded hills of San Francisco.

Ret turned off one of the main boulevards and onto a quaint residential block. He strode along the clean-swept sidewalk, with its uncluttered gutters and weed-free cracks, happily admiring the picturesque homes. Though their foundations had been poured generations ago, each house bore evidence of modern renovation: fresh paint, new lumber, snug windows. At each residence, a small set of stairs led from a little but well-groomed yard up to a raised porch. Ret particularly fancied one staircase where the forward-facing front of each step was covered in a sort of creeping, clinging vine. No two homes were identical—some with pairs of square windows or others with one large circular one; outdoor shutters rather than indoor drapes; grassy bushes instead of leafy shrubs—yet not one was unattractive or uninviting.

At the end of the block, Ret walked straight across the intersection and continued his pleasant stroll where the same street resumed on the other side. He shuffled along the dusty parkway, brushing aside the litter and trying not to step in broken glass. Blankets of smashed acorns obscured swaths of the street, run over by heavy tires, then neglected. Ret avoided the long, messy grasses and weeds, thinking they might harbor chiggers. The dwellings were shabby, with well-worn walls and ill-kempt corners. There were portions of porches where holes had rotted through, carefully avoided by those rocking in rickety chairs. Through shattered window panes, Ret spied cold inhabitants gathered around wood-burning stoves that belched black smoke through splotchy rooftops. A place whose palette was an over-whelmingly graying brown, some might call it condemned, though others called it home.

Ret reached another intersection, profoundly puzzled by what he had just observed. He made a quarter turn and walked a good ways to an entirely different street. He sauntered along another nice stretch of stunning houses, then crossed, continued, and hurried past another row of depressing shanties. He did it again and again, always selecting a new location at random. At one point, he stopped in the middle of a vacant intersec-tion, glancing back and forth at yet another pair of different city blocks. How was it that two groups of homes could be so different—technically on the same street but actually worlds apart? Ret hadn't seen such stark inequality since his tour of the levels at Sunken Earth or his visit of the floating islands at Lake Titicaca, yet here it was once again, but this time in his own backyard.

With head lowered and hands pocketed, Ret remained in deep contemplation all the way back to the office complex. He arrived just minutes before Ana returned to the lobby, shaking her head wordlessly when Ret stared at her for a report. With heavy hearts, they returned to the mall and waited for Pauline to pick them up.

"Why the long face?" Pauline inquired when Ana slid into the front. Ret was always content with the backseat.

"I tried dozens of places," an exasperated Ana explained, "and no one wanted to hire me. I'm a failure."

"Don't take it personally, dear," Pauline soothed. "You'll find your niche somewhere soon. The important thing is to keep trying."

Slouching, Ana propped her knees on the dash and sighed, "Let's go home."

The drive back to Tybee was silent, save for the loud hum of the old engine of the family car. Pauline frequently peered in her rearview mirror to check on Ret, only to find him gazing out his window, his face expressionless and his eyes half closed. Pauline knew the look: Ret was lost in his private thoughts again. For the entire journey, she desperately tried to think of something to say to him but couldn't come up with anything. She never quite knew how to help Ret.

Now only a matter of blocks from home, Pauline remarked, "You know, you could always apply at the Crusty Chicken." She said it mostly as a joke to get her children to snap out of their doldrums.

"Might as well," Ana yawned. "What've I got to lose?"

Surprised yet proud at her daughter's persistence, Pauline steered the car into the restaurant's parking lot, where Ana spilled out and lumbered inside.

"Say a prayer for her," Pauline whispered to Ret as they watched Ana slip through the door.

Perhaps brought on by the dinnertime rush, the Crusty Chicken seemed extremely busy in Ana's estimation, even though she claimed no experience in the food industry. Without haste, she entered the queue and waited patiently for her turn at the counter. While in line, she observed the swamped staff, each employee assuming multiple duties in a mad dash to meet the demands of clamorous customers. All in all, Ana felt like she was standing in the middle of a pinball machine.

"What can I get for you?" asked a weary cashier named John, whose badge claimed he was the manager.

"My name is Ana Cooper," she said, extending her hand to shake his, "and I'd like a job."

"You're hired," John proclaimed with a bit of relief, wiping beads of sweat from his forehead with the back of his hand. He reached under the counter and grabbed an apron that he quickly shoved in Ana's extended hand. Ana stood in shock for a moment, in disbelief at such a sudden turn of events. Before advancing to the next customer in line, John added, "Steve will show you how to use the fryer." He pointed behind at a strapping lad who was manning the many fryers. Ana instantly found Steve wildly attractive.

Her heart aflutter, she giddily galloped behind the counter, tying her apron and cheering, "He's everything I ever wanted in a job!"

CHAPTER 3

COY'S CONFESSION

Even though the official start of winter was drawing nigh, the weather wasn't the only thing that had waxed cold. The relationships among the members of the Coy and Cooper families seemed to grow a little more distant with every passing day.

Everyone was upset with Mr. Coy, of course: Pauline and Ana desperately yearned to learn the identity of the Jaret lookalike; Ret was worried about what torturous havoc Lye might be wreaking on Lionel; and Paige, caught in the middle, was once again embarrassed by her father's rash behavior.

There were other wedges, however, that were surfacing for the first time. Pauline was irked that Ana had ever mentioned the possibility of Jaret's survival, as it now was growing to consume her mind. Ret hardly spoke to Paige anymore, displacing on her the displeasure he felt for her father. What's more, Paige even felt estranged from Ana, who was working plenty of hours and making a new group of friends at her job.

To sum it all up, the product of so much less fellowship was a dreary feeling of overall division.

Pauline could sense a pick-me-up was needed and decided to plan a modest birthday party for Ana. It was a low-key gathering at best—an after-hours get-together at the Crusty Chicken. The guest list was simple: Pauline, Ret, and whichever co-workers happened to be closing the restaurant that night. Paige had also been invited, of course, but Pauline wasn't sure if she'd come. In fact, by the time the last customer left and the manager locked the door, Paige was nowhere in sight.

"You must be Ana's mother," John, the middle-aged manager, greeted Pauline.

"Why yes, I am," Pauline replied.

"Ana is a terrific employee," John complimented. "She's a hard worker and a great team player." He had many more positive things to say, which Pauline thoroughly enjoyed.

Ana was the star of the evening. The unique combination of her amicable attitude and down-to-earth personality meant she was well-liked by all of her fellow employees, each of whom was eager to participate in the celebration of Ana's sixteenth year: one young woman supplied a cake, another some candles, while others hung streamers, inflated balloons, and scooped ice-cream—not to mention the all-you-can-eat fried chicken.

There was one co-worker who apparently fawned over Ana more than anyone else. Steve followed her wherever she went—attempting to hold her hand, rub her shoulders, twirl her hair. It seemed a very tactile relationship, and while Ana embraced her hunk's flirtations with open arms, it was causing Pauline to squirm. Every minute (at least), she would steal a glance at the couple, almost attached at the hip, to ensure their behavior was still rated-G.

Meanwhile, Ret had become consumed in a very one-sided conversation with another member of the Crusty Chicken's staff—one who was Steve's opposite in nearly every particular. Long and lanky, he preferred thick books over Steve's barbells, and his wide-rimmed glasses half concealed his big, brown eyes.

"You're Ana's brother, Ret, ain't ya?" he asked as he slid into the booth, speaking with a heavy drawl in his voice that both slowed his words and prolonged their vowels.

"Uh, yeah," said Ret, caught a bit off-guard.

"You're in my statistics class," he explained. "That's how come I knew your name. I'm Leonard Swain, but most people just call me Leo"—then, as if ashamed by a less endearing moniker—"or Swain."

"Good to meet you...Leo," Ret replied, unsure of what to call him for a moment.

"Oh, the pleasure's all mine, sir," Leo responded quickly. "Ana talks about you all the time. Well, not *all* the time, 'course, but I reckon at least a fair bit, from the little I overhear her sayin'."

"Oh really..." Ret started to say.

"I can't wait for Ana to open the present I got her," Leo interrupted, clearly wanting to speak about a certain subject. "She's been talkin' for days and days about how much she wants a GPS for the car—ya know, since she says she's so bad with directions and all. 'Course, she also says she wants her *own* car, but I don't see nothing wrong with the one y'all came up in." He glanced toward the parking lot. "Yes, sir, she's gonna love it. Saved two weeks' worth of paychecks to buy it, I did."

Leo proceeded to rattle off a long dialogue covering a wide array of topics, but Ret noticed a common thread holding it all together: whatever he talked about, it always had something to do with Ana. Even though he clearly knew a great deal about her, Ret got the feeling Leo had gleaned it all from observation and not from interaction.

Eventually, Leo was summoned by the manager. He eagerly flew out of the booth and over the counter, stopping in the kitchen where he fetched his mop and began slopping a bubbly solution over the dirty floor.

Leo was the janitor, and he seemed to take great pride in his work, despite the grimy conditions and the subtle disrespect of his associates. At one point, John managed to pry Steve away from Ana just long enough to retrieve something heavy from a delivery truck. On his way to the backdoor, Steve purposely walked through the freshly-mopped part of the floor and then yelled, "Hey, Swain, you missed a spot," before kicking over the bucket of soapy water. Remarkably, Leo didn't seem to mind.

Although Ret was not easily intimidated by people, he was somewhat taken aback by this country boy. Leo was of a curious nature that Ret couldn't quite put his finger on. He seemed outgoing but not outspoken. He was the epitome of innocence but no spring pig. In many ways, he wore his heart on his shirt-sleeve but kept his mind tucked in. Perhaps helped by his thick accent and inborn propriety, there was an immediate guiltlessness about him. He was at peace with himself and with the world, and both parties knew it. True, he was a tad awkward and not much to look at (especially with the grease splatters on his glasses and the sauce stains on his apron), but his character was almost irresistible—even if he did smell like he bathed in fry oil.

Soon it was time to open gifts. Jewelry, clothes, gift cards—all the usual items, but then—

"Who's that one from?" someone asked as Ana grabbed another present from the dwindling stack.

She searched for a card, a name, anything. "It doesn't say," she concluded. She scanned the group, but no one came forward. Ana shrugged, tore it open, then screamed to find her much-desired GPS.

"No, really," she sobered up, "who is this from? Who—" She turned to face Steve. "It was *you*, wasn't it?" He didn't have time (or, apparently, the integrity) to respond before Ana leapt from her seat and hugged him. She might have kissed him, but Pauline grabbed her daughter's party hat and used the rubber band under her chin to yank her away.

Silently, Ret peered into the galley of the restaurant to locate Leo, the real bestower of the GPS. Leo had paused from his duties to observe the goings-on of the gift giving. Peeking from behind the soda fountain, his eyes were full of joy, not outrage. He was happy because he had made Ana so. To celebrate, he danced with his mop, painting sudsy hearts all along the tile floor.

Suddenly, there was a knock at the glass double doors. Everyone turned to look, straining to see who it was amid the darkness of the night. John somewhat cautiously undid the lock and confronted the visitor.

"Paige!" Ana cheered from across the room. "I'm so glad you could make it. Come in!" Realizing the stranger was Ana's friend, John politely granted her admittance.

As he quickly moved to shut the door, John was stunned to find a man's foot jamming it. When he pulled it open to see who was there, Mr. Coy came striding into the restaurant.

"Party's over," Coy announced. "I need everyone to leave—now."

"Who are you?" John asked indignantly.

"Unbelievable!" Pauline shrieked.

"No one invited you!" Ana barked.

"Not this again," Ret moaned.

"I repeat: I need everyone to leave," Coy restated. Then, with a smirk, he added, "And I ain't *lion.*"

Without any warning at all, a full-grown lion burst into the room with a deafening roar. With teeth bared, the ferocious cat stood next to Mr. Coy, ready to pounce.

The building erupted in chaos as everyone, save Paige and the Coopers, frantically sought out the nearest exit, looking much like a bunch of chickens with their heads cut off. In no time at all, the party had ended, with only one brave attendee refusing to clear out.

"Who is this crazy guy?" Steve wondered trepidatiously, standing in front of Ana to protect her. Neither the Coopers nor Paige looked very alarmed as Mr. Coy and his lion approached the booth where they were seated.

"Don't worry, Steve," Ana sighed. "He's just the biggest party pooper of all time."

"Why, thank you," Coy grinned.

"I won't let you hurt us," Steve promised, standing up to Coy. "You'll have to go through me first."

"Beat it, Stevie Wonder," Coy ordered. Then, as if on command, the lion let out another blood-curdling roar, and Steve, pale-faced, high-tailed it out of the Crusty Chicken.

"This is the last straw, Ben," Pauline declared, angry beyond all reason. "I am at my wit's end with you. I am going to file a restraining order against you, first thing in the morning—you and your lion."

"His name is Feathers," said Coy, scratching the cat's mane.

"Come on, Ret and Ana," Pauline beckoned. "We're leaving."

"Gladly," Ana obeyed, emerging from the booth.

"I have come to explain my actions from the other night," Coy stated.

"Oh, you mean when you gassed us all into unconsciousness?" Pauline sneered.

"And abandoned my dad?" Ana added.

"And broke your promise to save Lionel?" Ret reminded.

As if chewing something large, Mr. Coy thought for a moment before swallowing, "Precisely."

"Well, save it for someone who cares," said Pauline as the three of them made their way to the door.

"Yeah," said Ana bitterly, "who knows if you'd be telling the truth anyway."

"Very true, dear," Pauline agreed as she reached to pull the door handle.

Then, like slinging a spear of ice, Mr. Coy loudly proclaimed, "That place killed my wife."

The room fell silent. Everyone stood still. Not an eye blinked, incapable of breaking the trance produced by such cold words.

Pauline was a statue. For a moment that felt like eons, she stood in silent frenzy at a pivotal crossroads. With her hand, now clammy, still clasping the door knob, she had a decision to make: she could proceed with her aforementioned intentions and walk out on Mr. Coy, the Oracle, and everything else stained with his scent, or she could yet again go against her present passions and try to view, through the lens of forgiveness, a grander picture. And so, appealing to an embryonic change of heart, she slowly loosened her grip on the handle of the door while she quickly relinquished her grasp on the malice of the past.

Without haste, the Coopers turned around to face the poor soul from whom the shocking words had come. Mr. Coy was seated now, his back to the door, with Paige next to him, her face morose and head down. Hesitantly, the three Coopers returned to the booth.

"Her name was Helen," Mr. Coy started, his voice soft and subdued. "We were both in our mid-twenties when we met. She had recently completed medical school—first in her class. I was pursuing post-graduate work in the U.S. Navy. I was good friends with her older brother, Peter. He and I were part of a special ops mission behind enemy lines, which I cannot discuss, except that we were captured, imprisoned, tortured. Peter sacrificed himself to save the rest of us. I watched him die."

Pauline thought to mention similar acts of valor performed by her husband, but she decided to hold her tongue.

"I was invited to say a few words at Peter's funeral services in Washington, D.C., which is where I met Helen," Coy continued. "To say she was devastated would be an understatement. Her beloved brother's death had a profound and lasting effect on her. At first, our association was very businesslike: she would want to meet with me on occasion to learn the details surrounding her brother's martyrdom. I probably told her more than I should have, but eventually our relationship evolved from lecture to love. Initially, I thought she only wanted me around because I was a sailor who reminded her of Peter and helped to fill a gaping void in her life. As time healed her wounds, however, her questions stopped revolving around him and started focusing on me. Still, she kept the memory of her brother vibrant and vowed to do everything in her power for the rest of her life to relieve suffering and prevent premature death in this world."

Paige smiled to herself, swelling with pride at her mother and her noble ambitions.

"Me, on the other hand," said Coy. "Well, I was just hoping she'd marry me. I had never met anyone like her. She was so devoted—so motivated by this inner-drive to help people without any regard for herself. She possessed a brilliance that was free of arrogance, which is why so many people loved her. That, and she was beautiful—radiant, even." Mr. Coy's face had loosened up a bit at such fond remembrances, and the overall mood at the table seemed to perk up some. "To this day, I'm not sure why she ever consented to marry a guy like me. To be honest, I never thought I'd ever find a girl who could love me. I mean, you know," Coy shrugged, "I can be a little…well, odd."

His listeners snickered in agreement.

"She said I never failed to make her laugh," Coy reminisced fondly. "I loved her laugh, and her smile. As a scientist, she could become so rigid from her work and stressed from her studies, so I took it upon myself as often as I could to help her wind down by doing something spontaneous, out of the ordinary. I was the more carefree one in the relationship—the thrill seeker, the adventure lover. I'd say we complimented each other perfectly."

"Helen was an unstoppable force for good," said Coy. "After cracking the code on her first vaccine, she won international attention and all kinds of support. Charities, celebrities, even entire nations approached us and solicited our aid. Eventually, as part of a cooperative agreement between the United States and the United Nations, we were commissioned to travel the globe on a Navy vessel as a sort of nomadic humanitarian station. While Helen administered large-scale vaccinations and treated all kinds of ailments, I organized various construction projects ranging from schools and indoor plumbing to wells for water and power lines for electricity. We would spend weeks—even months, sometimes—in certain areas, and when we left, we had changed—saved—lives and transformed entire communities."

The narrative was like hearing the accomplishments of a great hero.

"Helen always wanted a family," Coy carried on, "and by the time Paige was born, we had assumed the roles of diplomats—ambassadors. We had established such a good name and reputation for ourselves that we were encouraged by world leaders to parlay our positive influence as a means for peace. We turned enemies into friends—hostile tribes into hospitable ones. We helped solve armed conflicts and get a leg up on political corruption. It was amazing—the doors that opened and miracles that happened. It was Helen: she had a way with people. They could feel her love and concern for them, even when we couldn't speak their language. And Paige softened hearts, too: oftentimes we were greeted by swords and spears, but as soon as they saw a child with us, they backed off."

As intriguing as was Mr. Coy's story, Ret couldn't help but keep a watchful eye on the unsettling beast at the head of the booth. The lion—or Feathers, as its owner had pointed out—hadn't moved a muscle since Ret had returned to his seat. In fact, the feline had scarcely blinked, and its blank stare made Ret wonder if the creature might be under some sort of hypnosis. Then Ret's eye caught something flickering in Mr. Coy's ear. It looked like a tiny hearing aid. Ret remained alert for whatever Mr. Coy might have up his sleeve.

"But then, one day," Mr. Coy explained, the gravity returning to the conversation, "something terrible happened—*I* did something terrible. We had just launched from Auckland, having met with some of New Zealand's top officials, and were heading out into the Pacific for an assignment in the Polynesian Islands. On the way, we came across a very strange-looking place. It was its vibrant colors that drew our attention, just like they did yours that day in my balloon. We weren't sure what it was—an island, an oil platform, a gyre of garbage. It was uncharted—we couldn't find it on any maps—so we decided to investigate. As we got closer, it became clear that it was, in fact, a landmass, but we still were puzzled by its rainbow-like appearance. I anchored our ship and was preparing to go ashore when Helen stopped me. She was hesitant. She told me that something about that place didn't seem safe to her. This was not uncommon, so I persisted. She obliged, somewhat unwillingly, but brought along some of her instruments to do a little research while I did a bit of exploring."

"As it turns out," said Coy, "the island was covered in hot springs. We couldn't take a dozen steps without encountering another circular pool of warm water, most small in size but some very large. Helen was giddy about our discovery; she hastened from spring to spring, collecting samples of bacteria and filling vials with water. It certainly was a breathtaking place; the pools were a dark, rich blue in the center, surrounded by thin rings of the brightest reds, yellows, oranges, and greens. They were truly like full-circle rainbows. In fact, every-thing about the island seemed new and fresh—almost fake. There was not so much as one yellowing leaf on any of the trees, and every flower was at the peak of blooming. But there was an eerie feeling hiding all around. We never saw another living creature, yet it was one of those situations where I felt as though we were being watched. We turned back, resolved to return in the near future when we would be better prepared and hopefully accompanied by a team of researchers and security."

"As you can probably guess, Helen immediately got to work. Right away, she knew there was something different about the water she had collected from the hot springs. She couldn't quite figure it out, but whenever she tested it on plants and rodents, an amazing thing happened: it reversed the effects of time. It healed wear and tear; it rejuvenated—restored life and vitality. When she sprayed some on a fading rose bud, it bounced back into full bloom in a matter of seconds. When she fed a drop to a lizard that had lost its tail, it grew a new one right before our eyes. It was incredible! She even fed a spoonful to herself, and her few wrinkles and gray hairs disappeared."

Ret's eyes began to widen.

"We both agreed not to tell anyone about our discovery until she had fully decoded the complex molecular structure of the liquid. She said it was unlike anything she had ever scrutinized under a microscope— that the atoms and molecules seemed to be alive and mutating in some sort of systemized pattern—almost like how a reptile sheds its skin. She said it would only be a matter of time before she figured it out and could mass produce it, but until that time, we knew we had to keep it a secret so that it wouldn't fall into the wrong hands. She was ecstatic: here was the ultimate vaccine! the elixir for all illnesses! It stitched any wound, healed any bruise, remedied any malady. This was what she was born to discover!"

Too enthralled in Coy's chronicles, no one inside the Crusty Chicken seemed to notice the behavior of its manager. John was still on the premises, unwilling to abandon his besieged restaurant. After peeking through the windows multiple times, he decided to retreat to the safety of his car and enlist the help of the local Animal Control agency.

"And then, in a terrible twist of irony," Coy recalled somberly, "Helen got sick. Really sick. In just a few days, she was bedridden. We thought it was nothing more than a bad case of the flu or something, but when it wouldn't go away and only got worse, we knew we needed help. We contacted one of our good friends and associates, Dr. Victor Cross, one of medicine's brightest minds with whom we had worked extensively in the past. He graciously came to our aid, watching over Helen day and night. He called in all kinds of specialists from all over the world. They tried their best, but nothing worked. She was fading fast."

"The water," Ret blurted out. "Why not use some of the water from the island?"

"We did," Coy replied hopelessly, "and it went right through her, as if it was just regular water. It was enough to convince me that it wasn't quite the cure-all we thought it was; in fact, it was my opinion that it was the strange liquid itself that had brought about Helen's condition. But she disagreed. None of her specimens had shown such ill side effects, so she still believed it was the miracle drug—that there was nothing harmful about it. She was sure of it. Even in her emaciated condition, she persevered in her effort to pin down the secret of the magical water. Confined to her hospital bed, she could hardly hold her pencil but was determined it could heal the world if she could just crack the code. But time was not on our side. In my desperation, I left Helen in the trusted care of Dr. Cross and set out in search of a cure for my ailing wife. I met with priests and apothecaries. I sought out potion masters and witchdoctors. I tried ancient tonics and homemade concoctions."

The Coopers glared at Coy, hoping for good news, but he shook his head.

"I'll never forget the day, though I've tried to," said Coy with regret. "I had gone home to tend to Paige when Dr. Cross summoned me back to the hospital."

"'Helen has something she needs to tell you,' Dr. Cross explained to me. 'She won't tell me what it is, but she said it's very important.'"

"I instantly knew what it was," said Mr. Coy. "She had cracked the code. I went to the hospital, as I had done so many times before. There I found Dr. Cross."

"'She could go at any moment,' he whispered to me."

"I crept into her room. The air was cold and stale. An infrequent beep was the only movement that stirred the deathly scene. As I drew near her bedside, I saw her books and calculations spread out amid the mess of tubing and wiring. Then I saw her hand cradling a folded piece of paper. I gently caressed her frail fingers. Sensing my touch, she cracked open one of her eyes and, with all her strength, reached out to hand the note to me. I was moved to tears, for here was a woman who, on the verge of death, was using her final ounces of energy in the service of others. I unfolded the slip of paper, expecting to see a complex equation or scientific formula, but was surprised when I found neither. Written in her shaky but familiar penmanship was one question: *How could you do this to me?*"

A quiet gasp escaped from Pauline's shocked mouth. Ana brought her hand to her lips in dismay. Ret glanced at Paige, finding a wet trail of tears underneath each of her eyes.

Benjamin Coy began to weep bitterly. The childlike tears of a full-grown man crashed and puddled on the tabletop. A numbing pain seized every breast.

"When I looked up to ask what she had meant," said Coy, "she was gone. But I already knew what she meant. It was true; *I* had brought this upon her. *I* was the one who insisted on going to that wretched island. It was *my* fault she ever came in contact with that mutated water. It was because of *me* and *my* foolishness. She tried to warn me, but I didn't listen. And now it's too late."

Pauline thought to advise Mr. Coy not to be so hard on himself, but she didn't think any words from someone like herself could reverse a decade's worth of rankling regret.

"In that singular moment," said Coy, "my entire world crumbled. Indeed, I wished *I* was the one who had died. I lost the will to live. I wanted to cease to exist. I couldn't live with myself; couldn't look in the mirror. I had extinguished one of the greatest lives—some of the best blood—to ever grace this world. I couldn't eat. I couldn't sleep. I couldn't even be at home. Every time I looked at my beautiful daughter, I was reminded of her darling mother and how I had betrayed them both. I had robbed my child of her mother. I couldn't face her. Paige would ask for Helen, wonder where she had gone, but what could I say? How could I tell a five-year-old that her mother was dead because of me? She would cry for her mother in the night; her screams of 'Mommy! Mommy! Where are you?' would echo in my head, and I had the same desire. I was going mad. Suicide would solve nothing, only make things worse. I had to distance myself; get my mind on other things. It felt like I had suffered the most agonizing death and somehow survived—survived death."

"I swore never to tell anyone about that island," said Coy. "The memory of that deplorable place with its murderous poison died with Helen. And that is why I had to turn around so abruptly when we came upon it several days ago: because that place killed my dear wife—and most of me, too."

The tragic tale of the late Helen Coy was hard to hear but necessary to know. The widower had always been an enigma of questionable character and mysterious motivations. He was a man who had been masked with a false identity, and the disguise prevented others from seeing through to the real person. Like an asinine mascot at a sporting event, his costume hardly mimicked the soul within, for the reality was Benjamin Coy was a remarkable human being—a Renaissance man of immense capacity—a truth to which the world became blind when he was redefined by one heartrending event. Two Coys died that day: one gave up the ghost, and the other became a ghost, living out the rest of his ruined life like a man within a man, mummified and misunderstood. What a double shame it would be if, after all these years, he were to discover that his secondary identity had been based on misinformation.

By the end of Mr. Coy's monologue, a strong fellowship was rising from the vinyl seats of the restaurant booth. Through his willingness to confide in his friends such personal matters, Coy got what he gave, as his listeners were restoring their own confidence in him. A warm bond was brewing, peeling away pride and melting old grudges along the way. For the first time, Pauline felt she shared something in common with Mr. Coy. That night, trust begat trust.

"So," said Coy with sudden renewed energy, snapping back to his usual self, "when is someone going to serve me some of that cake?" He pointed to the half-eaten pastry that had been pushed to the other end of the table. Paige cut a slice and passed it on a plate to her dad.

"You know, Mr. Coy," said Ana brightly, "you're not so bad after all—even if you did ruin my birthday party."

"Ruin?" Coy cried out, his mouth full of cake. "The party didn't start until *I* got here. And it's not over yet." Paige and the Coopers looked at each other with slight uneasiness at what might come roaring into the room next. "Since some of you have had trouble believing me in the past, I asked someone to come with me here tonight to corroborate my claims. You might know him." Then, as if speaking to the air, he ordered, "Bring him in."

The doors flew open, and in strode an unfortunately familiar figure.

CHAPTER 4

THE LION, THE WRETCH, AND THE MICROBE

Pauline shrieked, "Principal Stone!"

Automatically, Ret leapt from his seat and produced two streams of fire that encircled their common foe in a blazing ring of flames. Stone stopped dead in his tracks, tightly closing his stance so as not to get singed. The room had been transformed into an oven, so dramatically did the temperature rise.

Suddenly, a second individual whizzed through the open doors—a stranger to Ret, much larger in stature than Stone. Still in self-defense mode and, thus, oblivious to most anything else, Ret sent another pair of fireballs in the newcomer's direction.

But the unknown man was ready. With his bare hands, he ripped out of the ground the tables from two nearby booths and held them up to shield himself from the approaching infernos. Then, like a tomahawk, he heaved one of the charred tables at Ret, who quickly forsook his hold on any flames and called upon his power over earth to assemble a wall in front of himself, using the floor tiles at his feet. The table crashed into the barrier, which exploded into dust.

"Enough already!" Coy bellowed over the scene. "Cool it, Ret. We're not in any danger."

As they waited for the dust to settle and the smoke to disperse, the fire alarm began to ring, and then water started sprinkling from the fire suppression system along the ceiling.

"Conrad!" Coy shouted in response to the riotous circumstances. "Take care of this, would you?"

The stranger, who was apparently an agent of Coy, obeyed his orders. He hurried over to the blinking fire alarm and powerfully struck it with his fist, effectively killing it. With the noise gone but water still spewing, he then ran towards the restrooms and put his ear up against the wall. It looked like he was searching for something by sound. Without any warning, he pulverized a section of the wall, located a series of pipes, and squeezed them shut with his brute strength. The water promptly abated.

Meanwhile, out in the tranquil parking lot on a cool winter's eve, a representative from Animal Control had arrived, as summoned by John. They were about to carry out their plan of attack when the Crusty Chicken erupted in chaos. In silent terror, John watched, wide-eyed and jaw-dropped, as the belligerents burned the lobby, tossed the tables, tore up the tile, and flooded the floor. In fact, when the flashes of light and clouds of smoke were added to the rain and wildfire, it looked much like a complete thunderstorm had converged within the establishment.

"Sorry," Ret apologized to Coy, embarrassed by the damage he had caused. Then, pointing a wet finger at Conrad, "He's with you?"

"Of course he is," said Coy, a little annoyed as he tried to dislodge water from his ears. "Conrad is Keeper of Artifacts and Wildlife at Coy Manor." Coy walked to Conrad's side and put his dripping arm around him. "He hails from the land Down Under. Isn't that right, mate?"

Conrad gave an almost imperceptible nod.

The man called Conrad was truly something terrible to look upon—a most wretched human being. With head shorn as sheep and skin dark as night, he was a creature of great size and even greater might. His thick skin was not supple anywhere but scarred everywhere, and his body bulged with muscles, some of which Ret never knew existed. As streams of water dribbled down his curvature, he resembled a beast from the jungle—a pack animal on a farm. And yet, as terrifying as he was to behold, there was no emotion in his immediate appearance. He was every bit as stolid as he was solid. He stood, stiff as a board, in complete subjection to Mr.

Coy, like a soldier to his superior. In fact, save for the blinking of his eyes, he looked more like a piece of property—a sculpture, perhaps—than a real person. He could be described in one word: stoic.

At the same time, however, there was something about Conrad that couldn't be described in just a single word—or even in a thousand—and it was visible in his every feature. It found place in his posture, molded by years of discipline too servile for Mr. Coy's conscience. It was given prominence in his stillborn smile, dulled to death by never-found happiness. But nowhere was it more obvious than in his eyes—big, round windows to his soul, where something beautiful was buried deep within, for protection, underneath all the repulsive layers. Yes, there was something about Conrad that made you intensely interested in what he had to say. The trouble was, he never spoke.

"He's not one much for words," Coy informed the group as they continued to glare at Conrad, "but he's got it where it really counts." Coy gave him a solid slap on his muscular back, then glanced back at Principal Stone and added, "unlike someone else I know."

Stone finished ringing his suit free of excess water and slowly approached the booth, looking very much out of sorts.

"Ms. Cooper," he nodded in salutation, the air uneasy. "Children." He was greeted by stern stares of distrust.

"Rest easy, friends," Coy said cheerily, returning to his seat. "This is an armistice of sorts; we are meeting on peaceful terms. Besides, I'm sure Stone is well aware that, should he try any funny business, he will be crushed by Conrad, charbroiled by Ret, and fed to Feathers." As if on cue, the lion licked his snout with his long tongue. "And he especially likes dark meat," Coy added, petting the cat's thick mane. "Now, don't be bashful, Lester," Coy welcomed him, making space for him next to Feathers. "Pull up a chair." Stone warily obliged.

"Fried chicken?" Coy offered to Stone, shoving a plate of leftover food in front of him as he took his seat.

"No, thank you," Stone declined. "Gives me gas."

"Pity," Coy mumbled, taking a hearty bite of one of the cold drumsticks. "You might be interested to know," Coy continued, "Stone recently opened a correspondence with me and expressed his desire to exchange information." Pauline suddenly perked up a bit. "It will proceed much like swapping prisoners of war—that is, man for man. For every question we answer for Stone, he must answer one of ours. So choose wisely," he advised, shaking his half-eaten drumstick in their direction for emphasis.

"How will we know he's telling the truth?" Pauline accused, well aware of Stone's tainted integrity.

"I should wonder the same," Stone rebutted, their rivalry rekindled.

"We will begin the questioning, Pauline," Coy intervened, like a teacher trying to keep unruly students on topic. "If Stone is vague in his answers to us, then we will be just the same in ours."

"Fair enough," said Stone.

"Ret," said Coy pleasantly, "would you care to go first?"

Coy had caught Ret off-guard, as he was staring at a small, flickering circuit half-concealed in Conrad's ear. It was identical to the device that Ret had spied in Mr. Coy's ear earlier in the evening. He reasoned it must be some type of two-way communications system. How else would Conrad have heard Coy's instructions to bring in Principal Stone?

Suddenly, Ret noticed everyone glaring at him.

"Oh, me?" he blushed. Paige tried to suppress a smile.

Ret thought for a few moments, sifting through the many questions that were always on his mind, and then asked one near the forefront, "What has Lye done to Lionel?"

Puzzled, Stone quickly replied, "I don't know anyone by that name."

Ret was stunned. Perhaps Stone was bluffing. "You don't know any—"

"Wait a minute, Ret," Coy cautioned. "Remember: every question counts." Ret held his tongue. Coy, the mediator, carried on, "Who's next?"

"I've got a question," Pauline interjected. "What have you done with my husband?" Ana had been hoping her mother would make such an inquiry.

"Ah, you must mean Jaret," Stone taunted with a wicked smile. "He works for Lord Lye now."

"Liar!" Pauline protested, rising from her seat. "Jaret would never work for such scum!"

"No one speaks of my lord like that!" Stone snapped, rising from his own chair.

In response to the uproar, Feathers thundered a roar of his own, immediately quelling the ruckus. Paige and Ana covered their ears. An insulted Stone and frumpy Pauline quieted down.

It was in this moment when Ret became aware of an almost invisible connection between Conrad and Feathers. Besides standing as still as pillars, Ret saw both parties twitch ever so slightly just prior to the lion's booming growl. Curious, he studied the two of them intently before noticing how both had a pair of objects affixed to each of their heads. They were small and round objects, situated on each of their temples, almost like stickers, flesh-colored so as to render them almost unrecognizable. What's more, Conrad possessed an additional piece: some kind of wire that ran around his skull and attached to a tiny device at the base of his cranium. In Ret's estimation, it bore the brand of Coy.

"You've earned two questions, Stone," Coy calcu-lated. "Fire at will."

"Finally," Stone muttered. "Has a new scar appeared?"

The entire booth turned to face Ret.

At first, though only for a second, Ret mulled over this third question that had been put forth, and wondered if he ought to plead the Fifth. Of course, Ret made it a point in life to be perfectly honest in all things, but would it not be better to make an exception in this case? For one thing, who's to say Stone was honest in his own response to Ret's question regarding Lionel? And, for another, passing along clues to Stone (and, therefore, to Lye) didn't seem the noblest thing to do either.

It was clear, by now, that Stone had agreed to this meeting with a prescribed agenda and that any informa-tion gleaned would undoubtedly make its way back to Lye. For quite some time now, Ret had wondered if Lye already knew the locations of each element, and if, in fact, he did know, why would he care which one was next?

"Yes," Ret answered. Since he had never told anyone about the emergence of a new scar that day in the hot-air balloon, Ret's response in the affirmative earned a wide array of reactions from his tablemates. Stone was slightly surprised and instantly gratified, like a poker player dealt a winning hand. The women were dumbfounded and began a conversation solely voiced by facial expressions. Mr. Coy cringed, as he had hoped to have withheld such valuable information for a more opportune moment. Meanwhile, Conrad and Feathers appeared totally disengaged.

"Well, out with it!" Stone demanded, fully expecting Ret to expound beyond his one-word answer. "What is the next scar?"

"To answer your second question...," Ret said slyly. Outsmarted, Stone frowned in frustration. "...It's hard to say; I wasn't able to look at it for very long before falling asleep." He shot a displeased glance at Coy. "At first glance, I thought it was a Ferris wheel, or even a spider web. But then it started to look more like a weird type of star, with a base at the bottom and lines between each of the points. Like I said, I didn't have much time to study it."

Stone nodded his head, trying to look as though he was content with Ret's candid attempt at recollection but not so pleased with the nebulous information presented. Inwardly, however, Stone was elated because he knew exactly what Ret was referring to. He had just accomplished half of what he had set out to do.

Mr. Coy was also well pleased, though for an entirely different reason. As ambiguous as it was, Ret's description of the new star-shaped scar was so dissimilar to the new scar Coy had seen while Ret was asleep, Coy was convinced they had seen totally separate scars that night. Initially, he was a bit unhappy that Ret did not tell him about the new star-shaped scar; however, Coy was also a bit relieved that he himself had withheld the same from Ret, as Ret likely would have told Stone about both scars. Coy was secretly grateful that Stone had not asked his question in the plural, as he felt no moral obligation to inform Stone of the second new scar.

Unbeknownst to the interrogation squad, John and the agent from Animal Control had snuck around to the back of the Crusty Chicken and were observing the powwow through the rear door's mail slot. The agent had brought with him a tranquilizer gun and had slipped its double barrel through the horizontal slot, aiming it at the menacing lion. He fired, sending two darts speeding towards the cat. Miraculously, Conrad's senses picked up the approaching projectiles. In a flash, he grabbed a dinner plate from a nearby table and shielded Feathers from impact. The darts ricocheted off the plate, shot back the way they came, and struck both John and the gunman in the forehead. In no time at all, they slumped to the ground, where they slept peacefully for the next four to six hours.

Ret suddenly thought of another inquiry for Stone. "Has Lye collected any of the other elements?"

"No," said Stone. "He is unable to do so without you." Then, with a cruel grin, he added, "It's a good thing you agreed to collect them for him."

Stone's words hit Ret like a ton of bricks. Every ounce of him wanted to disbelieve Stone's statement—shrug it off as hogwash—but, for some reason, he couldn't bring himself to fully dismiss it. It resonated too soundly with one of Ret's most detestable fears—that he once worked cooperatively with Lye. And, since his memory only spanned the last few years, he had no way of knowing the truth.

Observing how his declaration was having its desired effect, Stone proceeded to pursue the second item on his agenda: "Did the Guardian of the Fire Element give you anything?"

Stone's questions were so pointed, loaded, and expertly worded that Ret was beginning to feel like his principal was taking advantage of him and that Coy's idea of exchanging information was extremely foolish.

"Yes," was all Ret said, giving Stone another dose of his own medicine.

"And what did he give you?"

"An hour glass," Ret answered, having learned not to divulge any more than he had to.

"I see," said Stone. "Very well." He moved as if to leave.

"I believe it's my turn to ask a question," Coy stated, trying to halt Stone in his flight.

"That won't be necessary," Stone protested. "I really must be going."

"Hold the phone, Stony!" Coy persisted. "You still owe us one answer. Real quick, tell everyone how you know Dr. Victor Cross."

Stone's face clouded over. His eyes became shifty. He looked sick to his stomach.

"I—I..." he stammered, "I've never heard of anyone named—"

"Nonsense!" Coy cried out. "I know for a fact that you know Dr. Cross."

"No, really, I—"

"There's a picture of you two, shaking hands," Coy urgently explained. "I saw it with my own eyes, on a table in your living room, next to that hideous chaise lounge."

"I don't know what you're talking about," Stone denied nervously, hastily making his way to the door. "Goodnight," he said, wiping sweat from his brow.

"You're a terrible liar, Stone," Coy shouted after him as the principal slipped through the double doors into the night.

"Run him down," Ret urged. "Have Feathers sic him. He owes us an answer."

"No," Coy sighed, "that's not my style; too direct. Besides, it's getting late. We should head for home. Come on, Paige." Without a word, Paige scooted out of the booth and hurried to her father's side. "Nighty-night, all," Coy called out as the two of them exited, holding hands, with the bodyguard and the beast following close behind.

Ret felt the room grow cold and dim as soon as Paige left it. As if she had been a candle, he was now sitting in the dark, and it suddenly felt foolish to still be there. It was one of those cases where it takes a thing's absence to realize it had been present. Now that everything of primary importance had vacated (Stone, Conrad, the innerving lion), Ret had a moment to reflect on what he had overlooked. When Paige had entered the restaurant, Ret was unusually captivated by her radiant beauty, but, amid all the excitement, he had forgotten to tell her. Ret kicked himself, lamenting his tendency to, as Lionel had put it once, see through the people he sees all the time. He resolved, then and there, to put a stop to that right away.

There was one individual in attendance, however, who had gone completely unnoticed. Leo, the jovial janitor, was hiding in the custodial closet. As soon as he learned there was a lion in the building, he booked it for the one place even humans hate to go, hoping the overwhelming scent of ammonia in the small room would keep the creature at bay. When it became obvious to him that Feathers was profoundly tame, he still wanted to wait for the restaurant to clear out, knowing the mortification that would be his if Ana saw him stumble out of the janitor's closet. As such, he witnessed the evening's entire exchange: Coy's story about his wife, Ret's ability to spontaneously combust, Stone's question-and-answer session. For Leo, who was all ears, it was like watching an intriguing three-act play, albeit a foreign one since he had no idea what was going on.

But no one was privy to the bitter tears being shed by Lester Stone as he stumbled to his vehicle in the parking lot. With fumbling hands, he located his car key and shakily started the ignition. He hardly paid any attention to the road on his drive home, too focused was his mind on other things. Due to the radio device in Conrad's ear, Stone had overheard Coy's recounting of Helen's death as the two of them stood outside the Crusty Chicken, awaiting their cue to enter. On this occasion, however, Stone had heard the other side of the story, and, for the first time in his life, he was experiencing guilt.

CHAPTER 5

TWO BURDENS WITH
ONE STONE

When Ana showed up for work the day after their meeting with Principal Stone, she was fully expecting John to fire her on the spot. Of course, she had not caused any of the damage to the restaurant, but, as a sort of liaison for the offending party, she couldn't help but feel at least somewhat responsible. That afternoon, as she sheepishly tiptoed into the Crusty Chicken, she was stunned to find that the dining area looked as good as new.

"Ana, I'm glad you're here," John greeted her cheerfully. "I was wondering if you could pass on my gratitude to your friend, Mr. Coy." The manager went on to explain how, soon after the night's questioning had concluded, a sizeable workforce from Coy Manor arrived at the site and immediately began making reparations. With lumber and drywall, they rebuilt framing and patched holes. Mops soaked up any extra moisture while fresh paint covered up the burn marks. By the time the institution's doors opened for business, the place was in pristine condition.

"It was in need of a good facelift anyway," John smiled. "And I'm sure Leo's relieved he won't have to clean up the mess." The custodian, who had been eavesdropping, ran and hid behind the freezer upon hearing his name inserted into the conversation.

When it came to preparing for her driver test, however, Ana was not so lucky. Over the last few weeks, Pauline had permitted her daughter to play chauffeur, ferrying the family to and from school and such. Each time Ret got in the car with Ana behind the wheel, he offered a silent prayer that he'd live to see another day. Still, it didn't seem right to call her reckless, since every day she managed to wreck more. She had already dinged every guide post and scratched every sidewall of the McDonald's drive-thru. She backed over the mailbox so many times that Pauline was prepared to switch to a PO box. She once hit a speed bump so fast that it launched Ret into the roof, where his head left a nice dent. Of course, it didn't help that the family car was a manual transmission, whose stick shift and clutch pedal only added to its driver's confusion. On one occasion, after halting at a stop sign at the top of a slope, Ana couldn't get the car in gear until they had rolled halfway down the hill backwards. That was one of the more terrifying episodes.

Whenever Pauline was able to turn down the radio, she was always full of advice:

"Slow down, dear. You're going a little too fast."

"Don't forget to use your blinker."

"Always keep both hands on the wheel, honey."

"Don't follow so close."

Still, Ana was determined to get her license. Ret looked on from the front porch the day she and Pauline departed for the Department of Motor Vehicles to conduct the behind-the-wheel portion of her exam. Like always, Pauline buckled her seatbelt as soon as she slid into the passenger seat, then gripped a handlebar and armrest to brace herself. Ana fired up the engine like a rocket ship and then bottomed out of the driveway, as usual, passing cleanly over the amputated mailbox that Ret had finally decided to just lay on the curb. As he waved goodbye, he was anxious to hear the outcome.

"I failed!" Ana dramatically announced upon their return. "I failed my driving test." She collapsed on the couch, as if her world had been totaled.

"How could you fail?" Ret wondered. "You're a terrific driver." Only Pauline noticed his sarcasm.

"I know!" Ana agreed. "Tell that to Captain Hook."

"Captain Hook?" Ret inquired of Pauline.

"The gentleman who rode with her to score her driving had a hook for a hand," Pauline explained.

"Yeah, and it totally creeped me out," Ana shuddered. "How is a girl supposed to concentrate when there's a guy with a hook in the seat next to her?"

"So you failed because of a guy with a hook...?" Ret scratched his head.

"No," Ana replied. "I failed because I backed into a car." Ret gasped. "And it was just my luck that the car happened to be a police car."

"Ouch," Ret cringed.

"Yeah," said Ana. "I was trying to parallel park, doing something like a twenty-point turn to get into this tiny little space; it was taking forever, traffic backed up in both directions for probably a mile—when good old Cap'n grabbed the wheel with his shiny hook for some reason, and I freaked out and pushed the wrong pedal and kaboom."

"Fortunately, our car made it out with only a scratch," Pauline looked on the bright side.

"Unlike the cop car," Ana rolled her eyes. "The entire front bumper broke off. Don't mess with the Coopers' clunker—that thing's built like a tank."

"Good thing, too," Ret mumbled to himself as he started up the stairs to resume his homework, foreseeing still more dangerous driving practice in the future.

○   ○   ○

Saturday, early in the morning, was one of Ret's favorite times each week. In the predawn stillness, he would arise and sneak out of the house, careful not to wake a slumbering Pauline and snoring Ana. He would tiptoe toward the beach as noiselessly as possible, striving to preserve the profound silence. The houses were dark; the traffic still garaged. No hustle and no bustle allowed him to know peace.

Ret's destination was no different on this first weekend in February than on any other: his secluded nook along the southernmost tip of Tybee's shoreline — the place of his first memory, as Pauline had once informed him. He hunkered down in his bunker there, clothed in a light jacket against the omnipresent breeze. It was a cold morning, the sky gray with wintry blues. In the sand in front of him, Ret telekinetically carved a crude pit, then, with fingers of flint, filled it with fire — all so quickly and effortlessly that it surely would have insulted even the cleverest of cavemen. He welcomed the additional warmth.

Something was troubling Ret. Ever since Principal Stone had alluded to an alleged alliance between Lye and Ret — that the lad had once agreed to help the lord — Ret had been plagued by a psychological pestilence. He knew Stone could not be fully trusted, but he also felt some of Stone's answers that night were genuine. Ret had encountered a similar predicament in the convoluted information that Lye had shared with him and the Guardian of the Earth element: what was fact, and what was fiction? It was a constant, back-and-forth battle for Ret, a riddle almost. It would make his life a great deal easier if Ret could just count on his enemies to be consistent—to either always yield to verities or else always employ falsehoods. Indeed, it was their preferred practice to mingle truth with lies that never failed to mess with Ret's mind. How was he supposed to discern the difference? And what if his deductions were incorrect?

"I thought I'd find you here," said an approaching voice. It was Pauline, her hands tucked in the front pockets of her sweatshirt as she cut through the sand towards him. "What's on your mind?" she asked as she sat down next to him.

"Oh, nothing much," Ret replied nervously, a bit startled, as if Pauline had somehow seen or heard what he had been thinking.

"Now Ret," Pauline prodded tenderly, "I think I know you well enough to suspect there's something going on up here." She playfully shuffled his hair. "Lately, you've been talking even less than you usually do, and you play with your food more than you eat it. So…let's hear it."

With a heavy sigh, Ret opened up: "I've just been thinking about what Stone said. You know, when he told us how I agreed to collect the elements for Lye."

"Oh, Stone, that old windbag," Pauline dismissed. "The man can't be taken seriously, you know that. Don't take it to heart, Ret."

"I know," Ret concurred, only half-believing, "but it's been true so far, hasn't it?"

"What do you mean?"

"Look," said Ret, eager to talk through his thoughts. He shifted his weight towards Pauline and readied his hands for emphasizing certain points. "At first, I thought Lye was out to get me—that I was getting in his way and messing up his plans. But I don't know if I believe that anymore. I mean, he knows where we live; with one wave of his staff, he could take us out." Pauline cringed at the thought. "And each time I've met him in person, he has tried to tear me away from the Oracle—as opposed to tearing me apart."

"So he just needs the Oracle then," Pauline suggested, trying to lift Ret out of his despondency. "Don't you have to have the Oracle in order to collect the elements?"

"Yes, but it's got to be more than that," Ret reasoned. "If all he needed was the Oracle, he could have collected the elements a long, long time ago. I mean, he's been doing this forever, basically."

"Then maybe he needs you to lead him to the locations where the elements are hidden," Pauline postulated.

"But he already knows where they are," Ret countered, throwing up his hands. "When we got to Sunken Earth, he was already there; at Fire Island, same thing. He probably knows where the other four are hidden, too."

"Well, if I were Lye," said Pauline, "and if I already knew where to go but just needed you to get there, then I would do more than just kill time and wait for you to figure out the clues on your own. If I were him, I'd—oh, I don't know—give you a call or write you a letter, anything with a big x-marks-the-spot."

"I know, right?" Ret agreed, Pauline's remark having the opposite effect of what she had intended. "So why is he stalling? What's he waiting for? It's like he wants me to figure it out on my own—to feel like I'm a step ahead of him. He must understand that, if he came right out and told me where to go and what to do, I'd think it was some kind of trap and would back off."

"So you're not working for him," Pauline tried to conclude.

"I know I'm not," said Ret desperately, "but maybe I am in a roundabout way—in a sort of indirect way."

"Is it your scars?"

"Yes and no," Ret answered. "The scars help me figure out where to go, which Lye already seems to know, but they also help me feel what to do and even cause the Oracle to open, so maybe that's what he needs from me..."

"Oh, Ret!" Pauline sighed. "You exhaust me! Just let it be."

"But I can't, Pauline. I can't!"

"And why not?"

"Because every time I collect an element," Ret replied emotionally, "I feel like I'm helping him." The air was silent for a few moments. Ret took a deep breath and sunk into a hunched position before continuing. "Lye is trying to collect the elements so he can achieve world domination—or whatever it is sick-minded, power-hungry people want. Every time I collect one of them, he collects one of them, too, and *I'm* the one who collected it for him. A win for us is a win for him. So the best way to stop Lye is to stop collecting the elements. If all he needs is me—or my scars, really anyone from my line—then I should just not let him have me. The best way to stop Lye is to never fill the Oracle; that way, he can never have it filled for himself. Maybe that's why none of my ancestors ever made any real progress in filling it: because they were smarter than I am, and they realized early on that if the Oracle remains empty, then Lye remains empty handed."

Pauline had taken part in enough crestfallen conversations throughout her lifetime to know how to turn the tide of despair in this one and return Ret to the realm of rational thought. Ret had begun his woebegone monologue as if he already believed in a possible truth that he really didn't want to believe in. When he mentioned it to Pauline, she naturally took the opposite position, hoping to talk him out of it. But, for a reason that Pauline had always noticed but could never explain, no matter how much evidence she presented to the contrary, the sorrowing party only became more and more entrenched in its stance. Over the years, however, Pauline had experimented with a different tactic—indeed, the opposite approach: instead of trying to talk someone out of something, she tried to talk him into it.

"Well, I guess you're right, Ret," Pauline shrugged, secretly smiling. "I guess you really are working for Lye, and the only way to fix it is to give up."

Ret paused to internalize Pauline's words and then laughed. Her ridiculous statement caused Ret to wake up and see how ridiculous he had been. He glanced at her appreciatively, embarrassed by his irrational behavior.

"I can't give up," Ret said, almost in a whisper, his head still lowered.

"I know you can't," Pauline returned tenderly, touching his chin with her finger to lift his drooping head. "That's why I said it."

Just then, with the tide nearly at its lowest point of retreat, Pauline saw a familiar object that reminded her of something.

"You know, Ret," she began quietly, her eyes shiny from restrained tears, "it seems to me like the whole reason you're still carrying on with this Oracle business is to stop Lye."

"Well, yeah," he returned, as if she had stated the obvious.

"But I'm not so sure that's the goal," said Pauline. "Is that why the Oracle exists—to prevent Lye from getting it?" Ret knew such logic was absurd. "Do you remember that parchment thing we read in Coy's house a while back—you know, the one with the poem? What did it say, again?"

Having committed it to memory long ago, Ret rattled it off, saying:

What now is six, must be one;
Earth's imbalance to be undone.
Fill the Oracle, pure elements reunite;
Cure the world; one line has the rite.

"Yeah, that's it," Pauline remembered. "Does it say anything in there about stopping Lye?"

Ret pondered for a moment before answering slowly, "No, it doesn't say anything about Lye."

"Right, it doesn't," said Pauline curiously, unsure of where she was going with her train of thought, as it was coming to her bit by bit. This was the first time she had ever given any prolonged thought to the prophetic words. "Fill the Oracle, reunite the elements—those are clearly Lye's goals." Ret patiently collected each of her piecemeal thoughts. "One line has the rite—so, like you said, he must need you and your scars."

"But it seems to me," Ret interjected, "that Lye would never want to undo Earth's imbalance," then with added emphasis, "or cure the world."

"Of course not," Pauline agreed. And then the light bulb went from flicker to flood. "Of course not," she repeated with newfound confidence, "because those are *our* goals, Ret." He was beginning to see, too. "Undo Earth's imbalance; cure the world—Lye wants to stop those things from happening; we need to make sure they *do* happen. All this time, we've been viewing this stuff as a means to stop bad things from happening, but it's so much more than that: it's a quest for good things—great things—to take place as well. Our goal is not to stop Lye; Lye's goal is to stop *us*."

"So, if Lye doesn't want those things to happen," Ret wondered, "why does he want to fill the Oracle?"

"Because he probably figures if he is in control of the Oracle when the final element is collected, then he can stop those things from happening. I'm sure Lye has realized by now that, sooner or later, someone is going to step up and find the elements. But if Lye can get there first and be ready to seize control at that pivotal moment, then he probably thinks he's got a chance." Ret was surprised by how much valuable insight Pauline was producing for someone who had never before vocalized her opinion on this matter.

"I'm not sure why it seems none of your ancestors ever took up the challenge to fill the Oracle," Pauline continued. "Maybe that was before Lye was ready or willing to accept the fact that someone like you might give him a run for his money, so he scared them off or threatened them or killed them. Or maybe your ancestors shared some of your earlier thoughts—that all they had to do to stop Lye was to ignore the whole operation— that they wouldn't have to devote themselves to a greater cause and could just live their own life." Now Ret felt a bit ashamed for entertaining the idea of shirking his responsibility. "So you're not helping Lye, Ret. Even if we give up and let the elements remain uncollected, he still wins. To *not* collect the elements would be to help Lye."

Ret had never thought of things in such light before, and it certainly was an empowering perspective. Suddenly feeling much better, Ret leaned over to give Pauline a hug. "Thank you," he told her. "Is that why you came down here to talk to me?"

"No, not at all, actually," Pauline admitted with a chuckle. "It was just something that sort of came to me, I guess," then, with a smile, she added, "once I saw that peculiar-looking rock out there." She pointed out to sea, where Ret spied Jaret's tombstone. "When I saw it, I was reminded of Jaret's favorite adage—the motto that he lived by every day of his life: the only way for evil to prevail is for good men to do nothing." Jaret was Ret's hero for so many reasons.

Pauline rose to her feet and started down shore. Ret followed a few steps behind. The sand was still wet and becoming more so the further they walked toward the sea. The clouds had not allowed the sun to come out and dry things off. Even the face of the tombstone was still slick and glossy. As they neared the marker, Pauline's pace slowed. Together, she and Ret stood in silence, their heads down in reverence.

"How do you feel, now that you know he's alive?" Ret asked delicately.

"I always knew he was," Pauline confessed. "I know that might sound corny, but it's true. There was something, deep down inside, telling me to have hope, to hold on. And then, when you came to us, it was sort of a lifeline to keep going. I just fear what Lye has done to him."

"Do you think Lye brainwashed him?" Ret wondered.

"Unfortunately, that's the only explanation I can think of. That would explain why Jaret never returned to us or sent anything our way. I know he would have tried to do something to ease my pain. Truthfully, he may have been brainwashed for his own good: Jaret probably would have rather died than serve someone like Lye."

Then Ret asked something that he had been curious about for quite some time: "Do you think Lye brainwashed me?"

"Possibly," Pauline replied, her thick hair swaying in the salty breeze. "I just hope he didn't do to Jaret what he did to you." Ret looked at her quizzically. "Your entire memory was erased, Ret. If the same happened to Jaret—" Her voice trailed off, replaced by tears. The implications were too tragic to put into words.

What Pauline said next took Ret by surprise. "I want you to know, Ret, that I am a full believer in the Oracle now. I support you 100%. I know it took me a while to get onboard; I hope you will forgive me." He already had long ago. "Now that I've seen what's at stake and what's already been done, I'm willing to do whatever it takes to make things right. We need Mr. Coy; we can't do this without him. I know he and I have sparred over virtually everything in the past, but I promise to change that. You have my word. This is what I came to tell you."

Pauline's words were so unexpected that Ret was a little suspicious. He almost asked her to explain her motivations. Still staring at the tomb of the unfound spouse, Ret wondered if the only reason for Pauline's sudden pledge of allegiance was because there was now something in it for her. Ret chose instead to relish the moment, preferring to convey gratitude rather than condemnation.

"All I ask is that you help me get rid of this rock," Pauline continued with a more liberated demeanor. She bent over and, with great effort, pushed the top of the tall stone to uproot it. When it had fallen on its side, she proceeded to roll it into the deeper water and turn it over to the will of the waves.

"Wait," Ret petitioned. Winded, Pauline gladly paused. "Why don't we keep it? I'll store it up shore, at my spot. That way, when Jaret comes back, we can show it to him."

Pauline obliged. "I think that's a terrific idea," she said, rising to her feet and putting a sandy hand on Ret's shoulder. "But I'm not carrying it all the way up there." They laughed. With a flick of the wrist, Ret made the rock roll like a bowling ball into his nook as the two of them started towards home.

"Who knows," said Ret, trying to buoy Pauline's hopes as she had done to his, "maybe this will be the place where Jaret's happiest memories start over, just like mine." In his heart, however, Ret had just committed himself to discovering a method to restore the brain's losses. It sounded like a task for none other than the amazing Benjamin Coy.

CHAPTER 6

RINGS A BELL

In the days following his beachside conversation with Pauline, Ret had his mind set on visiting Mr. Coy and asking some specific questions. With each passing day, his imagination seemed to multiply, with Coy's boundless possibilities acting as exponent. Early in the school week, Ret doubled up on his studies so as to free up an entire afternoon when he could finally make the trek to the Manor.

With the sun partly shining and the air somewhat biting, Ret set out for Coy Manor with a briskness that matched the weather. He clopped along the wooden boardwalk behind the house, his feet almost getting ahead of himself, and then freed the kayak from its fetters of dead twigs and cobwebs. Fortunately, Tybee was a place where Ret could sport his fraying shorts and well-worn flip-flops year-round, so it was without a second thought that he plowed into the shallow water and launched into Tybee Creek.

Reaching dry land, Ret ditched his dinghy and barreled up the hill, the dust and debris along the earthen trail hitching a ride on the wet soles of his footwear. As he neared the top of Little Tybee Island, however, he slowed his pace to listen to a familiar sound. It was the ringing of bells—the deep echoes of large bells fit for a tower. Then, as he reached the rugged plateau whereupon the Manor rested, Ret noticed the complex's bell tower for the first time. Its modest height caused it to blend in with the other high-rising and grotesque-looking features of the Manor.

The gong and bong of bells were nothing new to Ret or his fellow islanders, but the source of such resonating certainly was so. Until now, Ret had assumed the regular chiming originated from an aged church somewhere on Tybee, but, all this time, it had been ringing out from the proclaimed eyesore on the next island over.

In addition to announcing the time, the bells were also providing a little tune—a happy, festive jig of a familiar folk song. It brightened Ret's already-lively steps as he neared the Manor's main gate.

And then, as if to complete the cheery ambiance, Ret heard a voice—a beautiful, soothing voice, accompanying the melody of the bells. It was not a harsh voice, but dulcet, and neither was it loud, for Ret had to strain his ear in order to just catch a scant wisp of it. Pleasant and inviting, Ret followed this siren's sound—meaning mythological nymph rather than emergency personnel.

He shuffled along the property's perimeter fence or outer wall (for the design changed every few yards), careful not to drown out the lovely voice. Like a babbling brook, it led him on until he spotted the vocalist on the other side of some olive trees. To Ret's surprise, it was Paige.

Ret called out to her.

Startled, Paige abruptly fell silent. Exposed, she glanced at Ret. Embarrassed, she quickly spun around.

"Oh, hi," she managed to say. "I didn't know you were here."

"May I come in?" Ret asked through the fence's iron bars.

"Of course, of course," Paige graciously welcomed, hoping she had not chased Ret away with her chagrin. "I'll unlock the main gate—"

She had hardly taken two hurried steps when Ret formed a staircase from the periphery's brushy dirt. The last step matched the height of the tall fence, and Ret leapt over the pointed bars onto the lush grass within the compound. Then he forsook his hold on the stairs, letting the earth crumble back into its haphazard heaps.

"You're every trespasser's dream," Paige joked as Ret strolled up to her, having jumped the fence with ease. Upon saying he was someone's dream, they both glanced at each other, then laughed awkwardly before looking away. A few seconds went by, with Paige digging the toe of her shoe into the dirt.

"These are some, uh, beautiful flowers…you've got here," Ret struggled to say.

"Those are zinnias," Paige replied, identifying the bunch that had caught Ret's eye.

"These are cool, too," said Ret, spotting another variety with large, showy blooms.

"Dahlias," Paige pointed out. "Lots of people like those. But do you want to know which ones are my favorite?"

"Sure."

"Look over here," she instructed, lifting a low-hanging leaf out of the way.

After a few moments of searching, Ret asked, "Where?"

"Here," Paige chuckled, "right in front of you."

"These little blue things?"

"Yep," Paige answered proudly, pushing a curl of hair behind her ear. "They're called forget-me-nots."

"For real?" Ret wondered at the unusual name. "Why are they your favorite?"

"Oh, I don't know," she sighed as she admiringly

caressed the tiny, cerulean florets. "Most people tend to like the big, impressive flowers, and they *are* gorgeous, but I like the small forget-me-nots. You really have to be looking in order to see them. I mean, if you're not careful, you might not know they're even there — which would be a shame: just look how beautiful they are."

Ret, who had been looking at Paige more than the petals, then said, "Almost as beautiful as your voice."

"Oh, well," Paige replied nervously, rising from her stooped position, "I don't know about that."

Just then, Ret was struck with an idea that was entirely not his own.

"What are you doing for Valentine's Day?" he asked off-the-cuff.

Pleasantly surprised, Paige responded, "That depends." Unlike Ret, Paige possessed more technique in the dating game. "What did you have in mind?"

Paige's question caught Ret totally off-guard. "Well, um…," he stammered, trying to ad-lib, "it depends." He returned Paige's playful smile.

"Depends on what?"

"Depends on…how you respond to my first question," he said, almost as a question itself.

"Oh, Ret!" Paige laughed heartily. "You're so funny." He hadn't been trying to be humorous but reckoned he ought to just go with it since it appeared to be working. "If you're asking me out on a date, then my answer is yes, of course."

"Okay, cool," said Ret, nearly sweating. "I'll have Ana give you the details later," he breathed, already exhausted.

"Is that why you came all the way over here?" Paige inquired, assuming such to be the case.

Ret opened his mouth to answer but figured a bit of fabrication might go a long way. "Yes," he answered unconvincingly, "sort of. I also came over to talk to your dad. Is he around?"

"Yeah," she said. "He's in the belfry." She pointed at the bell tower, which was still sending forth its melodious music.

"You mean someone's actually in there?" Ret asked.

"Of course," said Paige matter-of-factly. "Someone has to play the carillon."

"Who's Carol Lynn?" said Ret, puzzled.

Paige erupted in laughter. "Dad will explain it better than I can. Go on up and see him."

So Ret withdrew from Paige, leaving her amid the flowers and feeling happier than she had been in a long time.

Paige had just disappeared from view when Ret wished he had asked her for directions. He had already walked a good distance around the west side of the

Manor but had yet to locate an entrance. The large double doors, through which he had always entered previously, were not right around the corner as he had initially presumed. He should have known better, as Coy Manor never stayed the same for very long.

In time, he arrived at a stretch of the Manor's exterior wall that was made of large stone blocks. Like strolling down the bread aisle at the grocery store, the rectangular blocks were mortared with considerable uniformity, except for one portion that appeared to have been sloppily constructed. In fact, with its numerous gaps and mismatched pieces, it resembled a poorly played game of Tetris. Upon closer examination, it occurred to Ret that the bricks in this section were loose, so he rather instinctively began to shuffle them around, filling holes here and closing crevices there. Before long, he uncovered a sort of secret passageway into the Manor.

Ret walked into the sewer-like corridor, his cautious footsteps echoing against the stone walls. The light of day quickly faded as he pressed on, so he conjured up a flame in his hand, holding it as would a torchbearer. Soon, Ret encountered puddles of water at his feet. Then came the emergence of several other corridors, branching off in multiple directions. But he did not begin to worry until he heard the distant trumpeting of an elephant—followed by the chirping of monkeys and then the squawking of parrots.

Ret stopped to check his ears. He noticed a faint light overhead: a sewer grate half-covered by overgrown grass. He pushed it up, lifted himself out, and replaced the dripping grate to its original position.

Ret found himself in the center of a broad savanna. He stood knee-deep in the dry brush of the grassland, whose flatness was interrupted by an occasional acacia tree and termite mound. Although it felt like he had just joined an African safari, the glass, domed ceiling far above him begged to differ. The room spanned longer and wider than many football fields, with what appeared to be wildebeests in one distant corner, gazelles in another.

Suddenly, a frenzied herd of antelope swarmed past Ret, darting to and fro like deer as they tried to dodge him. As the last of the group hurried by, Ret glanced behind himself to see if he ought to be fleeing, too. Sure enough, he turned around just in time to see a pouncing cheetah flying through the air toward him.

Ret fell to the ground as the cat soared over him. He was on his feet in a flash. The cheetah had abandoned his pursuit of the antelope and was now skulking in the grass, his shiny eyes fixated on a much tastier meal. Ret stood, feet apart and arms free, poised and ready.

Without warning, the feline attacked, springing fangs-first toward Ret. With impeccable timing, Ret tore a patch of earth out of the ground and flung it towards himself. The sod-like cutting would have hit him in the face had he not leaned way back to avoid it, like playing an extreme game of limbo. The cheetah landed on the cutting in midair and was carried away as if riding a magic carpet. Ret immediately tried to send the platform high above the floor so as to quarantine the creature, but it made an impressive leap back into the arena.

Ret knew he needed to escape, but he was also aware that he could not outrun such a beast. If he could somehow isolate or encage the animal, perhaps doing so would grant him enough time to find the nearest exit.

Out of nowhere, the cheetah charged. Ret lunged out of the way, onto the ground. Then he saw a pair of massive paws appear above the grass. He rolled as fast as he could but wasn't agile enough. Just as claws were closing in, Ret buried himself in soil. Like lying in his own grave, Ret listened as the cheetah struck his enclosure. The cat quickly scratched the layers away and broke through.

Rising to his feet, Ret watched as a second cheetah appeared on the scene—followed by a third, with hyenas not far behind. Ret had had enough. As his antagonists started to close in, he set the savanna ablaze. In a single motion, he encircled himself in a ring of fire. To his astonishment, however, the cheetahs leapt over the flames.

Suddenly, Ret began to feel the ground vibrating. The intensifying quaking frightened the cheetahs, bewildered by the flames that prevented them from seeing what might be approaching. When Ret saw a stampeding rhinoceros plow through the fire, he initiated combustion at his feet and launched himself a dozen feet into the air.

Ret was shocked to find himself hovering above an entire pack of rhinos, with Conrad riding the lead rhino like a horse. With the danger driven away, Ret dropped back down to the ground to thank his rescue party.

Conrad had slid off his beast to inspect the burnt grassland and ensure it was fully extinguished. Meanwhile, Ret observed the monstrous creatures roaming around them, each a striking sight to behold. Of the white species, these gray-skinned mammals stood as tall as Conrad, their length double their height. Each had a pair of horns, the front one much longer than the other behind it.

While the rest of the pack grazed nearby, the rhinoceros that Conrad had ridden refused to join the others; in fact, it didn't move much at all. It didn't even swish its tail to dispel the annoying flies like its comrades were frequently doing. Like Feathers the lion, this rhino was profoundly docile. Ret marveled how Conrad had been able to achieve such domestication with a wild animal, especially one whose imposing horn was as long as one of Ret's legs.

Soon, Conrad returned. With his usual straight-faced demeanor, the burly aborigine nodded affirmatively at Ret, mounted his beast, and turned to press on.

"Wait!" Ret protested. "How do I get to the bell tower?"

Conrad pointed to a giant boulder, about a stone's throw away. Then the taciturn man gripped his rhino and, without so much as a kick in its side or shout of "giddy up," the herd moved out.

Having just learned the savanna's top two rules for survival—that is, to watch your back and keep moving—Ret dared not to dawdle. He hastened toward the large rock, though, like most everything else in the Manor, he knew not what to expect. Fortunately, this puzzle was easily solved: Ret located a small, granite-colored button and pressed it. Two rectangular slabs of the boulder's face parted, revealing a square cavity within. Stepping inside, Ret considered the hollow opening to be an elevator, except for the fact that its walls were entirely blank. When the doors closed, he was enveloped in darkness.

Ret got a bit spooked when he felt something like a pair of tiny earmuffs slide gently onto his head, coming to rest on his temples. Suddenly, a question entered Ret's mind: "Where would I like to go?" No audible voice had uttered the query, yet the question pressed itself to the forefront of Ret's thinking.

The answer was simple: "The bell tower," he thought to himself. As if it had received a command, the earmuffs flew off his head, and the elevator immediately jolted into motion. With great speed, it descended for a ways, then rushed right, then left, then perhaps diagonally—Ret couldn't tell amid the darkness.

Eventually, the conveyor assumed a lateral motion, traveling neither up nor down but sideways. Suddenly, wondrous scenes began to flash before Ret's eyes as the elevator passed through the other arenas that constituted Coy's personal zoo. Through the glass walls of his people-mover, Ret saw rainforests of towering trees, with apes swinging on vines and frogs clinging to walls; deserts where coyotes and lizards darted among the cactus and sand; even a polar region where white-furred bear cubs fished among white-tusked walrus colonies in icy waters. Window after window, the earth's ecosystems were played out with astounding majesty. Only in Coy Manor could things that were worlds apart be only walls apart.

Then darkness—a few quick turns—stop. The double doors opened, and three additional riders entered. One was outfitted like an Eskimo, another like a bee keeper, and the third in scuba gear. Ret watched as three earmuffs lowered from the ceiling and came to rest on each of the newcomers' heads. Then the devices rose, and the elevator was off.

Since the beeman was masked and the diver was goggled, only the arctic agent glanced at Ret, giving him a funny look. Ret rejoined with a glare of his own, since the polar man himself looked like an electrocuted hamster.

The next few minutes were a tad overwhelming for Ret. Every few seconds, the elevator would stop to let off passengers and permit others to get on. Seemingly endless hordes of people were exchanged: bakers and cooks, and teachers with books; decorators with mirrors, and gardeners with shears; housemaids wielding wet mops, and butchers grasping pork chops; carpenters and exterminators, and even someone dressed like a clown and juggling turnips. Their destinations were equally as varied, with some stopping in offices and kitchens, others in freezers and workshops. Through it all, everyone seemed to know each other, hailing with a "hi there," or bidding with a "bye now."

In time, the last passenger had been dropped off, and the elevator began to travel directly upward. Ret felt his ears pop as the elevation increased, and he knew he was finally on his way to the belfry.

When the doors slid ajar, Ret stood in a complete stupor. Staring into nothingness, he didn't budge, too dazed by the whirlwind he had just experienced.

"Well, it's about time you got here," said Mr. Coy, his back to Ret. "I was beginning to worry."

Like an overloaded pipe finally draining free, Ret shook off his trance and sighed, "Sorry, but this place is crazy."

"Not crazy," Mr. Coy corrected with a tinge of offense, "just *coy*. It's a tough name to live up to, but I'd say I do it rather swimmingly, wouldn't you?"

"Wait," said Ret, backtracking. "You were expecting me?"

"Ever since you set foot on my property," Coy informed. "On this island, nothing goes unnoticed."

"Seems kind of overprotective," Ret muttered.

"Accurate information precedes inspiration, my young friend," said Coy soberly. "Nothing ever comes to light in the dark."

Ret didn't give the advice much thought, mostly because he didn't have much left to give. Rubbing his head, he staggered out of the elevator's cabin.

"Looks like you needed some 'protection' out there on the savanna," Coy snickered.

"Yeah," Ret replied, "your cheetah almost tore me to shreds."

"I do appreciate you not hurting the poor cats," said Coy gratefully. "Years ago, I saved their skins from a stubborn group of poachers. Same with the rhinos, though I couldn't get to all of them in time." Coy's voice trailed off, as if he had remembered something gruesome. "Anyway, I'm glad you're safe—knew you would be."

When Ret rolled his eyes at Coy's glib remark, he unintentionally did a visual sweep of his new surroundings. It was a small room, not unlike a stuffy attic. Mr. Coy, who still had yet to turn around, was facing the far wall, against which stood a strange piece of furniture, insofar as Ret could tell. It looked like an upright piano, except its keyboard was made of pegs, and its strings extended vertically through the ceiling. Mr. Coy was sitting on a wooden bench in front of the contraption, with his feet resting on a second manual of pegs.

"What is this thing?" Ret wondered, taking a few steps forward.

"Why, it's my carillon," Coy beamed. "Four octaves and 47 bells of pure musical bliss. I add a couple of bells every few months—keeps the staff busy, you know."

"So you don't actually ring the bells?" Ret asked, trying to understand.

"Each one of these batons acts as a sort of lever," Coy taught, placing a hand on the pegs that looked like table legs. "When I strike it with my fist, it pulls a wire connected to a metal clapper, and it's the clapper that hits the inside of the bell. The harder I press, the louder the sound." Coy hit a few pegs to illustrate his lesson, filling the room with vibrations that scemed to come from all angles.

"Impressive," said Ret admiringly.

"Yes, it is," Coy said of the apparatus, even though Ret was complimenting Coy's ability to play it. "One of the largest and heaviest of all instruments. This one is nearly 75 tons, I think."

"I'd love to watch you play something," Ret urged, standing at Coy's side. "How about this one?" He pointed to a stack of well-worn sheet music resting next to Coy on the bench. The top page read "Second Waltz" by Dmitri Shostakovich. Scribbled underneath the title were the words *Helen's favorite*.

"Maybe some other time," Coy suggested, a mixture of both heaviness and longing in his soft tone. "So," he perked up, anxious to change the subject, "what brings you to the Manor today?"

"I'd like to ask you about a few things," said Ret, "if that's okay."

"Of course," Coy cheered, turning away from the carillon to give Ret his undivided attention. "Ask away."

"Can Conrad control minds? Or, at least, does he have some kind of power over animals? I remember seeing a connection between him and the lion that night with Stone. I mean, Feathers hardly even moved, like he was some kind of robot. And then today, with the rhino: the one Conrad was riding behaved so differently compared to all the others in the herd. I wonder if it has anything to do with that headpiece Conrad wears..."

Coy smiled like a father proud of his son. "Very astute observations, Ret. Strictly speaking, Conrad cannot control minds, but he can influence them, all thanks to that headpiece—or, as I like to call it, the neuroscope." For Ret, the term rang a bell, but he was glad when Coy went on to explain it. "As you may recall, the neuroscope was the genius behind the subsuits we wore in the water to and from Sunken Earth. It sends an electrical current through the brain and intercepts the impulses being transmitted among neurons." Having been reminded, Ret now recalled the memory perfectly. "With the subsuits, the neuroscope transports thoughts *out* of the brain, but with Conrad's telepathic capabilities, the neuroscope transmits thoughts *into* the brain."

"So that must be what happened on your elevator," Ret inferred.

"Exactly," said Coy. "The headpiece that lowered from the ceiling was a neuroscope. After it came to rest on your head, it sent an electrical current into your brain. That current is an exact copy of the brain's own electrical impulse when it wonders the question, 'Where would I like to go?' That's what it asked, am I right?"

"Word for word," Ret responded.

"Now, with regard to Conrad," Coy continued, eager to share. "Neuroscopes can be linked together, very similar to people speaking on their cell phones, allowing thoughts and ideas to flow between minds. But herein lies a problem: just because you *think* something doesn't mean you have to *do* it. For example, all the elevator did was get you *thinking* about where you wanted it to take you, but you didn't have to answer. You could have ignored the thought, not responded to the question, and the elevator would not have gone anywhere. But very few minds are capable of totally expelling thoughts without first giving them some thought. The brain is not programmed that way naturally; it has to be trained. This is why the process works so well with animals; they have virtually no power of reason beyond instinct. When a thought flies into their inferior minds, they act on it—so when Conrad gives them a command, they do it. It's just like training a dog, but instead of shouting orders at the beast, the trainer merely needs to think them."

Ironically for Ret, so much talk of brains was beginning to fry his own.

"But only a person with immense composure is capable of thinking for multiple minds simultaneously," said Coy, "which is why Conrad is able to do it so well. He is a man of tremendous self-control who possesses a mental discipline as strong as steel. It's a self-taught self-mastery, no doubt the result of his experiences in life. What Conrad is able to do with the neuroscope is much more than mere multi-tasking; I'd say it even surpasses the dynamics of an avatar. It centers around the ability to purposely forget, and, believe me, it is very difficult to remind yourself to lose track of something." Ret could hardly fathom the concept. "So you see, the secret is control over self—to have conquered yourself enough to engage auto pilot and focus instead on what another life is going through." Then, as if contemplating his own words, Coy said, "Sounds a lot like motherhood, actually."

Like peeking inside a fire hydrant, Ret's simple curiosity had been answered by a flood of information from Mr. Coy. As grateful as he was for all the new material to chew on, Ret reckoned now was an opportune time to ask the real question he had come all this way to ask.

Said Ret, "So can you restore a person's memory?"

For a minute, silence prevailed. The room's sole window was slightly ajar, through which a gentle breeze carried the faint cries of seagulls circling below. Mr. Coy slowly turned to stare at Ret for a few moments, as if to see how serious he was. For quite a while now, Coy knew it was only a matter of time before Ret approached him with queries concerning his amnesia and if he could rectify it. Recent revelations regarding Jaret only compounded Coy's dread. Could there be integrity in a white lie if uttered for a person's own good?

"The *human* mind is a whole different animal," said Coy with a deep breath, treading carefully. "Indeed, the human brain is something akin to a miracle. It regulates body temperature and blood pressure; it controls breathing and heart rate. It interprets all the things we see, hear, smell, taste, and touch. It orchestrates the great movements of walking, talking, and sitting. And most of it at the same time. And sure, we've come to understand the basics of neurons, axons, and dendrites; but I submit there exists an entirely separate dimension to the brain that science will never comprehend unless it changes its platform."

"What do you mean?" asked Ret, intrigued.

"When I pinch my arm," Coy said, grabbing a clump of skin near his wrist, "my nerves send a signal to my brain to let me know what's going on. This is how it works with things that happen *to* us, or external stimulus. But what about internal stimulus? What gives us the power to think—the ability to reason? What is the grand idea generator—the source from which our thoughts flow?"

"Take this instrument, for example," he continued, turning to face the carillon. "Without someone to play it, it's useless. Like the brain, it is a complex system, with bells like neurons and wires like axons. But without some musician, working inside this claustrophobic cabin, striking the keys, the whole contraption is worthless. I suppose an external stimulus could create a good gong—a mighty wind or kamikaze bird—but without an internal force, the music will never ring out."

"So how does that relate to memory?" Ret wondered.

"When I see you," Coy carried on, "something in my mind reaches into its store of memories and tells me that you are Ret—that is, in the brain's carillon, it strikes the peg to play a B-flat. But when I see Ana, it knows to play a C-sharp. Where does it come from? How is it accessed? Who is playing the music? There is something up there—in there. It's a higher dimension of intelligence—a phantom in the attic, a specter from an unseen realm. It's the reason why I believe we never lose our memories, Ret. We may forget them, yes, but they are always there—somewhere. Just because we can't remember something doesn't mean it's gone. It existed once; even unspoken thoughts existed once as brain matter. The mind stores everything it receives; we're the ones who limit what it retrieves. Time is a great forgetter; ask someone with a broken heart. So is our own desire, whether to forget or to retain; ask someone holding a grudge. But your memory is not lost, Ret; it has just been forgotten. And all you need in order to remember it, piece by piece, is something that reminds you of it—something that rings a bell. And the more in tune you are with whatever it is that quickens the inner mind, the more clearly those bells will ring."

Ret was beginning to see the truth of Mr. Coy's words. Just moments ago, Coy's mentioning of the word *neuroscope* struck a chord with Ret's memory, and, by the time the concept had been explained anew, he had remembered it. Ret also recalled the experience he had aboard Coy's yacht last summer on their way to the submerged road when he was about to jump into the ocean to aid in the rescue of Pauline: the scene before him, with a ship sinking amid bubbling waters and billowing flames, did not feel entirely new to him, as if he had experienced it before. Indeed, it had a familiar ring to it.

"Yes, the human mind," Coy celebrated, rejoicing in its profundity. *"Mind*-boggling, isn't it?" At this moment, Coy felt quite content with the extent to which he had addressed Ret's question, having answered it without divulging all he knew. Of a truth, Coy did have a way of accessing the brain's forgotten memories, but he wasn't sure yet if he wanted Ret to know.

"Now *I've* a question for *you,"* said Coy broadly, anxious to change the subject. "Any leads as to what the next element might be?"

"No," said Ret thoughtfully, "I haven't had any weird encounters with things lately. But I know of a place we could go to maybe find some clues?"

"And where might that be?"

"That island we saw from your balloon," Ret explained. "It could have been the reason my scar lit up."

The conversation had reached another topic whose inevitable surfacing Mr. Coy had been loathing. He had hoped Ret would not have made the deduction that the wretched place might share a link to the Oracle.

"I'm sorry, Ret," said Coy sullenly, "but I cannot go there."

"But I really think—"

"You can go without me, of course," Coy suggested. "I'm afraid I'm just not ready to face that place again."

It was only for a split second that Ret even considered making such a voyage without Coy. It was out of the question.

"I can't do this without you," Ret pled, hoping to convince Coy to confront his fears.

"I know you can't," Coy replied, taking Ret by surprise. "Especially since I know something you don't know."

"Like what?"

"The scar you told Stone about," Coy went on, "was not the only scar that illuminated that night." Ret shot him a glare of near betrayal. Smirking, Coy reminded him, "Accurate information precedes inspiration, my boy."

"Well, what was it?" Ret hounded. "What did it look like?"

"I don't know," Coy admitted. "It was nothing more than a squiggly line, but it seemed incomplete— if that's all there was to it, then it would have a hard time aligning with its twin on the Oracle. It was on your right hand, to the left of the scar of the hook and triangle."

Ret held out his right palm. Coy's description meant this new scar was in the center of the palm, with the hook and triangle to the right toward the thumb and with a still-unknown scar to the left toward the little finger. Although the hook and triangle were easy to see, the other two scars were still too unpronounced to decipher.

"Well that's not very helpful," Ret shrugged.

"But wait—there's more!" Coy led on, impersonating an infomercial. "I bent our course a different way that night. Instead of returning home along the west side of the South American continent, I took us up the east side. The scar made its debut when we came upon the mouth of the Amazon River."

"So what are you thinking?" Ret asked with growing anticipation, though he was almost certain he already knew the answer.

With adventure flaring in his eyes, Mr. Coy said, "Don't bother packing an umbrella."

CHAPTER 7

LOVE IS IN THE AIR

By the time Valentine's Day rolled around, Ret had lost a considerable amount of sleep, lying awake at night in nervous anticipation of his date with Paige. By a stroke of genius, Ana had suggested that she and Steve join the occasion, thinking a second couple might relieve some of the pressure. Ret gratefully obliged.

Ana's confidence helped to calm Ret's worries. She dished out hearty servings of advice—what to do and what not to do. Together, they brainstormed what venue would be the most practical and what activities might be the most economical. Ana was well aware of Ret's amateur status when it came to all things romantic, so she was happy to unload her vast stores of expertise.

Still, in the hours leading up to showtime, Ret was beginning to regret the whole production.

"What if she gets bored? Or cold?" Ret feared.

"What if I say something dumb? Or stutter or—"

"Relax, Ret," Ana called out from the bathroom. She was sitting sidesaddle on the counter with her face an inch from the mirror. Ret always marveled at the countless steps of her makeup routine.

"How can I relax?" Ret balked. "I haven't even picked out what shirt I'm going to wear."

"You don't have very many," Ana pointed out. "It can't be that hard."

"How about this one?" Ret held out a bright yellow polo.

"That hideous thing?" Ana critiqued. "Your date would need sunglasses just to look at you. I still don't know why Mom got that for you."

"She said it was on sale," Ret recalled.

"Can't imagine why..."

"I kinda like it," said Ret. He brought it up to his face and found it softened his skin's own brightness. "It makes me look, you know, more normal."

"Oh, Ret," Ana rolled her eyes, "not that subject again."

"Right," Ret said coolly, returning the yellow shirt to the far reaches of his closet. "I just need to be myself."

"Don't just be yourself, Ret," Ana advised. "Be your *best* self. True love should bring out the best in each other. So just put your date's needs above your own— you know, show her you've been thinking about her."

"Right," Ret said, trying to reassure himself as he put on a shirt of a darker shade. "It's the thought that counts."

"But it's not just the thought that counts," Ana corrected. (Ret could never win.) "You've got to follow through with action. For instance, it's one thing to *think* about getting your date chocolates, but it's quite another to actually get them."

"Does Paige like chocolate?" Ret wondered in earnest.

"It was just an example, Ret," Ana laughed. "Girls love it when you show them that you listen to what they say. Like when Steve bought me that GPS for my birthday."

Ret was about to tell Ana the truth about the real giver of the gadget, but he was suddenly struck with a brilliant idea and made a mental note to stop by the florist on their way to the date.

The twilight of evening was still far away when Ret and Ana headed out the door. Pauline, who loved Ana's idea of a double date, requested they return home before nightfall. As such, the shorter days of winter called for an earlier departure time. Since Ana had yet to secure her driver license, they decided on a location within walking distance: the boardwalk, whose carnival-style attractions were sure to provide them with lots to do.

Within moments of one other, everyone had converged at the predetermined spot near the front of Tybee's beachfront promenade. Paige had asked her chauffeur to drop her off a block away from the gathering place, so as not to create a scene. As usual, her outfit was nothing fancy. Although he had never told her, Ret liked her unornamented approach to fashion, as it brought out the radiance of her natural beauty. Her long curls bounced about her simple scarf as she bounded up the street.

Meanwhile, a speeding car came barreling around the corner, commanding the attention of everyone in the vicinity.

"There's Steve," Ana sighed, rolling her eyes.

With a loud roar, Steve accelerated toward the boardwalk and came to a screeching halt in the parking lot. His set of wheels was the apple of his eye: an antique of an auto, salvaged from a former generation and fully restored by himself. With slick hair and sleek clothes, he stepped out and approached the Coopers, often glancing back with pride at his ride.

"It's a 1978 Chevy Nova, you know," Ana mumbled to Ret.

"Since when do you know anything about cars?" Ret asked in awe. "You can hardly drive one."

"All he ever talks about is that thing," she said with annoyance. "I could tell you everything there is to know about it. For example, did you know the gas tank plug is behind the rear license plate?"

"That's different," said Ret.

"You're telling me. The first time I pumped the gas, he didn't bother showing me where it was. He thought it was a good trick; still laughs about it." Their dates had nearly arrived now, so Ana quickly added, "He tells everyone how it's some kind of V8 car, but I don't see how it could run on something like vegetable juice; *I* can barely drink that stuff."

Ret was eager to present his fresh bouquet of forget-me-not flowers to Paige.

"Oh, Ret!" Paige lit up. "You're so sweet." She gave him a hug while Ana gave him a wink for a job well done.

An awkward silence ensued, as if it was Steve's turn to show his premeditated thought for Ana.

"And…uh…I got you a pair of guns," Steve told his date, coming up with something on the spot.

"Guns?" Ana questioned.

"Yeah, these guns." Steve flexed his biceps ostentatiously. Ret suppressed a humored snort while Paige blushed.

"Oh," Ana sighed with disappointment. "You shouldn't have."

The first order of business on the unwritten agenda was to get a bite to eat. As they approached the entrance to the indoor eatery, Steve suddenly scooped up Ana in his arms and carried her over the threshold. Ret, on the other hand, held the door open and let his lady go first.

"What do you feel like?" Ret asked Paige as they surveyed their options.

"I need a burger," Steve bellowed, rubbing his stomach.

Taken aback by such an executive order, Paige answered softly, "That sounds fine."

"I'll go find us a table," Steve told Ana. "Get me a burger with everything on it."

"Even onions?" Ana winced.

"Oh, and a large Coke," he added, walking away, as the three of them got in line.

"Steve seems like quite the charmer," Ret observed.

"He's just hungry," Ana said, trying to be optimistic. When they turned to see what table Steve had selected, they found him sitting at one that positioned him directly in front of a big-screen television.

Ana ordered first: a burger for her man, a salad for herself. Paige, not wanting something messy, liked the idea of a salad. But when she saw Ana foot the bill for Steve's plate in addition to her own, she changed her mind.

"I'm not very hungry," she whispered to Ret. "I'll just have some of your fries, if that's okay." Ret agreed; he didn't really like French fries anyway.

Throughout the entire meal, Ret felt like Steve was staring at him. Turns out, the sports junkie was only glaring between Ret and Paige, keeping a close eye on the game.

"So did you ever make it up to the bell tower the other day?" Paige asked Ret, trying to initiate conversation.

"Yeah, I did," Ret explained. "It took a while, but I finally did."

Ana admired how Ret and Paige were handling dinner—how Ret took appropriate bites of his hamburger, frequently offering some to his date in case her occasional pick at his shoestring fries wasn't satisfying her hunger. She also liked the subtle romance behind the couple's subconscious act of sharing the same plate.

"Would you like some of my salad?" Ana offered her date, copying Ret's style.

"Not a chance," Steve declined. "Not that rabbit food." He had consumed his meal both quickly and loudly, chewing with his mouth ajar and licking his fingers from time to time. The sides of his mouth bore evidence of grease, so Ana handed him a napkin, which he used to wipe his forehead. Then he downed the rest of his soda and belched.

"Now *that* was good," Steve said, slouching back in his chair.

Trying to shrug off her date's impropriety, Ana asked, "Why did you go to the Manor, Ret?"

"I needed to ask Mr. Coy a few things," he replied.

Recognizing there was one among them who knew nothing about the Oracle (and that it should stay that way), Paige put forth her question safely: "Did my dad tell you what you needed?"

"He sure did," Ret said with amazement. "Your dad's a genius."

"You mean that crazy guy with the lion?" Steve asked, having picked up on a portion of the dialogue now that the sporting event had gone to commercial. "What a weirdo!"

Paige's spirits were suddenly dampened. Ana felt ashamed and rushed to change the subject.

"Who's up for dessert?" she interjected.

With ice-cream cones in hand, the group began a stroll along the boardwalk. It was a cheery place to be, with its carefree mood and open-air setting. Bubbly, clownish music blared from the speakers of carrousels and merry-go-rounds. The pulsating sound effects and clang of cash-turned-coin spilled out from the arcade area. The lights of colorful neon and flashing bulbs were growing brighter with the approach of evening. Even the scent of buttery popcorn and sugary confections over-powered the damp and salty smells of the beach just a few steps away.

Still meandering, the two couples naturally broke off into pairs. Steve was quick to put his arm around Ana and pull her in close, but he was quite slow when it came to conversation. He seemed more interested in the festivities and passersby. Ana turned her attention to Ret and Paige, who were a few steps ahead. They were not making much contact physically (besides an accidental—playful—bump into each other), but they were connecting in practically every other way: talking, laughing, pointing to things of mutual interest. Ana could only overhear bits and pieces of their dialogue— something about a cheetah named Carol Lynn—but it didn't matter: she was much more intrigued by what she saw than what she heard.

In time, Steve couldn't resist the challenge of the carnival games any longer. His first stop was at the basketball booth. Despite a rim with no give and a ball with too much bounce, he managed to score a prize: a giant teddy bear, which he promptly bequeathed to Ana as a token of his love (or masculinity).

One by one, Steve knocked out every game along carnival alley: collapsing a pyramid of bottles with a baseball; landing a ring around protruding pegs; sinking a table-tennis ball in a vase; and, of course, the manifold variations of beanbag toss and dart throw. He had a bit of trouble trying to crawl up the rope ladder, but he restored his manhood with a few impressive rounds of the hammer striker.

Ana served as personal catchall for Steve's steady stream of winnings. Before long, she had become the proud owner of a paddleball, a polka dot bandana, a set of glow-in-the-dark scrunchies, a live (for now) goldfish, a hamburger yo-yo, a white tiger stuffed animal (too lifelike for Ana to look at), an Atlanta Falcons jersey (size XXL), a whoopee cushion (the only thing on which Steve called dibs), a pair of Groucho glasses (which Ana considered wearing to avoid embarrassment), and a Mickey Mouse bobblehead—oh, and the stuffed-to-scale teddy bear. Ana was relieved when a red wagon was added to the family, which she used to pull the loot behind her.

Ret and Paige, however, lost interest somewhere between paddleball and bandana. Though feeling sorry for Ana, they left the gaming duo at the midway and headed to the ticket counter. With childlike innocence, they patronized the rides and rollercoasters. From collisions in the bumper cars to revolutions on the Ferris wheel, the late afternoon transpired in pure bliss. With longing in her eyes, Ana watched the happy couple from the side of her burdensome bear while the stuffed one lounged in the wagon.

With tickets torn and energy spent, Ret and Paige concluded their rendezvous with a shared cup of hot cocoa. Using his straw, Ret pushed all the marshmallows over to Paige's side, since he knew they were her favorite part. Just then, a deflated Ana plopped into the empty chair at their table.

"Where's Steve?" Ret asked, noticing Ana's discontent.

"He's where he's been for the last 30 minutes," she muttered. She pointed inside the nearby arcade, where Steve was gripping a plastic gun and firing pretend bullets into the screen. "I reckon he'll come and find me when he needs more quarters."

"Looks like Steve won a few things for you," Paige observed, trying to make her feel better.

"A few?" Ret gasped, eyeing the bounty. "You hit the mother lode!"

"Yep, it's a jackpot, alright," Ana said without emotion. "A jackpot of junk."

"I'll take some of those scrunchies off your hands," Paige offered cheerily.

"By all means," Ana obliged. "Take 'em all. And here's a fish to go with them," she included, sliding the travel aquarium across the table. "All I am is a prize to Steve—some trophy to put on a shelf."

"Oh, Ana," Paige soothed, "don't take it personally. Maybe he's just not your type."

"You're right, just forget about it," Ana concluded, trying to smile. "He's not the reason we're here, anyway. Don't let my moping dampen the good time you two are having together. Just because my date's a deadbeat who's more interested in shooting zombies doesn't mean the two of you can't still have a good time. All I ask is one thing."

"What's that?" Ret asked.

"Can you buy me some hot chocolate, Ret?" she requested. "I'm broke." Ret was happy to help out.

As they sipped away the cocoa, Ret's mind was swept away in love. Tonight was the first time he and Paige had ever spent a large portion of quality time together, just the two of them. Of course, they had clocked countless hours in each other's company before, but this new capacity of courtship possessed the properties of a paring knife, peeling away outer layers that are so easily misjudged. And, as each shared moment revealed more of the bare bones beneath, Ret was realizing how he and she were very much alike.

For instance, Paige wasn't so shy and dull after all—in fact, she was fun and confident—but, Ret had realized, she came across as reserved and aloof for fear of being trampled. The airship of her very nature soared on a higher plane of thought and reason compared to the general populace. Her aerial views granted awesome vistas that demonstrated such depth in scope and such stability in judgment so as to defy the nonbuoyancy of her age and rise above the rat race of life. Consequently, she rarely shared her feelings and opinions with others because, more often than not, she felt like a bird trying to describe the wonder of flight to a buffalo.

Moreover, Ret already knew something of Paige's intellect and concern for others, but he hadn't been aware of the profound depth of such qualities. She possessed an intelligence that blasted through layers of bedrock and hit wisdom—a compassion that stretched across the strata all the way to unconditional love. Ret felt he could pour out his soul to her and, for once, be understood—hopefully even enlightened. He liked how gentle and kind she was—toward him, yes, but especially toward those who were of no real consequence. He liked how her words were neither cold nor harsh and never accusing; how her behavior seemed to transcend the pettiness of short-sighted gain and momentary pleasure, as if she had some far-off end in mind. Indeed, if Paige were a swimming pool, Ret had taken a few steps tonight into the deep end.

Just a few hours ago, Ret had still been a mere spectator of the magic of love. But, as he was realizing, the trick to love pertained little to what was pulled out of a hat but quite a lot to what came out of the heart. The allusion lay not in what was up his sleeve but what was down in his soul. In order to win Paige's heart, he first had to know it, and, since a magician never reveals his secrets, the only way to know her heart was for him to be of the same one. And so, after some on-the-job experience, Ret had finally come to wield the wand.

Suddenly, the faint chiming of bells began to stir the air. Though difficult to hear amid the noise of the promenade, Little Tybee Island's resident carillonneur was just starting the daily ritual of the evening carol, marking the end of another day with the strains of a well-known tune.

Ret jumped up from his seat. "Would you care to dance?" he asked Paige, extending his hand in a chivalrous manner that humored them both.

Paige was flattered. She recognized the song as Shostakovich's "Second Waltz," a family favorite. Still, a bit bashful, she petitioned, "But I hardly know how to waltz."

"Good," Ret cheered, grabbing her hand and helping her up. "Then you can teach me!"

Ret strode across the plaza, pulling Paige and her feigned unwillingness behind him. He stopped a good ways down the pier, which connected to the boardwalk and jutted a fair distance above the ocean. The isolation of their impromptu dance floor allowed them to escape the crowd and commotion.

There, in the center of the pier, Ret and Paige stood face to face. Although he had no idea how to waltz, Ret took the lead. He grabbed Paige's hand, put his other one on her waist, and began to bounce and twirl with neither grace nor technique.

"Oh, Ret!" Paige cried. They laughed away any embarrassment. To Ret's joy, Paige then took over. Though by no means an expert herself, she knew the basics. At a slow tempo, she guided Ret. Their feet collided occasionally, and their hips bent awkwardly, but both proved to be quick learners.

Meanwhile, back at the table that the lovebirds had abruptly vacated, Ana sat with harmless envy in her eyes as she watched Ret and Paige. With an elbow on the table, she held up her head with one hand while the other subconsciously stirred her cup of hot chocolate, whose marshmallows were quickly being whipped into cream. With satisfaction, she smiled contentedly at the happy couple on the pier, wishing the same would happen for her. She decided to give Steve one more chance to redeem himself.

She found him in the arcade, vigorously gripping the steering wheel of a fake racecar.

"Ret and Paige are out on the pier," she hinted with an open-ended tone. Steve said nothing. Then she bent over and added loudly in his ear, "They're dancing." He shifted gears in preparation for a hairpin turn. "It would mean a lot to me if you and I joined them."

"Dancing's for girls," said Steve coldly.

It was the last straw for Ana. She furrowed her brow, threw up her arms, and yelled, "Exactly my point!"

Ana marched back to the table. She yanked her wagon of winnings into motion, rolled it to the nearest dumpster, and dumped it all. Then she headed for home, more than ready for her date to be over. As lousy as her evening had been, she considered it worthwhile to have learned firsthand how no amount of GQ can compensate for a lack of IQ. Though initially wooed by Steve's affection, Ana was now certain that all he was willing to offer was a pretty face. Yes, as handsome a stag as Steve was, the buck stopped there.

Back at the boardwalk, a pair of dancers was in step with true love. After a bit of practice, they now waltzed like naturals. The soles of their shoes slid across the wooden planks while the water beneath waved up at them through the cracks and crossbeams of the pier. In the distance, the sun prepared to set as it saluted them with beautiful streaks of red between white clouds and blue sky. Great and small, the bells rang on and on, their vibrations flung far on the breeze.

Ret made it a point to master the movement of his feet so that he could stare instead at the beauty waltzing in front of him. Paige didn't care if the wind blew her hair in her face, so long as it didn't obstruct her view of her prince.

As if it had transpired in slow-motion, it was the perfect ending to the perfect evening. When the belfry's last bell had been struck in conclusion of the sunset carol, Ret and Paige set off for home—side by side, hand in hand, heart to heart.

Not far away, in the solitary bell tower, a lonely widower sat and wept bitterly.

CHAPTER 8

THE AMAZING
AMAZON

As winter entered its final stretch, Ret didn't seem to be as bothered as he usually was by the generally bland and stagnant appeal of his least favorite season. His mind was elsewhere, swallowed up in anxious anticipation of his upcoming trip with Mr. Coy to the Amazon Basin.

True to her word, Pauline was supportive and understanding when Ret explained the situation to her. This is not to say she had become a proponent of laissez faire parenting, however, for her infamous interrogating still ensued. Unfortunately, there was little Ret could tell her because there was little Mr. Coy had told him, and Ret worried she might revoke her blessing. Instead, Pauline caught herself, corked her questioning, and let her doubts yield to trust.

Actually, Ret shared many of the same questions. When it came to Amazonia, there was far more he didn't know than he did know. From what he had gleaned from library books and online articles, the rainforest was one of earth's final frontiers—with large swaths still unexplored, uncharted, and untouched by modern man, and with new species being discovered constantly. It didn't annoy Ret to be headed for a place that was overgrown with unknowns; he just wanted to know what he should pack.

In true Coy fashion, Ret was apprised of their departure without much warning. It was late in the afternoon when Mr. Coy appeared at the Cooper home to pick up Ret before continuing on to the airport. With Conrad as chauffeur, Coy added Ret's bags to the luggage in the trunk and then joined Ret in the backseat.

"We'll be traveling entirely by public transportation this time," Mr. Coy explained as they passed the power plant and then the high school on their drive into Savannah. "We don't know exactly what we're looking for yet, and I don't want to draw any attention to ourselves." So long as he was flanked by Ret and Conrad, however, Coy's prospects of blending in looked bleak.

"Where will we be flying to?" Ret asked.

"Our first stop is the city of Manaus, the capital of the Brazilian state of Amazonas," Coy explained, retrieving from his pocket a map of the region. "I have an acquaintance there who might be of help to us—or at least get us on the river." He used his finger to follow the course of just a few of the many tributaries. "Until we gather more information, we'll need to cover as much ground as we can, and the best way to do that is by boat, especially at this time of year."

"Why not use a plane—or helicopter?" Ret wondered, remembering former adventures.

"That's certainly an option," Coy acknowledged. "Without the help of aerial views, we likely never would have seen the submerged road or the lines in the desert, so feel free to scan the region before we land in Manaus—you can have the window seat." Coy smiled, then added, "But I have a feeling it's going to be different this time. The Amazon is unlike anything we've encountered together so far. It's much like the great deep of the ocean, where an entire world exists without showing much of any evidence at the surface. The same is true with the vast rainforest: if you want to learn what's in it, you have to get in it."

"I see," Ret stated with growing soberness.

"And getting in is the easy part," Coy said.

Ret hesitated with a bit of nervousness before asking, "Is there a hard part?"

"Yes," Coy replied. "Getting out."

"Oh," Ret said feebly, "sounds nice."

It suddenly occurred to Mr. Coy that this would be Ret's first excursion into the Amazon, and he hoped he had not given him the wrong impression. As such, Coy figured he ought to try and clarify.

"The Amazon is a place of tremendous beauty and majesty," Coy told him. "In many ways, however, it is also dangerous and uninhabitable, but I think it was purposely designed that way as a sort of self-defense." Ret gave him a look requesting explanation. "You see, I like to think of the Amazon as the heart of the earth—a fully self-sustaining system that is vital to the health of our planet. If we take care of it, it will take care of us. It is home to countless living things, and we are their guests. We should not act like we own the place." He folded up his map and returned it to his pocket as they neared the airport. "The Amazon should be a better place for our having passed through it, and we will be better people if we let the Amazon pass through us. Besides our footprints, Ret, the only thing we should leave behind is our ignorance."

The odd-looking trio traveled light and slept heavily (thanks to some sleeping pills) on their red-eye flight to South America. Before Ret drifted off to sleep, his mind was filled with thoughts of Paige.

Upon descent, the plane burst through a thick layer of clouds amid the bright morning sunshine. Lush, green rainforest dominated the landscape for as far as the eye could see. Ret felt like a tiny ant perched atop the tallest blade of a flourishing lawn. The only break in the heavy vegetation came from the many waterways winding their way like snakes throughout the territory. Finally, the cement of civilization appeared as the plane approached Manaus.

As the airport sat on the northwestern outskirts of the city, Mr. Coy flagged down a taxi and bade the driver take them south to the river—at least, that's what Ret assumed was communicated, since Mr. Coy spoke in Portuguese. Judging by the faded photographs strewn across the dashboard, the driver was a family man, and his weary heart seemed to find some relief in the impending payment from his passengers, who needed to go as far across town as anyone could go.

Their route took them through the heart of Manaus. It was a large city, with several skyscrapers scattered along the low-lying and mostly flat terrain. As they sped further into the city center, the road became more crowded and the stops more frequent. Colorful booths lined the streets as part of some city-wide and low-budget bazaar. Buses pulled up to crumbling curbs to unload throngs of riders and pick up the same. It was not necessarily a pretty place, with its tired buildings and littered gutters, but there were people everywhere, and everyone was doing something—peddling a product here, pushing a cart there, loading a haul and then hauling the load. Each person's individual scavenger hunt combined to look like some kind of organized free-for-all in the daily quest to make a dollar—or, in this currency, a real.

The taxi came to a halt at the river's edge—literally: the water nearly lapped its tires. Like towels and umbrellas snuffing out the sand on an overcrowded beach, vehicles lined the dirt shore of the river. Ret found himself surrounded by people engaged in the commerce of the day. He stayed close to Mr. Coy.

Coy made a pit stop at an outdoor fish market nearby. Ret watched as all sorts of crude crafts oared their way into the fray to get their catch on the counter. He also kept an eye on Mr. Coy who seemed to fit in with the locals in every way save skin color. With great kindness and graciousness, he combed through the aisles before returning with a large fish in his hand. It looked so fresh and ungutted that, at first, Ret thought it might still be alive.

They made their way down the riverfront, passing a row of ferries and tour yachts, not to mention a ship carrying hundreds of bushels of bananas. In time, a man in the distance up ahead turned and hailed Mr. Coy with a broad smile and a loud cheer.

"It is good to see you, Rodrigo," Coy returned as they embraced.

"Likewise, my friend."

"For your family," said Coy, presenting the fish he had recently purchased.

Rodrigo was almost moved to tears. "Tonight, my family and I will feast with friends."

Introductions ensued. Ret was relieved to know Coy's acquaintance spoke English—with a pleasant Portuguese flavor, of course.

"I don't mean to rush you," Coy insisted as Rodrigo began to make for his boat. "If you have business to take care of, please take your time."

"Oh no," Rodrigo dismissed, "I am done here. I just sold the two tambaqui I caught yesterday."

The traveling triad followed Rodrigo aboard his simple vessel, which was not much more than a hollowed tree trunk. Thankfully, it floated (barely), and the four of them shoved off into the river.

"What brings you to the Amazon?" Rodrigo asked his passengers once they had fled the commotion of the harbor.

"We're here to learn," Coy answered for them. Then, pointing at Ret, he added, "He has a special interest in this place."

"As do I," Rodrigo grinned, proud of his homeland.

"Rodrigo has lived here his entire life," said Coy. "If you want to know anything about the Amazon, he's the one to ask."

Rodrigo possessed a simple beauty. His short, black hair was neatly tucked in a tattered straw hat. He wore a plain shirt, with a hole here and a tear there, and a pair of shorts that stopped halfway down each thigh.

About the same age as Mr. Coy, his skin was like dark chocolate, rich and smooth, and his trim physique attested to much rowing and little gorging.

Not much later, Rodrigo was asked his first question. They had come upon a strange phenomenon in the water. It looked as though the river was composed of two separate liquids: half of it was dark blue and clear while the other was light brown and muddy. Like oil poured into water, the separation was so defined that Ret wondered if half the river had been polluted.

"It happens naturally," Rodrigo explained, "when the slower and warmer waters of the Rio Negro join the faster and cooler waters of the Amazon. It takes a few kilometers for them to fully mix."

There was no question that the Amazon was the king of rivers. Its sheer size was staggering. They were paddling through a stretch that, as Ret estimated, must have measured at least four miles in width. At times, it felt like they were floating in the ocean, though the current was not as choppy, and while the rainforest grew right up to the river's banks, the water even seemed to extend a great distance into the forest. To say Ret was in awe would be an understatement. This place was intimidating!

Ret quickly discovered why Rodrigo wore a hat. Since landing in Manaus, it had already rained twice. The sky, which seemed a great deal larger than any Ret had ever seen, was filled with clouds—great, big, swirling clouds of white and gray and every shade in between. The heavens were constantly moving, allowing the hot, equatorial sun to burst through amid a backdrop of the most dazzling blue. The sun, always directly overhead, seemed to evaporate the rain that had just fallen, only to be rereleased by the clouds in somewhat of an endless cycle.

What Ret experienced next was something that he heard, saw, and then felt—in that order. It sounded like the rushing of great waters, and, sure enough, such was the sight as they rounded another bend, where a treacherous tributary was spilling into the main artery of the river. Like a thousand fire hydrants, its white water gushed forth endlessly, pulverizing whatever lay in its path. Ret was grateful to be floating a safe distance away from the commotion.

In the face of such raw power, Ret felt rather insignificant, to say the least. In every direction was proof of nature's unmatched might and astounding order. Thus far, his one-hour jaunt down the Amazon had proven to be a very humbling experience. Granted, Ret was aware of his ability to control the elements— only earth and fire at this point, of course—but his attempts so far did not even begin to approach the magnitude of the scenes all around him. Whenever he had manipulated the elements in the past, it had been for only a brief moment, using only a tiny fraction of dirt or flame compared to what was available on the planet. It gave him great cause to wonder, then, what was directing all the other elements the rest of the time?

Ret's contemplation was interrupted when it came his turn to man the oar. While Rodrigo declined a reprieve, his passengers alternated using the second paddle. Mr. Coy passed it behind him to Ret, who happily began to row. As soon as Ret lodged the butt of the oar into the palm of his right hand, however, he felt an interesting sensation—not pain but a very slight and all-too-familiar numbness. He immediately inspected his hand. A portion of the new scar had appeared, but it was only that—just a portion. It looked like a small cutting of discarded thread, terribly unaligned with the other two scars on that palm. As Coy had speculated before, there was yet more of it to be revealed.

Noticing Ret's inattention to the oar, Mr. Coy turned around to see what was going on. Without a word, Ret held up his hand for Coy to see the scar. Coy immediately lowered Ret's hand and glanced forward to make sure Rodrigo hadn't seen. After a quick study, Mr. Coy was struck with an idea.

"Rodrigo, I think Ret would like to go for a swim," Coy announced.

"By all means," Rodrigo obliged.

"You want me to get in there?" Ret countered, staring wide-eyed at the water all around them.

"Why not?" Coy replied with a wink. He pulled a pair of goggles from his pack and tossed them in Ret's lap. "Just splash around a bit; you know, have a look around."

"Why don't you join me?" Ret petitioned, fearing the unknown.

"No thanks," he declined, smirking. "But I'll be right here if you need me."

"Can we at least go over to the water that's not so muddy?" Ret asked, motioning to the small sliver of the river where the water was still clear. Whereas they had been traveling down the middle of the river, Rodrigo promptly shifted course shoreward and stopped a few dozen feet from land.

Naturally, Ret was a bit apprehensive about going for a recreational swim in the Amazon. Like virtually all living things, it was the fear of the unknown that caused him to doubt. He hoped he would soon discover a newfound power over water, knowing there wasn't a great deal of earth or fire to be called to his aid amid so much liquid. Recalling Mr. Coy's counsel, however, he decided to get in, hoping he would be able to get out.

The water was remarkably warm, mimicking a bath more than a pool. Ret swam a few circles around the boat, resembling a sea otter, unsure of what to do. He glanced at Mr. Coy, who, like a baseball catcher, was giving Ret signs to tell him to dive. Ret inhaled and plunged out of sight.

He found himself literally swimming among the fishes, in quantities and with qualities that Ret had never before seen. These were neither trout nor bass; they were tropical creatures with long, spiky whiskers and short, thick snouts and wild, flowing fins. The great preyed on the small while the small prayed for mercy. There were crabs and krill and something that looked like an electric eel. Organic matter floated aimlessly amid the filtered sunlight, with Ret returning to the surface only to breathe.

Since the bottom of the river sloped upward as it neared the bank, Ret swam closer to shore so that he would be able to reach the ground in his dives. The floor was a whole new world in and of itself, hiding all manner of critters among the rocks and plant life. On accident, Ret startled what appeared to be a freshwater species of stingray, lying flat on the ground, camouflaged and motionless. It departed amid a flurry of dirt and sand. Despite the chaos, something shiny caught Ret's eye, but it quickly vanished as the disturbed dirt gently fell back to the floor.

Ret swam to the surface, breathed, and returned to the same spot. He began to push away the sand, searching for the metal coin or glass shard that had

drawn his attention. He soon uncovered a piece of gold,
buried under a layer of silt and mud. He continued to
dig, hoping to locate an edge where he could pry it free
and lift it from the ground. With a simple flick of his
wrist, he could have easily excavated the whole cubic
area like a backhoe but chose not to do so because he
didn't want to disrupt things any more than he had to,
remembering Mr. Coy's advice that they had come to the
Amazon as guests.

Surface, breathe, dive. He had now unearthed a
section about the size of a sheet of paper. At this point,
at least two things were obvious: first, that the piece was
actually quite large, and second, that it was some kind of
solid gold bar or plate because there were no decorative
designs or inscriptions on it so far.

Another break, only to breathe. But Ret's presence
had not gone unnoticed. After returning once again to
the spot to resume digging, he glanced up just in time to
see something hurtling towards him. On account of
being submerged, he didn't have the dexterity to get out
of the way before the animal plowed into him.
Disoriented and suddenly winded, Ret hastened toward
the surface for air but was prevented when something
latched onto his shorts and yanked him back into deeper
waters.

Ret's attacker was a river dolphin—a terrifyingly
ugly creature with a bottle-nosed snout and whitish-pink

skin. It was longer and larger than Ret and a great deal more flexible. Suddenly, the water was filled with high-pitched noises as several more river dolphins converged on the scene, each calling out to the other. Like an angry mob, they descended on Ret, jabbing him with their snouts, slapping him with their fins, and body slamming him away from his dig site.

Back at the boat, Rodrigo had perked up in alarm. Through the water, he had seen the dolphins dart by and now heard their shrieks of echolocation. The trio hurried over to where Ret had been diving and were distraught when they saw him being harassed underwater. Immediately, Conrad leapt from the boat and entered the fight. Like a boxer hitting great slabs of meat hanging in a butcher shop, he punched and elbowed his way to Ret, who would soon drown. Conrad pushed Ret up to the surface, where Mr. Coy and Rodrigo hauled him into the boat. With difficulty, Conrad escaped and pulled himself aboard.

But the river dolphins were relentless. With their great size and body mass, they rocked the boat violently, determined to capsize the craft and drag its human cargo to a watery grave. Rodrigo desperately tried to maneuver the boat out of the sea of enraged beasts. Mr. Coy smacked them away with his oar. Conrad picked them up indiscriminately by the tail and flung them as far as he could in any direction, like a dog tearing up a turnip patch. But it was to no avail, with more dolphins appearing every second. Like protectors of an ancient secret, they had been provoked by intruders, and the penalty was death.

CHAPTER 9

LEGENDS AND LESSONS

"Conrad!" Mr. Coy shouted above the chaos. "Get us out of here!"

Sitting at the rear, Conrad gripped both sides of the boat and raised himself up. Then, with impressive agility, he extended himself horizontally and laid flat on his chest, with the lower half of his body hanging out the back of the craft. Hinging at his waist, he put his legs and feet close together in the water and began to flap them up and down like a fin. With immense power, he repeatedly plunged his legs into the water, colliding with river dolphins and forcing them out of the way.

With the advent of their heavy human propeller, the nose of the boat rose slightly, allowing Rodrigo to oar his way over the dolphins. Conrad's brute strength created great splashes and deep, booming sounds as he plowed through the onslaught. Breaking free, the vessel skimmed across the water at a fairly quick clip, thanks to the oarsmen up front and the merman in the back.

Knowing it would require nothing short of a miracle to outswim a pack of enraged dolphins, the party summoned all the energy they could to put a safe distance between themselves and the beasts. Eventually, however, they came to the conclusion that they were not being pursued. With the threat of danger gone, Conrad climbed back inside the boat, and they resumed their normal pace.

"What were those things?" Ret asked out loud in consternation.

"The Amazon river dolphin," Rodrigo answered. "They are usually harmless. I have never known them to be so violent around people. Perhaps the legend *is* true."

"Legend?" Coy wondered.

"Oh, yes," Rodrigo replied. "There is an ancient myth in our culture about the boto, as we call them. At night, they transform into beautiful men and women. They go on land and cause all kinds of mischief. By morning, they return to the river and become dolphins again."

"Seems they also cause mischief *in* the water," Coy pointed out.

"Are there any legends about gold?" Ret inquired, curious to know what it was he had uncovered on the river floor.

Mr. Coy spun around and gave Ret a perplexed look.

"I'll explain later," Ret whispered to him.

"Yes, of course!" Rodrigo laughed, as if it was common knowledge. "I take it you've never heard of the city of gold?"

"He could use a refresher," Coy told their guide. "Ret doesn't get out much."

"Gee, thanks," Ret muttered.

"The legend of the city of gold is nearly as old as the Amazon itself," Rodrigo began amid his incessant rowing. "From generation to generation, the story has been told of a great city that once existed, deep in the jungle. It had large buildings that rose above the treetops; wide bridges that crossed the rivers; statues and idols of men and kings. Gold was everywhere to be found—streets of gold, temples of gold, jewelry and dishes and altars and shrines. It is said that even the leader of the city was coated in gold dust for certain ceremonies."

"That's a lot of gold," Ret observed.

"But there wasn't just gold," Rodrigo informed. "Silver and copper and precious stones—anything that shined and pleased the eye."

"So where is this place?" Ret wanted to know.

"It has never been found," came the ghostly reply. "For hundreds of years, explorers from all over the world have come here to seek for the city of gold. In the past, they came in the names of their kings and queens; now, they say they are in search of a better life. But whatever the reason may be, they all come with one real motive: greed. They cannot resist the lure of riches. Over the centuries, all kinds of people have come to our land to try and locate the fabled city. They befriend us, ask us questions, show us their maps, exchange goods for information. We tell them what we know, but in our hearts we weep for them. Over and over again, we watch as they become obsessed, consumed. Many are never heard from again, lost in the jungle."

"Do you think such a place exists, Rodrigo?" Mr. Coy asked.

"Maybe, maybe not," Rodrigo shrugged. "It makes no difference to me. What would *I* do with a city full of gold? I have everything I need right here." He stretched out his arm to sweep the landscape all around them. "Like our ancestors, we tell the legend to our children to teach them how this land, with its river and forest, is our city of gold. It provides us with everything we need, and we never take more than what we need. Live here long enough and you'll see how it is never Amazonians who go looking for the city of gold; it is always others from distant lands who come searching for it. We do not worry whether it exists or not; if we were to find it, we would have little use for it anyway. Greed does not exist in our culture, but the foreigners who come here must be taught something different in theirs."

There came a point in their easterly trek along the main channel of the Amazon when Rodrigo bent their course northward. As they approached the riverbank, it appeared they would collide into the vegetation, but instead they simply drifted into it. Remarkably, the waters extended inland for miles, and they were now traveling through what was literally a flooded forest. They navigated around tree trunks, half submerged in the monsoonal waters. Monkeys and birds darted through the canopy overhead. Seeds occasionally fell from branches, only to be slurped and shelled by strong-jawed fishes. More than once, Ret saw a slender, slimy-looking fish leap several feet into the air to nab an unsuspecting insect clinging to a limb. Like strolling through a zoo on another planet, everything seemed so new and different.

Somehow, within the labyrinth of the flooded forest, Rodrigo found his way home. Built on stilts, the habitation barely rose above the height of the floodwaters, resembling a sort of stationary houseboat. The tin roof was more shoddy than shingled, and the wooden side paneling was fresh with rot rather than paint. Weeks ago, the front yard had been replaced by a swift current. All in all, the ramshackle dwelling took the term *humble abode* to a new level.

Suddenly, the cries of happy children filled the humid air.

"Mr. Coy! Mr. Coy!" shouted Rodrigo's family as they jumped up and down on the rickety, planked patio of the house. With what seemed to be a melted heart, Mr. Coy returned their cheers with a series of vigorous waves.

Rodrigo moored the boat to a shabby dock and lent a hand to help his passengers step out. Mr. Coy was immediately swarmed by four elated children.

"My, how you've grown!" Coy remarked as he knelt down. He greeted each of his admirers by name and began to assess their individual conditions as he had done in the past.

"Looks like your arm healed just fine," he said to one; then, to another, "How's that lip doing?" To a third, "I trust you're taking good care of those teeth"; and to the last, the youngest and most rambunctious, "And to think, there was a time when we didn't think you were going to make it." It was obvious by now that Mr. Coy had met this family on one of his former humanitarian trips.

Rodrigo introduced Ret and Conrad to his family. The older children were polite to the strangers, while the younger ones timidly retreated to their mother.

"Maria, my dear," Mr. Coy addressed Rodrigo's wife. "How are you?"

"Good, good," she replied.

"Something tells me you've been using those English tapes I gave you years ago," Coy observed upon hearing Maria speak.

"We have all been using them," she explained bashfully.

Mr. Coy was overwhelmed. Ret had never seen him so happy.

"Well then, it sounds like you're ready for more," Coy reasoned, unzipping his pack. He pulled out a plethora of supplies: workbooks on math and phonics, paper with pencils, even batteries and a few shiny-wrapped candies. Ret marveled at how eager these children were for schoolwork.

With evening setting in, Rodrigo took the fish gifted to him by Coy and prepared it for dinner. Ret had never seen someone fillet and gut a fish before. As if an everyday thing, Rodrigo fingered his way through the innards and organs. He emptied the stomach of its half-digested seed kernels and set them aside in a bowl. Then he went around the corner, dumped the contents of the bowl, and unlocked the pig pen. A family of swine descended on the seeds. A few minutes later, Rodrigo corralled them back into the pen to keep them from falling into the river and drowning.

The meal was cooked over a crude fire. Rodrigo and his family were more than gracious to their guests, even serving them the fat of the fish. Ret was surprised when none of the children complained about the menu; he didn't think kids were generally fond of seafood, but it was clear that they either liked it or starved.

When night fell, no lights came on. There was no electricity, just a kerosene lamp and a few candles — and a flashlight that Mr. Coy had brought, which the kids used to light up their math worksheets. As soon as Mr. Coy had a spare minute, Ret told him the details about the strip of gold he had discovered at the bottom of the river before being attacked by the river dolphins.

"It sounds like we need to get back in the water," Coy concluded after hearing what Ret had to say.

"I'd rather not go back to where we stopped the first time," Ret cringed.

"Has your scar changed at all?" Coy asked.

Ret inspected his hand. "No, it's still the same as when I showed it to you earlier."

"When I saw your scar that night in the hot-air balloon," Coy remembered, "the illuminated portion was about five times the length of what it is now. I say we get back on the Amazon, get moving again, and see what happens. Sound like a plan?"

"Sounds like a plan," Ret agreed.

"Good," Coy sighed, "because I'm exhausted."

The fatigue was mutual, which was a blessing since their beds were about as comfortable as a wooden floorboard.

The next morning, following a flurry of farewells, the fearsome foursome boarded their familiar boat and set sail. Per Coy's instructions, Rodrigo carried them to the edge of the flooded forest, where the three travelers disembarked and continued their trek on foot. According to Rodrigo, it was just over a day's hike to the nearest road, where they could hitch a ride into the closest town.

Ret found refreshment in standing on solid ground. Together, the three of them blazed a trail in the jungle, shuffling through the leaf litter that covered the forest floor. Sunlight flickered through the leafy treetops, which partially shielded them from the intermittent rainfall. Ret paid close attention to his footing, trying to spare bugs and avoid anything poisonous. There was much activity in the canopy, and great noises filled the air. Prehistoric trees stood with roots as large as cars and trunks as wide as homes, with snakes slithering along thick boughs amid trails of oversized ants. The rainforest was rife with life, radiating an unfathomable amount of nonstop energy.

As the afternoon wore on, Ret was pained by a recurring psychological plague that had recently come out of remission during his rendezvous with Rodrigo and his family. Their sorry situation reminded Ret so much of the oppressed people who once lived in the slums of the lower level of Sunken Earth; of the outcasts eking out a meager existence on the floating islands of

Lake Titicaca; and even of the polarized streets he had seen in Savannah on his daytrip during Ana's job search. He felt an acute anxiety for the impoverished and under-privileged peoples he continued to come across in his travels to places known and unknown. He was troubled by their troubles and yearned to fix them but was at a total loss of how to do so.

Daylight came and went. Coy sectioned off a flat space to set up camp, and Conrad gathered fallen limbs and branches to construct a lean-to for shelter while sleeping. For his part, Ret moved some dirt into a circular mound and fashioned a pit, then flicked his fingers to add a fuel-less fire.

Even at night, the Amazon was wide awake, showing no signs of weariness. The faint glow of the firelight revealed the impenetrable darkness all around them. Now, the jungle was no longer a painting for the eyes but a nocturne for the ears. All manner of shrieks and howls and sappy pulses rang through the shadows as a new set of creatures clocked in for the night shift. It was a bit unsettling for Ret to be able to hear all but see none of the activity surrounding them, though he found some solace in Conrad who was sitting upright and alert in his vicarious vigil as onsite sentinel.

A simple meal. An easy cleanup. A fireside chat.

"Mr. Coy," Ret asked, with great concern in his voice, "why is there so much inequality in the world?"

Mr. Coy, who had been writing in a journal, looked up at Ret with a slightly confused face. "Inequality?" he repeated, wondering if he had heard correctly.

"Yeah," Ret reaffirmed. "You know, why are there so many poor people, like Rodrigo and his family?"

Mr. Coy drew in a long breath. "Poverty is a point of view, Ret. It's a status assigned by society; a measurement meted by men; a rank, a value. The richest and second richest men in the world are both very rich to you and me, but to each other, the second is poorer than the first."

"But wouldn't you say Rodrigo is poor?"

"When it comes to money and assets," Coy prefaced, "yes, he is very poor."

"I realize not everyone can be rich," said Ret, "but why are there so many more poor people than rich people?"

"The world of wealth is a pyramid," Coy taught, being careful to present objective information rather than preach a sermon so that Ret could draw his own conclusions, "with the poor along the base, the rich at the peak, and everyone else in the middle. Technically, everyone is free to move around—all it takes is money. In reality, however, it's usually much harder to move up than it is to move down—unless you win the lottery, of course."

"Or find a city of gold," Ret added. The two of them exchanged humored glances. "But why does the bottom of the pyramid have to be so big—and the top so small? Why can't it be an upside-down pyramid—or at least more like a rectangle?"

"Now you're starting to sound like a Marxist, Ret!" Coy joked with a hearty laugh.

Ret wasn't entirely sure what that term entailed, but he knew it didn't sound good, so he tried to clarify: "Everywhere I go, I see so much inequality. At first, I thought it only belonged to places like Sunken Earth and Fire Island, but lately I've been noticing it all over *our* world, too—even in my own backyard. It wasn't until we visited those places that I realized I had been living in a bubble, sheltered from seeing what's really out there—like Rodrigo: he lives in a shack, Mr. Coy," Ret put it bluntly, sounding upset by the honest truth. "No electricity, no plumbing—I have neighbors back home with storage sheds that are nicer than where he lives."

"I hear you," Coy concurred. "Rodrigo lives a convenience-free life. He has to catch his food and eat it all on the same day because he has no refrigerator. They have a protein-rich but vitamin-deficient diet. They have no doctor and couldn't pay to see one anyway. Their first child died of malaria. When I met them for the first time, they had never heard of a vaccine. As you could probably tell, there is no formal schooling."

"I see these things, and it breaks my heart," Ret interrupted. "I meet these people, and I want to help them—so badly. I want to give them a better life; I want to do something—anything. But what can I do? I'm just one guy, and I'm not much better off than them, really. I guess I've just been luckier in life—born luckier…I don't know."

Despite the grim gravity of the subject, Mr. Coy looked down and grinned slightly at the goodness in Ret's heart. He prayed for help as he proceeded in his attempt to address Ret's concerns.

"Let's think this through together," Coy began, closing his journal. "Why is Rodrigo poor?"

"Because he doesn't have any money," Ret stated matter-of-factly.

"And why doesn't he have any money?"

"Because he doesn't have a job," answered Ret again.

"And why doesn't he have a job?" Coy asked.

Ret wasn't as certain this time. "Because he doesn't have a skill—an education?"

"And why doesn't he have an education?"

"Because he can't go to school."

"And why can't he go to school?" Coy said with closure.

"Because he," Ret paused, having come full-circle, "doesn't have any money."

"Hence the cycle of poverty," Coy mourned.

"Then why doesn't anyone fix it?" Ret wondered.

"Don't think you're the first person who has had these concerns, Ret," Coy cautioned with a hint of offense. "There are numerous organizations in this world that have done remarkable things for the under-privileged: charitable and humanitarian foundations that give of their time and service; celebrities and philan-thropists who donate great amounts of money and resources; churches, missions, and rescues that care for and take in the needy; education funds with their loans, grants, and scholarships—"

"Then why are there still so many poor people?" Ret inserted smartly.

"Because they far outnumber the benefactors, Ret," Coy said sharply. His slightly raised voice signaled his frustration with the global dilemma, not with Ret's insatiable inquiries. A few moments of silence followed.

"But I'm trying," Coy sighed. "I rescued Conrad from the black-market slave trade." He motioned to the brute seated nearby, still as speechless as ever as he maintained his watch over the campsite. "On one of my trips overseas, I met him and liked his work ethic, so I bought his freedom and put him to work at the Manor. It's a similar story with Ishmael and his sister: they needed a new lease on life, so I took them in."

"Same with—" Mr. Coy paused abruptly before resuming, his voice subdued, "—Ivan." Ret lowered his head in sorrowful remembrance of the late butler. "Did you know he was royalty?" Coy said with a tearful laugh. "He was ostracized by his family because of his speech impediment. They were ashamed of him—said he wasn't fit to be affiliated with the blood of nobility. He fell into deep depression and became a drunk. Helen and I met him at a café in Moscow. He came up to us, begging for money. He was so inebriated that he could hardly speak; so hungry, he could scarcely stand. We fed him a warm meal, gave him something non-intoxicating to drink, and then put him up for the night in the hotel room next to ours."

"That night," Coy retold, "Helen brought up the idea of hiring Ivan as our personal assistant. For the safety of my wife and daughter, I was always wary of inviting strangers into our personal lives, but Helen was a much better judge of character than I ever was. She possessed the rare ability to look past a person's sketchy present and see the light within—what he once was and what he could become. And she was always right."

"I've tried to perpetuate Helen's legacy by estab-lishing the Manor," said Coy. "Every staff member is someone who either desired a second chance or simply needed a first one. The Manor is essentially a miniature university—a trade school of sorts—where people are taught a skill and given the means to master it. That's why the Manor is always changing. Most of the staff members stay for only a season and then go back home to start a career and family. Some stay longer and send their wages home. A few, like Ivan and Conrad, become family."

"So the Manor isn't just your house?" Ret inquired, somewhat in shock.

"That monstrosity?" Coy balked. "No way; Paige and I live in two distant rooms, away from most of the action. I've never cared much for temporal things, apart from what I need for science and exploration. When Helen and I began our humanitarian work, we sold most of our possessions and stored the rest in her parent's garage outside of Milwaukie. But, as Paige grew older, I figured it would be best for her if we settled down somewhere. I still wanted to continue my labors, though, so I guess you could say I started working from home." He paused briefly to smile with satisfaction.

"So, no, the Manor isn't really my house at all," Coy concluded. "It's a place that opens closed doors and turns the third-world into a new world."

"That's pretty awesome, Mr. Coy," Ret said admiringly, having never known the true identity of the misshapen chateau that had always been condemned by the public eye.

"It's also pretty expensive," he rejoined. "But you know something? The more I give, the more I seem to get. I tell you, it's a phenomenon that defies logic. Every time I accept a new staff member or take on a new program, I get another grant from some charity or an old friend bequeaths his estate to me. It's amazing how often former staff members will call and say they want to give back to the cause that turned their lives around. I mean, it's remarkable. It has taught me that, if done right, you can never become poor by giving; in fact, it's by giving that we become rich."

"So what about Rodrigo?" Ret reminded him.

"Rodrigo is perfectly content to live and die as a hunter-gatherer on the Amazon River," Coy stated. "And if that's what he wants, then that's what he should do. Some people are like that, and that's their prerogative. However, I'm not so sure that's what his children will want, which is why I am doing everything in my power to give them options—to feed their thirst for knowledge without overstepping my bounds. Rodrigo and Maria are good parents who undoubtedly want their children to be better off than themselves; they just don't have the resources. So far, I've managed to help them learn English—just that alone will be a great asset to them."

"So only the rich can help the poor?" Ret surmised.

"Absolutely not," Coy countered, "but it certainly helps. I've always considered it a privilege—an honor, a duty—to put my resources to good use in the service of my fellowmen. So I wouldn't say only the rich can help the poor, but I might say they should feel in their heart a greater obligation to do so."

"Let me tell you why," Coy offered. "The interesting thing about the pyramid of wealth is that we all depend on each other—each brick, each level, each side leans against another for support. For example, Rodrigo is on the very bottom level; he depends on the ground, literally—he told us himself how he lives off the earth, the river, the rainforest. On the level above him, however, is a merchantman who counts on people like Rodrigo to supply him with fish, who then counts on someone like a restaurant owner to buy the same fish from him. The owner then depends on a customer to eat at his restaurant. This is where another side of the pyramid comes in: the customer needs money to eat at the restaurant and, thus, depends on his job and employer. Depending on the type of employment, we could insert the corporate world with its many levels and ladders. Ultimately, however, it peaks at executives and shareholders, and while everyone below them depends on their investments, they themselves wouldn't see any return on their investments without the people below them. So, you see, we're all in this together. We all need each other."

"But just because that's the way it is now," Ret returned to the dialogue, "doesn't mean it has to stay that way—that is, in the shape of a pyramid. I mean, what if everyone would reach down to help someone up—you know, be a little more generous, a little less greedy. Then the pyramid would turn into something taller and thinner—you know, like a...like a skyscraper. Then we'd all be higher up and better off by shrinking the base and swelling the body."

Before Ret could say any more, Coy was quick to add with a sweeping voice, "But there is a universal warning in all of this that cannot be emphasized enough, and it is this: you cannot force equality. All people must be free to choose for themselves. Next to life itself, the greatest gift we've been given is the freedom to direct our own lives. When we do anything that might infringe on that freedom, we toy with the very underpinnings of the universe."

"So you shouldn't even force people to do *good* things, like help the poor?" Ret said in search of a loophole.

"No," Coy bellowed. "Compel someone to be generous? It's an oxymoron. Coercion breeds resentment, and we have a natural resistance to it for good reason. It deprives us of the blessings we get for using our own freewill. Force someone to help the impoverished and that person will come to despise the poor. It backfires; instead of fostering goodwill, it kills it.

"But Lionel forces things to happen," Ret rebutted. "That day in the nuclear power plant, he showed me how they force uranium atoms to split and how that releases tremendous amounts of energy for all of us to use. That's a positive example of coercion, isn't it?"

"That may be true," said Coy, his interest in the conversation suddenly fading at the mention of Lionel, "but did he also show you the byproducts of those reactions? All the toxic, radioactive waste that can take thousands of years to decay?" Coy prepared to retire for the night. "Yeah, sure—apply nuclear fission to global poverty; that'll really cure the world."

Whether or not he intended to say them, Mr. Coy's final three words rang true in Ret's ears like a fire alarm. *Cure the world.* That was the exact phrase from the Oracle prophecy written on the piece of parchment paper stolen from Principal Stone's office a year ago. Those three words—*cure the world*—continued to be the most puzzling to Ret. With Coy checked out and Conrad keeping watch, Ret relinquished the fire and lay down to rest. As usual, however, he didn't drift to sleep for a long time, there being so much on his mind.

CHAPTER 10

PAULINE TO THE
RESCUE

Pauline had just pulled into the driveway from taking Ana to school when she saw the mailman bounding up the sidewalk with a heavy bag full of mail draped over his shoulder.

"Good morning, Ms. Cooper," he greeted her cheerily.

Though she preferred *Mrs.*, Pauline replied, "Why hello, Don. What've you got for me today? Something besides bills, I hope."

"Looks like the usual," Don answered, sifting through his bundles of letters and flyers. Then, eyeing the Coopers' mailbox, which was still sitting on the curb so as to escape Ana's haphazard back-outs, he added, "How's Ana doing behind the wheel these days?" He was secretly grateful he could simply hand-deliver today's mail to Pauline, as it meant he didn't have to

○ 179 ○

walk down to the street, kneel on the asphalt, and use the jaws of life to pry open the contorted mailbox.

"She's getting better every day," Pauline smiled. "I suspect you'll be delivering her license to us very soon."

After handing Pauline the day's mail, Don proceeded to tell her everything he knew about driving. Blessed with the gift of gab, it was not uncommon for Don to slip in a lengthy conversation with each resident's letters. Pauline normally welcomed the lighthearted chitchat, for she found Don to be a very knowledgeable individual who had been around the block. Having served the island since Ana was a baby, he knew everyone and was known by just as many. And although his daily attire of shorts and sunglasses (rain or shine) made him seem like a mail carrier incognito, his daily devotion to the tight-knit community did more to promote the neighborhood watch than provoke it.

On this day, however, Pauline became disengaged from the dialogue when she discovered a curious piece of mail among the stack that had been handed to her. There was an envelope addressed to Ret, written by hand. He almost never received mail, and when he did, it was usually from one person: Lionel Zarbock.

"I'm sorry, Don, but I really must be going," Pauline confessed in sober tones as she retreated towards the house. As far as she knew, Lionel was still a prisoner in the wicked hands of Lye. Therefore, anything that he needed to communicate was undoubtedly very important and urgent. But she also knew that Ret had just embarked on his journey with Mr. Coy to the Amazon and would not return for a few days at best. Even if she could reach Ret by phone and read the letter to him, she would still need to open it. So she tore open the envelope and unfolded a single piece of paper:

Dear Ret,

I hope this letter finds you soon. I am being held captive against my will by Lye at a place he calls Waters Deep. He has tortured me a great deal, but I am otherwise okay. His fortress here is heavily guarded, but I have managed to find a way to escape for no more than one hour each night, beginning at midnight. I need you to come and rescue me, Ret—please, as soon as you can. I'll be ready and waiting for you.

Your friend,
Lionel Zarbock

P.S. Based on my observations of the stars, I am likely located near these coordinates: 31°42'08"S 172°33'03"W.

Pauline's heart began to beat rapidly. A swarm of thoughts buzzed about her brain. Like a conveyor belt in an assembly line, her mind processed a flurry of ideas in a matter of seconds: "Lionel's alive!—but he's in trouble. And he wants Ret to help him?" She scanned the letter: "Hmm...'fortress'...'heavily guarded'—no, he might get hurt...or worse; I couldn't live with that. Oh, what to do? Ret won't be back from the Amazon for days, but Lionel needs help now. I could call Ret—I should call—read the letter over the phone—let him decide," she thought, taking a quick step to find her phone. "No, not a good idea," she abruptly halted. "Even if I could reach them in the Amazon, I know them: Coy's too spontaneous, Ret too loyal to Lionel—they'd leave in an instant for that 'heavily guarded' 'fortress'..."

Given the sudden stress of the situation, Pauline would have regretted opening Ret's mail had it not been for one idea that dwarfed all the others:

"Wait!" her mind froze in epiphany. "Wait— 'Waters Deep': could that be where Lye's fleet was headed—the place we saw from the hot-air balloon? Lionel was on one of those ships, no doubt, and that means..." She gasped, bringing her hand to her mouth. "Jaret—my Jaret was in that fleet! I know it!—he helped Lye aboard one of those same ships, I saw it—well, *Ana* saw it—but this place, 'Waters Deep'—that could be— no, that *is*...that's where he is!"

She fell into a few faltering steps forward, preventing herself from collapsing with elation. Then, pressing the letter to her chest in dismay, "That place— oh, no!—not *that* place: Coy shunned it like the plague; he blames it for killing his...—no, no, no! He would never go back, never take me!" Then her mercurial emotions flip-flopped again at the realization, "But he's not here—he's miles away in the Amazon. He doesn't have to know." She smiled, then chirped, "Ishmael! Ishmael will help me—I just know he will!" Overjoyed, she embraced the letter and pressed it to her heart, "Oh, Jaret, just hold on, dear! I'll come! I'll rescue you!"

Never mind it wasn't Jaret who had solicited a rescue.

Yet, as unprofessional as it was to open someone else's mail, it seemed to suit the intent of the sender for Pauline to intervene, for just about anyone else would have wondered how Lionel could have managed to send a letter while imprisoned. Knowing Pauline, however, she would likely have attributed the eerie impossibility to, if asked, either Lye's liberal incarceration policies or some transoceanic carrier pigeon.

With a newfound priority at the top of her list, Pauline dropped everything she had planned for the rest of the day. Locating her phone, she shakily typed a text message to Paige, who was her only link to accessing the Manor. Pauline told her that she needed to speak with

Ishmael right away and that she would be coming to the Manor immediately. While packing a few overnight provisions in her worn purse, Pauline received an affirmative (though likely bewildered) reply from Paige that Ishmael would be expecting her.

On account of her prolonged surge of adrenaline, Pauline braved the cold waters of Tybee Creek as she stepped into the kayak and rowed herself toward Little Tybee Island. There was neither grace nor technique to her rowing, a method that was literally madness. With hair flaring and water splashing, it looked like she was fighting with the oar rather than using it to her advantage. Had the current been any swifter, she may have been carried out to sea. In the end, as she neared the shallows, Pauline gave up trying to row and simply rolled out of the boat and walked the rest of the way to shore, pulling the kayak behind her.

Out of breath and sopping wet, Pauline arrived at the main gate to the Manor. She could see Ishmael through the iron bars, waiting for her. He cracked open the gate and greeted Pauline as she stepped inside.

"Paige said you needed to speak with me?" said Ishmael politely, though a little distracted by the water dripping from Pauline's face and clothes.

"Yes," she panted. "Read this." She handed Ishmael the letter from Lionel. It was damp but still legible.

After a few seconds of silent reading, Ishmael looked up at Pauline with suspicion in his face and asked, "How could Lionel have sent this? How did this get to you?"

"It came in today's mail," Pauline answered, wringing her shirt sleeve. "Ishmael, I need your help. I need you to take me to this place—Waters Deep."

As if slightly stunned by her upfront request, Ishmael said hesitantly, "I think we should wait until Mr. Coy and Ret return from the Amazon."

"But that could take days, Ishmael," Pauline persisted, "and this can't wait. Ja—Lionel needs our help *now*. You read what he said, didn't you? He found a way to escape for a very small window each night. It's only a matter of time before he is discovered. There's not a moment to lose. We can take the hot-air balloon."

"I would feel better if we ran it by Mr. Coy first," Ishmael returned calmly, "especially if we were to use his equipment. I can try to reach him by phone, if you'd like."

"No," she interjected, as if doing so would jeopardize everything. "Coy loathes Waters Deep. Remember how he acted when we saw it from the balloon? He would never go there himself, and he probably wouldn't let any of us go there either."

"Then you have my answer," Ishmael sighed, handing the letter back to Pauline. "I'm sorry," and he was, for he truly wanted to help.

Not willing to let go, Pauline turned up her nose and snatched the letter back. "Humph!" she snorted. "Fine then. I'll go by myself." Then she spun around on her soggy heels and began to march back downhill.

But Pauline was caught in a verbal bluff as unstable as the physical one she was descending. She could hardly paddle across a creek, let alone circumvent the globe: for starters, she would need to realize the digits included in the letter's postscript referred to coordinates of latitude and longitude and not a range of oven temperatures in a cooking recipe. Yes, she was totally at the mercy of Ishmael. By preying on his pity and wishing for a weak will, she hoped that somehow her dream trip would materialize from her guilt trip. As such, it was not with much surprise that she heard Ishmael call out from behind her, "Wait!"

"Yes?" she rejoined with feigned innocence.

"I'll take you," Ishmael said with a pitiable look on his face. Knowing something of Pauline's unconquerable spirit, he figured any alternative avenue that the battle-ax might take to realize her objective would be utterly disastrous, even fatal. And so, against the certainty of a stern rebuke from Coy, Ishmael reckoned he ought to step in and conduct Lionel's rescue mission himself, hoping to return before his boss could ever find out.

Worn down and defeated, Ishmael instructed, "In order to make it to Waters Deep by midnight, we need to

leave within the hour. I'll meet you back here ASAP."
Then, having walked a safe distance away, he muttered,
"That woman is impossible."

Seeing no sense in challenging the kayak to a
rematch, Pauline contentedly found a nearby bench by
the lawn and took a load off, counting on the salty breeze
to dry out her wet clothes and hair before departure.

Moments later, Pauline felt the ground at her feet
begin to vibrate. A bit alarmed, she stood and paced
across the property, feeling like a tardy traveler during
final boarding call. On the other side of the grounds, the
large lagoon was draining. When the last of thousands of
gallons of water had fallen through the retractable
bottom, Pauline peered over the rim and into the
Manor's underground hangar. Like an expensive sports
car, the hot-air balloon was covered in a protective tarp,
but unlike a sports car, there was not much to gawk at
once the tarp was removed. In fact, there was nothing to
see at all: although the airship's large envelope was in
the traditional shape of an upside-down raindrop, it was
covered with special solar panels that reflected their
surroundings like a mirror without inhibiting the interior
silicon mixture from absorbing the sun's warmth.
Similar to a glass skyscraper, an observer had to really
be looking for it in order to see it.

Ishmael maneuvered the balloon out of the hangar
and onto a wide stretch of lawn where he secured it to

the ground with the guy-lines. Knowing the airship needed to literally warm up, he let the contraption soak up the bright, mid-morning sunshine, allowing the panels to collect and convert at least enough solar power to launch. Hanging below the wicker basket was the repurposed jet engine that needed charging if it was to take them roundtrip in a matter of days and not weeks. Additionally, hanging above the basket was the hot plate that needed warming if it was to heat the air inside the balloon enough to create condensation that would drip back down to the hot plate in a steamy, self-sustaining cycle.

While Pauline waited patiently on the ground, Ishmael was several feet above her in the cabin, bustling about in his final preparations for their impromptu voyage. Eventually, he heaved the ladder over the side of the wicker basket so Pauline could climb aboard. But something was bothering Ishmael; he was not his normal self. He still helped Pauline step into the basket, of course, but he seemed to do so with a slight air of resent-ment. It was as if he was being forced to do something he didn't really want to do, and his displeasure went totally undetected by Pauline.

Once aboard, Pauline became aware of a third person who would be accompanying them on their journey: a dark-haired, plain-faced woman sitting in one corner of the basket. Surrounded by an assortment of tools and trinkets, she was engrossed in her task at hand, mincing all kinds of pebbles and petals while mixing them with just as many leaves and lotions.

"My sister, Lydia," Ishmael paused to say dryly once Pauline had taken notice of her.

"Oh," Pauline cheered, happy to have another woman in their company. "It's a pleasure to meet you. I'm Pauline. Will you be joining us for our trip?"

Lydia stopped her work just long enough to turn and nod at her inquirer. In her dispirited face was evidence of a life that had seen as much grinding as her own mortar and pestle. But Pauline's gaze quickly shifted to something that was even more captivating: a large, metal clasp around her neck, as stiff as steel but not so snug as to choke her. Like the collar of a turtle-neck shirt, it was a few inches tall, though it seemed more an emblem of punishment than a symbol of fashion, no matter the culture. Despite her curiosity and slight worry, however, Pauline felt it best not to probe, and Lydia returned to her work without ever saying anything.

In fact, few words were spoken among the three of them for almost the entire trip. The one exception occurred when Ishmael asked to see Lionel's letter again. He quickly jotted down the coordinates and promptly handed it back. He was impressed (and still a little suspicious) how Lionel had been able to determine his exact location while being held captive: 31 degrees, 42 minutes, and 8 seconds south of the equator; 172 degrees, 33 minutes, and 3 seconds west of the prime meridian in Greenwich, England.

The afternoon wore on slowly, but any sight of land went away quickly. With an endless tide below and an eventide above, Pauline spent the entire day with her head in the clouds, her mind fixed on what joy the future hours would bring. Could it be? Could this really be the day when she would finally be reunited with her long-lost love? For years, she had been wishing and waiting with unfailing loyalty and untiring patience, but it was these final moments of anticipation that were most agonizing of all. Oh, how ready she was to end this saga of sorrow!—to resurrect her shipwrecked marriage!—to resuscitate her broken heart! Like a prenuptial bride, Pauline's fantasies of a fresh start to a new season of life stretched as infinitely as the boundless Pacific Ocean all around them.

Meanwhile, Ishmael had his own anxieties. Their destination was a "fortress"—a prison, no less—and he was willing to bet visiting hours, if any, didn't fall within the witching hour. Neither was he so foolish as to believe such a "heavily guarded" place would be void of surveillance and security. What was he to do? While the aircraft's camouflage provided some relief against detection, how stealthily could he traverse the terrain of a place he knew nothing about? Would this be as quick and painless as fly-by and pick-up, or would he be expected to park it and sneak in? Ishmael wished Mr. Coy were with them; he was so much better at this kind of stuff. Fortunately, he had the next best thing: his sister, Lydia, and her potions.

Ishmael's tension seemed to relax slightly when a new moon rose to replace the old sun in the darkening sky. As little light as possible would make them all the more unnoticeable, and even though it meant all they could see were silhouettes, it was worth the risk.

About an hour before midnight, Lionel's coordinates were reached, and Waters Deep crept into view. With vision by starlight, it was difficult to distinguish the landmass from the blackness of the ocean and sky. Only on account of the white, frothy waves crashing against its many erratic shores could Pauline make out the general layout of what appeared to be an island.

For what a curious shape it was! Extending from its circular center were five protrusions: four were long and skinny, like peninsulas; the fifth was just as long but much wider, like a trapezoid. After studying it for several minutes, Pauline came to the conclusion that Waters Deep was indeed an island but in the form of a star—a star that would have had six arms if the gap between two of them wasn't filled in. In this way, it also resembled the framework of a Ferris wheel, with the

filled-in portion acting like a base and the four peninsulas like the beams that carry riders. It was really quite
strange, not made by man but perhaps influenced by
him. But besides this, neither Pauline nor Ishmael could
identify any other distinguishing characteristics.

At the stroke of midnight, Pauline became antsy,
contemplating what their next move should be now that
the clock was ticking. She glanced around the cabin for
help: while Lydia (aided by candlelight) seemed to be
packaging her mysterious pyrotechnics, Ishmael
continued to circle the area, staying a safe distance away
and maintaining a generous altitude above the island.
Wondering how Lionel would reveal his location,
Pauline peered over the side of the wicker basket and
scanned the scene below. Suddenly, she saw a tiny flash
of light flicker amid the darkness.

"I saw something!" she yelled in a whisper.

Ishmael strode to her side and glanced down. Sure
enough, a few seconds later, another faint flash of light
appeared in the same spot.

Ishmael deemed the discovery worthy of investi-
gation. He lowered the invisible balloon and slowly
advanced toward the island, ready to reverse course at
the slightest provocation. Pauline kept a watchful eye on
the consistent flashes of light. Once within a safe
distance, Ishmael retrieved a pair of high-tech goggles to
take his first real look at Waters Deep.

Penetrating the darkness through his night vision scope, Ishmael could view the general topography of the foreign landscape. The peninsular arms of the star-shaped island extended like oversized jetties into the ocean, with great waves crashing against them with tremendous force. Unlike its bare and rocky appendages, however, the body of the mainland was densely vegetated, with thick growth and dense fog obstructing any view beyond the perimeter.

Ishmael adjusted his instrument to slide a thermal lens in front of the night vision scope, enabling him to see objects emitting heat. He was hoping to be able to find Lionel this way, but, to his surprise, the scene before him lit up with activity. The entire place was brimming with warmth, which was consistent with Mr. Coy's claim that the isle was home to hordes of hot springs, as he had mentioned in his retelling of his and Helen's one and only visit.

With no other option, Ishmael blindly resumed his progression toward the mysterious, flashing light. Low and slow, he eased the balloon into the space between a pair of peninsulas, decreasing in elevation enough to feel the spray of the waves. The blinking light seemed to be coming from the point where the two arms met. With each passing second, the distance between the jetty-like barriers grew narrower, the jarring roar of the fearful breakers only adding to their suspense. Ishmael didn't like the idea of getting so close to the mainland; he knew every inch forward meant an eventual inch in retreat. But the light seemed to lure them in—closer, deeper.

Very quickly, the scene fell silent. The peninsulas had nearly met now, and the shallower water underneath them had turned from rage to ripple. The noiselessness was most unsettling. Even their breathing seemed loud.

After a few moments that felt like hours, they learned the source of the flashing light. Directly in front of them, on par with their approach, was the figure of a man. He was standing several yards from the edge of the ledge where the two peninsulas came together, holding a blinking flashlight out in front of him. At his back was what looked like a fallen tree trunk, as if he was using it to hide from any watchmen who might be lurking in the woods behind him.

"That must be him!" Pauline spoke softly, her nerves causing her to tremble.

Though they didn't know for certain, Ishmael agreed. He brought the balloon as close to the ledge as possible, stopping when the top of the basket was even with the ground.

"Lionel!" Ishmael called out with a stifled yell. "Lionel, it's us!"

"We're here to rescue you!" Pauline said more loudly.

"Shhh," Ishmael quieted her.

But there was no movement in the shadows. As far as they could tell, Lionel (if it indeed was him) couldn't hear them.

"Lionel!" they tried again, but still there was no response.

"Okay, I'll go and get him," Ishmael volunteered.

"I'll help you," Pauline suggested eagerly, though the offer was uncharacteristically daring of her.

"I need you to stay here," Ishmael countered.

Pauline thought to herself, *"Just how am I supposed to see Jaret if I stay here?"*

"You'll be safe here with Lydia," Ishmael told her.

"Oh, sure," Pauline scoffed in her mind, *"what's the silent scientist gonna do?"*

Ishmael explained, "The basket is hidden below the ledge, and the rest of the balloon is already invisible, so no one will know we're here."

"But I want Jaret to know I'm here!" she mentally protested.

"In case I run into any trouble," he continued, slipping his arms into a vest with all kinds of pockets and latches, "I'll need you to do exactly as I say." Pauline was trying to concentrate amid all the zipping and snapping going on as Ishmael armed himself with a stockpile of gadgets. "Okay?"

"Okay," she agreed. *"Once you rescue Lionel, then we'll concentrate on finding Jaret.* Got it."

Ishmael climbed onto the edge of the basket and leapt up onto the rocky ledge. He hunched low and stood still for a moment, waiting for any surprises. When the coast seemed clear, he hurried towards Lionel.

But, for some reason, Lionel was unresponsive. Arriving at his side, Ishmael grabbed the blinking flashlight and shined it on Lionel to see what was going on. It was in that moment when Ishmael discovered that a squirming Lionel was tied up and gagged.

Suddenly, a spot light engulfed Ishmael's position, and the sound of an alarm filled the air.

"A trap!" Ishmael shrieked.

CHAPTER 11

RESCUING PAULINE

In an instant, armed men converged on the scene and swarmed around Ishmael. They appeared from the shadows, spilled out of the nearby forests, and emerged from underground passageways. With great speed, the squadron formed a semi-circular barricade around their bait and its catch, cutting off any possibility of retreat. Ishmael quickly found himself backed up against the large tree trunk to which Lionel was tied. He was cornered and slowly put his hands in the air. Since he was the object in the dead center of every gun's crosshairs, none of the troops seemed yet aware of the hot-air balloon in their midst.

In no time, a single armored vehicle pulled into the semi-circle, and a decorated man stepped out. Obviously the commander, he was carrying a most peculiar weapon, one which Ishmael had never seen before. It was as long as a shotgun but bulkier, as if the chamber housed something much more complex than a bullet. Most curious of all, however, was a lead shield positioned near the midsection of the stock, probably to protect its wielder from what came out of the barrel. Whatever the odd-looking firearm was or did, the commander seemed to treat it with great care, and Ishmael didn't like the look of it, especially as it came closer towards him.

The commander scrutinized Ishmael, pacing around him in dizzying circles while maintaining his penetrating stare. He quickly became dissatisfied with what he saw, however. Finally, he grabbed one of Ishmael's hands and inspected the palm.

"You're not him!" the commander growled with hot displeasure.

Ishmael wasn't sure if he should be relieved or dismayed.

The commander touched a telecommunications device in one of his ears and said, "Lord Lye; come in, Lord Lye—can you hear me?" But the only thing anyone could hear was Lionel squirming nearby in his chains. "Lye, are you there?" Frustrated, the commander gave up trying to report to his superior, asking rhetorically, "Where *is* he?" He signaled a soldier next to him to return his special weapon to his vehicle. Then, turning to Ishmael, he barked, "Who are you?"

Ishmael was about to speak when he saw the commander whip out another weapon. This second device was much smaller than the first one, yet there was an exposed electrical current at the end of its muzzle. Obviously meant to stun rather than kill, it reminded Ishmael of some kind of deluxe edition of a Taser, apparently outfitted with both short- and long-range firing capabilities. As soon as the commander grasped it in his hand and ignited the current, his men followed suit, forsaking their lethal weapons and finding their stun guns.

"Who are you?" the commander repeated with failing patience, his ever-ready finger on the trigger. "Say something!"

Just then, something beyond the unfriendly face-off caught Ishmael's attention. Lydia was peeking over the ledge, staring at her brother. As soon as they made eye-contact, she deliberately blinked, as if to communicate instructions. Then she quietly ignited the fuse of a small capsule and heaved it toward the center of the circle.

Ishmael grinned and, as ordered, said something: "Have you ever—*Ben Coy?*"

Without any warning, a brilliant light flooded the area as Lydia's capsule exploded upon contact with the ground. Consisting mostly of magnesium and potassium perchlorate, the combustion of the flash powder produced a brief but powerful burst of illumination that temporarily blinded everyone standing on the ledge.

Everyone except for Ishmael, of course. He opened his eyes as soon as the lightning-like luminosity had faded and immediately turned his attention to Lionel. The poor prisoner's hands and legs were bound with iron cuffs, and he was fettered to the tree trunk with a thick chain that wrapped around his torso multiple times. While his antagonists were still seeing stars and stammering in their steps, Ishmael ungagged Lionel.

"Where's Ret?" Lionel immediately blurted out with concern that approached anger.

"Nice to see you, too," Ishmael replied sarcastically. Ignoring Lionel's ungrateful inquiry, Ishmael retrieved a small, pen-like device from his vest. It emitted a carbon dioxide laser, which made quick work of the chain. Then he dragged Lionel, who was also temporarily visionless, to the rear of the tree trunk for protection while he worked on removing the clasps around Lionel's ankles and wrists.

Meanwhile, Lydia was utilizing the guards' light-induced daze to her advantage. She lobbed two fistfuls of mechanical marbles onto the ledge. Like burrowing insects, they hit the ground rolling and then harnessed that kinetic energy to dig into the dirt and continue their subterranean mission toward the troops. Just as the soldiers' vision was returning, they became airborne, being launched at random as Lydia's landmines exhausted their strength and exploded under the earth. The ground became deformed and the men half-buried by the geyser-like eruptions that filled the air with dirt and rocks.

Knowing the men would quickly rebound, Lydia was already moving on to her next idea in her plan to buy her brother time. She was pouring a silvery potion into a refillable device that looked like a boomerang. When finished, she hurled the curved instrument into the air. As it made its wide arc over the heads of the fallen troops, it released its contents, which was a blend of liquid silk that was coated in magnetic material. It looked like it was raining spider webs as the silk dried in the air and was drizzled on the guards below. Then, on account of the magnetite and neodymium coating, the wispy fibers began to adhere to the men's guns, tunics, and everything else that was magnetic or could become so. As more magnetic fields were activated and compounded, the troops' situation became so icky and sticky that they were of no use at all by the time the empty boomerang flew back into Lydia's hand.

The commander escaped the misfortunes that had foiled his forces, however, thanks to his proximity to Ishmael and Lionel in the center of the fray. His intruders were still finding refuge behind the tree trunk.

Hoping to drive them out, he tore a can of tear gas from his belt, pulled the pin, and chucked it at their shelter.

Ishmael had already freed Lionel's ankles and was just about to do the same to his wrists when he heard something land in the dirt nearby. With dread, he and Lionel watched as the commander's shell rolled towards them and began to wildly release vapors into the air. Unaware of the contents of the can but figuring it couldn't be good, they knew they only had a few seconds to act before the unknown gas would overtake them.

Suddenly, a shield of water enclosed the chaotic can. Like an upside-down bowl, it covered the shell and its emissions, sparing the air of any additional gas and smoke. Just as the liquid cage was beginning to burst from the mounting pressure, Ishmael reached in, grabbed the can, and hurled it away. After a few bounces, it rolled underneath the commander's vehicle, where it continued to spew.

Assuming Lydia had conjured up the shield of water with one of her many potions, Ishmael remarked, "Thanks, sis."

Now that Lionel was ambulant, Ishmael decided to make a run for it, counting on his sister to continue to watch his back. He sprung from behind the tree, pulling a somewhat reluctant Lionel behind him. With his prey on the move, the commander pointed his stun gun at the fugitives and prepared to fire.

Lydia was repositioning the balloon in preparation for a quick getaway. She had already turned it around when she saw the unflinching commander aimed and ready to pull the trigger. She raised the balloon just enough to bring the jet engine above the ledge. Then she revved it at full power.

Like standing behind an airplane on a tarmac, the commander found himself caught in hurricane-strength winds. The gales leveled him flat, knocking him to the ground. His weapon fired upon impact, sending a pair of needled barbs into the air. Like a doctor's syringe, each of the two probes was connected to several feet of high-voltage wire that conducted the electrical pulse to whatever poor object happened to be in the line of fire. The twin barbs flew into the growing cloud of tear gas that had engulfed the commander's vehicle.

Ishmael and Lionel continued their beeline for the balloon. Just as the commander was rising to his feet in pursuit, he was sent to the ground again by an unexpected explosion. The front of his vehicle had suddenly erupted in flames. The electrical current provided by the stun gun's misfire served as the spark that ignited the fumes of the aerosol can. Suddenly stricken with terror, the commander flocked to the scene and retrieved something from the backseat. In his hands was the strange-looking weapon he had unveiled earlier. Relieved to have found it intact, he quickly moved it to safety.

"What in the world is going on out there?" Pauline wanted to know. Several moments ago, when she had heard Ishmael yell the word *trap,* she fled to a corner of the basket and cowered in fear. By now, she had idly witnessed streaking lights, shouting men, and violent explosions, with Lydia throwing things on the field like a cheerleader. Hoping her chances of searching for Jaret were not being jeopardized by any of the commotion, she finally stood up and looked for herself.

She had scarcely viewed the scene when she saw Ishmael pulling Lionel behind him and running full-speed towards her.

"Get down!" Ishmael ordered as they dove into the basket, which Lydia had lowered back down to the level of the ledge to grant them easy access. "Get us out of here!" Ishmael breathlessly told his sister.

The commander stood in shock for a moment. His enemy had either just disappeared out of thin air or leapt headlong over the side of the ledge. Then his puzzled gaze turned to something burning in the sky above. Looking more closely, however, he realized it was the reflection of his own vehicle, which was still aflame. When he saw the wicker basket begin to rise from beneath the safety of the ledge in its attempt to flee, he finally became aware of the elephant in the room.

"It's an airship!" the commander proclaimed. "Engage the turrets!"

Instantly, the forest came alive. Amid the bending of branches and the twisting of trunks, several massive missile turrets rose above the treetops. When the cracking of wood and the clanging of mechanical gears had ceased, the towers' operators waited for a single word from their commander.

"WAIT!"

It was Pauline. She was leaning over the side of the basket, staring unblinkingly at the commander.

"Jaret!" she called out to him. "Jaret!" Though the basket was a few feet above the ledge and gradually rising, she fearlessly rolled over its side and flopped onto the ground.

"Of course," Lionel moaned, as if regretting something.

"What is she doing?!" Ishmael cried out in disbelief.

Pauline pushed her hand against her knee to pick herself up. "Jaret, it's me," she celebrated as she staggered towards her husband. "It's me—Pauline!" She slowed and then stopped several yards in front of him, moving as little as possible to afford him a good, clear look.

For a brief moment, the world stood still as all nature held its breath. Every noise died, and Pauline's heart seemed to stop. Caught off-guard, Jaret slowly lowered his weapon. He furrowed his brow in vexation, staring intently at the wild woman standing before him. In some strange way, she seemed familiar to him. Something about her — her thick hair, her slightly irritating voice, something — felt vaguely, distantly familiar.

And then that moment ended.

"Come back, Pauline!" Lionel hollered from the basket.

Shaken from his trance, Jaret resumed operations: "Fire at will!"

At those words, Pauline's heart died.

But the turrets came alive. They began to fire immediately, and the skies lit up like a fireworks show. Initially, the shells seemed to be coming at random, for the men at the controls couldn't see what they were supposed to be firing at, and all the reflections from the solar panels did little to help in the cause of orientation. Still, a few rounds made contact, and the intense heat and shrapnel were enough to cause considerable damage to several solar panels.

Ishmael heaved the ladder over the side of the basket and slid down its sides, bypassing the rungs so as to expedite his rescue of Pauline. By the time Jaret had reloaded his stun gun with a fresh cartridge, Ishmael had arrived from behind Pauline. As Jaret fired, Ishmael dove into Pauline, pushing her out of the way. But it was a double hit, with one of the twin barbs lodging in Pauline's shoulder and the other in Ishmael's.

Pauline instantly went limp, perhaps a combination of being rejected by her husband and only half-hit with the tranquilizer. Ishmael, on the other hand, resisted with whatever residual stamina he could summon. After yanking the pair of projectiles out of their respective shoulders with his good arm, he found the whip on his vest and used it to latch onto Jaret's leg, sweeping him off his feet. Then, again employing the whip, Ishmael grabbed Jaret's gun and flung it far away.

When Ishmael tried a third time to strike Jaret, the commander stuck out his arm to block. The whip wrapped around his wrist, and Jaret pulled it from Ishmael's possession. But before Jaret could use it, Ishmael brought out a pouch of granules and smeared them in a line in front of him. Like strike-anywhere matches, they immediately caught fire from their friction against the sandy dirt, and Ishmael flung the burning embers in the direction of Jaret's face.

Again, it was time to flee. Even though half of his upper body was incapacitated, Ishmael hobbled back to the balloon with every last ounce of energy he could muster, dragging a lifeless Pauline behind him. He knew the ladder would soon be out of reach. Just as he was about to grab hold of the lowest rung, however, he was dealt a dose of his own medicine. Jaret had wielded the whip to grab hold of Ishmael's ankle, preventing his escape. The ladder quickly rose beyond his reach.

As Jaret lumbered toward his fallen prey, Ishmael resorted to his last hope. Seeing the basket directly above him, he deployed a grappling hook from the back of his vest. Like a harpoon, it torpedoed upwards until it crashed through the basket. With an ending like a fishhook, it lodged securely within the wicker fibers. Grasping Pauline tightly, they began to be lifted away as the balloon rose heavenward.

But, with a desperate leap, Jaret latched onto one of Ishmael's dangling feet, wrapping his hand tightly around it. The grappling hook threatened to give way under the stress of so much weight. With strong hands, Jaret began to inch his way up Ishmael's leg.

"You're as stubborn as your old lady," Ishmael observed as he tried to free himself from Jaret's powerful clutches. Finally, after using his other foot to deal repeated blows to Jaret's relentless grip, the commander relinquished and fell to the ground.

With renewed strength, the cord resumed rewinding itself. Ishmael reached for the ladder and climbed to safety within the basket, collapsing on the floor with exhaustion.

But there remained an effectual struggle to be made.

"Deploy heat-seeking missiles," Jaret ordered on the ground. "Bring down that ship!" He was beginning to panic now, fearing the wrath of Lye if he failed to retain his prisoner and detain the rescuers.

Lydia was maneuvering the balloon at full throttle, intent on maximizing her distance from Waters Deep as quickly as possible. As the envelope filled with hot air, they soared into the cooler skies of the night, while the engine propelled them further out to sea.

They had almost breathed a sigh of relief when Lionel announced, "Heat-seekers at six o'clock."

Ishmael spun around to see half a dozen heat-seeking missiles hot on their trail. He rushed to the controls and pressed a seldom-used button on an obscure region of the panel. It lowered a pair of flare dispensers, each on either side of the jet engine underneath the basket. Ishmael pushed a second button, deploying the flares, which fanned out across the sky.

"Now dive—dive!" Ishmael shouted to his sister. Lydia obeyed. Like a spouting whale, the balloon exhaled, releasing much of the warm air within its envelope.

"Hold on tight!" Ishmael advised. As if on a thrilling free-fall ride at an amusement park, the balloon plummeted. "Pull up! Pull up!" Just before plunging into the ocean, the balloon stabilized, and its riders watched from below as the outsmarted heat-seeking missiles chased the hot flares instead of their original target.

For several uneasy moments, the sibling pilots scoured the skies, waiting for ballistic missiles or fighter jets or whatever else Waters Deep had in its impressive arsenal. When nothing appeared on the horizon, they breathed a true sigh of relief.

"We're lucky Lye was missing in action," Ishmael observed, putting his good arm around his sister. "He doesn't make mistakes."

"Where is Ret?" Lionel wondered with great earnestness, even frustration. "Why didn't he come?"

"What does it matter?" Ishmael replied, disliking Lionel's tone. "We rescued you, didn't we?"

"Yes, but where *is* he?" the ingrate demanded. "Can you at least tell me where he is?"

Unfortunately for Lionel, Ishmael shared the same distrust for him as did Mr. Coy. As such, he answered, "Maybe you should ask Pauline," knowing Lionel wouldn't be able to squeeze any information out of her.

For she was lying in a corner of the basket, as mute and motionless as death, hiding her face from mankind. Curled up and trembling, the effects of the stun gun were wearing off, and feeling was returning to her body, though not to her heart. She was not so shaken up by the shot as she was by the shooter. Lionel threw his arms up in defeat, assuming sleep had already overtaken her. But she was wide awake—and would be for hours—silently weeping over her world that had just come to a bitter end.

Back at Waters Deep, Jaret was standing alone on the wind-swept and war-torn ledge, staring out to sea.

He had been watching his heat-seeking missiles and was strangely relieved when the airship had out-maneuvered them. He could easily have initiated and won an aerial pursuit but decided not to for the sake of the raving woman onboard—the one who had approached him, screaming his name. He knew her; he was sure of it. But how—from where? A dream, perhaps—or maybe a former life? There he stood, long after the basket had been swallowed in the darkness, still reaching for answers in the distant recesses of his memory.

For, in his brainwashed mind, that woman rang a bell—a bell that would not stop ringing.

CHAPTER 12

AN OCEAN RUNS
THROUGH IT

Ret was jolted into consciousness by a large, black beetle crawling up his arm. He shot up from his makeshift bed, flinging the critter away. Ret took it as a sign that it would be an exciting day.

Continuing their northern trek, it didn't take long for Ret, Conrad, and Mr. Coy to reach the road that Rodrigo had mentioned to them the day before. They flagged down a friendly truck driver who allowed them to climb into his cargo of Brazilian nuts and ride into the nearby town. It was a small place—a village, really. Situated right on the river, it was the equivalent of a truck stop along an interstate highway. Still, it was slim pickings for watercraft. In the end, Mr. Coy struck a deal with a man who was trying to sell a used airboat. Its modest platform accommodated the three travelers, and its large rear fan, encaged above the water, would provide propulsion far superior to rowing. After securing a few spare gallons of gasoline, they set off once again down the Amazon.

At Mr. Coy's urging, Ret maintained a weather eye on his scar, pledging to alert him if there was any change at all as they glided downriver. A few dozen miles later, the scar reawakened. Obviously prompted by something that was still unknown to them, the scar was added upon, illuminating another piece that was connected to and about the same size as the first one. Despite this addition, the meaning of the scar was still a mystery. Whereas it had resembled a sort of squiggly line, now it just looked like a longer squiggly line. It seemed the scars all possessed the same trait of being difficult to decipher.

"Time to swim," Coy announced as the airboat slowed to a stop.

Reluctantly, Ret glanced over the side of the boat and into the murky water. From shore to shore, the entire river was muddy now. Memories of the river dolphins swam into his mind.

"Can Conrad come with me this time?" Ret wondered hopefully. Mr. Coy liked the idea, and Conrad never said anything to the contrary.

The two of them stepped into the water, hoping to attract as little attention to themselves as possible for fear of what secret sentinels might be lying in wait this time. On account of the cloudy water, Ret couldn't see a thing. It was almost like swimming in the more fluid portion of paint when it hasn't been stirred in ages. Frustrated, Ret wished he could somehow remove the dirt from the water. It then occurred to him that he could probably do that.

With a wave of his hand, he dismissed the suspended particles of earth that befuddled his view. Like taking a wet rag to a dusty television screen, the river was wiped clean. Having watched from above as the water changed from brown to blue, Mr. Coy stuck his fist underwater to give Ret a thumbs-up.

However, Ret was focused on some residual matter that persisted in the water. It was not nearly as prevalent as the dirt had been, and it seemed to sparkle and glisten in the dancing sunlight. It reminded Ret of a certain activity in science class in which he had panned for small flecks of gold. In his squirming efforts to tread water, the shimmering flakes seemed to follow his right hand, collecting into thick strands like clearing cobwebs with a feather duster. He appeared to have some amount of control over the particles.

Ret continued to whisk away the golden dust obscuring his view. Conrad probably thought he resembled a sorcerer casting a magical spell with a wand. Then, with a grand and sweeping finale, Ret threw out his arms, expelling dirt and flecks away from him in every direction. The water was instantly washed clean, and, like a bomb making impact with the river bottom, the topmost layer of sediment began to roll back in low plumes.

Suddenly, something shiny appeared on the river floor. Being uncovered before Ret's eyes was a thin slab of pure gold, and it was growing. In the clear water, he could see how it stretched from bank to bank, perpendicular to the river's flow but following the natural contour of the river bottom. About as wide as a typical cement sidewalk, it almost seemed to form a ring inside the river, but it stopped as soon as it reached each outer rim of the river. If the river were ever to be parted or dammed, its steep and narrow form would create the ultimate half-pipe challenge for a skateboarder.

Once again, however, Ret had tripped the alarm. To their left, Conrad and Ret watched as a fast-moving wall of bubbles began to appear. The oddity was also being replicated on their right, coming toward them from the opposite direction. Like the jaw of some great sea creature, the walls were quickly closing in when they realized they were about to be consumed by swarms of piranha.

With all haste, Ret darted toward the surface. While Conrad pushed him up, Mr. Coy anxiously pulled him out. Conrad emerged amid dozens of ferocious piranha leaping towards him in the frothy water, their small but sharp teeth bared. The thick-skinned aborigine had taken a few bites but paid them little notice.

"I found something," Ret panted, eager to report his discovery to Mr. Coy.

"So did I," Coy replied, pointing upward. Directly above them was a golden archway. It was the mirror image of the inverted arch that Ret had just uncovered beneath them along the bottom of the river. The reflection had been made possible once the submerged arch had been revealed and the river water had been cleansed. With beauty and radiance, it spanned across the river like a rainbow, connecting on either side with the golden kink on each bank. At its zenith, the golden arch reached high into the sky.

"What did *you* find?" Coy asked amid the awe of the golden arch. "A McDonalds?"

While Ret was explaining his own discovery, the reflection of the golden arch began to fade away as a result of the never-ending flow of the Amazon. In a matter of seconds, the muddy water pouring into the area from upstream had overtaken the clean water and reburied the immersed arch, completely concealing the phenomenon from view.

Despite the disappearance, the piranha apparently did not get the memo. Unabated, the unruly, carnivorous fish totally encompassed the airboat and occasionally flopped on deck. Mr. Coy fired up the boat and sped away. Like the river dolphins, the piranha remained at the dive site and did not chase their trespassers.

After over an hour of cruising downriver, a third segment of the scar appeared. They stopped the boat in a somewhat secluded area, but instead of going for a swim, Ret simply immersed his head. Like before, he waved his hand, separating the dirt from the water, and uncovered the golden, subterranean half-pipe. Then, as they had before, they watched as the golden reflection of the upside-down arch materialized overhead.

One by one, this pattern was repeated nearly half a dozen times in their progression down the Amazon River: a new segment of the scar would appear, so they'd stop the boat, and Ret would dunk his head; he'd uncover the golden half-pipe beneath, they'd watch the golden arch light up above, and then the scene would be swept away by the river. The only variation was in the protectors that were unleashed to assault them. These faunal foes seemed to become more dangerous each time, ranging from a massive flock of sharp-beaked birds to a stealthy colony of caiman crocodiles.

According to their theory, the scar manifested itself literally line upon line, for that's all it was: a line— not a straight line, but one with a gradual curve here and a slight crinkle there. Once a handful of segments had been revealed, Ret noticed how the shape of the scar mimicked the course of the river. Where there was a gradual bend in the scar, Ret remembered there being a gradual bend in the river. Each new piece summarized the path they had taken since the previous one. The scar was like a GPS that highlighted the route they had already completed. Eventually, Mr. Coy and Ret came to the conclusion that the scar was charting their course. The scar was a direct reflection of the river. Simply put, the scar was a map.

With the setting sun behind them, they eventually floated into the delta where the mighty Amazon River spilled into the boundless Atlantic Ocean. For Ret, it was a perplexing experience, akin to going up through the narrow portion of a funnel. There was a definitive point when the river opened up and fanned out. Unlike most deltas, this one was many times wider than the river itself, shaped like a triangle. Adding to the confusion was the presence of large islands directly in the middle of the delta with the river sprawling around them on all sides in its drive toward the sea. Erosion might explain the islands but not the incredibly wide mouth. Had a tectonic wedge been driven in the side of the continent? Had a great chunk broken off?

They resolved to keep moving until they either reached the ocean or the scar grew one more time — whichever came first. Strangely enough, however, they both came at about the same time. Mr. Coy shut off the engine and then looked around to make sure none of the boats or barges in the vicinity was watching them. They weren't doing anything illegal, of course, but he knew he would have a pretty hard time explaining what three foreign tourists were doing on a flimsy airboat without a guide in the middle of the delta—especially if one of them was bent over, doing a face-plant and flailing his arms in the water.

Ret had his work cut out for him on this occasion. Besides being slightly colder and saltier, there was much more commotion in the water, with currents colliding and stream after stream of silt and dirt flowing from the river and rolling out to sea. Waving his hands back and forth, Ret brought order to the bedlam until he finally began to see strips of gold shining back at him.

But it was different this time. Something was wrong. Instead of lying in a straight, continuous line, the submerged, inverted arch was broken, with large gaps and jagged edges. Like a piece of chewed gum that had been stretched too far, it lay strewn in fragments along the rugged floor of the delta.

Ret surfaced and copied Coy in looking heaven-ward. The golden rainbow was a direct reflection of the disjoined fossil resting beneath them. They stared at each other in a profound stupor.

Ret was about to say something when he saw Mr. Coy's eyes focus intently on something in the distance.

Then they began to shift from side to side, scanning the water as his face clouded over with worry. When Ret spun around to see what was the matter, he saw a speedboat accosting them, with several more heading in their direction.

"Is that the police?" Ret asked.

"No," Mr. Coy replied suspiciously, staring at the men aboard the oncoming vessel, getting a better look at them the closer they came.

"The military?"

"No, not them either," said Coy softly. "I know them when I see them."

"Then who are they?" Ret pressed.

"Vigilantes, Ret."

"Are we in trouble?"

Eyeing their firearms, Coy observed, "Judging by the size of their guns—"

Suddenly, the boat nearest them fired on the airboat.

"—Yep, we're in trouble," Coy said, taking cover.

Coy leapt to the controls, and the airboat zoomed into motion. At the sight of their target making a run for it, the advancing patrol sped up to give it chase.

At full throttle, the lightweight airboat reached a respectable cruising speed. Mr. Coy zigzagged in the water, trying to lose their pursuers in the treacherous wind and wake being created by the large fan. Such maneuvering proved futile, however, and the first speedboat of vigilantes was nearly upon them.

As the small and unprotected airboat made its riders easy targets, it was obvious by now that their enemies were aiming at the fan and engine, trying to kill the craft instead of them. When one round of artillery came dangerously close to their gasoline reserve, Coy knew it had to go.

"Conrad!" he yelled. "Ditch the fuel!" Then, addressing Ret, he said, "You ever shot skeet before?"

"Once," Ret answered hesitantly, "in a video game."

"Good enough," Coy hollered back amid his strategic steering. "Conrad will throw the gas cans for you to shoot. Use the bullets." He pointed to the spent ammunition scattered across the deck.

"But I don't have a gun," Ret stated.

"I think the next element is metal, Ret." They cowered at another onslaught of gunfire as it ricocheted off the fan. "I would highly suggest you give it a try."

Ret picked up a bullet. It was still warm.

"Yell 'pull' when you're ready," Coy taught, "and don't shoot until it's just about to hit the water. And make sure to send a little fire with each bullet: containers don't explode just by being punctured."

Ret figured it was worth a shot.

"Pull!"

Conrad heaved the first jug of gasoline into the air, its trajectory directly in line with their closest assailant. Thrown with astounding accuracy, the container was on par to make a direct impact with the speedboat, but it jerked to the side at the last minute. Just as the jug was about to plunge into the sea, Ret power-flicked a bullet toward it, making sure to keep it enveloped in a small flame. As if shot from a silent gun, it made contact. The fuel exploded, causing the speedboat to capsize.

Amid Mr. Coy's cheers, Ret stared at his palm in shock. It was a literal handgun. Pleased, he extended his index finger and pretended to blow away exhaust from the smoking barrel.

One boat down, with many more to go. Soon, in like manner, they had taken out two more. But their enemies were catching on. Conrad discreetly slipped the last fuel canister off the side of the airboat, leaving it half-hidden in the churning water. Then Mr. Coy purposely maneuvered the boat until their closest antagonists were directly on course with where the jug was bobbing. Finally, at the right moment, Ret launched a fiery bullet, purposely exploding the improvised mine.

But the race was to the swift. Soon, a fifth speedboat came up alongside the airboat. Like the others before them, the vigilantes directed their fire at the rear of the airboat, trying to kill the engine and knock out the fan. At one point, the speedboat came close enough that one of the vigilantes leapt aboard the airboat, but Conrad promptly picked him up and threw him back. In self-defense, Ret fired bullet after bullet, shattering the speedboat's windshield, tearing up the upholstery, and scuttling the hull. Soon, with so much water filling the bottom of the vessel, the speedboat trailed behind and began to sink.

By the time a sixth enemy boat caught up to them, Ret had grown tired of acquiring his own ammunition and simply started rerouting the bullets that were coming out of the vigilantes' guns. Unlike the ruffians, however, Ret could cause his bullets to stop, turn around, and change direction. He repelled every bullet that came their way and sent them back in every direction, much to the bewilderment of his foes. Ret concentrated his attack on the control system, and once the steering wheel had been blown to bits, he watched as the speedboat drifted away aimlessly.

Meanwhile, the airboat riders failed to notice yet another speedboat that had snuck up on them and was straddling their other side. Having witnessed the fruitless attempts of his comrades, the driver of this second craft got close enough to the airboat sufficient to lodge the barrel of a gun through the cage and in the path of the fan blades. Following a deafening noise, there was a short struggle before the fan abruptly died, and the airboat slowed to a halt.

Additional speedboats surrounded them immediately, hemming them in on all sides and eliminating any possibility of escape. With every gun aimed in their direction, Mr. Coy and Conrad put their hands up, with Ret quickly following suit.

The vigilantes were a rough-looking lot, with rounds of ammunition hanging from their belts and unhappy scowls painted across their faces. They looked native to the region, as if hired as part of some secret operation—the kind that pays well and carries out its mission at any cost. They wore no uniforms, and their vessels were equally varied and mismatched.

No one moved until a final speedboat arrived, carrying an austere man who was obviously chiefest among the secret band. He stepped aboard the airboat and slowly walked around his three captives, giving each a hard stare, though he seemed to glare at Conrad and Ret the longest. Ret was relieved when it appeared his scar went unnoticed. Eventually, the ringleader returned to his boat and picked up his phone.

Ret couldn't tell who he was speaking to or what was being said. Not long into the conversation, however, an unpleasantly surprised look came over the leader's face. He glanced at his three prisoners multiple times, as if confirming their distinguishing features. In time, he replaced the phone, turned to face his subjects, and barked a disappointed command in Portuguese.

"What did he say?" Ret asked Mr. Coy. "Why are they lowering their weapons?"

"He's letting us go," Coy translated, lowering his hands. Without any explanation or apology, the vigilantes fired up their boats and prepared to depart. Within seconds, everyone had fled the scene, leaving the broken airboat alone in the outer reaches of the delta.

"What was that all about?" Ret wondered with vexation, rubbing his head. "Who was on the phone? And do you think those thugs were guarding the final arch?"

"I don't know," Coy replied, "but that last golden arch was very peculiar. It appeared...incomplete—all broken up and torn apart. There was definitely something missing." They stood in silence for a few moments, trying to think through the anomaly.

"It's too bad the Amazon doesn't keep going," Ret regretted, looking at his scar. "If it did, we could keep following it and find out what this scar becomes."

As if formulating a sudden idea into words for the first time, Mr. Coy said slowly, "Maybe it does keep going." He was gazing out into the endless Atlantic Ocean.

"In the ocean?" Ret said with absurdity.

"Not in the ocean, but maybe on the other side of it," Coy postulated. "Didn't you say once that one of the Guardians mentioned something about a great river?"

The wheels were beginning to turn in Ret's head, too. "Maybe the great Amazon River continues on the other side of the ocean."

At the thought, Mr. Coy and Ret turned and stared at each other wide-eyed, both with their next destination in mind: Africa.

CHAPTER 13

FRIENDSHIPS GAINED
AND STRAINED

When Ana learned about her mother's urgent request to meet with Ishmael, she naturally became quite curious. She pressed Paige for greater details, but her friend regrettably had none to give. It wasn't until after school that day, while Ana was walking to work, when Paige texted her, explaining how she had heard from the staff at the Manor that Ishmael had left hours ago in the hot-air balloon with his sister and some other woman, but no one knew where they went or when they would return. Paige offered to pick up Ana after work and bring her to the Manor for the night, depending on what happened by the end of her shift.

As the hours transpired, however, Ana's suspicion turned to worry. On her break, she repeatedly (though fruitlessly) tried to contact Pauline, wondering why her mother apparently hadn't attempted to do the same. On account of her anxiety, Ana was not her typical, talkative self as she went about her duties at the Crusty Chicken, and there was one co-worker who seemed to notice her unusual demeanor more than anyone else: the quaint and quiet custodian, Leonard Swain. Ever mindful of Ana, Leo watched her from near and far. He saw a bit too much concern in her eyes for a task as remedial as frying battered bits of zucchini, and he noted the waning cheeriness of her pretty smile whenever she helped a customer. Something was troubling her, and it was bothering him, too.

Leo decided the time had finally come for him to strike up a conversation with Ana. For the rest of his shift, he agonized over what he ought to say, scouring his mind for the right words as hard as he had the restroom tiles for the perfect shine. When it came time to clock out, however, everything he had come up with either seemed too corny or too silly or just plain dumb, and, as a result, he stood speechless as Ana strode out the door.

For several moments, however, Ana stood between storefront and parking lot, waiting for her ride. Pauline had always been very prompt when it came to picking up her daughter from work, but Leo couldn't see the Coopers' car anywhere. After another visual sweep of the lot, Ana sighed heavily and took out her phone to take Paige up on her offer.

Leo smiled. The Fates had dealt him a second chance. Calling on his courage, he puffed up his chest and girded up his loins, reassuring himself that he would succeed. In the midst of so much zeal, however, he forgot the restaurant's double doors opened from the inside with a pull, and, after a hearty push, his momentum caused him to crash into the glass.

Despite the sudden noise and his embarrassing fall, Ana didn't seem to notice. Leo dusted himself off and resumed his resolute composure.

"Evening, Miss Ana," Leo began, his nervousness adding a slight trembling to the drawl in his speech.

"Oh, hi," Ana replied, a little surprised. "It's Leonard, right?"

"That's right," he said eagerly, encouraged to learn Ana knew his name. "But most folks just call me Leo." With his shaky hands, he was subconsciously wringing his greasy hat in front of him. "Your mom'll be here soon to pick you up, won't she?"

"Not tonight," Ana explained. "She went out of town."

"But you do have a ride, don't ya?"

"Yeah, my friend, Paige, said she'd come and get me," said Ana, "if she would just respond to my text." She checked her phone again for a reply. "You know Paige?"

"I know her," Leo answered. "We're in the same

chemistry class, she and I."

"Oh, that's nice," Ana remarked politely.

An awkward silence ensued as Leo groped to prevent the conversation from dying. He wondered if he had made a mistake in speaking about another girl. Finally, he thought to say, "So where'd your mom go to?"

"I don't know; she didn't tell me," Ana said, opening up a bit now that she had someone to talk to about the situation. "I hope she's okay. She's not very good when it comes to places and directions—kind of like me, I guess—so I hope she took my GPS or something. 'Course, she's not very good with those types of things either, and there's probably no where for her to plug it in anyway, so—"

"Then it could run off the battery," Leo informed her. "Your model came with an extra battery, so it ought to last for a good two, maybe three, hours. But, really, all you need to do is stick it in one of the car's power outlets."

"I know," said Ana, "but they didn't take a car; they took the—" She stopped abruptly, worried that she had said too much in her rambling.

"—the balloon?" Leo finished her sentence.

Ana stared at him incredulously. He quickly glanced away. It made him nervous to know she was looking at him. He hoped she wouldn't notice him turning a bit red in the face, but she did and, flattered, thought it was rather cute, so she kept looking at him. She had never really paid much attention to Leonard the janitor before, yet it was an oversight that she was just beginning to regret, for there was something truly charming about him.

"How do you know about Coy's balloon?" Ana quizzed him with a raised eye brow and a playful grin. "And how do you know so much about my GPS?"

With ever greater boldness, Leo suggested, "How 'bout I tell you while I walk you home?"

"It's a deal," Ana smiled. She quickly typed an updated text message to Paige, apprising her of the change in plans and arranging for the pickup to take place at the Cooper residence.

For the next several minutes, Leo found himself with no shortage of things to talk about. He explained how he had hid himself in the janitor's closet when Mr. Coy had barged into the Crusty Chicken with his lion, allowing him to overhear the entire discussion that night. When he admitted he didn't really understand what they were talking about, Ana helped to fill in the details. She told him more about Ret and his powers, the Oracle and its purposes, and just a sampling of the adventures they had experienced thus far. It was all very intriguing to Leo, who began to ask lots of questions.

"Wait," Ana stopped him, "you never told me how you know so much about my GPS."

Leo had evaded the inquiry on purpose. It was neither his style nor intention to remove the anonymity of gift-giving. "Well, you see," he started bashfully, "I'm the one who sorta got it for ya."

"Really?" Ana asked with delight. "Oh, Leo, that's so sweet! I had a feeling it—" Again, she halted her speech.

"—wasn't Steve?" Leo winced.

"Yeah, *him,*" Ana sneered, rolling her eyes.

"I noticed you don't work when he does anymore," Leo pointed out.

"Yeah, I talked to John about it, and he said he'd make sure our schedules wouldn't overlap anymore," Ana explained. "Steve and I kind of had a falling out, I guess you could say."

A broad, hopeful smile developed across Leo's face, which he quickly wiped away. "Oh, that's awful," he fibbed, as he was cheering inside.

"Yes, he is," Ana clarified. "But enough about that." A jubilant Leo gladly obliged.

Both were a bit disappointed when the Cooper house came into view.

"Well, good night," Leo said at the front door.

"Thank you for walking me home, Leo," Ana told him. She gave him a quick hug, during which he stood as stiff as a board, too awestruck to move. "It was really sweet of you."

"Uh…you're welcome," Leo replied. "Maybe we can do it again tomorrow, if you're working, that is."

"Yeah, I'd like that," Ana smiled, as she stepped into the house to fetch a few things before Paige arrived. "Good night."

And it certainly had been. In fact, it was the best night that Leo could ever remember having. True, his worn-thin jacket did little to keep out the cold of the evening; and, yes, walking to the south end of the island was totally opposite the direction he needed to go. But he didn't mind—he didn't care. For something wonderful was stirring in a cobwebbed corner of his humble heart— something he never knew was missing because he never knew it existed. That something was love, and it warmed every one of his steps as he skipped amid the twilight, all the way home to the Center Street Orphanage.

It was a scene that was to be repeated in the few days that followed. During her mother's rendezvous with heavy artillery in the South Pacific and her brother's escapade with armed vigilantes on the Amazon River, Ana was a world away, enjoying the beautiful blossoms of her budding friendship with Leo. He was smart, though not arrogantly so, and funny—pleasant to talk to and easy to be around. He possessed a great deal of compassion, in word and in deed, not to mention a fair bit of mystery—mostly about his past, which he seemed to avoid for fear of embarrassment.

Behind Leo's glasses and within his big, brown eyes, there was a depth of soul that only seemed to grow deeper the more Ana spent time with him. She began to notice him more, at school and at work. She hadn't realized he was in two of her classes, and she no longer took for granted how clean the Crusty Chicken always seemed to be. The highlight of each day quickly became the moments they spent walking to wherever or talking of whatever—the specifics never mattered as much as the time spent together. For, as Ana was learning, Leo was more like a starchy food than a sweet candy, and although his lack of refined sugar did little to quell a craving or induce a rush, the extra time spent breaking down his complex carbs yielded something much more satisfying.

All was well until one night, at the end of the week, when Leo and Ana turned the corner and noticed there were lights on in the Cooper home. Assuming it was either Pauline or Ret, Ana bolted for the house while Leo, hoping it wasn't an intruder, darted after her. Ana burst through the front door and flew into the front room, where she was shocked to find Lionel sitting calmly on the couch.

"What are *you* doing here?" Ana wondered. Upon hearing Ana's voice, Ishmael came in from the adjoining room. She turned to him and, with growing vexation, addressed him with the same question, "What are *you* doing here?"

Before anyone could answer, however, Ret arrived at the house and stepped across the threshold, carrying a suitcase. He was just returning from his trip to the Amazon and, like his sister, was surprised by their visitors. "Leo?" he saw first, standing near the door, followed by "Ishmael?" across the room, and then finally, though with more elation than bewilderment in his voice, "Lionel?! What are *you* doing here?"

The last to enter was Mr. Coy, bringing in the rest of Ret's luggage. Like pouring water on hot grease, he erupted as soon as he saw Lionel.

"What in the world is *he* doing here?" Coy bellowed more loudly than anyone else. Ishmael quickly shut his eyes in pain, looking as though he would rather not be alive at the moment.

Coy's indignant roar seemed to rattle everyone to silence for a few moments. With great uneasiness, they all glanced back and forth at one another, wondering what strange set of circumstances had brought them all together. Just then, in the calm before the storm, Pauline appeared from the kitchen. In her face was a look beyond depression that seemed to say she didn't care about anything anymore, especially whatever was going on or about to go down in her house at the moment. Without looking at anyone, she strode past the gathering like a zombie, with a Coke in one hand and a box of Twinkies in the other, and headed upstairs for her room.

And then, as if the situation couldn't get any more bizarre, the massive man Conrad tried to come inside, but his broad shoulders got stuck in the doorway.

Eventually, Coy continued, "Would somebody please explain what is going on here?"

Excusing herself, Ana yelped, "Mom!" and ran upstairs after her.

"*I* can explain," Lionel volunteered.

"No, you *can't* explain because you're not supposed to be here," Coy protested condescendingly. "As far as I'm concerned, you're *not* here, and I'm talking to this couch right now." Lionel rolled his eyes.

"Lionel sent a letter to Ret," Ishmael began with a sigh that was heavy with regret.

"You did?" Ret jumped in.

"I didn't write that letter," Lionel clarified.

"Couches are to be sat on and not heard," Coy insisted, not even glancing at Lionel. "And what did this letter say, Ishmael?"

"Lionel said he was a prisoner to Lye and needed Ret to rescue him—" said Ishmael.

"I told you I didn't write—" Lionel tried again.

"Overruled," Coy judged.

Ishmael continued, "But Pauline got to the letter first, of course, and then she came to me and asked if I would take her in the balloon. And since you and Ret wouldn't be back for at least a few days—"

"You took her?" Coy presumed with disbelief.

"Lionel said he found a way to escape for only a small amount of time each night," Ishmael began to rationalize.

"I said I didn't write—"

"But you *took* her!" Coy fumed. "Without my permission—even without my knowledge!"

"I had to, sir," Ishmael pled.

"In *my* balloon!"

"You know that woman," Ishmael reasoned. "She's impossible!" Coy's frustration seemed to subside at that statement, since he was well aware of Pauline's obstinate and conniving tendencies.

"And where was this place that Lionel told you he was?" Coy asked, rubbing his forehead.

"For the last time," Lionel declared, "I did *not* write—"

"Alright, alright," Coy conceded, reigning in like a parent over an annoying child. "The couch didn't write the letter. We got it. Then who *did* write the letter?"

"I think it—" Lionel attempted to speak.

"Ishmael," Coy interrupted, totally brushing Lionel aside, "who wrote the letter?"

"It was probably Lye or one of his men," said Ishmael. "The whole thing was a setup. They were ready for us as soon as we got there. But it was Ret who they really wanted."

"Me?" Ret said softly.

"There was a struggle; Lydia helped me," Ishmael said, including more details. "And Pauline saw Jaret—"

"Jaret was there?!" Ret interjected.

"—But he didn't recognize her," Ishmael added morosely. It was an unfortunate fact that caused everyone to gasp. A solemn gloom seemed to permeate the room.

"Hence the Twinkies," Coy remarked. Then, returning to his earlier question, "And where was this place?"

"Some place called Waters Deep," Ishmael replied, pulling the letter out of his pocket. "Here, take a look for yourself. The coordinates are at the bottom."

Mr. Coy was about to grab the letter from Ishmael when Lionel leapt from his seat and snatched it for himself.

"What do you think you're doing?" Coy asked threateningly.

"First tell me where you and Ret just got back from," Lionel said, setting his terms, "and then you can see the letter."

"That's blackmail!" Ishmael argued.

"Literally!" Coy agreed. "And you didn't even write that letter, remember?"

As if he hadn't heard their complaints, Lionel restated, "Where did you and Ret go on your trip?" He dangled the letter in front of them tauntingly.

"I'd rather squirt lemon juice in my eyes than tell you, you overgrown piece of lint," Coy sneered. "Now give me the letter before I order Conrad to sit on you."

"Perhaps I should ask the only honest person in the room. Tell me, Ret," Lionel said kindly, "where did you and Mr. Coy go?"

"Don't tell him, Ret," Coy immediately cautioned. With great sincerity in his voice, he repeated, "Do *not* tell him."

Ret was suddenly thrust to the forefront of a difficult situation, standing in the middle of a vicious, verbal tug-of-war, with Lionel on one side and Mr. Coy on the other. But how could this be? Each of them was his friend—a helpmeet, a mentor—and here they were, pulling Ret in opposite directions? Were they not all on the same side, pulling for the same team?

Ret had been here before. The unpleasant circumstances felt all too familiar. His mind reached back to a distinct memory in his recent past: he was inside the peak of the great mountain at Sunken Earth, standing between the Guardian and Lye, listening to both of their versions of the truth. The grand question on his mind then, and which had resurfaced now, was simple in statement but profound in consequence. The question was this: who could he trust?

Ret was deeply pained and intensely torn. Could he not trust both? Perhaps he should trust neither? Did they not all have the same end in mind, even if they espoused differing means of getting there? Why, then, was Ret the one who was caught in the middle? Did his choices really make that much of a difference? Was there something he didn't know?

In the end, he decided he would simply need to ask.

"Why do you want to know where we went?" Ret asked Lionel without bias.

"Because I want to help you, Ret," Lionel responded with words laced in genuine concern. "Do you remember when we walked home from the power plant together, and I told you I wanted to help you in any way I can?"

"Yes."

"Well, I meant it," said Lionel. "I also asked you to tell me whenever something happens, remember? How can I help you if you don't share things with me? Like this trip—I feel like you're hiding something from me. Why? Is it because it's just too good to share? Or are you plotting against me—should I be worried? It's just a simple question, Ret. Why won't you tell me?"

Feeling slightly guilty and very much swayed, Ret put forth the question, "Didn't Pauline tell you?"

"He was going to ask her," Ishmael chimed in, "but she hasn't said a word since she saw Jaret."

Puzzled by Coy's dogmatic declaration, Ret then turned to him and asked, "Why don't you want me to tell Lionel where we went?"

Mr. Coy stood still for a moment, his brow still furrowed in fury and his eyes still squinted in skepticism. He sighed, put his hands on his waist, and let his gaze fall to the floor. When he looked up, there was an entirely different expression that had washed over his face. Instead of malice, there was misery; in place of hardness, there was hardship; despair in lieu of desperation. It was a hallowed sort of harrowing that, in some surreal way, neither hindered nor hampered his handsomeness, making it all the more authentic. In many ways, it was as if he had just taken off a mask, and, for some reason, it reminded Ret of a certain woman named Helen.

"You can do what you want, Ret," he told him softly, sounding suddenly deflated, "but if I were you, I wouldn't tell him."

Ret was still too undecided to cast his vote. Yet, he was leaning toward the party that wasn't leaning into him. In other words, he was slightly turned off by Lionel's aggressive approach and more inclined to Mr. Coy's freedom of choice. So he said nothing, which, in most cases, says a lot.

"Unbelievable," Lionel muttered, shaking his head in disgust at Ret's silence. "All I want to do is help—all

I've ever wanted to do is help you, Ret. Even though I'm a very busy person with a lot on my plate, especially now that I've been gone for months—still, I just want to help you, but, for some reason, that doesn't seem to mean anything to you." He readied to leave. "So you know what? If that's what you want, then fine. I don't need this. Good luck, Ret. I am very disappointed in you." Lionel promptly vacated the premises.

Lionel's words stung Ret's heart. He felt as though he had just betrayed one of his best friends and greatest allies. What had he done? What was he thinking? How could he be so foolish? Oh, the aggravation!

"You did the right thing," Mr. Coy reassured him in sober tones, putting a supportive hand on his shoulder.

"Then why does it feel so wrong?" Ret asked dejectedly before heading upstairs for the night. Coy was glad when Ret didn't wait for a response because he had none to give to such a searching question.

"Well, what a way to end the day, eh men?" Coy clapped with sudden cheerfulness. "Ishmael, I know it was all you could do to keep your mouth shut about our trip, so I thank you. You have redeemed yourself—a little." Ishmael bowed his head in appreciation. "And Conrad," he said, turning to the gentle giant in the doorway, "well, let's just say I think your speechlessness is one of your greatest attributes. So never change." Conrad quickly nodded.

As Mr. Coy moved toward the door, he noticed a young man standing up against the wall in the entry, looking rather shell-shocked.

"You look like you've just seen a ghost," Coy observed, sizing him up. "Who might you be, sprout?"

"Leonard Swain, sir," came the respectful reply. Leo erected his posture, almost feeling the need to salute.

"Have you been here this whole time?" Coy wondered.

"Yes, sir," Leo said promptly.

"So you heard every word?"

"Yes, sir."

Mr. Coy thought for a moment. As much as he didn't like the idea that another party was now privy to the content of the conversation, he was somewhat impressed by what he saw.

"Swain, was it?" Coy asked to be reminded.

"Yes, sir."

"Swain, I like you," said Coy. "We'll be going to Africa in a couple of weeks. How would you like to join us?"

The forthright invitation took Leo by surprise, causing him to wobble in his posture for a moment. "I would love to, sir."

"Wonderful," Coy beamed as he left Leo's side and stepped into the night. Then, with Ishmael and Conrad following, he muttered, "We need someone to carry our bags across the desert, don't we?"

CHAPTER 14

THREAT OF
LIQUIDATION

It was suppertime at the Stone residence, and the air smelled like chili. After letting her concoction sit and stew all day, Virginia gave it a final stir and switched the stove to simmer before setting out in search of table-mates. She quickly paged Charlotte, wherever she might be housekeeping, and then stepped out the backdoor to locate Lester.

She already knew where she would find her husband. With her well-used apron tied in a knot and her light-brown hair pinned in a bun, Virginia slipped her feet into a pair of loafers and strode across the lawn. Her destination was the enclosed gazebo, which housed the avian menagerie with its extensive assortment of birds. It was Lester's retreat of choice at the end of a long week, and, knowing he had been under an unusual amount of stress lately, she wasn't surprised to find the lights on as she rounded a corner and paced ever closer along the dew-smitten grass.

"How did I know I'd find you here?" Virginia said tenderly as she gently pushed the door open. With round walls and domed ceiling, the single-roomed establishment was modest in size but stunning in display, featuring fowl from all parts of the world. In one corner, cardinals roomed with blue jays while, in another, orioles roosted among robins. Fine-feathered finches hopped in the presence of curiously-colored canaries, and dazzling macaws mingled with vibrant toucans. From the local to the exotic, there seemed to be a bird from every territory and tropic.

Lester made no reply to his wife's salutation. Though aware of her presence, he kept his back turned to her, remaining focused on his task of scattering feed throughout the cages. With great care, he dropped berries and sprinkled seeds into the many trays and troughs. Unafraid, the hungry birds swarmed around their caregiver, who seemed to take pride and find pleasure in his work.

Slowly, Virginia advanced toward her husband. The birds seemed unthreatened by her as well. With a loving smile, she wrapped her arm around him and leaned her head at his shoulder. For days now, she had gotten the sense that something was troubling him, so she hoped her supportive embrace would provide some comfort.

After a few moments of nothing but chirping and tweeting, Lester said, "This one's my favorite." He motioned to the rainbow-colored lorikeet that had come to nibble at the fruit in his cup-shaped hand. It was a marvelous creation, beautiful and dainty, and it sported nearly every color across its plumage.

"And why is that?" Virginia asked affectionately.

"Because it reminds me of you," Lester replied endearingly. Then, laying his head on hers, he said, "I love you, Virginia."

With her heart warmed by his sweet words, she also pledged, "I love you, too." Then she added, "Supper's ready, if you're hungry."

"I'll be there in a few minutes," he told her as she prepared to exit, "as soon as I finish up here." Hoping to have eased his unspoken burdens, she left the bird keeper's side and flew the coop.

Just as Virginia was returning to the house, someone else's shadow emerged on the property, though there was neither love nor compassion in this newcomer's swift stride. With the unneeded help of a white and spiraled cane, he paced with hurried haste toward the mansion house, coming from up the street and sending leaves and dust scurrying in his wake. As he approached the force field that he knew encapsulated the premises, he lifted his cane and fired a brilliant bolt of electricity, temporarily disbanding a portion of the shield and granting him unobstructed access. With ever increasing speed, he bypassed the front door, headed straight for the well-lit menagerie.

Lester had concluded his task and was preparing to leave his fowls in peace when they suddenly erupted in commotion. As if spooked by an evil presence, these birds of ill omen began to squawk and squeal and fly in frenzy. Lester froze in place, wondering what might be provoking such chaos.

Then, with a blinding flash of light and a thundering clap of noise, the door to the menagerie burst open. Lester was thrown to the ground. When he arose, he couldn't believe who he saw standing before him.

"Lord Lye!" Stone gasped from the floor. He found himself trembling, not only from the shock of his superior's unannounced visit but also because Lye was something truly terrible to look upon—a horrific sight that no amount of viewing could ever soften. Against flowing robes of darkest black lay long strands of white hair from head and beard. His skin was as pale as milk and his lips as thin as straws. With unflinching loyalty, he kept his talon-like hand clutched atop his twisted cane, his pointed fingernails like daggers. He was the epitome of elderly—the archetype of ancient—and his every breath seemed to sing an ode to being old.

And yet, the full measure of his hideousness rested in his eyes—terrible, miserable eyes that acted like windows into the most wretched and deplorable of living souls. With whites of yellow and pupils of white, whatever thing Lye's eyes beheld surely wished to be beheld by them no longer, so cursed was even the gaze of this miscreant among men.

"I...I wasn't expecting you, my lord," Stone said fearfully. "What—what are you..."

"So *this* is what you've been doing, eh, Stone?" Lye shouted insultingly, glancing around the gazebo. "Tending to your birds?!" With an angry grunt and a quick flick of his wrist, he ruptured all the water dishes and drinking bottles throughout the cages, sending a wet spray into the air. "While *I*'ve been trying to track down that blasted boy, *you*'ve been here playing house with your pretty little wife?!" A stream of electricity shot from the top of his cane, connecting with the overhead lights in the room and causing several bulbs to violently explode. The birds were ballistic now, each one wildly aflutter in hopes of escaping the showers of shards and sparks raining down on them.

Somehow finding the courage to speak, Stone said, "But the letter—what about the letter? I thought—"

"The letter was a complete failure," Lye told him flatly, displeased to be reviewing the flop.

"You mean Rct never got it?" Stone asked incredulously. "But I snuck it into the postal system, just like you asked."

"*Some*one at that house got it," Lye grumbled.

"So Ret never came to Waters Deep like you—like we—thought he would?" Stone wondered, as this was all news to him.

"No!" Lye cried with a menacing wave of his cane, which rattled the cages and ruffled the birds.

"But he's been missing school, just like I told you," Stone inserted, desperate to clear himself of any blame.

"Only after I reminded you to check the school's attendance rolls," Lye revised.

"Then perhaps Ret has fallen ill?" Stone timidly suggested.

"He isn't sick, you fool!" Lye rebuked. "He went somewhere—I'm certain of it! He left town with Coy, and they just got back tonight. Ret was never even aware of the letter. Had he known about it—that his precious friend Lionel was my prisoner and needed help escaping—Ret would have dropped everything at the chance to rescue him. But he was somewhere else, Stone, and I must know where! Where? WHERE?!"

A sudden calmness seemed to come over Lye, silenced by frustration like a lost driver who kept turning down wrong streets and arriving at dead-ends. Stone hoped his fiery indignation was cooling.

Seeking to solve his problems by retracing his steps, Lye commenced a summary of recent events. With a subdued voice and a methodical walk, he began, "I asked you to offer to exchange information with them."

"And I did, sir—"

"And you told me the next scar would lead them to Waters Deep. Right? Isn't that what you told me?"

"Yes, my lord," Stone confirmed, relieved by his leader's softer tone. "Ret described the next scar to me that night in our meeting at the restaurant, and it matched perfectly with—"

"So all this time," Lye interrupted him, "I've been expecting them to show up on my shores. For weeks— months now—I've been preparing to meet them head-on." Suddenly, Lye's wrath returned. He grabbed Stone by his lapels and, with uncanny strength for a geezer, lifted him up off the ground. "But no one ever came!" he shouted. "No one!" Lye shoved Stone into one of the nearby cages, further scattering the startled birds.

"Then," Lye resumed, "we noticed how Ret was skipping school. We thought he was finally on his way. But still," Lye paused, as if to accentuate his disapproval of a pattern, "he never came. Perhaps he was lost—maybe he couldn't figure out how to get to Waters Deep. So then we tried the letter—the bait, the lure," Lye continued to recall their unsuccessful attempts. "We gave him the exact coordinates of where to go. It was fool proof."

"Perhaps Pauline intervened," Stone thought, anxious to be helpful. "She's always getting in the way."

"Exactly, you fool!" Lye rebutted. "That meddle-some mother was the crux of the whole scheme. I knew she would intervene. Why else would we send a letter to Ret if we believed Ret wasn't even there? We needed her to intercept it, and she did just that."

"You mean she was the one who—"

"Yes, yes!" Lye hissed. "It was she who fell into my trap—she and two of Coy's cronies. And they got away—with Lionel!" With ever growing anger, Lye shot currents of electricity on either side of Stone, purposely singeing him without directly striking him.

"I weep at such a loss," Stone stuttered. "Surely, I do. But I had no way of knowing what that woman would do. You know as well as I do how unpredictable she is."

"But it's your fault, Stone," Lye blamed. "If Ret really was on his way to Waters Deep, don't you think the mother would have told him about the letter? Told him the coordinates? At least informed him about Lionel? Hmm? Why, then, didn't she tell him?"

"I…I don't…"

"Because they weren't going to Waters Deep!" Lye roared. "They went somewhere else! And you, Stone, are the one who should know where they went. That's why I've come to this pathetic place of yours: so you can tell me in person why I don't know where they went."

Stone was speechless.

"I purposely put you here to keep a close eye on Ret," Lye said. "That was your main responsibility—your top priority: to watch him like a hawk. I built you this house, gave you charge over the Keep, secured you as principal. I placed you at the helm of my extensive surveillance teams all over the world. I have eyes everywhere, and all of them were to report to you. You were to tell me wherever Ret went, whatever he did, whomever he associated with. Now, Ret has gone somewhere, and—"

"Please, my lord," Stone begged, trying to quell his master's growing anger. "I've done everything in my power—"

"Power?" Lye scoffed. "You have no power, Stone. Do you remember when you came to me? You were a desperate lowlife—putrid scum—and you groveled at my feet, pleading for me to help you." Lye was now standing over Stone, reenacting the scene he was retelling. "So I did. I gave you a new life. I taught you my ways, took you under my wing. I put you in authority, gave you everything you have. And what did I ask for in return? Hmm? What is the only thing that I ever ask for in return?"

"Total loyalty," Stone answered from his knees.

"Supreme allegiance," Lye embellished with a broad tone. "All I require is that you do exactly what I tell you to do. Complete obedience, Stone—that's the program."

There was an eerie pause in the evil lord's lecture. With feigned compassion, he brought one of his hands to his subordinate's chin (the hand that wasn't glued to his cane) and gently raised Stone's head until their eyes met. The touch from Lye's emaciated flesh felt like ice on Stone's rosy skin.

"But for some reason, my dear friend," Lye caressed, "I get the feeling you wish to renege on your oath. I see you wavering in your commitment."

"Why, sir, I would never—"

"Perhaps I haven't made myself clear enough?" Lye suggested to himself, pretending to be at fault.

"No, my lord—"

"Or maybe I'm jumping to conclusions?"

"I am doing the best I can," Stone affirmed. "Please, be fair, Lye. Have mercy—"

"BE FAIR?!" Lye fumed, lunging at Stone and gripping his neck. "HAVE MERCY?!" Stone began to struggle for want of air. "Mercy is for the weak. It's nothing but an excuse for failure—a copout. Only the guilty beg for mercy, Stone. *I*'m the one who should be demanding things here—not *you*." He released his grasp, as if he was being soiled by Stone's filthiness.

"I require justice—the only fair course," Lye taught. "Mercy robs justice—what's *fair* about that?"

"Nothing, my lord," Stone mumbled in between gasps for air.

"Right: nothing!" Lye yelled. "You see, mercy is a flaw; it doesn't work. I extended mercy to you once, Stone, but never again."

"Forgive me, lord," Stone asked, trying to regain some credibility.

"Humph!" Lye snorted in derision. "Forgiveness: another fault of the weak. Unfortunately for you, it's a fault I do not possess."

"Yes, the fault is all mine," Stone confessed.

"Of course it is," Lye concurred. "It's *your* fault we don't know what Ret's been up to. It's *your* fault the letter failed. It's *your* fault I lost my prisoner." Stone seemed to sink lower to the ground with each accusation. Then, as if Lye had reminded himself of a serious blunder, he gave a guttural growl and wailed, "Lionel—lost! No one ever escapes! I make no mistakes!"

"I am to blame—"

"Do you know why I must know where Ret went?" Lye hissed. "Do you?"

"I'm afraid I—"

"Of course you don't," Lye chided him. "I must always stay one step ahead of Ret. It should be obvious to you by now what happens to the places where the elements are located once Ret collects them."

Stone remained silent, unsure if Lye wanted him to answer.

"They implode, you fool!" Lye rejoined. "As soon as the element is procured in the Oracle, the whole place is kaput. So far, we've been lucky: Sunken Earth and Fire Island were disposable; I had limited operations in those locations. But now the odds are against us. Waters Deep is my lair—the source of my longevity in this life. And the Vault is my treasury—the source of my influence in this world. They cannot be destroyed."

"But the Deep and the Vault are each guarding an element," Stone bravely pointed out. "Isn't their destruction imminent?"

"Of course it is!" Lye snapped. "They have to give way if I ever expect to fill the Oracle. That is why I must know which element is next. I must be ready; I must prepare. And, if possible, I must prevent it from happening for as long as possible." Then, remembering the purpose of his visit, Lye turned on Stone, "Which is why I must know what Ret has been doing!"

"I understand, my lord," Stone bowed. "I apologize for my ignorance, which is far inferior to your great wisdom and knowledge."

"Don't blow smoke at me, Stone," Lye wheezed. "Your failings have worn away my confidence in you. It is very difficult to regain my trust, but it can be done."

"You have my word," Stone promised, making obeisance by bowing before his master.

"Let's hope so," Lye said. Then, noticing the wedding ring on Stone's outstretched hand, he added with a sinister smile, "for your sake and for those you love." He forcefully placed the end of his cane on the ring to ensure Stone got the point.

"Virginia," Stone gasped almost inaudibly. "She knows nothing about any of this—nothing! I've kept her out of this, and I beg of you to do the same."

"*I* am the one who sets the terms," Lye reminded him. "Don't forget your place. May the wellbeing of your wife be your motivation to never fail me again."

"As you wish," Stone prayed pitifully. "Just keep her safe."

"Ah, love," Lye sang in contempt. "The greatest collateral of all. I knew I was wise to let you keep her. Love always allows the most leverage."

"I'll do anything—whatever you ask."

"Case in point," Lye said with satisfaction. "This has been a very productive evening. We have exposed man's greatest vices: mercy, forgiveness, love. Once you purge your heart of these hallmarks of weakness, then you will be on the path to becoming great like me. But should you fail," he warned grimly, "I will make you wish you had never been born."

"It would be an honor to die at your hand," Stone said.

"Die?" Lye questioned with a laugh. "You have so much to learn, Stone. Death is a reward, not a punishment. A dead man is of no use to me: I cannot make him bleed, I cannot cause him pain. To put a man out of his misery deprives me of enjoying it myself. There's something sweet about watching another man suffer." Then, coming in close enough to whisper, Lye said, "So you see, Stone, the only death *I* am interested in is the kind that brings the most agony to the living."

It was in this moment, while staring unwillingly into Lye's heartless eyes, that Stone got his first preview of eternal torment. He was nose-to-nose with the literal face of evil, and even though he had just reconfirmed his standing at the pit of perniciousness, he had never quite realized the bottomless depth of the maleficent ways of secret darkness. And it scared him.

Finally, Lye moved toward the door that he had stormed through not long ago, now hanging haphazardly on only one hinge. Relieved to see him leaving, Stone was about to rise to his feet when Lye suddenly stopped. Something had caught his eye. He turned to his side and glanced at one of the birds buzzing fitfully in the cage next to him. It was the lorikeet—the fowl with florid feathers, the apple of Stone's eye. Commanding the water within the creature's small and frightened frame, Lye grabbed a hold of it and forced it from its place of refuge. With manipulation born of sheer mind power, he held it out in front of Stone with perfect subjection.

"Did you know, Stone," Lye asked pleasantly, "that approximately 75% of a bird's body consists solely of water?" Stone was too worried about his favorite fowl to answer the question. "Would you like to know what makes up the other 25%?"

In an instant, the bird vanished before Stone's very eyes as Lye vaporized all of the water molecules within its body. In answer to his own question, the non-liquid portion slowly fell to the floor, accumulating in a heap of dust and feathers at Stone's quivering feet.

"Don't toy with me, Stone," Lye concluded coldly. "I will not be mocked." Then he strode out the door and into the night.

Falling to his knees, Lester scooped up the remnants of his beloved bird and let them sift through his trembling fingers. Tears began to stream down his cheeks, and he put his face in his hands. But his weeping was spurred not in mourning of his bird but in fear for his wife, for after the feathers had fallen away, he saw his wedding ring on his finger. Thinking of Virginia and remembering Lye's threat, he became hopelessly aware of the dire situation in which he found himself. He had already mocked Lye, for he knew exactly where Ret and Coy had gone: not long ago he had received a phone call and freed them from a band of Lye's vigilantes at the mouth of the Amazon River.

CHAPTER 15

PIECING TOGETHER
THE GREAT RIVER

Ret was sick—not the kind of sick where he couldn't keep anything down in his stomach but the kind where he couldn't keep something from coming up in his mind. Ever since the unplanned faceoff between Mr. Coy and Lionel in the Coopers' living room, Ret had been burdened by poignant feelings of remorse. He wasn't looking to point fingers—in his mind, the entire exchange had gotten out of hand. Rather, he regretted not telling Lionel anything about his trip to the Amazon, and his pain only seemed to increase with time. It was his first thought when he awoke each morning, his last thought when he retired each night, and just about every other thought in the intervening hours.

Ret knew his friendship with Lionel would never be the same—irreparably impaired if not already ruined. He felt as though he had foolishly severed an important lifeline in his quest to fill the Oracle, for Lionel had played an instrumental role in collecting the elements thus far. His mere involvement seemed to grace their adventures with good fortune: Lionel was the reason their escape from Sunken Earth's jailhouse was a success, and Lionel was the means by which Ret arrived at the slopes of the great mountain; it was Lionel who had suggested they visit the Nazca Desert, Lionel who had identified Machu Picchu, and Lionel who had called Ret's attention to the shadow cast by the Intihuatana Stone. Yes, whether by providing key information or imparting wise instruction, Lionel had repeatedly proved to be an invaluable investment, and now Ret worried he had jeopardized his hopes of receiving any future dividends.

But that was only the half of it, for Ret also felt guilty for being dishonest. Of course, he technically hadn't lied to Lionel, but he *had* withheld the truth from him, meaning any presumed commission was in the silent omission. Ret was realizing how saying nothing often speaks volumes. By remaining mute, Ret had demonstrated a lack of trust, and he knew of no one in his personal Rolodex who was as undeserving of such treatment as Lionel Zarbock.

At the same time, however, Ret had also shown an increased measure of trust—in Mr. Coy, that is. Ret had acted according to Coy's urging that night even though he personally disagreed with it. Had the situation taken place months earlier, it might not have played out the same way, for Mr. Coy was different these days. His reasoning seemed more rational, and his opinion carried greater weight. He was still a bit kooky, yes, but also a little less cocky; he had become more like a rare bird as opposed to an odd duck; now quite extraordinary, no longer so extraterrestrial. The change had not happened in his appearance but rather in others' perceptions, and the more they learned about the man behind the mask, the more they understood him and what it was that predicated his often unpredictable nature.

Still, Ret's inner plague raged on, festering and cankering within him like an incurable cancer. He couldn't help but feel he had made a grave mistake, but the outcome seemed to be rotten no matter which way he sliced it: if he could redo the past and instead side with Lionel, then Ret would feel just as guilty for blatantly going against Coy's advice—it was a lose-lose situation! And Mr. Coy was no less valuable an ally in Ret's procurement of the elements than Lionel. Oh, what to do? What to do!

Such mental turmoil seemed to consume Ret's thinking and jade his senses. He preferred not to carry such emotional baggage with him all the way to Africa, where he knew he would, no doubt, need to have his wits about him. At length, he decided to write a letter to

Lionel and tell him the truth, hoping that getting it off his chest would relieve his heavy heart.

Ret kept the letter short. Besides offering a word of apology and including an open-ended request for any future assistance, he wrote little more than where they had gone and where they were going. Perhaps by being concise and sparing details, Ret reasoned, he wouldn't feel any guilt for now going against Mr. Coy's wishes. It was hard work trying to appease both parties, which was really impossible since pleasing one meant displeasing the other, even if done in secret. Ret hurriedly stuffed the letter in an envelope, hoping neither Pauline nor Ana would spy him scribbling at his desk and start asking questions. He located the business card that Lionel had given to him when they had walked home from the power plant together and used it to address the envelope to Lionel's office at the headquarters of the International Atomic Energy Agency in Vienna, Austria. Unsure of overseas mailing rates, he was generous with postage.

"Let's go, Ret," Ana called to him from downstairs. "We need to be at the Manor in fifteen minutes."

"Coming," Ret hollered back. He jammed the letter in his pocket, grabbed his suitcase, and headed downstairs, where he found Ana sitting on the couch next to Leo. It wasn't a very strange sight, as she and Leo were spending a fair amount of time together these days. Ret's curiosity was piqued, however, when he saw Leo holding a ragged old backpack on his lap.

"Hey, Leo," Ret greeted him pleasantly. "Come to wish Ana bon voyage, eh?"

"Didn't you hear?" Ana put forth. "Leo's coming with us."

"Really?" Ret said with surprise.

"Mr. Coy invited me," Leo explained, hoping he wasn't intruding.

"Cool," Ret replied with delight, gladdened by the idea of having another guy around.

Just then, Pauline came into the room from the kitchen.

"He'll be taking my place," she stated somberly while drying a pan with a frayed dish towel.

"What?" Ret asked. "You're not coming with us?"

"I'll go with you to the Manor to see you off," Pauline told them, "but I'm afraid I'm just not feeling up to traveling this time." Although it came as news to Ret, Ana wasn't too surprised by her mother's pronouncement. They were both shocked, however, when Pauline said, "You'll be safe with Mr. Coy." You could have knocked the Cooper kids over with a feather to hear Pauline speak so favorably of Mr. Coy. After a few moments of stunned silence, she reminded them, "We'd better get going. We don't want you to be late."

In turning toward the door, Ret laid eye on Ana's slew of luggage for the first time.

"What *is* all of this stuff?" Ret balked.

"Unlike you *guys,*" Ana said stiffly, pinching Ret's shirt, "*I* don't wear the same thing every day." Ret and Leo glanced approvingly at each other and shrugged. "It's a tough job being beautiful," she said, throwing her hair behind her shoulder, "but someone's got to do it."

Ret rolled a large suitcase to Leo's feet and then heaved a bulging duffle bag on top of it. "I'm glad you're here to help with Ana's junk," he mumbled.

Thanks to Ana's belongings, two trips were needed to transport the passengers and their possessions across Tybee Creek without the kayak sinking. After hiking up the hillside, they arrived at the Manor's main gate, where Paige was waiting for them. Pleasantries were exchanged, and the group made their way toward the grand double doors.

As this was his first visit to Coy Manor, Leo was experiencing a little bit of visual overload. Like the rest of the general population, the only structures that Leo had ever been able to see of Little Tybee Island's infamous acropolis were weird walls and tall towers. Now, however, as he absorbed the architecture and landscaping from up-close, he could fully appreciate the edifice's marvelous workmanship.

Stepping into the semi-circular entry, Ret noticed the awe on Leo's face. As they crossed the foyer toward one of the many archways, Ret smiled and warned him, "Watch out for Mother Coy." Then, while passing through the center of the room, Ret briefly raised his hand into the air, purposely blocking the sunlight in just the right spot so as to partly reveal the invisible bust of Mr. Coy's mother.

"What? How?" wondered a flabbergasted Leo.

"It's called a black mirror," Ret answered, retracting his hand. "Maybe Coy will tell you about it— if you're lucky." Ret grinned in remembrance of his encounter with the tiger sharks during his own first visit to the Manor.

Very shortly, they came to an elevator. It was a tight fit, but once all the bodies and bags had been squeezed inside, Ret paid particular attention to what happened next. As he was expecting, he watched as five sets of neuroscopes descended from above, each one gently coming to rest on the temples of each of the elevator's occupants. Because the prongs were so tiny and made contact within the hair of his scalp, Ret barely even felt the device slip onto his cranium. In fact, the only reason Ret realized it had occurred was because he had been anticipating it.

Pauline, still engulfed in gloom, paid no heed to the neuroscope, which was not surprising since not a single word had escaped the woebegone woman's lips in the last several minutes. Neither did Ana, still enveloped in conversation, take any notice of the device, which was typical since there had been no shortage of words from her lips in the last several minutes as she told Paige of her excitement to be spending their spring recess from school in such a place as Africa.

Obviously an old pro, Paige quickly communicated her desired destination through thought, and her neuroscope noiselessly returned to the ceiling. It was only when Leo observed something flying away from Paige's head that he became aware of the neuroscope on his own brow.

"Uh, Ret?" he whispered. "What *is* this thing?"

Smiling again, Ret told him, "It's called a neuroscope." Leo watched as the one on Ret's head returned to the ceiling. "It just asked you where you wanted to go, didn't it?"

"Yeah," Leo said, though a little spooked.

"Just tell it you'd like to go wherever Paige is going," Ret informed, having just done the same. Leo obeyed, and the neuroscope relinquished its hold.

For the next few minutes, while the elevator continued to plunge into the bosom of Coy Manor, Ret answered Leo's questions about the workings of the neuroscope. He explained the science and touched on the neurology. He mentioned Conrad, Feathers, the rhinos, and even a bit about the subsuits. It was all very fascinating to Leo, who began to feel a growing respect for Mr. Coy and his genius.

When the elevator doors parted, the group found themselves gazing into the vast, underground hangar. Though mostly dark, there were a few spotlights on an airplane nearby. Paige strode toward it, with the others following amid the roar of tiny luggage wheels rolling on pavement.

As they came to the aircraft, its cargo hold opened, and Mr. Coy jumped out.

"Oh happy day!" he cheered. "Callooh! Callay!" His jovial spirit sent chuckles throughout the oncoming caravan, and Ret thought he even saw Pauline crack a smile. "All aboard for our trip to Africa!" He immediately relieved the ladies of their bags. "It looks like Ana plans to stay a while," he joked, accepting the largesse of luggage she handed over to him. "And I'm glad to see you'll be joining us on this expedition, Mrs. Cooper."

"Actually, I'm going to sit this one out," Pauline informed him softly. There was very little emotion in her voice, and it was clear to Coy that she was still depressed from her heart-wrenching meeting with Jaret. "I'd rather not be a burden to you. I'll just spend the week at home, by myself."

Mr. Coy was no psychiatrist, but neither was he a novice when it came to dealing with grief, and Pauline's plan to mourn her loss in loneliness didn't seem like the best remedy for her anguish. In fact, it had the potential to make matters worse. He knew she needed to be around friendly people and to somehow get her mind off her sorrow. Suddenly, he was struck with an idea.

"Why don't you stay here at the Manor until we get back?" he suggested. "I've got some staff members who could really use some pointers in the kitchen. Maybe you could show them a thing or two. I hear you're a black belt when it comes to culinary arts."

Pauline's entire countenance appeared to perk up at Coy's offer. Elated, she replied, "I would really enjoy that, actually."

"Wonderful," Coy said. "I'll call the staff down here immediately." Within a few minutes, a pair of student-chefs waltzed out of the elevator, clad in their black-and-white checkered pants and big, fluffy hats. The two young ladies lovingly linked their arms with Pauline's and escorted her off.

"Bye, Mom!" Ana yelled. "Have a good time!"

"You, too, dear!" she returned, waving goodbye. "Send me a postcard!"

Ana whispered to herself, "It's so good to see her smiling again." Coy was smiling, too.

While Mr. Coy's airplane fell short of a jumbo jet, it was no Piper Cub. With its slender body and sleek wings, it was a beautiful bird. Ret and Leo lifted the luggage onto the edge of the cargo hold, where Conrad received it and placed it among a myriad of other supplies and provisions for their journey. Deeper inside the hold, Ret could see what appeared to be a pair of vehicles, the lower half of their thick tires left uncovered by a hefty tarp. He was about to ask Conrad what they were but figured it wouldn't do much good.

Mr. Coy welcomed his fellow travelers into the cabin and invited them to make themselves comfortable. Ana immediately plopped down in a seat and reclined it, then threw her hands behind her head and propped her feet up. "This is the life," she sighed. With a beckoning wave, she stated, "Take me to Africa."

The pilot must have heard her plea, for as soon as she uttered it, the plane's engines roared to life. Mr. Coy shut the door to the cabin and made his way to the cockpit, where Ret could see Ishmael at the controls, along with some other woman. When the plane became mobile, Ret turned his sights to the window. There was nothing to see until there came into view two rows of lights, with a wide gap between them. Ishmael steered the plane into the space between the lines of lights, which ran parallel to each other and outlined a sort of runway. Then Ret leaned back as the plane began to climb a gradual incline.

Suddenly, Ret was thrust into the padding of his chair as the plane propelled itself forward like a rocket.

Despite the slight upward slope, the aircraft greatly multiplied its speed. The lights on the ground had now morphed into a single line, so fast were they traveling. Knowing the underground tunnel couldn't be very long, Ret was relieved when he saw light up ahead, spilling into the corridor. He planted his face against the window, straining to see what was happening. They were quickly approaching an exit, where a bright opening was growing like the rolling back of a garage door. When the partition had parted just wide enough, daylight flooded the cabin as the plane shot out of the hangar, over the ocean, and into the sky. Ret glanced back at the exit, which promptly closed and became unrecognizable as it blended in with the island's hillside.

For several minutes, conversation was quieted by the wonder of flight. The view was simply dazzling, with sunlight streaking through the gaps between great, fluffy clouds and then shimmering on the swells of the Atlantic's waters below. Leo was glued to his window, as if he had never been airborne before. But Ret could understand, as taking to the skies had yet to become a trite experience for him, too. It was only when he began to see harmless shadows in the ocean, whether from seaweed or cloud cover, that Ret lost interest in the panoramic vista. His thoughts quickly digressed to a certain submerged road that led to a certain sunken civilization, all of which had been swallowed whole in certain death. They were likely passing over the under-water morgue now. Ret pulled down his window shade to shut out the view from sight, though it did little to shut out the pain from his heart.

When the plane had leveled out and reached its cruising altitude, Mr. Coy returned from the cockpit, carrying something in his hand.

"Perfect timing, Mr. Coy," Ana rejoiced, arising from her relaxation. "I could really go for some peanuts and a Sprite right now—on the rocks, of course."

"I'm afraid you're the only nut aboard this plane, sprite," Coy returned, possibly the only person who could out-whit Ana. "There'll be plenty of time for snacks later, after I show something to you." Mr. Coy stepped up to the front of the cabin, where he fired up some kind of computerized tablet in preparation for what appeared to be an in-flight presentation.

"What's he doing now?" an ever-inquisitive Leo asked his comrades in hushed tones, wondering if he should brace himself for something.

"He's going to show us how our seat cushion can be used as a flotation device," Ana kidded.

"In just a few hours," Coy began, "we will land in Africa." As he spoke, a faint stream of light appeared from his tablet and then expanded to create a three-dimensional hologram of the entire earth in midair. "Our first stop is Monrovia, the capital city of the west

African nation of Liberia." Sensitive to his touch, Mr. Coy could manipulate the global graphic at will. He effortlessly rotated it to focus on the African continent, then pinched his fingers together and pulled his hands away to zoom in on Liberia. "We will leave the plane in Monrovia (in the safe keeping of an associate of mine) and travel by land into the country of Mali." He adjusted the view to follow his description of their trek. "In northern Mali is the home village of Ishmael and his sister, Lydia, our co-pilot. They have agreed to take us there."

"Why don't we just fly straight to Mali, Dad?" Paige asked.

"In a perfect world, that would be perfectly fine," Coy answered. "Unfortunately, we're headed directly into one of the most imperfect places in the world. Besides the brutal conditions of the Sahara Desert, there is also civil unrest and instability in many parts of the region." Then, in all seriousness, he added, "Since Pauline isn't here, I'll be frank: Saharan Africa is downright dangerous."

"Now he tells us," Ana mumbled, rolling her eyes. "Guess I'd better put this baby on," she said as her seatbelt came together with a click. Mr. Coy's candid assessment had an unsettling effect on Leo, who seemed a bit uneasy, as well as Paige, who looked a little queasy. Ret, on the other hand, furrowed his brow and met the

warning with a face of fearlessness, trying to reassure himself that he had done the right thing in writing his letter to Lionel as now he would have greater clarity of mind in the likely event of danger.

"So, to answer your question, honeycomb," Coy continued (though Ana shot Paige a disgusted look upon hearing her father's term of endearment), "I feel it would be best to get out of the air as soon as possible, and since Monrovia is a large city right on the western coast of the continent, it will be the ideal place to do so. Once on the ground, we'll look like nothing more than a bunch of innocent tourists with two locals (Ishmael and Lydia) as our guides."

"Why are we going to their village?" Ret inquired, curious to know how such a visit related to their ultimate objective of locating the next element.

"An excellent segue, Ret," said Coy. "When we returned from the Amazon, I did some research and discovered this." He scrapped the globe and replaced it with an obscure picture that resembled a beginner's poor attempt at sand art. "This is a modified satellite image of the Sahara Desert. Using radar, it shows a layer of rock far beneath the sand that blankets the surface. These black grooves," he pointed out, "were carved into the rock long ago by the waterways of an ancient river." Ret was listening with rapt attention. Judging by the look on his face, Leo was relishing it as well.

"Here's another image," Coy said, advancing to the next photograph in the slideshow. "This is from an entirely different part of the desert, but it shows evidence of not only an ancient river but also an ancient lake." He cycled through several more snapshots, each one adding more credence to his point. "When I approached Ishmael and shared my findings with him, he told me it was consistent with what he and his people have believed for centuries, namely that a great river once existed in the desert, although it wasn't a desert then, of course. In fact, they think the river still exists— underground somewhere. Lydia once believed she was on the brink of discovering it, but then the—"

Mr. Coy abruptly stopped, unsure if he should say what was on his tongue. Then, in a subdued tone, he said, "I should not be the one to explain what happened to her. Ishmael should do that, if he so chooses." Ret's eyes met Ana's with mutual curiosity. They both glared at Paige for information regarding this new person named Lydia, but she held her tongue in obedience to what her father had just spoken. "Anyway," Coy concluded, "hopefully by going to their village, Ishmael and Lydia can fill in some of the blanks about the great river, and maybe we can dig up a few leads as to where we'll find the ore element."

"What the heck is ore?" Ana whispered to Paige. "Are we talking, like, a canoeing oar?"

"No," Paige replied softly, as if in class, "raw metal."

"Gotcha."

So much talk of a "Great River" reminded Ret that it was a borrowed term, first heard from the mouth of Argo, the Guardian of the Fire Element. After Ret had met him in the magma chamber of the volcano at Fire Island, Argo gave him an odd relic: a small hour glass whose contents seemed to defy gravity by refusing to fall from top to bottom even when Ret turned it upside-down. Ret recalled how Argo didn't know the purpose of the trinket but had mentioned how its flecks of gold undoubtedly came from the Great River, which existed before the Oracle's elements were scattered and the earth was thrown into upheaval. This tidbit of dialogue, though seemingly meaningless when spoken, was now an important piece of information.

For a brief second, Ret felt a piercing throb in the palm of his hand that confirmed his train of thought. He glanced down at the scar. It was only half illuminated, no further than it had been in the Amazon River delta. The squiggly line still meant nothing to him.

"Mr. Coy," Ret spoke up, "would you mind going back to that view of the world real quick?" He stepped toward the front of the cabin as Mr. Coy retrieved the globe. For a brief moment, Ret watched it slowly rotate. Though much larger, it reminded him of the Oracle.

When the Atlantic Ocean was passing in front of him, he stopped it. He put his left hand on the South American continent and his right hand on the African continent. Manipulating the landmasses like two pieces of a jigsaw puzzle, he brought them toward each other until they fit snugly together.

In awe, Leo mouthed the word, "Pangaea."

"Wow," Ana observed when she saw how naturally the two continents became a single landmass. "Fits like a glove, almost like—"

"—they used to be one giant continent," Paige chimed in. Then, vexed, she added, "But it looks like it was broken apart somehow."

"Do you think it's possible," Ret wondered of Mr. Coy, "that South America and Africa used to be joined together—that the Amazon once connected to the dried riverbeds you just showed us?"

"I see you're beginning to catch my continental drift," Coy quipped with a pleased grin as he watched the wheels turning in Ret's head.

"So the scattering of the elements caused the continents to break apart," Ret persisted, thinking through his theory aloud, "and when that happened, Africa's half of the Great River dried up—hence the Sahara Desert."

"And Bingo was his name-o!" Coy cheered on.

Zooming in on the globe, Ret observed, "And it looks like the Amazon would empty right into—"

"—the city of Monrovia," Coy finished. "What a coincidence!" It was obvious that Mr. Coy had previously solved the puzzle and was now simply presenting the remaining hints needed to give the rest of them the opportunity to piece things together on their own and learn for themselves.

"That's all fine and dandy," Ana interjected, "but what do all of these rivers and deserts have to do with metal?"

Leave it to Ana to be real. It was a fair question, one which Mr. Coy wasn't entirely sure how to answer. Seeking help, he turned to Ret, who stole a glance at his scar. There was no change. He returned Coy's blank stare with one of his own.

Looking Ana straight in the eye, Mr. Coy said, "We're about to find out."

CHAPTER 16

DANGER IN THE
DESERT

As soon as the Atlantic Ocean ended, the city of Monrovia began. The sprawling Liberian capital had been built directly on the edge of land. For miles up and down the crooked coast, evidence of settlement abbreviated the sand of beaches, with establishments extending out of sight into the African mainland. Ret marveled at the earth. Insofar as he could recall, here was a continent on which Ret had never set foot, and yet it was home to hordes of humans who, just like him, called the blue planet their home. He was excited to get on the ground and see what he could learn.

They landed on a thin stretch of runway in the thick of the city. Ishmael maneuvered the plane into a private hangar where a welcoming man stood waiting for them. When the aircraft came to rest, Mr. Coy promptly exited and greeted the man with a friendly embrace, followed by a stack of paperwork. As Ret observed the reunion through his cabin window, he was grateful for Mr. Coy and his repository of international contacts, which provided at least a sliver of security in places fraught with so many unknowns.

Within minutes, the riders disembarked and congregated near the cargo hold, where Conrad was busy preparing for the next leg of their journey. As if they were filled with air, he effortlessly retrieved the passengers' suitcases and handed them down to Ret and Leo.

"What's that thing on Conrad's head?" Leo asked Ret discreetly when the aborigine had paced away to fetch more of the luggage. "Is it one of those, you know, scope things you told me about?"

"Yep, it's a neuroscope," Ret replied. "He's always wearing one, whenever I've seen him at least."

Just then, Ishmael and Lydia arrived at the rear of the plane. They climbed into the cargo hold and began to unpack their personal effects. As this was the first time Leo and the Coopers had ever seen Ishmael's sister up close, they were somewhat startled by what they saw, and although they knew it was impolite to stare, there was something about Lydia that seemed to encourage it. As if the result of serious burns, her skin was scarred in multiple locations, including her face, and the large metal clasp around her neck gave her the appearance of a recently escaped prisoner. Her long, black hair fell past her shoulders, which helped to hide a few of the blemishes and the back half of her unfashionable choker. As if some public example, she seemed marred in all the wrong places.

The temptation to stare at Lydia abated when a great whoosh came from the rear of the cargo hold. Conrad had whisked away the heavy tarps covering the two sets of wheels, revealing a pair of the most peculiar-looking vehicles Ret had ever seen. Should he have been expecting any less from the man called Coy?

"Ah, I see you've unveiled the CAVEs," Mr. Coy proclaimed after bidding farewell to his acquaintance and rejoining his crewmates

"The what?" Ret asked.

"CAVE," said Coy, as Conrad slowly drove the first one down the liftgate. "It's an acronym, which stands for Coy's All-terrain Vehicle Extraordinaire." He beamed with pride as it rolled by. "Land, sea, air—this puppy can tackle it all."

"Then what does the 'extraordinaire' part mean?" Ana wondered.

"Well, let's just say it's been 'coyed' with," he replied with a sly grin. "Normal people might call it customized; you know, outfitted with all the bells and whistles."

Ana shrugged with approval and announced, "Shotgun!"

"More or less," Coy added, under his breath.

The CAVE looked more like a tank than a car. Except for a few small windows of the thickest glass, its body was more brawn than beauty. The metallic shell seemed highly impregnable, capable of surviving anything from blizzards to bullets. Apparently, the all-weather make and model came standard with all-terrain wheels, each with a circumference so wide and tread so thick that not even the most cumbersome of quagmires could slow them down. Like a beefy—albeit unsightly—motorhome, the CAVE wasn't exactly pretty on the outside, but it was the envy of the road from the inside.

"Sure beats riding a camel," Ana remarked as she made her way to claim the front seat. "This monster's a regular Winnebago. How many miles per gallon—like four?"

Before Ana could get comfortable, Mr. Coy strode over to one of the vehicles and said, "Ishmael and I will drive the CAVEs the long way around town. We'll pick the rest of you up on the outskirts. I don't want to make a scene driving down the main roads. These behemoths tend to stick out like a sore thumb."

"Why don't we just go with you, Dad?" Paige asked.

"And deprive you of experiencing the beautiful city of Monrovia?" Coy replied as he sat down in the driver's seat. "Nonsense! Just stroll down one of the main streets. It's only a few miles. You'll be safe with Conrad and Lydia." He shut the door and started the ignition. Like the gargling of a great beast, the engines roared to life, and the two CAVEs rolled away.

Now stranded, the motley band of international "tourists" commenced a leisurely jaunt through the city center. As the local skin color was overwhelmingly black, the four white youth rightly earned many curious glances. Ana's simple beauty, Paige's blonde curls, and Ret's still-brighter features begged for yet more attention, to say nothing of Lydia and her own uniqueness. For once, however, it was Conrad who seemed to blend in the best, an anomaly that left him speechless.

Based on his initial impression, Ret wasn't sure "beautiful" would be the first word he would use to describe Monrovia, as Mr. Coy had done. In fact, he wasn't sure it would be the second or even the third word. It certainly was *busy*, with its kamikaze motorcycle taxis weaving in and out and around and through every lane of the already hit-or-miss traffic. So yes, busy—and, along the same vein, *daring*, with pedestrians clogging streets by crossing wherever they so desired, giving new meaning to the term rush hour. And it was quite *colorful*, too, with its flags and umbrellas and upbeat music. Next came *hot* and *humid*, rounding out Ret's top five.

But *beautiful?* Where? Was it in the crumbling curbs or the cluttered gutters? The shabby shanties or the slanting slums? The clotheslines hanging above yards of mud or the rodents hanging out near the alleys of rubbish? The storefronts were dingy, the buildings dirty, and every surface looked as though it needed a fresh coat of paint—or its first coat. In all, it seemed the city had been assembled from the random remains of a pick-your-part auto salvage junkyard. The days were long past when Ret could innocently say such sights were new to him.

"This place is a zoo!" Ana gasped as a speeding motorcycle nearly ran over her.

"Maybe you'd have more luck getting your driver's license here than back home," Leo joked playfully.

"Ha-ha, very funny," said Ana with a grin as she flirtatiously bumped his shoulder.

But there were no smiles on the faces of the other young couple.

"What do you think?" Ret wondered of Paige after several minutes of silent observation. "Remind you of anywhere else we've been?"

"Yeah, Sunken Earth," Paige told him soberly. "Liberia still has a long way to go."

"I'll say," said Ret. "This place is trashed."

"But what do you expect from a country that

recently emerged from two back-to-back civil wars?" Paige pointed out. It was a detail that Ret hadn't known but put everything into sobering perspective.

Entering a sort of open-air market that had been amassed along the dusty sidewalk, the group rather unintentionally divided in half according to gender, with Lydia keeping close watch behind the girls while Conrad did the same with the guys. As they meandered deeper into the assortment of booths on boxes and stands on stilts, the pair of trios gradually drifted apart as they stopped to look at merchandise according to their interests.

"I want to get something for Ana," Leo told Ret once the girls were without earshot.

"Like what?" Ret wondered.

"Oh, I don't know...something nice," Leo explained. "Something to show her how much I care about her."

"How about one of these?" Ret suggested sarcastically, pointing to a platter of fried insects.

"Maybe a necklace," Leo thought as they strode past a person selling jewelry. "That way she'll always think of me when she wears it." Then, approaching a cart of homespun textiles, "Or what about one of these?" He held up a flamboyant item made of colorful cloth.

Cringing, Ret commented, "Well, it certainly matches her personality. But what is it?"

"I don't know," Leo admitted, staring blankly at it. "Some kind of hat?"

Just then, the woman running the display informed them, "It's a purse."

"Right, of course," Leo corrected himself quickly, turning the item right-side-up. "A purse." He promptly returned it, looking a little embarrassed.

"Don't worry, we'll find something," Ret tried to console him. "Let's keep looking."

Meanwhile, Ana and Paige were engaged in a bit of shopping themselves.

"Maybe we should get a small souvenir?" Paige suggested.

"You mean besides a sunburn?" Ana complained, rubbing the back of her neck as it baked under the midday heat.

"Here we go," said Paige, stopping under the umbrella of a young woman selling handmade crafts. "I'll take that one," she said, pointing to a simple bracelet of colorful threads.

"Ten dollars, please," the seller told her customer.

"Ten dollars?!" Ana balked. "That's just a couple of pieces of yarn tied together. I could make the same thing right now with the lint in my pocket."

"It's alright, Ana," Paige said quietly. "I don't mind. It's for a good cause…"

"No, it's not alright," Ana continued. "This lady

thinks she can swindle us just because we're young and naïve." Then, turning to the vendor, Ana said, "How about three dollars?"

The vendor was visibly taken aback by her American customer's bold approach to business. She must have been desperate for sales, however, so she timidly countered, "Four?"

"Done," Ana closed the deal before turning toward the street.

Paige quickly slipped a ten-dollar bill to the vendor and whispered "I'm sorry" to apologize for her friend's forwardness.

"What would you do without me, Paige?" Ana spoke triumphantly.

Paige replied, "You're quite the saleswoman."

"That's nothing," Ana told her. "I could sell sand to an Arab."

Not far from the end of the marketplace, the two CAVEs were parked under the leafy boughs of a large tree, where Mr. Coy and Ishmael stood like cab drivers waiting for passengers. The three women were the first to exit the street shops, followed soon thereafter by the men.

"I got something for you," Leo told Ana when the groups had rejoined, presenting a small paper bag to her.

With a pleasant look on her face, Ana received the gift and reached into the bag. She pulled out a small bottle of liquid.

"Oh," she said with a bit of perplexity. "What is it?"

"It looks like perfume," Paige informed her.

"Do you like it?" Leo inquired anxiously. Ret snuck him a reassuring wink.

Ana sprayed a sampling on her wrist and then took a whiff. As soon as the scent entered her nostrils, she coughed in disgust.

"This smells terrible!" came her honest review. Ret frowned while Mr. Coy walked off a fit of inner laughter. "Here, smell this," Ana said, offering her wrist to Paige.

"Oh, wow," a repulsed Paige agreed, her face looking as though she had just bitten into a lemon. "It's not so bad," she fibbed, "just a little pungent, that's all."

"It smells like urine!" Ana asserted.

"That's because it probably is," Ishmael mumbled to Coy.

"Didn't you smell it before you bought it?" Ana asked.

"The lady wouldn't let us," said Leo.

"Smart lady," Coy muttered to Ishmael.

"How much did it cost?" Ana questioned.

Leo swallowed hard and reported, "Forty dollars."

"Forty bucks?!" Ana blurted out. "You spent forty bucks on rancid perfume?"

"I wanted to get you something nice," Leo rationalized.

"You and I can't afford stuff like this—stuff that we don't need," said Ana. Her words sounded familiar to Ret, as if regurgitated from a conversation with Pauline on the same subject. "Do you know how many zucchini bites I have to fry at the Crusty Chicken to make forty bucks?" There was a lull in the conversation when Ana realized Leo's disappointment. "Look," she said in a gentler tone, "it was very sweet of you to think of me, but next time let's both talk about it first. Okay?"

"Yes, ma'am," Leo responded, receiving Ana's hug.

"Good answer," Coy said under his breath. Then, with a clap of his hands, he announced, "Let's get this show on the road, folks! Lydia, Ana, and Paige: you'll come with me. Ret and Leo: you'll go with Ishmael and Conrad."

"Why are you splitting us up, Dad?" Paige wondered, displeased that she wouldn't be riding in the same CAVE as Ret.

"Ishmael will drive in front with the men while I follow behind with the women," Mr. Coy explained. "That way, if he runs into any trouble, you three ladies will be safe."

"And so will you," Ana added, as if accusing Mr. Coy of also looking out for himself.

"And, should anything happen to *you*," Coy rebutted, shooting Ana a firm stare, "I, and I alone, shall be held responsible."

"Aye-aye, captain," Ana saluted as she ducked to enter the CAVE.

Before Paige followed Ana into the backseat, she held onto Ret's hand for as long as she could. There was worry in her face as she stared longingly into his eyes— worry that gave him cause to wonder. Why was she so concerned? And why was Mr. Coy being so cautious? Perhaps, in Pauline's absence, he was filling in as over-protective parent.

Taking the lead, the man CAVE hadn't gone far when Mr. Coy's voice was heard.

"If we need to communicate with each other, there is a two-way communications system in each CAVE," said Coy. "When you want to say something to the passengers in the other CAVE, just make sure to flip the switch before you speak." Ishmael pointed out the location of the switch on the center console. "Over and out."

As they reached the city limits, Ret pondered on the brief time he had spent in Liberia's capital. He came to the conclusion that if there was any beauty in Monrovia, it was to be found in its people. The glint in their eyes stood in brilliant contrast to the grime in their streets. There was hope for change in their hearts despite the heaps of ruin in their midst. But nowhere was there beauty more bounteous than in the children—huddles, hordes of children, some more clothed than others but each with a copious and contagious optimism in their bright and shining faces.

Perhaps this was the beauty to which Mr. Coy had been referring.

For all their bulkiness, the CAVEs more than proved themselves on the open road, clipping along at a remarkable speed. The only stops came when entering large cities or crossing national borders where, thankfully, Ishmael always seemed to say the magic words to the armed guards.

As the hours transpired, Ret was grateful for the wide variety of scenery, especially when they crossed a bridge over the Niger River. A large waterway, it was lined with all sorts of boats and barges, some transporting goods and others ferrying passengers. It was obviously the lifeblood of the land—literally, as Ret could see family gardens planted along the river banks while women washed clothes and children played games in the water. Ret thought of Rodrigo, Coy's acquaintance from the Amazon, and how he lived off the gifts of the land in his simple existence at the bottom of the pyramid of wealth.

The sight of a river also reminded Ret of his scar. He quickly inspected his hand, curious to learn if the Niger River bore any connection with the Great River or at least with the eventual location of the ore element. To his surprise, there indeed was some activity with his scar. Another small length of it had illuminated, but when he opened his mouth to inform Mr. Coy, the new portion suddenly disappeared. Ret flipped the intercom switch and explained to Mr. Coy what was going on with his scar.

"My guess is we're continuously crossing over parts of the underground river," Mr. Coy hypothesized.

"Do you think we should stop for a while?" Ret wondered. "You know, get out and see what we can find?"

"No, not yet," Coy advised. "It's way too dangerous in these parts. Let's wait until we get to Ishmael's village."

It wasn't the answer Ret was hoping to hear, and even though he still didn't see any signs of immediate danger, he trusted Mr. Coy's judgment.

As the afternoon wore on, the landscape gradually changed from green and lush to brown and barren. In fact, by the time they were passing through central Mali, they were surrounded by sand as far as the eye could see.

In nearly every conceivable way, the Sahara Desert was the exact opposite of the Amazon Rainforest. Whereas the Amazon was the epitome of life, the Sahara seemed the ideal definition of death. Except for a very rare tree, there was virtually no vegetation. In fact, a cursory glance revealed no signs of life anywhere. It was a sea of sand, with waves of heat and dunes like swells, yet no water at all.

Despite its inhospitable conditions, however, the Sahara was home to a few brave souls who belonged to cultures that had long ago tamed the wiles of the wilderness. Once, Ret saw a pair of tribal men skinning what appeared to be a slaughtered goat. Occasionally, off in the distance, he could see caravans of camels trekking across the sand, with their fully-dressed masters leading them along with rope. Each dromedary had rectangular slabs of salt draped over its humped back, the wind quickly erasing their footprints in the ever-changing sands.

Seen even less frequently were the wells, where parched people dipped their buckets and bags deep inside the underground reservoirs of water. Judging by how little liquid was retrieved, Ret reasoned the wells were nearly depleted. His assumption was confirmed when, through the CAVE-to-CAVE intercom, he overheard Paige informing Ana of the unmerciful drought that had smitten the land. Ret writhed in pain as he watched school-age children balancing vessels on their heads during the long walk home, careful not to waste even a single precious drop. Ret knew he would never look at bottled water or a garden hose in quite the same way.

"Now passing by Timbuktu," Mr. Coy announced as they drove past a sign heralding the famous destination.

"You mean it's a real place?" Ret asked in shock.

"Either it's real or that city over there is a giant mirage," Coy answered, pointing to the compound of earthen edifices in the distance.

"No way!" said Leo, straining to see.

Ana snapped a photo with her phone and cheered, "Best Facebook status ever."

"Can we stop and—"

"Sorry," Coy interrupted Ret, "but it's not safe."

"Not safe?" Ret questioned, obviously annoyed. "The whole city is made of dirt. I could level it with one wave of my hand." He was tempted to shut off the intercom and persuade Ishmael to take the men on a detour. "How are we supposed to figure out where the element is if we stay cooped up in this tank the whole time?"

"Mr. Coy is right, Ret," Ishmael asserted. "There are unseen dangers all around. Trust me; this is my homeland." Ret sighed with a frown. "But don't worry; we're almost to my village." Then, pointing to a gradual climb in the path ahead, he announced, "It's just over this hill."

It was dusk now, and the sun, blood red in the sky, looked like a ball of fire.

"It's been years since Lydia and I have been back," Ishmael told the group with fondness in his voice, obviously excited to be returning home. "We'll spend the night with our family. You'll love them. They fawn over guests." The prospect of a warm meal and soft pillow seemed to gladden the weary travelers, and Paige noticed how Ishmael's words even brought a faint smile to Lydia's thin lips.

All Ret wanted, however, was to feel the sand between his toes. He longed to get out of the CAVE and into the desert, anxious to see what clues he could uncover or leads he could locate among nature's elements.

As they neared the top of the hill, Ret wasn't sure if he should be anticipating a large town with tall buildings or a quiet community with simple huts. But when he gazed into the small valley below, he saw something that he never would have expected. To everyone's astonishment, a scene of total ruin lay before them. The village had been completely destroyed.

CHAPTER 17

THE POTION MASTER'S CURSE

A sudden coldness gripped the air, as still and silent as death itself. For several moments, the two vehicles paused at the crest of the hill, idling side by side. Every passenger was watching, some were wondering, and two were weeping at the devastation. Ishmael and Lydia looked at each other through their respective windows. The siblings, though clearly heart-broken, did not seem entirely surprised.

They pressed on. Resuming the lead, Ishmael slowed to a crawl, allowing him to survey the damage as they drove toward his homestead. When they reached the outskirts, he parked the CAVE and promptly exited, Lydia following close behind. Walking shoulder to shoulder, Ishmael wrapped a loving arm around his sister as they strolled into the leveled town together.

It was a disturbing sight. Whatever misfortune had befallen the borough was clearly the work of man. There were small craters in some parts, marking places where bombs had exploded. The few remains that hadn't already burned to ashes were peppered with bullet holes. It had been a small place, though its boundaries were now growing ever wider as the wind dispersed its soot and cinders in all directions across the sand.

"Keep your eyes peeled, Conrad," Mr. Coy warned ominously from the other CAVE. "Watch for anything that moves."

Ret suddenly wasn't so anxious to get out and walk the sand anymore. There was something about seeing an entire village burnt to a crisp that cast a pall on his investigative plans. He was in shock, to say the least. Perhaps this place wasn't as safe as he had assumed it to be.

"There's nothing for us here now," Ishmael declared once he and Lydia had returned after several minutes of rummaging. "Nothing was spared, and it looks like looters have already come through."

"Any survivors?" Coy asked.

"If there are any," Ishmael sighed, "they are few." He pointed to an irregular berm in the sand where a mass grave had been dug and buried.

"I'm very sorry," Coy mourned.

"As am I," Ishmael returned morosely, "but I'm afraid it's just the way life is in this cursed land." Ret added yet another question to his growing list of things he wanted to ask.

"We'll rest here for the night," Mr. Coy said, announcing their change of plans through the intercom.

When Ishmael had returned to the driver's seat, Ret felt he should offer his condolences. "I'm sorry for your loss, Ishmael," he said gently, copying Coy. "I really am. Honestly, I'm kind of in shock. I mean, things like this actually happen? In *our* world?"

Ishmael smiled slightly, warmed by Ret's empathy and also his innocence. Before starting the ignition, he looked back at Ret through the rearview mirror and, with a loving chuckle and a flavor of wisdom, taught, "What world are *you* from, Ret?"

The CAVEs came to life, and their drivers relocated to a clearing several yards away where there was flat ground and good visibility. Ret watched as the site was prepared for their overnight stay. Each CAVE transformed into a sort of backhoe. The front and rear bumpers were flipped over and extended outward using simple hydraulic booms. The one in the front did the plowing while the other in the rear did the digging. After only a few minutes of earthmoving, two rectangular dugouts had been created in the sand. Like underground parking, each CAVE pulled into the space, concealing it from view and shielding it from the plunging temperature.

"Just a sampling of the *extraordinaire* part you asked about earlier, Miss Cooper," Mr. Coy said with satisfaction once the excavation had been completed.

"Impressive," said Ana. "Now, if I could just get this seat to recline…"

While everyone else was trying to get comfortable, Ret was eager to start asking some of his questions. Like his associates, he was also exhausted from their long day of traveling, but he longed for answers more than sleep.

"Ishmael," Ret spoke softly, once the noise of everyone getting settled had died down, "can I ask you a question?"

"Of course."

Ret proceeded, "What did you mean when you called this land 'cursed'?"

There was a brief pause. Ishmael inhaled deeply, followed by a long sigh. Clearly, Ret's query touched on a heavy subject. Ishmael turned off the intercom and then repositioned himself in his seat.

"This village—or what's left of it—is where Lydia and I were born and raised," Ishmael began, glancing out the window at the obliterated settlement, which had now been swallowed from view by the darkness of the night. "Starting early in our childhood, we were educated in all the learning and lore of our ancestors. The history of my people begins long ago, before the days of the desert."

"You mean this place wasn't always a desert?" Ret asked incredulously.

"Oh no," Ishmael confirmed, though he was quick to add a skeptical caveat, "according to the tales of my ancestry, at least. We were taught how this land used to be rich and plentiful—a land of many lakes and fountains, with vast forests of great trees. There were all kinds of animals, birds, and fish, and a Great River that was the source of all life. Pretty hard to believe, huh?"

"No, not at all," Ret replied, hoping Ishmael would continue with his narrative. Upon mention of a Great River, Ret was silently overjoyed with the direction of the conversation. "Especially when you consider those satellite images of underground riverbeds in the Sahara. You know, the ones Mr. Coy showed us?"

"Yes, I know," Ishmael returned, seeming somewhat displeased by Ret's reference to the evidence that substantiated his own ancestral traditions. Ret was getting the feeling that Ishmael either didn't believe his own folklore or didn't want to believe it. In fact, there was a lull in the dialogue, as if Ishmael would rather not proceed. Ret hastily thought of something to say to keep the discussion alive.

"So...how did this place become a desert?"

"Well, as the story goes," Ishmael resumed, perpetuating his doubtful tone, "things began to change—and not very gradually. There was something different about the earth. It rained less. The rivers shrunk. The forests grew sparse. The whole face of the land changed. Once the Great River dried up, nearly all life died out, everything turned to dust, and just like that," he snapped his fingers, "the desert was born. Sandstorms became common—dry, rainless storms of nothing but sand, carried on the wind like blankets, burying everything along the way. As the desert grew wider, most people left. Those who stayed, however, were determined to bring prosperity back to their homeland. They knew it was a rich region whose treasures had just been buried under layers and layers of sand. So they stayed, hoping to restore the glory of the past by digging it up. Many tried; all failed. With each passing generation, the claims became more and more exaggerated: what once was just a river, with some fresh water and a few precious stones, turned into an entire city of untold wealth, hidden somewhere under the sand. Such an overblown description was enough to keep the hype going, and some people devoted their entire lives to it. This is when the tribal masters intervened."

"Tribal masters?" Ret besought clarification.

"You know, the elders or judges," Ishmael explained. "They're the wise, old patriarchs who watch over and protect all of the tribal communities throughout our region of the desert. There's at least one from each tribe or village—kind of like delegates or senators, but in our primitive form of self-government, we call them masters. Some are elected; others are appointed, especially if they're an expert in a certain field or skill, like weaponry, masonry…"

"So what did the masters do?"

"They saw how many of their descendants were spending their whole lives in search of the Great River and its rumored wealth, so they decided to change their society's attitude toward the endeavor. It was no longer a noble aspiration but a vain ambition. It took some time for the viewpoint to take hold because the gold diggers, as they came to be called, had good intentions and seemed to be getting closer and closer to solving the mystery. But the masters condemned it, claiming it had already consumed too many lives. So they changed it from fact to myth. Eventually, the belief of the Great River turned into a legend, always accompanied by a lesson about the woes of greed. Nowadays, we pass the legend down from generation to generation, along with ample discouragement to try to find it."

"But it's still true, isn't it?" Ret wondered optimistically. "You believe the Great River really exists, don't you, Ishmael?"

"Not as much as Lydia," Ishmael admitted. "When we were young, we dreamed of finding the Great River. (You know how much kids enjoy tales of buried treasure.) As I got older, I was obedient and shunned any desire to prove the legend true. But not Lydia. She was going to do whatever it took to unravel the mystery and bring prosperity back to her people. In her spare time, she studied the land and traveled the desert, following leads and building upon the research that countless others before her had compiled. Eventually, she correctly used a series of clues that led her to some ancient ruins, way out in the middle of nowhere. Of course, ancient ruins aren't that big of a deal in this part of the world, but there was something unique about these that intrigued her. The site runs right up against a large bed of quicksand—the dry kind, not the wet stuff." Ret was not aware there were different classifications of quicksand. "Lydia calculated it to be about the size of a small lake, but full of sand. She tried to explore it— dredge it, tie men to a rope and let them sink—but nothing ever worked. In my opinion," he said, checking the intercom to make sure it was still disengaged, "she went way too far; she even lost a good friend in that quicksand."

"Have you ever seen it?" Ret asked.

"She showed it to me once," Ishmael explained, "but I didn't want to get involved. I never felt at peace with her quest, and I even asked her to stop. Seeking out the legend of the Great River is condemned in our culture now, and the tribal masters strictly warned her to abandon her search. But she was stubborn and continued her research anyway—in secret. She was sure she was on to something this time, mostly because she had found gold in the quicksand."

"Gold?" Ret repeated with great interest. (He wanted to add, *"Now* we're talking.")

"Yeah, gold flecks mixed in with the sand," Ishmael confirmed. "If she couldn't drain the bed of sand or get to the bottom of it, then she figured she could at least extract the gold from it and use it as proof. But whenever she tried to scoop out a sample, the quicksand wrought havoc on her tools. She even created a new potion to dissolve the sand, or something like that."

"A potion?"

"Didn't you know? Lydia is an apothecary. She can make all sorts of medicines and potions."

"Really?"

"In fact, she was such a talented potion maker that she was the apprentice of the tribal potion master. The Sahara Desert is home to some of the best ingredients in the world: horned viper venom, scorpion blood, precious gemstones, and other rare materials that are impossible to find anywhere else in the world. So she created a potion that separated the gold from the sand. All she had to do was throw it out over the bed of quicksand."

"Did it work?" Ret was eager to know.

With a tone of dissatisfaction, Ishmael said, "Yes; unfortunately, it worked very well." He paused for a moment. "The potion dissolved the sand and created a sort of cavity through which the flakes of gold fell like a funnel. When she shined a light through the conduit to see where the gold had gone, she saw that she had discovered some kind of underground basin: beyond the base of the cavity was an empty space, and beyond the empty space was a sandy floor. She could see the gold accumulating on the ground, several feet below her. She poured more of the potion on the quicksand to enlarge the cavity enough for her to drop through it. As she kept adding more and more of her potion to the growing cavity, some of it dripped down onto the floor of the basin. It started to dissolve the sand on the bottom floor as well, revealing a large strip of gold."

Ishmael's description reminded Ret of the inverted arches along the bottom of the Amazon River. "What happened after that?"

"She was attacked," Ishmael said with some uncertainty. "Just as she was preparing to descend through the cavity, a massive colony of flesh-eating bats began pouring up through the opening. She said there was no end to them—they just kept coming and coming, swarming around her, suffocating her, biting her profusely. She had no choice but to flee for her life. Strangely, the bats didn't pursue her. From a distance, she watched as they flew back into the opening Lydia had created in the bed, recovering her work with fresh sand.

Despite Lydia's traumatic experience, Ret was ecstatic. He remembered his own, similar run-in with the Amazon's river dolphins, among the many other predators who were protecting the golden arches. Based on Ishmael's retelling of the bat-born bedlam, Ret was now certain they were on the right track.

"Did she come back better prepared?" Ret asked.

"No," said Ishmael. His voice was suddenly subdued. "She has never been back." In shock, Ret waited for an explanation. "As you can probably imagine, Lydia was covered in bite wounds, which were difficult to hide. It didn't take long before her secret was found out. The tribal masters were indignant, especially her potion master mentor. Not only had she made a mockery of the basic mores of our society by willfully searching for the Great River but she had also made the mistake of using extract from the Nile lotus flower in her special, new potion."

Ret entreated, "The Nile lotus flower?"

Employing vigor to underscore its importance, Ishmael said, "Yes," as if it was something Ret really ought to know about if he didn't already, "though sometimes it's called the blue water lily. They're native to the Nile River, where they rise above the surface of the water in the morning before submerging again at night. The lotus flower has deep, religious meaning, particularly in ancient Egyptian culture. The fact that

Lydia used such a sacred symbol for such a (purport-edly) vile purpose was seen as an instance of great sacrilege. The masters even deemed it a security threat, seeing as clans in the desert aren't always on the best of terms with each other and will use any excuse to stir up trouble. What's more, she really *had* discovered something, which the masters feared would only lead to more problems and renewed interest in the legend if they didn't come down hard on Lydia. At any rate, she had done something very serious and highly dishonorable, so they punished her."

Ishmael was suddenly overcome with emotion. In his nervousness, he checked the intercom again. Haltingly, he carried on, "The punishment was carried out by the potion master, which was only fitting since he was Lydia's mentor as well as our village's representa-tive among the tribal masters. First, he scarred her skin with liquid acid. Then she was forced to drink a cleansing solution, which burned her esophagus and robbed her of her voice. And, as if that wasn't enough, he administered a blue cursing potion that inflicted her with an acute kind of palsy, bewitching her hands with muscle spasms and convulsions so that they would cause her to strangle herself to death. The tribal masters warned our village to learn a lesson from Lydia—to not be greedy, that greed will strangle you if you let it. That's why she wears that clasp around her neck—to keep her from choking herself. Over the years, she has developed better control over her hands, but we keep the clasp in place, just in case."

Ishmael sniffed and lamented, "All Lydia wanted to do was help her people—bring prosperity back, lift them from poverty, just find new sources of water. Life can be so difficult here. There is very little certainty— with food, disease, the government. All she wanted to do was relieve some of that. But she had gotten too close; she had discovered something that someone already knew about but was unwilling to share. She had shed a faint light on a conspiracy, Ret; an ancient conspiracy— a secret society that's guarding something. That's what I think, anyway."

"I don't mean to pass judgment on your tribe or anything," Ret carefully stated upfront, "but what your masters did—doesn't that seem, you know, unusual to you?" He wasn't sure he had picked the best word. "I mean, I would think they'd be overjoyed at Lydia's discovery."

"You're not the only one," Ishmael told him. "In recent years, my people have been torn apart—rebels attempt to overthrow the masters while the masters try to maintain control. That's what life here has become—an eye for an eye, guerrilla-style, with a coup every other month it seems. That's why Lydia and I fled—well, that and she was already ostracized by society. So who knows? Who knows why my village sits in ashes today? Who knows who's right and who's wrong? Or are they all wrong? You're never quite sure if you can trust the people in charge here. It's the sad history of this land, Ret: secret societies that enforce their agendas at any cost, all for the sake of money and power. They are the reason this land is cursed. Their greed is a scourge that afflicts entire nations. The economists call it the 'resource curse'—how a country with vast natural resources can be so economically undeveloped, how its people can be living in such poverty while living among such riches. And it's true: this land is loaded with natural resources, just like my ancestors believed. My people don't have the means to harvest them or even find them (except for maybe a few salt mines), so they don't benefit from them. Only the greedy moguls have access to them, and when we try to change that by bringing fairness and equity to the system, people like Lydia suffer. Wars, civil wars, terrorist plots, government takeovers—these are the only things that are constant in the lives of the people here. That's why there is a curse in this land, Ret. It's the curse of greed."

Ret was drawing several parallels between Ishmael's ancestral tale of the underground river of wealth and Rodrigo's legend of the lost city of gold. He figured there might be a reason for the striking similarities, seeing as how the great rivers of both the Amazon Rainforest and the Sahara Desert were once theoretically the same, connected waterway.

"Do you think we can go to the bed of quicksand that Lydia found by those ancient ruins?" Ret inquired with great desire.

"Unfortunately, I suspect that's the reason why we are here," Ishmael said with a hint of disappointment. "Mr. Coy asked me that same question not too long ago. I told him it was a bad idea. But maybe there's a bigger reason why both of you have expressed the same interest. Hold on, let me ask Ben if he still wants to go there."

Ishmael reached to engage the intercom. As soon as he flipped the switch, however, the air was filled with snoring. There was almost a rhythm to it.

"That must be him," Ishmael identified the deep snores.

"And that's Ana," Ret said of the more high-pitched tones. They both chuckled.

"Glad I'm not in *that* CAVE," Ishmael said as he shut off the intercom. "We'll ask Mr. Coy in the morning." He yawned. "But until then, I'd better get some sleep. I don't want to be falling asleep at the wheel tomorrow. It was good talking with you, Ret." He slouched over to lean against his door. "Goodnight."

"Goodnight."

Yet, despite his comfy seat and the balmy temperature, Ret didn't do much sleeping. There was simply
too much on his mind—so very much to think about—
that he couldn't file it all away in tomorrow's to-do pile.
He wasn't the only one who was sleepless—either that
or Conrad always slept with his eyes open.

As the hours passed and his information-induced
insomnia persisted, Ret watched the shadows begin to
tremble and then flee as the sun rose to start another day.
There was something beautiful about dawn, that daily
blessing from the heavens. It was such a gradual thing,
so simple in some ways but cosmically complex in
others, and the varying amounts of light allowed him to
see things from different perspectives.

In fact, the same could be said about Ret's scars.
He scrutinized the ore scar yet again, hoping its meaning
would somehow burst upon him and finally come to full
light, but it didn't. This scar—the squiggly line—had no
doubt been the most unhelpful so far. Sure, it confirmed
they were on the right path, but only after they had
traversed it. In some ways, it was more mature than its
predecessors because it only came to light bit by bit—
here a little and there a little. As frustrating as this learn-
as-you-go method was at times, perhaps there was some
wisdom in it. After all, if the meaning of the scars could
be discerned as easily as night and day, Ret would have
missed out on a lot of experiences along the way.

Suddenly, the sound of music shattered the morning's solitude. Ret immediately recognized it as Ana's wake-up alarm on her cell phone, which she obviously had forgotten to adjust for spring break. For several seconds, the desert rang with her ringtone, which was an excerpt from Donna Summer's hit song "She Works Hard for the Money." Ret rolled his eyes; he was very familiar with it, as it was something he heard through the wall every morning back home.

Persuading Mr. Coy to allow a visit to the bed of quicksand was an easy sell. In fact, all Mr. Coy said in response was, "Lead the way." And with that, they were off.

The Sahara Desert was truly colossal in size and seemingly endless at times. Still, it wasn't all dunes and sand. There were very large sections of hard ground, like a dried up lakebed. On these flat stretches, the CAVEs picked up considerable speed, which was helpful because it felt like they were trying to get to one of the most remote locations on the planet. In the many miles they covered, they never saw another living soul.

It was true that the desert could play tricks on the mind. On occasion, Ret had to stare long and hard at things to properly identify them. Most of these mirages were caused by waves of intense heat that made it look like there were pools of fresh water in the distance. What a sinister place!

Somewhere near the borders of Algeria and Libya, Ret could see what looked like ancient ruins, and this time they were no mirage. They parked the CAVEs and prepared to step out.

"Hold it," Coy ordered before Ret opened his door. "Do you see how hot it is outside?" All eyes focused on the temperature reading on the center console.

"49 degrees?" Ana read aloud.

"That's Celsius," Paige pointed out. After Mr. Coy converted the measurement to Fahrenheit, it read 121 degrees.

"Ouch!" said Leo.

"And it's only going to get hotter, so drink plenty of water," Mr. Coy warned. Then, just before getting out, he quickly added, almost under his breath, "Oh, and watch out for snakes."

"Snakes?!" Paige shrieked.

Opening the door of the CAVE was like opening the door of an oven. An intense wave of warmth washed over Ret as he took his first steps on the sand. The sun delivered immediate heat and blinding light.

"Here," Ishmael told him, handing over some black charcoal. "Smear some of this under your eyes. It'll help with the glare and keep your corneas from frying."

"Nice place," Ret remarked sarcastically.

"Home sweet home," Ishmael smiled.

The party fanned out to explore the ancient ruins. If there had once been a ceiling, it was now long gone. The floor was buried in so much sand that any still-standing walls could easily be stepped over. Stone pillars, some more intact than others, cast the only shadows. Mounds of rubble were everywhere, and anything of significant value had either been buried deep or carried off by raiders.

Ret made his way to the backend of the complex. As he neared the edge of the property, he noticed a long line of columns standing along the perimeter. They were taller and more substantial than the pillars he had seen previously, and they were erected with remarkable uniformity. At the top of each one, an arm extended out across the open sand, away from the ruins, though nearly all of them had broken off. They reminded Ret of the cranes at a seaport that lift cargo from the decks of great barges.

Suddenly, Ret felt someone grab him from behind. It was Lydia. She held onto Ret tightly, a look of alarm on her face. She pointed at the ground in front of Ret. He was standing on the edge of the large body of deadly quicksand, and she had saved him from stumbling into it.

"Thank you," Ret told her as she released him. The wordless woman nodded her head in reply.

There was something strange about the expanse of quicksand in front of Ret. Contrary to what he had seen or heard about quicksand, there was nothing marshy or boggy about the grainy terrain at his feet. In fact, it didn't look much different from all the other sand in the desert, except that it seemed more refined, as if it had been sifted like flour. Moreover, the bed was slightly lower in elevation compared to the distant, surrounding area, creating the perfect contour for a giant puddle in the rare event of rain.

Just then, Mr. Coy arrived at Ret's side and joined in gazing out over the depression of fine granules. He hadn't looked long, however, when he bent down and picked up a small rock, about the size of a golf ball. Then he extended his arm over the edge of the embankment and dropped it into the sand. Without any resistance, the sand swallowed the rock whole. There was no battle with buoyancy, no waiting for it to sink—it immediately disappeared upon contact, as if thrown in water, launching a thin jet of sand particles vertically into the air behind it.

"What was that?" Ret wondered.

"It's quicksand alright," said Coy, *"dry quicksand."*

"What's dry quicksand?" Ret asked, as Ishmael came and stood next to his sister.

"I learned about it from a group of engineers who helped with the design of some of the spacecraft used in the Apollo missions to the moon," Coy explained.

"Unlike its wet cousin, *dry* quicksand contains no water. It is loose particulate matter that loses its density when air is blown through it—or, in this case, when there's a sandstorm."

"But the wind is constantly blowing sand every-where here," Ret said. "Why isn't there dry quicksand all over the desert?"

"There is," Ishmael interjected, "in some parts."

Mr. Coy leaned over the edge of the ruins, looking left and right, and then said, "Do you see those date trees out there?" He motioned to several vegetated clumps where huddles of palm-like trees were swaying above the sand. "Do you see how they're all growing in a straight line—the same line as the edge of the foundation for these ruins?" He tapped his foot on the ground. "A tree grows where water flows," he rhymed, then added, "or at least where water *used* to flow."

"You mean we're standing on the bank of the Great River?" Ret questioned with absurdity.

"Or the shell of it, at least," Coy clarified. "It seems that's what those palms are trying to tell us. But what does *your* palm have to say about it?"

It took Ret a moment to realize Mr. Coy was referring to his scar. Once it registered, he eagerly consulted his hand, hoping for some kind of sign or sensation. To his joy, the squiggly line had grown.

"There's more!" Ret rejoiced. "Look! Look how much longer it is now!" He held out his palm for all to see. Lydia seemed especially curious.

"What does it mean?" Ishmael asked. This was the first time he had seen the scar, and he couldn't quite understand how something as bland as a curvy line could be so thrilling.

"It means we're standing on the bank of what used to be the Great River," said Coy. Lydia's eyes lit up with exhilaration. "When it dried up, it became completely filled with sand. The sand had been blown in by the wind, but when it hit the trees and structures along the riverbank, the sand fell to the ground. Over time, layers upon layers of sand built up—airy, wind-blown sand— creating these pockets of dry quicksand. I'm willing to bet there are similar pits of dry quicksand near each of those groups of date trees."

Lydia nodded her head in agreement.

"But what does a dried river full of sand have to do with ore?" Paige asked, arriving at Ret's side. Ret liked how she kept her mind on the ultimate goal.

Eager to participate, Lydia stepped forward and knelt in front of the sand. She held out her hand, in the palm of which was a powdery potion. Ret immediately flinched and turned away, bracing for a barrage of frenzied bats, but Lydia grabbed his hand and drew him back. She showed him how she was only using a pinch of the potion this time, not fistfuls like before. Like a witch sprinkling ingredients into a cauldron, she scattered the powder onto a nearby section of the dry quicksand. Everyone watched with great interest as the mystic concoction interacted with the sand, drawing out small flecks of gold to the surface, similar to how Pauline removes molecules of fat from gravy.

"Amazing," Leo said to himself, having snuck up to the group to see what was going on.

All of a sudden, the tiny, golden flakes fled from view as they sunk into the sand. Lydia frowned.

Rather instinctively, Ret reached out with his hand. Even though he held it a few feet above the sand, he could distinctly feel the specks of ore. It was like he was a puppeteer, and each fleck was tied to a string that was attached to his fingers. He lifted each piece of metal out of the sand, gathered them into his palm, and then molded them together like tiny bits of Play-Doh until they become one solid mass.

Ret was overjoyed, and Mr. Coy was well-pleased. Paige was impressed, but Leo was mesmerized. Ishmael was dumbfounded, while Lydia was speechless. Conrad was refueling the vehicles, and Ana was ready to go.

"Can we leave already?" Ana moaned, the last to rejoin the group. Her cheeks were bright red, and she looked a bit peaked.

"My thoughts exactly," Coy sang, tossing Ana his bottle of water. "Everyone, to the CAVEs!"

As the party began to migrate back to the CAVEs, a perplexed Ret pulled Mr. Coy aside and asked, "Where are we going now?"

"For a swim," Coy replied with a grin.

"I like the sound of that," said Ret, remembering their similar adventures on the Amazon.

Mr. Coy started to walk away but then stopped to say, "Would you do me a favor and fashion a pair of ramps right here near the edge? Nothing fancy, just something to give us a bit of a boost, that's all." Ret obliged, moving sand and rock into the shape of a ramp, even employing a bit of flame to heat things up and glue it all together.

Ana was the first to make it back to the CAVEs, where she cranked the air-conditioning to full blast. When the last door had closed, Mr. Coy's voice was heard over the intercom.

"Follow my lead, Ishmael," he instructed.

"Yes, sir."

Mr. Coy slowly maneuvered his CAVE until he lined it up head-on with one of Ret's ramps, clear on the other side of the complex. Once Ishmael had done the same with the other ramp, Mr. Coy floored the gas pedal. The CAVE hurtled forward, crashing through debris and narrowly missing pillars.

"Uh, Dad?" Paige said with a shaky voice. "What are you doing?" She watched the speedometer fly by 20 miles per hour, then 30, then 40. "Dad?!"

Mr. Coy showed no signs of slowing. Paige glanced out the window. Ishmael was obeying his orders to mimic his boss's every move. Soon, the CAVEs were neck and neck, side by side, speeding to an uncertain future.

They were running out of ruins. The bed of dry quicksand was in sight. Mr. Coy engaged the vehicle's emergency thrusters, greatly increasing its speed as they hit the ramp and became airborne.

"DAD!"

They were launched into the desert air, flying out into the region of dry quicksand. Floating within the confines of her seatbelt, Paige looked at the other CAVE to their side, where she saw Ret and Leo cheering as if on a rollercoaster.

The apex was reached. The decline began. For several uneasy seconds, they fell back toward the earth until they plunged into the quicksand and disappeared.

Chapter 18

River of Ore

In some ways, falling through several stories of dry quicksand was like driving through a very suspenseful carwash: it was dark (though the windows were covered with sand instead of suds), and strange sounds came from unseen objects as they passed by. Like patrons of a thrill ride, the eight passengers in the two CAVEs were all alarmed but had different ways of showing it—some choosing to hold their breath, others trying to hold onto their lunch—not to mention the occasional, high-pitched shriek.

For several seconds, they experienced an unobstructed drop until, like a hiccup, they briefly made contact with a harder surface and immediately broke through it. An even faster free fall ensued, this time amid air instead of sand. After just a few more seconds, the CAVEs touched down on solid terrain, the brunt of the rough impact being absorbed by the thick tires and sturdy shocks.

But the wheels were still rolling. Having landed on a downward slope with so much momentum, the CAVEs began to skid out of control. In their respective vehicles, both Mr. Coy and Ishmael gripped the gears and pumped the brakes, trying to curb the wild swerving. After a long and bumpy slide amid total darkness, the ground leveled out, and the CAVEs finally came to a stop.

"Well, that was fun," Mr. Coy said brightly. He glanced at the girls in the backseat through his rearview mirror. Paige and Ana were clutching each other, frozen stiff and terror-stricken. "Let's see if we can find out where we are," he said, searching for a button at the controls. "Go ahead and turn on your floodlights, Ishmael."

In the moment just before the lights came on, Ret had little idea what he should expect to see. He wanted to believe they were sitting on the underground riverbed of the Great River, and he was almost certain they were, but there was no telling what might be hidden in the blackness. It reminded him of a time when they were in a similar situation, swimming in darkness down the submerged shaft that led from the Bimini road to the lost city of Sunken Earth. On that occasion, when Mr. Coy had briefly illuminated the scene by way of his underwater flare, it had shed light on many human skeletons dangling from the walls. Ret was hoping now for happier, less haunting interior decorating.

And, truth be told, what the floodlights revealed was a bit anticlimactic. There really wasn't a whole lot to see. The bright, parallel beams shot several hundred yards over a desolate wasteland, flat and barren like a prairie plagued by drought. A few minutes passed by in silent anticipation as the group watched for something to bestir the stillness, but there was nothing—no people, no animals, not even tumbleweeds.

"This reminds me of something out of a Jules Verne novel," Paige whispered to Ana as they continued to survey the limited scenery.

"Yeah, and just watch," said Ana. "Any minute now, the tongue of some giant monster is going to flop on the windshield."

Ret was the first person to get out of the CAVEs. The air, cool and windless, was stale and tasted like dust. The floor's brittle squares of dehydrated dirt, laid out like a chessboard, crunched beneath his feet. He felt like an astronaut exploring a new planet, which was home to nothing but thick, impenetrable shadows.

One by one, the four other men and Lydia followed Ret's lead and ventured into the unknown. Those without flashlights stayed close to those who had them.

Upon seeing a vacant spot at Ret's side, Paige turned to Ana and asked, "Want to look around?"

"No thanks," Ana replied contentedly, also recalling the chute they had to swim through in order to reach Sunken Earth. "I've already checked off 'explore a dark and mysterious underground tunnel toward the center of the earth' from my bucket list."

"Suit yourself," said Paige, who vacated the vehicle and scurried off toward Ret.

The frequent crackling created by their footsteps made it difficult for the group to hear the only other noise being made. It was Mr. Coy who took notice of it first. Sweeping the vicinity with his flashlight, he quickly discovered the source of the sound: two steady streams of sand pouring through a pair of large holes in the ceiling. They were obviously the spots where the CAVEs had broken through.

"Hey, Ret," Coy called out. "Mind using your masonry skills to patch up those holes?" He shined his flashlight up at the ceiling, which was nothing more than a hardened layer of crusted sand.

It was a simple fix. Ret removed two broad sections of earth from the nearby ground, raised them high into the air, and then manipulated them until they fit snugly into the gaps in the ceiling. In very little time and with hardly any effort, the holes had been plugged and the sand stopped.

"Easy enough," Ret said of his work, wiping his hands as if they had gotten dirty.

The noise of falling sand had scarcely ceased when a new sound fell faintly on the adventurers' ears. Ret looked up quizzically at his patch job of the ceiling, but he could detect no leaks. Then he stared at Mr. Coy, who was standing perfectly still, straining to hear the curious new sound. Whatever it was, it was getting louder—and closer.

Suddenly, Lydia burst into a full sprint toward the CAVEs, a look of terror on her face. It was in that moment when the others realized the source of the mysterious sound.

"It's the bats!" Ishmael cried.

"Everyone, back to the CAVEs!" Mr. Coy ordered. "Now!"

While everyone else hurried back to the safety of the CAVEs, Ret ran with suspicion over to the part of the floor where he had removed the two large slabs to repair the ceiling. He knew the bats would not have been provoked unless the golden arch had somehow been uncovered. When he arrived at the spot, he held out his fist with the thumb extended like a hitchhiker and conjured a small flame above it as if holding a lighter. Using it to illuminate his view, he saw how, sure enough, he had exposed a small swatch of the upside-down golden arch. Ret smiled, for he was sure of it now: they were in the dried bed of the Great River.

"Ret!" Paige yelled from the CAVE when she saw he was far from the safety of his own. She was tempted to run out to him, but before she could do so, her father ushered her into the CAVE.

"He'll be fine," Coy reassured her before shutting the door.

When Ret looked up to see who had called his name, something caught his eye. His improvised flashlight was casting a dim light on an object several yards in front of him. It was an old piece of lumber. When he picked it up, it left behind small deposits of gold dust on his hand. He rose and enlarged the flame at his thumb to enhance his view of the immediate area. He was standing at the base of the incline that led all the way up the riverbank. Littering the hillside were many more pieces of petrified wood, each reflecting its own share of gold dust.

Ret was about to hike up the slope to investigate when, with a howl like the whistling of a teakettle, a stray bat came barreling into him. It was the first of thousands closing in on him. When the winged harbinger returned for a second snip, Ret dodged the creature, which flew straight through the large flame at Ret's hand. With a whimper, the burned bat fell dead to the floor.

Ret reached back to massage the part of his shoulder where the bat had collided into him earlier. There was a slight tear in his shirt. It was very close to the spot where he had been struck by the initial river dolphin in the Amazon River, and although he hadn't been able to kindle any fire there (being immersed in so much water), he certainly didn't have that problem here. Ret furrowed his brow in self-defense. There was still much more he wished to investigate at this newest arch location, and he wasn't about to let a bunch of bats scare him off.

Choosing fight instead of flight, Ret readied his stance in preparation for the bombardment of bats. The flying foes' shrill cries filled the air, echoing off the enclosed channel. Coming towards him was chaos in the form of a swarm. He couldn't discern individual creatures, only a solid mass that was disturbing the darkness.

"What's he doing?" Ishmael wondered, speaking the words that were on everyone's lips as they watched Ret from inside the CAVEs.

The events that happened next took place in rapid succession. Still holding onto his pilot light, Ret brought both of his hands together, high above his head. In an instant, he sent a pillar of fire all the way to the ceiling. Then he stretched his arms out on each side, parallel to the ground, widening the pillar lengthwise as far as it could go. Finally, as if clapping, he rushed his hands together in front of him. Like serving a tennis ball, Ret had explosively created a massive wall of fire in a continuous motion. The blazing barrier billowed forth, scorching everything in its path. The advancing adversaries flew directly into the flames and never flew again.

In addition to purging the pestilence, Ret's firewall also lit up the underground chamber in its totality. Like a mass of gas passing through the intestinal tract, the inferno expanded to fill the total width of the riverbed as it moved along the length. For a few fleeting moments, the group was blessed with panoramic vision before the flames fizzled out. It was as if an enormous camera had flashed and captured a photograph.

And the picture was worth a thousand bats. It unveiled a scene that was much different than the restricted one provided earlier by the limited floodlights: true, the riverbed was waterless, with not so much as a pond, pool, or puddle anywhere in sight, but it wasn't lifeless—or at least hadn't always been, for it was abounding with evidence that man had come and conquered. There were dozens upon dozens of tunnels that had been dug into the sloping sides of the river. Strewn down the center of the bed were great heaps of excavated dirt and large loads of rubbish. There were tire treads, car parts, and even remnants of what looked like a train track. Whatever it had been, it was now abandoned.

With dead bats falling all around, Ret commenced a leisurely walk back to the CAVEs. Despite the downpour of death, he did not seem the least bit hurried or bothered but really quite pleased with himself.

"You uncovered an arch when you fixed the ceiling, didn't you?" Mr. Coy guessed correctly as he opened his door and re-exited the CAVE.

"It was my fault the bats came," Ret admitted, "so I figured I should be the one to get rid of them."

Just then, a dead bat floated into the CAVE through the door that Mr. Coy had left ajar. It bounced off the driver's seat and landed in Ana's lap.

"Ahh!" she screamed, followed by a fit of hysteria.

"Don't worry," Ret told her. "It's dead."

"I'll worry all I want, *bat* man!" she sneered. "Just get this thing off of me!"

As Ret picked it up and prepared to fling it away, Paige joked, "But, Ana, it's just how you like your wings: extra crispy." A CAVE away, Leo was snickering to himself.

When the excitement had subsided, Ret explained to everyone, "I saw something over here, before the bats attacked, that I'd like to check out."

He made his way toward the site where he had found the pieces of petrified wood bearing gold dust. Several junk piles were now aflame thanks to Ret's firewall, providing a comfortable level of light as he began to comb through the scattered debris. He focused on the large sections of wood since they shared some connection with ore. They resembled plastic tracks for

Hot Wheels cars, though much bigger, with a flat bottom and raised edges, and they even seemed to fit together.

"It's called a sluice," Mr. Coy said, arriving at Ret's side. Ishmael was standing a few steps back, still in shock that his culture's legend of the Great River was actually real. Meanwhile, Leo was steadily making his way toward them, trying hard not to step on any bats.

"How does it work?" Ret asked.

"It's a long channel for conducting water, used by miners to separate gold from sediment," Coy explained. "Do you see those footings up there?" He directed Ret's attention to several foundational stones near the top of the riverbank. "Those probably supported the stilts that held up the sluice." He pointed to some of the wooden beams that had fallen nearby. "It looks like these miners laid the sluice at the surface and used the natural flow of the river to sift the gold. So they'd put a load of mineral-rich soil at the top, let the water carry it down the sluice, and then these riffles," he said, indicating the slightly raised ribs along the bottom of the sluice, "would catch the heavier gold particles as they passed by."

"I wonder if this sluice has anything to do with those ancient ruins we were just at," Ret stated, directing a faint light toward the ceiling, "the ruins that are now above us."

"Most likely," said Coy, "but this sluice, these pieces of petrified wood, and those ancient ruins above us don't seem to match up with the rest of the scene down here."

"What do you mean?" Ret questioned.

"A Great River full of water is good for a sluice but bad for dozens of mines and connecting tunnels," Coy answered. "This sluice may very well date back to the days of peace and plenty before the elements were scattered and when the Great River was still full. But these mines and tunnels could not have been created until the Great River went dry. So I think we're seeing evidence of at least two separate operations down here, each from very different generations."

"So why is this place deserted now?" Ret wanted to know.

"I would imagine it made little sense to sluice once the water stopped flowing," Coy deduced, "and the mines must already be completely harvested." He shined his flashlight into the mouth of one of the many tunnels, as if to see if any untapped lodes shined back at him. When none did, he said with suspicion, "It seems like this was quite the sophisticated operation." Then, turning to Ishmael, he said, "Didn't you tell me no one ever discovered the Great River?"

"No one in *my* ancestry did," Ishmael reaffirmed. "It is now very clear, however, that someone else knows about it—and has known about it for a very long time."

"We'd better keep moving," Coy suggested soberly. "We may not be the only ones down here."

Very shortly, they were back on the road again, blazing their own trail along the dried river basin. They followed the natural course of the river, which took them in a principally eastward direction. Unfortunately, the vehicles' high beams supplied enough light for traveling but not enough for sightseeing. Besides the occasional stretches of emptiness, much of the path ahead was littered with junk. Some of it, like rusty pipes and rotted barrels, was easily plowed through with the help of the CAVEs, while other obstructions, such as scrap metal and heavy machinery, were safer to avoid altogether. It made for an exciting ride, with the drivers dodging and swerving as if on an obstacle course.

At Mr. Coy's urging, Ret kept a close eye on his scar and announced each time another bar was added to the squiggly line on his palm. After a while, he began to feel like the bird of a cuckoo clock, reemerging every hour to make known the completion of another cycle. When he wasn't watching his palm, Ret looked at the GPS on the CAVE's center console. It traced the route they had traveled, which was essentially identical to the shape of his scar. He desperately wanted to know what it all meant, but, until then, he would have to be content. He tried to be patient, reminding himself that as long as the scar was growing, they were getting closer to the element.

"Looks like we just crossed into Egypt," Mr. Coy broadcasted after several hours of nonstop driving.

"Can we at least listen to the radio or something?" Ana begged with boredom.

"All the stations are probably in Arabic," Paige told her.

"Tell you what," Coy compromised, "let's get to one more golden arch, and then we'll stop for the night. Looks like it's getting late anyway." He must have been looking at his watch because there was no way of knowing where the sun was in the sky.

"Good," Ana sighed, "because my bladder's about to burst."

The final arch of the day could not have come any sooner. When Ret made the announcement, both CAVEs slowed to a halt. As the weary travelers got out to stretch their legs, Mr. Coy scanned the area with his flashlight to make sure it was secure. As soon as he gave the all-clear, Ana grabbed a flashlight of her own and set out to relieve herself.

"Come on, girl," she said, pulling Paige along with her. "Let's see what kind of amenities this rest stop has to offer."

"Be careful not to uncover anything!" Coy called out after them.

It almost felt like they were camping. Mr. Coy prepared a quick, cold dinner while Conrad serviced the vehicles. Ever intrigued by the actual existence of the Great River, Ishmael and Lydia roamed nearby, equipped with their flashlights and curiosities. The four youths were glad to spend a few minutes together before it was back in the CAVEs for some shuteye.

"I'm turning off the intercom now," Mr. Coy warned. "Goodnight, everyone."

A hush fell over the group. There was absolute silence—not even the chirping of crickets. Paige noticed Ana's eyes were still open.

"What's on your mind, Ana?" she whispered.

"Just thinking about Mom," Ana said thoughtfully. "I miss her a little. I hope she's okay. It's weird not having her along with us this time."

"Yeah," Mr. Coy yawned, "I kind of miss the old bat." Upon mentioning the word *bat,* Ana jumped in her seat, the memory of a dead one falling in her lap still fresh in her mind.

Paige waited for her dad to drift off to sleep before resuming her conversation with Ana. It didn't take long before his heavy breathing was heard.

"Do you think Ret's been thinking about me much?" Paige asked.

"Beats me," Ana shrugged. "I never know what's on that boy's mind."

"What do you think they're talking about?" Paige wondered. "You know, in the other CAVE?"

"My guess is nothing," Ana stated flatly.

"They've got to be—"

"Are you kidding? We're talking about Ret, Ishmael, and Conrad—three of the most un-talkative guys I've ever met. Best case scenario, Leo's over there talking to himself."

Paige breathed a heavy, disappointed sigh.

"Listen, P," Ana said, trying to be more supportive. "Ret may not talk much, but he sure does a lot of thinking, so odds are you've crossed his mind."

"It's just sometimes I feel like I get pushed to the side by all of this Oracle stuff," Paige confessed. "I was hoping we'd spend some real quality time together on this adventure, but so far we've spent almost no time together."

"So your romantic getaway turned into a business trip, huh?" Ana summarized.

"I understand he's got a job to do, especially now that we know the element is somewhere around here," Paige tried to explain, "but I want him to remember that *I'm* here, too. Like Leo—he thinks about *you:* he bought you that perfume."

"You mean the urine?"

"I just wish I—"

Suddenly, Ret's voice was heard over the intercom.

"Do you think I should have bought something for her like you did for Ana?" said Ret.

"I'd say you were smart not to," Leo's voice came in reply, "judging by how Ana didn't exactly fawn over that perfume."

"You mean the urine?" Ret joked.

Ana and Paige glared at each other without making a sound. Almost inaudibly, Paige mouthed, "Who turned on the intercom?" Ana raised a finger to her lips to shush her, and the two of them tuned into what was being discussed in the man CAVE.

"I just hope she doesn't get the wrong impression," Ret expressed. "I really like being around her—she's intelligent to talk to, she's not annoying or demanding. Most of the time I feel so comfortable around her that I worry it comes across as I'm not giving her any attention."

"Sometimes it's the small things that mean the most," Leo advised.

"Like what?" Ret supplicated. "You're good at showing you care—like when you got Ana that GPS for her birthday. What can I do to express myself better—you know, turn my thoughts into actions, put a face to my feelings?"

"You could tell her you think she's beautiful?" Leo suggested.

"I already did that," Ret said.

"Recently?"

"A couple months ago."

Leo laughed. "Well, tell her again!"

"But she already knows it."

"Look, when it comes to romance, I'm about as inexperienced as they come," Leo conceded unabashedly. "In fact, I didn't even know what love was 'til Ana brought it into my life. And ever since then, I've never wanted it to go away. So I nurture it and care for it—ya know, kinda like a stray cat: if you keep feeding it, it'll keep coming back."

"So you're saying I should treat Paige like a stray cat?" Ret said with confusion. Ana and Paige giggled silently in the other CAVE.

Upon realizing how odd that sounded, Leo restated, "Like I said, I ain't the best at this kind of stuff. I just try to treat Ana special because that's how she makes me feel. How does Paige make *you* feel?"

After considering the question for a moment, Ret answered, "Stronger—she makes me feel like I can do just about anything."

"There you go," Leo said encouragingly.

"That's why I'm glad she comes on these crazy trips to find the elements," Ret continued. "It really helps to know I have her support, especially when I have to go it alone."

"Now all you need to do is tell her—show her—how you feel," Leo counseled.

"How do I do that?"

"Good question," Leo said, yawning and turning over in his seat. "Let's sleep on it."

"Alright," Ret smiled. "Goodnight, Leo."

When nothing was said between the two of them for a while, Conrad reached down and turned off the intercom that he had purposely turned on a few minutes ago.

Just a CAVE away, two young women swooned with joyful hearts and slipped into sweet dreams, happier than a pair of stray cats with a new home. Their inadvertent eavesdropping had yielded information that was more precious than gold.

But the slumbering crew was in for a rude awakening. Just inches below them, small pools of liquid were accumulating beneath each CAVE's under-carriage. The steady dripping was not the result of any leak or malfunction but rather the condensing of cool air against hot metal, thanks to many hours of uninterrupted operation throughout the course of the day. This would have posed no threat had they not unknowingly parked directly over the golden arch. As the puddles grew larger, they spilled over and ran together, taking the dust and flakes of the parched dirt with them. It didn't amount to much erosion, but, unfortunately, it was just enough to sound the alarm.

Ret's eyes shot open. His head still resting against the window, he could feel the thick glass rattling.

Through the space to the left of the driver's seat, he could see the needles shaking on the speedometer and other gauges. Soon, the entire CAVE began to tremble, jostling everyone else into consciousness.

Ishmael flipped the intercom switch and asked, "Ben, do you feel that?"

"Yes," said a slightly groggy Mr. Coy, "feels like an earthquake—or that bean dip we had for dinner."

The answer came when they turned on the headlights. In the distance ahead of them, they could see the ground rippling as if it were water. Like critters crawling underneath a rug, a large wave of something was traveling quickly through the topmost layer of sand and dust, and it was coming straight at them.

Ret opened his door and stepped outside to get a better look. When his foot hit the ground, he heard a splash. He looked down. There was a puddle. Getting on his knees, he peered underneath the CAVE, where he saw how the streams of liquid had carved tiny canyons in the ground and exposed a golden arch.

"Not again," Ret moaned. He looked out across the wave, hoping to learn the identity of this arch's predatory protector.

"What's your prognosis, Ishmael?" Coy asked.

Peering through a small pair of binoculars, Ishmael assessed, "Keep your distance. Looks like red spitting cobras to me—a whole colony of them."

"*Spitting* cobras?" Ret asked.

"Right," Ishmael confirmed. "They'll sometimes spray venom at an intruder's face."

Ana gasped, "Flesh-eating bats, red spitting cobras—what's next?"

"I'll handle this," Ret said. He shut his door, sending a loud boom echoing throughout the channel, and began to walk forward.

The entire riverbed was quaking now, specks of sand bouncing at Ret's feet. Needing some light in order to see what he was up against this time, he sent out two streams of fire on either side of himself, which blazed along the ground in both directions. For as far as he could see, the floor was quivering. The red, scaly bodies of the snakes were now coming into view as they slithered with great speed through the sand. The wave was knocking down everything in its path.

Knowing he couldn't easily burn the burrowed serpents, Ret tried another approach. About halfway between him and the advancing surge, he focused his attention on a spot of earth and began to create a crack in the ground. He concentrated on growing the gap— widening it, deepening it. He could feel the dirt between his fingers; it was exceptionally dry and brittle, very easy to break apart. The fissure flourished. Long and narrow, it spread far across the riverbed.

The cobras were oblivious. They plunged headlong into the cleft, spilling over the edge like floodwater until they disappeared. Satisfied, Ret turned to head back to the CAVEs.

But his victory march was premature. Cobras were climbing up the sides of the gap and onto the other side. They seemed even more agitated as they resumed their assault, hissing loudly and flaring their hooded heads.

Ret wondered if the CAVEs could fly. Just then, however, out of the corner of his eye, he saw something flickering—far from him, about halfway up the sloped side of the river bed, lying in the gully that Ret had newly formed when he divided the ground. Though mostly buried in sand, it looked like a boat, obviously uncovered by the splitting of the floor. The flames of Ret's light source were being reflected by the metallic exterior of the ship, which gave Ret an idea.

Not sure if his power over ore was strong enough yet, Ret mentally reached for the boat. With the deep groaning of a whale, it began to budge. He pulled harder, slowly sliding it free from where it was lodged. It was enormously heavy. The snakes were unsettlingly close now; the cobras along the frontline looked poised and ready to spit their venomous saliva. But there was still more ship to be unearthed—it was massive—and Ret wondered if he ought to abandon his plans and make for the CAVEs.

When he was finally cradling the craft from stem to stern, Ret realized it was much more than a boat—it was a barge. With all the mental energy he could summon, he raised the barge into the air above the riverbed. There was no time to waste, and it didn't help that the anchor had never been rewound and was now being dragged along. Clenching his teeth and dripping in sweat, Ret was shaking under the barge's weight as he moved it into position. The snakes' incessant hissing threatened to thwart his concentration as they prepared for their attack. Then, near exhaustion, Ret dropped the barge on top of the carpet of cobras. Forsaking his hold, the ark-like vessel crashed to the ground with an ear-splitting sound and a knee-knocking tremor. A plume of dust burst from the base and swallowed Ret, who remained perfectly still and calm.

Back in the CAVEs, the others were watching the proceedings in shock and awe. When the air had finally cleared, they breathed a collective sigh of relief to find Ret unharmed, though completely covered in dirt. He was standing just a few yards in front of the barge, staring at a large gash in its side. Whether or not it had been created at Ret's hand, he did not know, but he could see something shining back at him through the opening. He lifted a finger slightly and started peeling away the metal siding like the lid of a tin can. Inside, he saw several piles of gold and silver ingots—bars and blocks that had once been stacked neatly but had since fallen over. This barge had been hauling ore.

Hearing Mr. Coy's footsteps close behind him, Ret pointed out, "It's just as Argo said." Coy recognized the name as belonging to the late Guardian of the Fire Element. "He told me they used to get all of their precious metals from the Great River. That's what this is," Ret said, holding out his arms to take in the landscape. "It's one great river of ore."

"This barge must have been at port," Mr. Coy observed. "Why else would it be near the bank with its anchor down? And those ancient ruins we were at earlier before we dropped into the basin—I bet those used to be some kind of shipping dock."

"And the golden arches?" Ret was eager to know.

"I'm thinking they probably marked where each port was," Coy supposed. "Remember how the arches in the Amazon created a sort of golden rainbow in the air? I'm sure the ones down here did the same until they were swallowed by the desert."

"Then why are these arches covered up?" Ret wondered.

"To keep the bats and snakes away, of course," Coy replied.

"But if the arches used to indicate where the ports were," Ret reasoned, "then I'm sure they weren't always protected like they are today."

"Good point," said Coy. "The Amazon's arches stay concealed naturally by all of the silt and sediment, but the Sahara's may have been deliberately covered up. I think there's much more to this than meets the eye, Ret—the tip of the iceberg, as they say. And *I* say we keep moving until we figure it out."

"I agree."

It was more of the same as they journeyed farther and farther along the river of ore. Eventually, and to everyone's supreme relief, there came some variety into the monotony when they approached a great bend in the riverbed. It took several minutes to complete the leftward turn, which changed their route from east to northeast, and, as expected, it was reflected in the scar on Ret's hand.

When they had at last rounded the bend, they beheld a sight that was truly mind-blowing. Ishmael was the most surprised of all, now realizing *all* the legends of his family lore were true. With wide eyes, he described it best: "The city of gold."

CHAPTER 19

THE CITY OF GOLD

The scene was exquisitely bright—briefly blinding, even. Having grown accustomed to the darkness of the underground river basin, it took a few seconds for Ret's eyes to fully adjust. The source of the light was the subterranean city's backdrop, which appeared to be an enormous wall of pure gold. It seemed to taper slightly in its reach toward the ceiling, and it stood directly behind a bustling urban center. The entire sight was a bit bewildering. Ret wondered if they had reached the end of the Great River, culminating in a golden, impassable wall.

Where are we? What is this place? What's going on down here?

These and similar questions raced through the minds of the out-of-towners as they sat in the CAVEs, idling outside the city limits. Given the cornucopia of things to look at, Ret was slightly annoyed by a faint throbbing that was afflicting his hand. He attempted to shake it off, trying to focus instead on figuring out where they were, but the numbing feeling of something gnawing at his nerves refused to go away. In frustration, he averted his gaze and glared at his hand.

There it was—the complete scar, fully illuminated in the palm of his right hand. His eyes lit up. His heart began to beat a little faster with excitement. Like the course they had traveled, the squiggly line had made a sharp curve and then continued upwards briefly in a mostly straight line. At its end on the top was a curious shape, resembling a funnel or an upside-down cone. Ret still didn't know exactly what it meant, but he *did* know it was complete. He could feel it.

"This is it," Ret told everyone. "We're here."

"What makes you think that?" Mr. Coy asked from the other CAVE.

"My scar," Ret replied. "It's totally visible now."

Ret listened as Mr. Coy eagerly opened his door and hastened across the dry dirt to come and see the completed scar. The other passengers followed, forming a huddle in the space between the vehicles.

"What is that thing?" Paige inquired as they all stared down at Ret's outstretched hand.

"It's obviously a triangle," said Leo, "but what's this hooked object in the corner?"

Realizing Leo was examining the hook-and-triangle scar of the earth element, Ana pointed out, "Wrong scar, Leo; *that* one was so two elements ago."

"What do *you* think it could be, Ret?" Paige asked, reaching to hold his other hand.

"I'm not sure," he told her.

"If you ask me," Ana mumbled, "it looks a lot like that ugly recumbent flower vase Mom keeps on the piano."

As if sparked by a word that Ana had said, Lydia retrieved a pen and a piece of paper from her pocket and began to write something down.

"I still think it represents the original course of the Great River," Ret explained, "but I don't know what this thing on the top could be." He pointed to the inverted cone at the top end of the scar.

"It's the delta of the Nile River," Mr. Coy stated with certainty. Everyone stared at him, hoping to hear more. "Here, I'll show you." He stepped toward the CAVE and repositioned the GPS screen for all to see. "Let's zoom out." He did so until they could see the entire country of Egypt. "Now we'll switch to satellite view." Like looking from space, the map became colorful as it showed the natural geography of the globe. "This green line," he said, following a vertical strip in the eastern half of Egypt, "is the Nile River and the vegetation that grows along its shores. Up here," he pointed to the north end of the river, "is the Nile delta, where the river empties into the Mediterranean Sea. We are right *here*." He identified the small dot that marked their position, a fair distance south of the delta. "As you can see, we are only a few miles from the banks of the Nile."

"So the Great River connects with the Nile?" Ret postulated.

"It would seem so," Coy returned.

"Wow," Ret said with awe. "It really was a *Great* River, wasn't it?"

"My guess is," Coy continued, "once the continents split, the Amazonian half of the river was no longer able to feed the Saharan half, creating the Sahara Desert. But the Nile originates from different headwaters, further south of us, which probably allowed it to survive."

"Sorry to interrupt," Ishmael entered the conversation, "but Lydia wants me to tell you that, in her opinion, the scar looks just like the Nile lotus flower." He was holding the small piece of paper on which Lydia had written the words that she couldn't speak.

"See?" Ana whispered. "What'd I tell you about the flower vase?"

"Interesting," said Coy pensively. "Yes, they do bear a striking resemblance, don't they?" He stood in silent thought for a moment, his mouth askew as he considered Lydia's observation.

"What's the Nile lotus flower?" Paige inquired, ever eager to learn. Leo was glad she asked, as he was wondering the same thing.

"A type of water lily," her dad answered. "They used to be easy to find along the Nile but not so much anymore. The locals believe the flower has some kind of medicinal, spiritual powers."

"And Lydia used it to separate the gold from the sand when she discovered the underground river," Ret added. A sense of satisfaction fell upon Lydia's otherwise melancholy face, as if Ret was praising her accomplishment.

Glaring at Ishmael, Mr. Coy assumed, "You must have filled him in on the details." Ishmael nodded.

"Whatever the scar means," Ret summarized, "the ore element is somewhere in this city of gold."

"'Somewhere' is right," Mr. Coy said with gravity, gazing upon the sprawling city. Then, with a military air, he began to issue orders. "Conrad, get the CAVEs wet— use the extra water in the trunks." Conrad promptly sprung to action. "Ishmael, follow my lead—and lights off from here on out."

"Yes, sir," Ishmael obeyed. Everyone turned to reenter the CAVEs.

"We'll approach slowly—from the side," Coy said, still studying the landscape. "And Ret, be ready to redirect any bullets that might come our way."

"Bullets?!" Paige shrieked as she and Ana jumped into the backseat of the girls' CAVE.

Once Conrad had returned from spraying down the CAVEs, Mr. Coy asked Ret to fully coat each one in a thick layer of dust. As if his hand was a giant broom, Ret swept the ground outside and plastered the vehicles with a blanket of brown powder. Their homemade camouflage would not only shield them from view but also prevent the metallic exterior of the CAVEs from reflecting the brilliant city lights.

Leading the way, Mr. Coy proceeded toward the city. There was obvious alertness in his eyes, and the tires of each CAVE rolled slowly with caution. They steered directly to the closest side of the basin and climbed a good ways up the sloped riverbank, hoping to go unnoticed along the periphery. Their elevated position afforded them a bird's-eye view of the city.

It didn't take long before Ret realized the massive, golden wall at the rear of the region was not really a wall at all—it was a portion of one of the four sides of a giant pyramid. At least, Ret assumed it was a pyramid because, strangely, it bore no signs of having a traditional, pointed top. In fact, there was no real top to it; insofar as Ret could see, it was only the bottom half of a pyramid. As if the top had been chopped off, the sides were trapezoidal in shape, not triangular, and each one rose the entire height of the underground basin, making contact with the ceiling. Whether or not the structure extended past the roof, Ret couldn't tell, but he was pretty certain the decapitation was not the result of poor planning on the part of the architect.

For being just the base, the pyramid was colossal in size. It filled the width of the riverbed and dwarfed everything else in the vicinity. Amazingly, it was every bit as stunning as it was substantial. It was a structure of pure gold, whose every block was shining and shimmering with splendor. There was something mesmerizing about the pyramid—besides its greatness and beyond its spaciousness, there was something about the building that commanded one's attention and excited one's senses. Easily the most dominant feature of the city, it wanted to be looked at and admired, somehow infringing on the foreground though situated in the background. A part of Ret refused to let him take his eyes off of it, but there was so much more to see.

Immediately in front of the pyramid sat a large and lively industrial complex, about a mile square in size. It was clearly a very well-organized system for extracting natural resources. The wide mouths of open mines dotted the ground and slopes. Grungy workers hacked away at the soil like termites, searching for all kinds of ore and stone. Large loads of raw, metalliferous earth were being raised out of pits by cranes and then lowered to the floor where an army of pickax-wielding men descended upon them. Once separated from the dross, the valuables were hauled onto open-top hopper cars and transported from the site.

An impressive network of highways snaked through the entire compound. These were not beautiful boulevards carrying commuter cars; they were dirty roads for large trucks and trailers. Despite their number, however, every street eventually led to one, main, access road. The largest and most heavily trafficked, the access road appeared to be the only avenue for entering and exiting the basin. At a steady incline, it climbed the side of the riverbed and took its travelers to the world above-ground.

"I wonder what all of those towers are for?" Ret asked after losing count of the tall, scaffolding-like structures scattered all throughout the area.

"Those are derricks," Mr. Coy identified. "They're harvesting liquid gold."

"Liquid gold, sir?" Leo besought clarification.

"Yeah," said Coy in sober tones, "oil."

Suddenly, Ret became aware of the many oil tankers on the roads. These fuel-filled vehicles easily outnumbered all the other types combined.

As overwhelming as all of this was, it only pertained to what was happening on the ground. There was an entirely separate, though related, operation taking place on the ceiling—or at least on the other side of it. A large section of the underground basin's roof above the industrial complex was transparent. Ret could see directly through it into some sort of office building, whose employees looked down and monitored the scene below. What was a bottom floor for some constituted a glass ceiling for others.

And so, the legend of a city of gold was true after all. To be honest, Ret had never fully believed the myth, no matter how many cultures claimed it, and what lay before his eyes differed from what he had imagined in his mind. Based on how Rodrigo and Ishmael had described it, Ret had envisioned something of a cross between the Court of Versailles and the Greek Parthenon with a taste of Taj Mahal, but in reality it was more like a combination of Sunken Earth and Fire Island with a hint of Giza.

As it turned out, the city of gold was, by no means, a golden city. It was overflowing with opulence, yes; but in every other regard, it was as dry as the Great River in which it lay. For being such a rich place, it was staffed by the poorest of hirelings, each so filthy as to blend in with the ground. Meandering in a continuous circle was a manmade waterway, though its brown and murky water gave it the look and feel of a sewage line.

And then, rising high above the ugliness, was the mighty pyramid. So pristine and polished, its golden bricks stood in mocking contrast to the slaves at its feet.

At times, they would pause for a breath and, with idle eyes, look up at the pyramid. It was their taskmaster, and they hated their love of it. Every scoop of the shovel was an ode to the shrine; every nugget and jewel, a gift to the king. And even though they never received anything in return for their worship, oh how happy they were just to feel its golden gleam upon their faces!

Needless to say, it was a lot to take in for first-time visitors.

The CAVEs came to a stop. They were just outside the city now, still unseen in the shadows. Mr. Coy got out to take a closer look at the city.

"Where do you think I'll find the element?" Ret asked, arriving at his side.

"Well, seeing as the first element was in a mountain of earth and the second, a volcano of fire," Coy recalled, "I'd start looking in the pyramid of ore, if I were you."

"That's what I was thinking," said Ret.

"Oh," Coy added, "and you might need this." He handed Ret the Oracle.

It always made Ret feel happy to see the Oracle. He couldn't help but smile a little. It was like meeting an old friend—the kind of friend who is a silent giant, radiating an inner strength and peace of mind. The emotions surrounding the Oracle were antithetical to those of the pyramid. One was small and unobtrusive;

the other, huge and imposing. The ball seemed to say, "With me, all will be well," while the bricks threatened, "Without me, all will be lost."

"So you're not coming with me?" Ret assumed.

"I'm afraid this is where we leave you," Coy stated. "As soon as you collect the element, this whole place is going to collapse, so I need to get the rest of us to higher ground."

"By way of the access road?" Ishmael inquired, joining the group. "Looks like it's the only way out of here."

"Yes," said Coy pensively, "I don't think we have a choice. The CAVEs might fit right in with all the other utility vehicles on these roads, but I think we'll have a better chance of going unnoticed if we split up."

"How will Ret know where to find us?" Paige asked with concern, striding to Ret's side.

"Paige, dear," said Ana confidently, "remember last time, how you were about to be swallowed by that lava, and Ret came flying out of the volcano to save you?" Paige blushed. "Don't worry; wonder boy here's got it covered."

"Just be careful," Paige petitioned.

"I will," Ret pledged.

"You promise?"

"I promise." There was an awkward moment of silence, during which Ret thought he should at least give

Paige a hug, but with everyone else standing around and watching, he decided not to.

With the Oracle in one hand and the scar in the other, Ret set out down the sloped side of the riverbed toward the city of gold. He hadn't gotten far when he felt something nagging at him. This time, however, it wasn't his scar. He could feel Paige staring at him, still standing where he had left her. He kicked himself for missing another opportunity to show how much he cared for her. His thoughts rewound to his midnight chat with Leo. Suddenly, he was struck with an idea.

Paige was the last one to return to the CAVEs. She had stood exactly where Ret had left her, hoping that he would suddenly turn around, rush to her side, and kiss her like he had done at the rim of the volcano on Fire Island. But there was no kiss before the plunge this time. With a bit of dejection, she dragged her feet and heart back to the CAVE.

And then, off to the side, flames began to appear along the ground, where there was neither litter nor brush to fuel any sort of combustion. It was like a small-scale version of an airplane pilot drawing characters in the sky. Assuming it to be the work of Ret, the group watched as the letters R and P were formed, with a vertical line in between them.

"RIP?" Ana read. "Rest in peace?"

"Well that's morbid," Mr. Coy muttered.

Several steps away, Ret turned to glance at his work and realized he had forgotten to cross the vertical line in the middle.

"Oh, R + P," Ana reread. "Ret plus Paige!"

"Good save," Leo smiled, recalling the advice he had given Ret in their conversation.

Her heart relieved, Paige whispered with joy, "Go get 'em, Ret."

Now with one less passenger, both CAVEs approached the city and then parted ways, each taking a different course to enter the complex. Driving as inconspicuously as possible, they safely passed by a few excavation sites before joining the nearest road and merging with the flow of traffic.

"Everything alright, Ishmael?" Coy asked through the intercom.

"So far, so good," he replied.

There were no other vehicles on the roads that were quite like the CAVEs, but the sheer volume of trucks and tankers helped them to get lost amid the masses. Plus, the fact that they were still covered in dirt made it seem like they belonged.

Both CAVEs had entered the main access road and were proceeding smoothly when traffic began to slow. In fact, it slowed way down. The longer they were bumper to bumper, the more uneasy Mr. Coy became.

"You stopped, too, Ishmael?" he asked.

"Yes, sir."

"I can't see you," Coy stated, consulting his mirrors. "Are you behind me?"

"Yes," Ishmael reported, "quite a ways behind you. I can see *you* though." Thanks to the access road's continuous incline, Ishmael could see the other CAVE on a higher point of the road.

When the tractor trailer in front of him changed lanes, Mr. Coy was given his own glimpse of what was up ahead. He was struck with dread by what he saw.

"It's a checkpoint!" he lamented. "They're checking every vehicle!"

In her infinite wisdom, Ana said, "They're probably just going to ask if we have any fruit or something."

"This is bad, this is bad," Mr. Coy murmured to himself. His worry seemed strange to Paige. "Do you see any place to turn around, Ishmael?"

"I'm not seeing anything, sir," Ishmael told him. "What do you suggest we do?"

Biting his lip and tapping the steering wheel nervously, Mr. Coy searched around him frantically. Then, several yards ahead in the lane next to him, he saw a truck with a double-decker trailer for hauling multiple vehicles. To his delight, the trailer was full except for one space at the tail end of the bottom deck. It looked big enough for only one CAVE.

"Ishmael," said Coy, keeping an eye on the checkpoint as it grew ever nearer, "do you see that double-decker trailer in the far right lane?"

"Uh," he said, searching for it. Finally, "Yes, I see it." It was close to Coy but far from himself.

"There's room for one of us on there, so—"

In a rare move, Ishmael instructed his boss, "You take it, Ben. It's our best bet, and you need to keep the women safe."

It was not what Mr. Coy had been planning to do, but he knew Ishmael was right. He also knew he couldn't trade places or ask the three men in the other CAVE to cram into his own, as that would give them away.

The checkpoint was only a handful of car lengths away and coming up fast.

"We'll be fine, Ben," Ishmael reassured. "I'm too far behind; I'd never make it in time. Besides, I'm from this part of the world; I look like most of the men down here. I think I'll be able to sneak by. I'll just be *coy.*"

Mr. Coy was too preoccupied to smile. It was either now or never if he was going to take his place on the trailer. When his line had advanced a little further, he wedged his way into the right lane, putting him directly behind the trailer. He crawled toward the rear until the thick tread of his large tires was touching the metal of the bottom deck. Then, timing it with a bump in the road, he revved the engine and lunged forward, keeping his foot lightly on the gas so that the truck driver would not feel any drag. Then he slowly rolled onto the deck.

"Everyone, get down!" Mr. Coy whispered when they arrived at the checkpoint. The trailer paused briefly, then continued forward. They stayed frozen for several suspenseful moments. When the coast seemed clear, Mr. Coy peered over the bottom of the window. They were traveling at a normal speed now, with lots of other traffic around and still a considerable length of access road to go before they would be aboveground.

"Ishmael?" said Coy. "Where are you?"

"We're approaching the checkpoint," he informed. "Here goes."

Mr. Coy waited in silence, having an ear in Ishmael's CAVE thanks to the intercom.

"Hello, sir," Ishmael greeted the guard, who had two rifles strapped across his back and a pair of pistols at his belt.

The guard gave Ishmael a frustrated look, as if the checkpoint was common protocol and he ought to know what to do.

Finally, after getting nothing but a blank stare from Ishmael, the guard barked, "Sign?"

"Uh," Ishmael groped, "what kind of sign?"

Then, taking stock of the CAVE, the guard interrogated, "What vehicle is this?"

Things weren't looking good.

"Pull over to the side," the guard ordered. "Now!"

"Wait, wait," Ishmael implored patiently, "I found my sign." The guard peered through the window with a confused frown on his face. Ishmael leaned back and muttered to Conrad in the front seat, "Knock him out." Conrad promptly punched the guard in the face, sending him flying into his station.

They made a run for it. With a screech, Ishmael sped out of the checkpoint.

"How'd it go?" Coy asked.

Suddenly, bullets were heard ricocheting off the CAVE. The guard at the checkpoint had rebounded and was firing at the fugitives.

"That well, huh?" Coy surmised, having heard the gunshots.

Ishmael sped further up the access road, weaving in and out of traffic. He was feeling hopeful until he saw two armored vehicles pop up in his rearview mirror. A barrage of artillery was descending on the CAVE. Leo ducked in the backseat as the bulletproof glass of the rear window began to give way.

Ishmael spotted a long trailer up ahead. It was carrying a backhoe and other heavy equipment on its bed. Catching up to it, Ishmael pulled a lever on the control panel, deploying dagger-like knives attached to the center of each of the CAVE's wheels. He rammed into the trailer until he punctured one of its rear tires. The tread spun off, slanting the bed and sending the equipment rolling onto the road. The armored vehicles came to a halt to keep from crashing into the obstacles.

But there was no time to celebrate as three more foes appeared on Ishmael's radar. They had been behind the first two, and when the road had become blocked, they plowed through the cement barrier that divided the access road. The trio traveled on the wrong side of traffic before breaking through the divider again and resuming their pursuit of Ishmael. On the roof of one of the pursuing vehicles, a man with a rocket launcher was aligning the CAVE in his crosshairs.

Thinking fast, Ishmael swerved in front of an oil tanker. The driver moved from lane to lane, trying to get his tanker out of the line of fire, but Ishmael stayed with him. Ishmael was getting closer to escape every second; all he needed to do was buy time. Unfortunately, his merciless enemies knew this, too. They grew tired of Ishmael's game and fired on the oil tanker to get it out of the way. It burst into flames and fell back, exposing Ishmael.

With nothing to hide behind, Ishmael knew he either needed to face his foes or face death. Still speeding along, he pulled the emergency brake, sending the CAVE into a spin. In a split second, they had spun

180 degrees, and Ishmael shifted into reverse. Though they were still moving forward, they were now facing backward.

While keeping an eye on his mirrors to see where they were going, Ishmael looked through the back window-turned-windshield and fired off a few rockets of his own, effectively ending the pursuit.

Still backwards, Ishmael watched as a pair of helicopters rose from the mining grounds and into the air. He looked in his rearview mirror and saw the end of the access road approaching. He was almost there, still determined to make it. Then he saw the double-decker trailer. He was catching up to Mr. Coy's CAVE, which had still gone unnoticed. Ishmael reasoned that if he got much closer to the second CAVE, he would jeopardize the safety of his friends. Ishmael knew he couldn't do that, and although he wasn't aware of it, he had read Mr. Coy's mind. With bittersweet emotion, Mr. Coy watched Ishmael get closer and closer to him and his still-undetected CAVE. He wanted the others to escape, of course, but now that they were wanted men, Coy hoped to distance himself from them as much as possible.

Ishmael slowed down and maneuvered over to the edge of the road, still moving in reverse.

"Jump out!" he told Conrad and Leo. "Save yourselves!"

The two passengers hesitated for a moment, unwilling to leave Ishmael and unsure about self-ejection.

But the helicopters were closing in.

"Do it!" Ishmael yelled. "Now!"

Conrad and Leo pushed open their doors and leapt out of the CAVE. They landed on the dirt and began to roll down the hillside. When they finally managed to stop themselves, they both looked back to see if Ishmael was safe. Just as their eyes fell on the access road, the helicopters fired, and the CAVE exploded.

CHAPTER 20

THE PYRAMID OF WEALTH

With considerable pep in his step, Ret hiked down the hillside and into the industrial complex. Even though the situation was dangerous and the outcome unknown, he derived a measure of strength from knowing he had the support of his friends.

An up-close view revealed the excavation grounds to be somewhat of a wreck. In fact, the site looked much like the littered sections of the underground riverbed that they had traveled through on their way to the city of gold. Scrap metal, bent parts, trash, railroad ties, rusted tools, dozens of tires—it reminded Ret of a cross between a dilapidated barnyard and a messy machine shop.

As he crept through the compound, Ret was probably more cautious than he needed to be. No one seemed to notice him. Like circus roustabouts, the scruffy men stayed focused on their menial tasks at hand. They were too busy manning messy oil drills or scooping large payloads to give much attention to the outsider in their midst. And so, without resistance, Ret wound his way through the mess of trucks honking, cranes creaking, and workers shouting.

Where the grime of the industrial complex ended, the gleam of the pyramid site began. The distinction was like night and day. The ground went from being dark and icky to bright and smooth. It reminded Ret of walking to the beach back home, when the terrain changes from coarse asphalt to soft sand. There was a long stretch of nothingness before the first blocks of the pyramid began. Ret felt like an unsuspecting deer wandering into a quiet meadow as he walked out onto the dusty stone floor, instinctively glancing all around to make sure there were no watchtowers with snipers monitoring him.

Ret was but a tiny ant compared to the massive pyramid. It made him dizzy just looking at it, not only due to its overbearing size but also its exceeding luster. Keeping his gaze on the path ahead, Ret saw a small opening to the pyramid, near the middle and along the base, with a long corridor leading up to it. Ret bent his course in that direction. The corridor's floor followed a declining plane, and Ret strode the length of the downward ramp, like a car entering an underground parking garage.

When he reached the open doorway, Ret was greeted by a stunning sight. The pyramid was filled with riches. There was treasure everywhere, from corner to corner and from top to bottom. The architecture was equally impressive. The pyramid was mostly hollow inside. From his studies, Ret knew pyramids needed substantial amounts of interior support in order to keep from caving in on themselves. But this one seemed to defy gravity. Ret was more pleased than paranoid about the precarious design, however, as it meant the ore element was somewhere inside. He painfully recalled how both Sunken Earth and Fire Island had imploded when they no longer had their respective elements to uphold them. He quickly thought about something else.

Ret wondered if it might be more appropriate to refer to the six original elements as *powers* instead, for both the earth and fire elements—and now ore—exuded extraordinary amounts of real and raw power. This was in addition to their influence over like substances. This was a tangible energy, like heat from a campfire. It was living. That's how Ret felt as he entered the pyramid: he felt more alive—his senses more acute, his reflexes more accurate. Every cell and fiber of his body and mind seemed enhanced.

Due to a curious feature in its design, there were multiple stories within the pyramid. Off to Ret's right, a wide walkway began at the floor and slowly curved upward, like a ramp. It was connected to the inside walls of the pyramid and rose to the top like a spiral staircase without any steps. Because of the pyramid's size, the slope of this ramp was very gradual, and a great deal of the building's treasure had been stored along it like commodities on a shelf.

With awe as his guide, Ret began a slow-paced tour of the treasury. Gold was everywhere to be seen, alongside several different kinds of metal: silver, iron, copper, nickel—and many others that Ret couldn't even identify. They had been bent and molded into countless shapes and designs: coins and candlesticks, silverware and chandeliers, bars and bedrails. There were massive stockpiles here, neatly stacked ingots there—

And the jewels! Precious stones sat in heaps like laundry: diamonds so clear and rubies so red, next to sapphires of blue and emeralds of green; pearls, and the pink and purple hues of...of (Paige would know the name)—yes!, amethyst, that's it. The collection had the makings of a rich man's scavenger hunt: a diamond-studded dagger, a king's bejeweled diadem, a topaz-crested hand mirror, a gold serving tray, a silver goblet, a marble elephant with copper tusks—

Ret began his ascent to the second level, where there was much more than metals and stones. There were fine linens and lavish silks; royal rugs and imperial tapestries; large pieces of ivory and the purest of porcelain; even postage stamps and pottery—any and all kinds of artifacts of ancient date that would fetch a modern fortune. Then came the cash—stacks and stacks of nothing but bills and coins of every denomination and from every economy—booming or extinct. Dollars and pesos, euros and yen—even currencies that had long since been out of circulation: the denarius from ancient Rome, the daric from ancient Persia. The pyramid was literally a world bank.

Ret picked up a coin bearing the face of Caesar Augustus. He flipped it into the air with his thumb and let it fall into the palm of his hand. As if it belonged to him, the antique brought him a sense of pride, but it was covering up a strange mark on his palm. He moved the coin to the side. The strange mark was the lotus flower scar.

Ret came to himself. He took a step back and looked around. He had unknowingly climbed a great distance up the ramp of riches, admiring all the different treasures. He wasn't sure how much time had passed. He stood still for a few moments, breathing deeply and blinking repeatedly. He was feeling a bit frightened by how easily he had become consumed by the wealth all around him.

As he returned to the ground level, Ret seriously questioned if he could handle the power over ore that the procurement of the element would bestow upon him. Unlike previous elements, there were two powers at work here. The earth and fire elements could wield great power, yes, but at the end of the day, all they could really do was bury and burn stuff. Earth could reclaim, as in compost; and fire could purge, as in impurities. But ore could corrode—not so much its outer shell as its owner's soul. Ore could influence people; it carried greater weight; it was of more value. Metal seemed to have a mind of its own. Unlike earth, money is power; and unlike fire, cash talks. Did power over ore come with power over greed?

For the first time, Ret wasn't sure he wanted to collect the next element. With doubt as his new guide, he continued his tour of the resplendent riches of the great pyramid, this time with more worry than wonder. What had previously been a thousand gold mines and a million bank vaults was now, for Ret, one big problem. By collecting the ore element, he could easily become the world's richest man. Could he trust himself?

Of course, Ret knew it was no sin to be rich; prosperity was often the natural result of hard work and honest toil. But that's not what was troubling him. He feared that too many run-ins with decadence would put him on the outs with reality—that too sharp an increase in rich things would dull his sensitivity to poor people— people like Rodrigo and his family.

Ret recalled something the Amazonian had said: "What would *I* do with a city full of gold?" Ret asked himself the same question. Truth be told, if he inherited a city of gold, Ret would probably give it all away: a few gold bars to Rodrigo, a silver dollar to every citizen in Monrovia and Manaus, maybe even a couple bucks in the jar for Ana's car fund back home. That's what Ret would do with a city full of gold; he didn't have the heart to spend it on himself. He would give it to those in need.

Problem solved. The pyramid had revealed the inner thoughts and intents of his heart, and once they were made manifest, Ret knew he possessed the self-control and continence to procure the element and, thus, have power over all the ore in all the earth.

And so, it was within the wanton walls of the pyramid of wealth where Ret became acquainted with a new kind of power—a force more important, perhaps, than anything the Oracle or its elements could exert: the will of one's heart.

Just then, a strange object caught Ret's eye.

"Was that a camel?" he said to himself with absurdity. He glanced back for a better look. In between two heaps of treasure, he saw what appeared to be a statue of a camel. Unlike the dozens of other animal figurines he had seen in the pyramid, this one was neither gold nor silver; in fact, the dromedary had been hewn from rock, hump and all. Ret decided to take a closer look. His scar seemed to agree.

The camel was standing on a wooden floor. The planks, old and splintering, were all different shapes and sizes and had been laid in no particular pattern. There was not so much as a single gold coin on this section of the floor. On one side stood the camel, built to actual size but obviously chiseled by an unskilled hand. On the other side, across from the camel, there was a post with a simple oil lamp resting on top. It was an old, clay lamp, the kind that looked like the residence of a magic genie. The post was taller than Ret, but the lamp was not beyond his reach. In all, the complete scene (with camel on one end, post on the other, and wood in between) looked like a poorly-funded miniature basketball court with nontraditional hoops. It was ugly and terribly out of place amid so much beautiful gold. Ret wondered why anyone would care about an old oil lamp and a crudely-carved camel when there was so much treasure to be enjoyed.

He was beginning to think like a Guardian.

Ret walked up to the post. He reached to the top and brought down the dusty lamp. Except for a few cobwebs, it was empty and dry as a bone, with not even a wick to light. On the tip of the lamp, however, a needle had been driven into the clay. It stood straight up and was much larger than the ones Ret had seen Pauline use in her sewing. In fact, the opening for its eye was so wide that Ret reasoned this was a needle that even *he* could thread. Despite the absence of fuel, he kindled a small flame in the center of the lamp, behind the needle. Then he returned the lamp to the top of the pole.

When he turned around to address the camel, Ret saw something dancing on the floor. It was a shadow— a very faint one at that. A thin, dark line extended about halfway into the wooden court, and at its end was a large, hollow oval. Ret recognized it as the shadow of the needle that had been stuck in the oil lamp. The flame that he had conjured was casting the needle's shadow onto the wooden floorboards.

Ret walked along the line that represented the body of the needle. The floor felt unstable beneath his feet and creaked under the weight of each step. When he got to the part of the shadow that represented the needle's eye, he stood in the middle of the circle and stopped. Not sure what he was doing, he felt a little foolish, like a child playing hopscotch. The floor seemed to wobble in this circular spot, even more so than the others. He jumped in place, and when he landed, it teetered unmistakably, like standing on top of an in-ground utility box. There was clearly some kind of hole in the ground, and he was apparently standing on its lid as if it were the cap to a sewer. Whether buried treasure or some secret passageway, it seemed O marked the spot.

Ret walked over to the nearest treasure heap and dug out a golden rod. Using it as a crowbar, he tried to pry open the circular lid, hoping to lift it up. It was large, about the length and width of a small car, and he could only get it to bob back and forth. It was connected to something.

If he couldn't pull it up, perhaps he could push it down. Again, he jumped up and stomped down, but he didn't weigh enough. He needed something heavier.

And then Ret looked to the camel for help. It was staring back at him with a pathetic look on its face, as if it was disappointed that Ret hadn't solicited its assistance sooner. Ret was grateful it was made of rock, as he could use his power over earth to easily move it despite its great weight.

Suddenly, the peculiarity of the situation made perfect sense. Ret remembered how Argo, the Guardian of the Fire Element, had placed a boulder over each of the entrances into the lava tubes that led to the magma chamber and the fire element. Purposely placed in the way, it was an obstacle that the person with the scars could move with his previously-acquired power over earth. Argo had explained how Ret's First Father told the six Guardians which elements would be collected before each of theirs. And here it was again: Ret needed power over fire to light the empty lamp, which would cast a shadow as a hint, and then he needed power over earth to move the stone camel.

Knowing the element couldn't be far now, Ret hastily hauled the camel toward the round wooden lid.

The heavy statue dug into the wooden floor as its sturdy feet slid along the crumbling boards. In order to apply all the weight equally, Ret lifted the camel a few inches off the ground and set it gently in the eye's shadow. His heart skipped a beat as the circular slab of wood began to sink beneath the floor.

Slowly, Ret continued to shoulder less and less of the weight. As the camel descended deeper, it also pulled down the long stretch of floor that fell within the shadow of the needle's body. It was the narrow part that also felt unsteady as Ret had walked along it, and now he knew why. It was connected to both the circular platform and the post, and it became a sort of ramp as it went down on one side, still hinged to the base of the post. It was like Ret was in an attic and was now preparing to exit by means of a drop-down walkway.

When the load had become very light, Ret let go, and the camel pushed the platform a few more inches before it landed on solid ground. Ret gazed down into the long, rectangular opening that had just been formed. It looked a bit like a freshly dug grave for a very tall person. He walked over to the post where the ramp began. The darkness ahead was quiet and damp, but he wasn't scared as he started down the slanted walkway. Finding the final hiding place of each element seemed to be getting more and more difficult. Had he relied on the pyramid's treasure, he never would have found the entrance but would have spent an eternity wandering aimlessly. In the end, however, it had proven easier for a camel to go through the eye of a needle than for the riches to lead him to his goal.

When Ret reached the end of the ramp, he patted the camel gratefully and stepped in front of it. He found himself in a room that had the look and feel of a typical chamber in a normal pyramid—one that didn't rely on an element to support its weight. The place wasn't terribly large, covering the area of an average gas station, and looked like it had been scooped out of the very bedrock underneath the Great River. For a moment, Ret wondered if he had stepped inside the domed containment structure of a miniature nuclear power plant, for not only was it round and walled on all sides but he could also sense a great deal of raw power in the room. The rough, stony floor had all kinds of colorful lines cutting through it. There were gold lines, silver lines; some that showed a hint of green, others a touch of red; and several others that covered every shade of gray. They resembled veins and arteries as they bent and swooped across the floor, then up the walls and out of sight. There even appeared to be some type of solid material slowly moving through them. Each line led back to one main source in the center of the room.

And then Ret saw the ore element. On account of their small size, the elements were easy to overlook, but once Ret laid his eyes on them, he never wanted to look away. They were just plain glorious, but the ore element was even more magnificent than either the earth or fire elements. It was essentially a gold nugget, shining exquisitely as it floated in the air between the floor and ceiling. As if it were a beautiful piece of expensive jewelry rotating behind thick glass, the ore element was moving. It was gradually molding and remolding itself, like a glob in a lava lamp, aided by gold's soft and malleable properties. The element was alive.

Like the others before it, there was no solid ground below the lump of ore, just a bottomless hole that seemed to stretch all the way to the earth's core. As Ret unhurriedly advanced toward the element, he observed how all of the lines along the floor traced back to about two dozen main lines that were coming up through the chasm under the element. They almost looked like pipes—a gold pipe, a copper pipe, a lead pipe. It finally dawned on him that each line was pumping a different type of metal. In a constant stream, every different kind of pure metal—from aluminum to zinc—was flowing up from the inner layers of the earth and out into its crust. As the veins snaked away, they split and branched out, sometimes combining and mixing with other lines to create different alloys. It was like one giant plumbing system. Little wonder the Great River was once the source of all ore: it acted like a massive pipeline for the ore that seeped into its waters!

As Ret continued to admire the element, he waited for the Guardian to show himself, anticipating his sudden debut at any moment. Ret waited, stalled, even tapped his foot a time or two. But there was no sign of the Guardian. Ret wondered if he ought to just collect the element and leave, but he was really looking forward to meeting the Guardian. To be honest, their conversations had become one of his favorite things—a sort of reward for all of Ret's hard work in tracking down the element. Their dialogues always yielded so much new information—like last time, when Argo had given Ret that faulty hour glass and explained how Ret's First Father had given each of the six Guardians something that they were to give to the one with the scars. That was another reason Ret couldn't leave without first speaking with the Guardian: he needed to get whatever the Guardian had to give him.

Ret set out on a one-man search party to find the missing Guardian. Perhaps he was napping, as elderly people are known to do. Ret took a few steps away from the element and began a deliberate walk along the periphery of the room. The element and metallic veins didn't exactly light up the cavernous place, but it was enough for Ret to make out silhouettes among the shadows.

Finally, across from the camel and on the other side of the room, Ret saw something. There was a large hole in the wall, and it looked like the mouth of a long tunnel. Standing just inside the mouth was a dark figure, in the shape of a person.

"Guardian, sir," Ret called out to the shadow, "is that you?"

Ret held up his fist and kindled a flame above his thumb, but it didn't shine far enough to reveal the person's identity.

The mysterious individual began to walk towards Ret. It was the slow shuffle of a senior citizen. Relief flooded over Ret.

"You had me worried, sir," Ret said with a happy sigh. "It didn't seem right for me to collect the element without first speaking with its Guardian."

The figure made no reply but was coming closer to Ret with each step. Ret held out his arm as far as it could go, hoping his flame would shed some light on the stranger.

"Sir?" Ret said with growing suspicion.

A few more steps.

Now only a few yards away, Ret could see that the man was severely hunched over and walking with the aid of a cane.

"There's no *Guardian* here, Ret," the man finally spoke, his cold voice raspy and full of scorn. A horrifyingly familiar face came into view. "Just me."

It was Lye.

CHAPTER 21

MIND OVER MATTER

From the safety of their still-undetected CAVE, Mr. Coy and the girls watched Ishmael's failed escape attempt with great anxiety. With startled confusion, they saw the man CAVE slow down and pull over to the side of the access road, becoming an unmissable target for the pursuing helicopters. The choppers scarcely fired their missiles when the trailer that Coy and the girls were riding finally arrived aboveground, just before a large emergency gate made of solid steel sealed the access road shut.

They heard a loud explosion and felt a slight rumble. The CAVEs' intercom system went dead. They could see nothing and feared the worst. Mr. Coy tried to keep a shred of hope alive.

"Ishmael is smarter than that," he told the girls, trying to sound confident. "I'm sure he had something planned. And it takes much more than an explosion to slow down Conrad." His words provided little comfort.

The world above the ground looked much the same as it did before they went under it. They were still in the Sahara Desert, surrounded by a sea of sand. The inescapable sun caused their eyes to squint and their skin to burn, without a cloud in the sky.

The truck, with its double-decker trailer full of vehicles, drove a short distance beyond the mouth of the underground access road before coming to a stop near a large warehouse. The driver climbed down from the cabin and walked inside the building, providing a perfect opportunity for Mr. Coy to dislodge the CAVE. He shifted into reverse, slowly rolled off the end of the trailer, and drove away.

"Don't worry, ladies," he reassured his distraught passengers. "I'll find a way to open that gate and get back down there. I'm sure the guys are okay. We'll save them." Then, catching his daughter's worried eye in his rearview mirror, he added, "All four of them," making sure to include Ret. But it was a promise that Mr. Coy did not yet know how he was going to keep.

They found themselves in an office complex of sorts, something of a cross between a company's corporate headquarters and a retailer's distribution center. The many buildings were long and low. They all looked largely the same, unmarked and unnamed, so as to draw little attention to themselves (and the activities taking place therein). At times, Mr. Coy felt like he was driving in circles as he navigated the dirt roads that snaked throughout the compound. He wasn't sure what he was looking for exactly, and whenever the main gate to the access road came back into view, he checked to see if it had been reopened. No such luck.

Still roaming the roads, it came as no surprise to see a large pyramid not far from the group of buildings. It matched the many Egyptian pyramids that Paige and Ana had seen in pictures and movies. Though placed with astounding uniformity, its dusty blocks looked old and worn, with some even crumbling in a few places. This was an edifice of stone, not of gold like the one they had just seen on the underground riverbed. However, it was quite obvious that the pointed pyramid before their eyes was the top of the one now below their feet. So, in actuality, it was the same pyramid, not a different one—not a separate pyramid, just a separated one—with nothing but a thick layer of hardened sand keeping them worlds apart.

Suddenly, the CAVE came to an abrupt halt. Mr. Coy had turned a blind corner and rear-ended an improperly parked car. Uttering a grunt of dissatisfaction, he struck the steering wheel with a frustrated fist and stepped out to assess the situation. He worried that his blunder had put them in danger of being discovered.

The girls watched from the CAVE. Although they couldn't hear what was being said, they could see everything that transpired. While Mr. Coy's tank-like vehicle had sustained no damage, the other car looked like an elephant had sat on it. It was some kind of fancy SUV, no doubt carrying a VIP. A well-groomed chauffeur emerged from the driver's seat. He did not look happy as he marched, with arms crossed, to meet Mr. Coy.

As the irate chauffeur continued to rant, Mr. Coy seemed to be paying more attention to who was sitting in the SUV than what was being said to him. He repeatedly glared through the tinted windows, which appeared to anger the chauffeur even more. Eventually, the drivers returned to their respective vehicles.

"Lydia, quick," Mr. Coy said hastily as he leaned into the CAVE. "Do you have any sleeping gas?" Lydia immediately rummaged through her stash of potions and retrieved a couple capsules. She rolled them into Coy's outstretched hand.

"What's that for?" Ana asked.

"It's my proof of insurance," he replied with a hopeful smile.

"Oh boy," Paige said, rolling her eyes as her father paced away.

Mr. Coy strolled up to the driver's door. As soon as the chauffeur rolled down his window to exchange information, Mr. Coy threw the capsules into the SUV and scurried away. In an instant, sleeping gas filled the SUV's cabin, spilling out the chauffeur's window. When the gas had cleared, Mr. Coy returned to the SUV and entered the backseat. A few moments later, he exited, wearing a sports coat and carrying a briefcase.

"Did you just mug someone?" Ana accused when Mr. Coy had rejoined them.

"Not just someone," said Coy. Then, reading the name on the briefcase, "George V. Peck, to be exact."

"Who's that?" Paige wondered.

"Apparently, he's the guy who's taking a nap in the backseat of that SUV," Coy admitted, "and, I must say, he's got good taste in blazers." He held out his arms to admire the fine coat. Mr. Coy set the briefcase down in his seat and opened it. After sifting through a few papers, he concluded, "Looks like Mr. Peck is a Swiss chocolatier who came here to do some investing"—then, upon seeing financial figures, he added—"a whole lot of investing."

"Did Sir Peck happen to bring any chocolate with him?" Ana inquired.

"Actually, he did," said Coy, tossing a few samples into the backseat.

Closing the briefcase, Mr. Coy turned to face Paige and Ana and stated, "I need you two to stay here while Lydia and I have a look around. Hopefully we can find a way to reopen the access road and get back underground. We've got to find Ishmael, Conrad, and Leo and get to some place safe before Ret collects the element."

"What if someone notices us, Dad?" Paige asked.

"I'll put the CAVE in lockdown mode," Coy told her. "It'll be pretty much impenetrable. If you think you're in trouble, just give me a buzz, and we'll come back right away. Okay?"

Mr. Coy waited for either of the girls to say something. Finally, Ana said, smacking her lips, "This is really good chocolate." Mr. Coy smiled.

Once Lydia had disembarked, Mr. Coy made final preparations and then fully secured the CAVE. The two of them made an odd pair as they approached the nearest building. Lydia opened the door for Mr. Coy who, employing his best rich man's swagger, waltzed right inside.

"You must be Mr. Peck," a bubbly receptionist immediately greeted them.

"Please, call me George," Mr. Coy told her with a debonair tone.

"Pleasure to make your acquaintance, *George*," she said, charmed. "If you'll please follow me." She emerged from behind her desk and led them to a nearby elevator, her high-heels rapping against the hard floor. "The masters have been expecting you. I'll let them know you have arrived. The board room is on the second floor." The elevator doors opened with the sound of a bell. "Just keep walking until you see the double doors."

Enjoying the VIP treatment, Mr. Coy winked at the receptionist and said, "Thanks, doll face." Then, reaching inside one of his coat pockets, he grabbed a few small pieces of finely-wrapped chocolate and handed them to her before the elevator doors closed. "I'm a natural," he sighed to Lydia.

The elevator opened to a long and eerily empty hallway. Mr. Coy and Lydia moved forward slowly and cautiously. About halfway down the hall, a much shorter corridor turned off to their right. Before rounding the corner, Mr. Coy stopped and gently held out his arm to halt Lydia. He peered around the corner and down the corridor. It ended in the aforementioned double doors, each of which contained a large viewing window of transparent glass.

"I'll go in and talk to the bigwigs," Mr. Coy whispered to Lydia. "Maybe I can use Mr. Peck's money to get them to do what I want. You stay here." He back-tracked a few steps and opened the door to a custodial closet they had just walked past. "You'll be safe in here until I'm done." Then, with a sober expression, he said, "Put this on." He extended a curious headpiece to her. "It's a neuroscope." He placed one on his own head. "Yours is linked with mine, so we'll be able to commu-nicate with each other purely through thought. We've scarcely used them human-to-human before, but desperate times call for desperate measures."

Mr. Coy waited for Lydia to attach the neuroscope to her forehead, near each temple.

"Do you read me?" he thought, looking her in the eye but without speaking a word.

"Yes—yes, I do," Lydia thought back, in awe of the technology.

"Good," Coy spoke. "Then wish me luck."

"Good luck."

With all the confidence of a moneyed man, Mr. Coy stuck up his chin, puffed up his chest, and marched down the corridor. Then he pushed open both doors and waltzed into the room.

"Gentlemen!" he hailed broadly. "How do you do?"

Four men immediately rose from their seats at a large table and came forward to greet their guest.

"Good afternoon, Mr. Peck," one of them said, shaking hands.

"Welcome to the Sahara Desert," said another.

From the third, "It's a pleasure to meet you in person."

And the last, "You are much more jovial than you sound on the phone."

"I get that all the time," Mr. Coy explained with a laugh.

They rolled a fifth chair from the end of the table that was closest to the door and invited Mr. Coy to sit down. Then each returned to his own seat.

The board room was an exceptionally stately place that reeked of wealth. It was in the shape of a semicircle, and the long wall on its arc consisted of a single sheet of glass. There were no streaks or smudges on this wide window, permitting an unobstructed view of the complex outside. Fine marble pillars supported a high ceiling, and there was little need for lighting on account of the vast amount of natural light pouring through the window. The entire expanse of the floor was the see-through lid of a terrarium, where all kinds of creatures lived in captivity. It proved difficult for Mr. Coy to ignore the sight of tarantulas and scorpions crawling just inches under his feet, and he tried not to hear the sound of sharp-fanged snakes striking the glass in their attempt to attack him.

Mr. Coy propped his elbows on the table. It was a handsome piece of furniture, its rich wood a dark red color. There was a large silver pitcher in the center, next to an icebox and a small glass cup. The four men each sat so as to be facing their investor. They looked older than Mr. Coy, though not too advanced in years yet. Each had black, cottony hair and a short, untrimmed beard. They wore suits but without ties, choosing to leave the topmost button of their white shirts unfastened.

A nameplate sat on the desk in front of each of them, turned away from them so that Mr. Coy could read each of their titles: weapon master, commodity master, artifact master, and potion master.

"Potion master?" Lydia thought with sudden frenzy. Thanks to the neuroscopes, everything that was being processed by Mr. Coy's mind was being transferred to Lydia's mind. The window, the pillars, the terrarium, the desk, the masters, even the brightness of the light and the scent in the air—every piece of information that Mr. Coy's senses were picking up was being converted by his brain into electrical impulses that his neuroscope was intercepting and transmitting to Lydia's brain through her own neuroscope. Though separated, they were like human cell phones—living walkie-talkies, or two networked computers—freely sharing their experiences.

"The potion master is there?" she thought again in disbelief.

"It may not be the same man," Mr. Coy responded, worried how Lydia might react if the master who had cursed her was in the room.

"It IS him!" she thought with rage. *"Half-moon glasses and a wart by his nose—it's him alright."* Mr. Coy wished he hadn't looked back and stared at the potion master, as Lydia had seen the man through Coy's eyes. This was one of the many complications to using

the neuroscopes human-to-human: they were all but impossible to keep under control.

Suddenly, a flurry of angry emotions flowed into Mr. Coy's mind, pouring in like floodwaters through Lydia's neuroscope. Mr. Coy could see the memories that were flashing before Lydia's mind. He could feel her pain and taste her sorrow.

"Lydia, control your thoughts," he instructed gently. *"I can hardly think for myself."*

"Yes, sir." The flood abated and was replaced by boring observations of a mop in the janitor's closet.

Thinking with someone was much more efficient than *speaking* with someone, as Mr. Coy and Lydia's mental conversation had consumed a grand total of just a few seconds.

"We're glad you could meet with us today, Mr. Peck," said the weapon master. "We thank you for your initial investment of 500 million Swiss francs."

"As you can see," the commodity master interrupted, proudly handing a spreadsheet to Mr. Coy, "your funds have already turned a sizeable profit."

"Yes, indeed," said Coy, studying the paper. He was amazed by the large sums on the sheet. "I wonder, gentlemen, if you might be able to tell me a little bit more about your operations here—your history, your future?" Since he didn't know what the masters may have already told George Peck, Mr. Coy chose his words carefully. The men seemed leery of their associate's motives, so Mr. Coy let Mr. Peck's money do the talking. "Before I invest further in your business, I would like to know much more about it. It's good due diligence, as I'm sure you can relate."

The masters took turns glancing at each other warily.

"How much more money are you willing to invest, Mr. Peck?" asked the artifact master.

"That depends on how much information you are willing to disclose," Mr. Coy said without hesitation, employing a sly smile. The masters exchanged greedy grins; they were willing to spill all of their beans if it meant they could take every last one of his.

"Do you see that pyramid over there?" the artifact master began, pointing out the window toward the ancient edifice that towered above the other buildings. "That structure is but the peak of a much larger pyramid, most of which is hidden underneath the sand. It was built thousands of years ago in the dried basin of a Great River, which used to flow through this desert, according to our lord." Upon referencing their lord, each of the four masters immediately closed his eyes, bowed his head, and put his hand over his heart. They held the pose for a second or two, clearly as a sign of reverence.

Ignoring their strange ritual, Mr. Coy pretended he had no idea concerning the information that was being presented. "A river? In the Sahara?" he marveled. "You can't be serious."

The artifact master continued: "Our lord"—again, the sign of adulation—"is very old and very wise. He remembers the days when the Great River spanned the length of the supercontinent, many millennia ago. Soon after the landmasses divided and the Great River became extinct, he discovered untold treasures all along the banks of the dried riverbed and even a mother treasure underneath it, completely unknown to the rest of the world. He created an underground vault at this very spot, where he stockpiles precious metals and stones in all their varieties—all collected from different regions along the dried river basin. He knew this priceless vault of ever-increasing treasure must be protected at all costs, so he convinced the pharaoh of his day to construct a magnificent pyramid on top of it to keep it hidden and safe. Of course, he told the Egyptian king nothing about the vault but instead promised that the structure would serve as the pharaoh's private burial place. The pharaoh loved the idea and spared no expense to build himself a glorious tomb."

"Sounds like a man after my own heart," Coy said in the spirit of Peck. The masters laughed with delight, obviously in agreement.

"The concept of building pyramids worked out even better than our lord"—the sign—"had planned," said the artifact master. "Each succeeding pharaoh wanted a pyramid for himself—a pyramid that was bigger and better than the one before it."

"So would I," Coy inserted.

"But it took a long time to perfect the design. The pyramid of our lord"—sign—"had been relatively easy to build; it miraculously did not need any inner support due to the immense power of the mother treasure. But the subsequent pyramids were a different story. It took years for the pharaohs just to figure out how to prevent the pyramids from caving in on themselves. The shape of the foundation, the slant of the walls, the type of stone—it was a trial-and-error endeavor that spanned hundreds of years, required thousands of workers, and drained the kingdom's coffers."

Suddenly, the commodity master took control of the conversation: "And therein lies the genius of our lord"—Mr. Coy was getting tired of the signs—"because the pharaohs' obsession with pyramid-building made them blind to just about everything else, including the riches to be found in their own land. When the Great River's basin became completely buried by the sands, our lord"—Mr. Coy looked away in disgust—"was able to greatly expand his operation, totally in secret. He tapped into the basin's vast natural resources, finding gold and silver, precious stones and coal, even oil—from here all the way to the Atlantic coast. He had a monopoly, and no one knew it."

"But the original river of ore had never been designed to be hidden," interjected the potion master. "Before it ran dry, it was a heavily traveled waterway that was the lifeblood of the supercontinent. There were inverted golden arches placed in regular intervals all along the riverbed, marking the many ports and towns and shipyards, and when the sun or moon shined through the pure water to the arches, a reflection would appear like a rainbow above the river—inviting, beckoning one and all to come and see and freely partake of its riches. But our lord"—Mr. Coy mockingly joined them in making the sign—"knew this could not continue if he was to retain his dominion. The arches were too generous, too revealing; they would lead anyone and everyone to the river's great wealth. So he called upon the local species—the river dolphin, the piranha, the caiman, the bat, the cobra—and cursed them to forever be protectors of the golden arches. The massive arches still line the riverbed to this day, but they have been buried by centuries of silt and sand. I am honored to be the one who maintains the curses on those chosen, lethal creatures, should the arches ever be exposed."

As soon as the potion master had begun to speak, Mr. Coy could sense a resurgence of bitter feelings entering his mind. They were not his own; they were Lydia's.

Mr. Coy reached across the desk and grabbed the pitcher. Then he dropped a few ice cubes in the single glass and poured himself a drink. When he looked at the bluish liquid coming out of the pitcher, Lydia immediately warned:

"Don't drink that!"

"Why not?" he thought back.

"It could be poison," she told him. *"It looks identical to one of the potions my master used when he cursed me."*

"I'm glad you told me," Coy confessed. *"I just thought it was Kool-Aid."*

Now that he had poured himself a drink, Mr. Coy couldn't just let it sit there without drinking it. Maybe if he stirred it for a while, the masters would forget about it. He reached into Mr. Peck's designer jacket to see if he could find a straw or a pen—any long thing he could use for stirring. All he could find was a couple of chocolate-flavored suckers, each packaged in a lovely gold wrapper. Leaving the wrapper on, he dipped the sucker in his glass and began to stir.

Meanwhile, the weapon master continued the lecture: "In more recent times, once the infatuation with building pyramids died and the ancient empires were broken up, our lord"—Mr. Coy decided to start making his own signs, beginning with a thumbs-up—"saw the need to enter an alliance with the rulers of the neighboring nations. Although he liked the fact that most of them were tyrants and despots, he knew they would likely pose a threat to his enterprise unless they were in league with him. He won them over easily, showering them with all manner of riches. The leaders actually preferred the arrangement because while they effortlessly inherited loads of dirty money, their hands looked clean, insofar as their people could tell."

"So if I were to invest further," Coy put forth, still stirring his potential poison, "what would happen to my investment if the people were to throw off our friends, the tyrants, and establish a more democratic form of government?"

The weapon master laughed and said, "Haven't you ever heard of the golden rule, Mr. Peck? He who owns the gold makes the rules." The other three masters snickered. "The masses can revolt all they want, but money always wins. In his infinite wisdom, however, our lord"—Mr. Coy made a peace sign—"foresaw the possibility of the fall of certain dictatorships. That is why he joined with us, the masters. You see, we are the leaders of tribes, not nations. We purposely keep our people primitive, outside the confines of countries and the rule of law. We are the real authority in this land, a truth already understood by our lord"—Mr. Coy tried a hang-ten sign. "Some of our tribesmen have rebelled; one even came close to discovering the Great River basin."

"But we took care of her," the potion master inserted with a fiendish smile. Mr. Coy could feel Lydia's gall mounting.

While the masters were chuckling at the potion master's comment, Mr. Coy thought it was a good opportunity to finally stop stirring his drink. When he lifted the sucker out of the blue beverage, he was stunned to see nothing on the submerged end of the stick: it had been completely dissolved, and the remnants of the golden wrapper and chocolaty candy were sitting on the bottom of the glass.

"Told you," Lydia thought.

Still, Mr. Coy was dying to taste any sucker that was wrapped in foil that contained real flecks of gold. Fortunately, he found a backup in his pocket, unwrapped it, and popped it in his mouth.

"Gentlemen," Coy put forth, after a hearty lick of his lollipop, "does your lord"—he cringed at his folly, shaping his hand in the form of a gun and putting it to his head—"have a name?"

"He insists we call him our lord," explained the artifact master before the group executed the sign, during which Mr. Coy fanned out his hand, put his thumb on his nose, and fluttered his fingers as a token of his respects.

"And has he," Coy inquired, making sure to use the pronoun, "ever told you anything in particular about

the so-called 'mother treasure' that is hidden underneath the pyramid?" By this point, Mr. Coy already
knew their lord was Lye and that the mother treasure
was the ore element, but he wanted to know what Lye
had told them.

"He has not," the commodity master explained,
"but we think we know what it is."

"Oh?" said Coy. He was very curious to hear their
theory.

"We think it is the mother root of the Nile lotus
flower," the weapon master said. Mr. Coy had to fake a
cough to cover up his laugh, though he wasn't surprised
that Lye hadn't told them everything.

"Excuse me," Coy begged. "The what?"

"The Nile lotus flower," affirmed the potion
master after his three associates turned to him in
deference. "It is a blue lily, native to the Nile, and
maintains some sort of affinity with ore. It has the
unique ability to dissolve solids without harming any
metal that might reside within said solids. Since it grows
in water, it made the Great River a literal goldmine,
preventing the majority of the river's ore from being
trapped in rock and mud. Long ago, our lord"—Coy
stuck his finger up his nose—"commanded that all lotus
flowers be removed from the Nile and stored in his
pyramid. Consequently, the lotus species has been
virtually eradicated. It would be devastating if the flower

became common again; then anyone could become rich—and at *our* expense!"

"Though you've become rich at ours!" Lydia sneered.

"Am I correct to assume that this blue drink in front of me is a product of the Nile lotus flower?" Mr. Coy wondered.

"Precisely," beamed the potion master.

"And you were just going to let me drink to my death?" said Coy with more amusement than offense.

"We would have admonished *you*, Mr. Peck," the commodity master chortled. "We only use it as leverage with our more frugal donors."

As interesting as all of this information was, none of it really helped Mr. Coy in realizing his original purpose of devising a way to reopen the access road and save his friends. He knew it was only a matter of time before Ret procured the ore element. Struck with a brilliant idea, Mr. Coy decided to ask the masters for a tour of the underground site as a means of getting back down there.

"Before I cut you a check," said Coy, "I was wondering if you—"

"No more questions, Mr. Peck," the artifact master said sternly. "We've divulged quite enough of our secrets already. It's time for you to reimburse us for our generosity."

"Lydia, I need you to get me out of here," Coy thought as he stared into the unflinching faces of the four masters. *"Do you have any potions on hand?"*

"Always."

"Okay, sneak up to the double doors, and let me know when you're there," Coy told her. *"On your way, think of a plan."* He got lost in Lydia's thoughts as she sifted through many different options of escape.

With a deep breath, Mr. Coy smiled broadly at the four frowns across the table. He folded his hands together and rested them on the edge of the desk.

"Just one last question," he told them.

"I'm here," thought Lydia.

With a slick grin and a raised eyebrow, the Peck impostor removed the sucker from his mouth and asked, "Have you ever—*Ben Coy?*"

In a flash, the double doors flew open, and Lydia rushed into the room. Mr. Coy chucked his sticky sucker at the masters, and it stuck to the window. Lydia grabbed Coy's wheeled chair and pulled it backwards. As he rolled to his exit, Mr. Coy waved goodbye to the masters. Before he passed through the double doors, however, Lydia removed the neuroscope from his head and retained it in her hand. As soon as Mr. Coy had safely rolled out of the room, Lydia quickly sealed the double doors with a pasty potion, locking herself inside with the masters.

"Lydia!" Coy shouted, springing from his chair and sprinting back towards the room. "What are you doing? Get out of there!" Though he was banging on the doors, Lydia pretended not to hear him.

The masters had risen to their feet, their faces awash with alarm as if they had just been tricked by a fraud. The weapon master pressed a button underneath the desk. A small panel on the tabletop retracted, exposing a secret compartment where a loaded gun was hiding. Before the weapon master could grab the firearm, however, Lydia blew through a small dart blower and stuck him with a tranquilizer. He fell back into his seat, unconscious. Then Lydia lodged darts in both the artifact and commodity masters, who fell to their knees and then slumped to the ground.

"Well, well, well," the potion master slowly said, loud and proud. "Who do we have here?" He waited a few seconds for a response. When none came, he put his hand to his ear. "I'm sorry; I didn't hear you. Oh, wait! That's right: you can't speak, can you, Lydia?" He chuckled with sick pleasure. "Is that your friend out there?" The potion master motioned to Mr. Coy, who was watching the showdown through the glass panels in the door. "Did he bring you all the way here—just so you could see me? Oh, Lydia," he crooned, "my heart is touched."

Lydia shook her head.

"No?" the potion master continued. "Then why *are* you here? To seek revenge? For vengeance?"

Again, Lydia answered in the negative.

"Then you must have come to die!"

Suddenly, the potion master attacked. What happened next, from Mr. Coy's point of view, looked like a battle between two sorcerers, each hurling potions at the other like wizards wielding wands. The inside of the master's coat was lined with dozens of tiny jars and flasks, as colorful as a box of crayons. One after the other, he flung them at his former apprentice. They shattered and exploded, created streams of sparks and flashes of light. As if playing a game, he laughed as he lobbed each solution, losing track of his opponent amidst the flames and smoke.

Meanwhile, Lydia was desperately trying to protect herself from the onslaught of toxic tonics. Mr. Coy watched as she cast up temporary walls and fiber-glass barriers to block each attack. Like fireworks, the flaming and fizzing fluids ricocheted off Lydia's defenses, colliding with lights on the ceiling and coloring the walls with scars of a warzone. One potion struck the curved window and shattered it to pieces. Another splattered on the double doors, prompting Mr. Coy to take cover.

Eventually, the floor at Lydia's feet began to melt, due to all the volatile potions that were puddling up in front of her blockades. Just before the glass at her feet broke away, she leapt from her haven and rolled behind the pillar that was furthest from the potion master.

A hush fell over the scene. The potion master suspended his assault and waited for the air to clear. He saw how the floor had given way where Lydia had been standing. There were critters crawling out of the terrarium, but there was no sign of her. Assuming she must be hiding behind one of the thick pillars in the room, the potion master walked towards the pillar closest to him. On the way, he swung by the table and picked up the gun that was still resting in the hidden compartment.

"You know, Lydia," he teased as he neared the first pillar, "it's a shame you lost your voice. I'm sure there's so much you'd like to say to me."

Suddenly, he stepped to the backside of the pillar and fired the gun. Had Lydia been there, he would have taken her by surprise, but the space was vacant. The master moved on to the next pillar.

"Even if you *could* speak, I wonder what you would tell me," he continued to taunt. "That you hate me? That I ruined your life?" Like before, he spun around and fired behind the pillar. The bang echoed against the high ceiling, but Lydia wasn't there.

"You know, I really hated cursing you," said the master, advancing to the third pillar. Along the way, he went around the hole in the floor and passed by the double doors, where Mr. Coy was still observing the brawl through the glass panels. "You were my most gifted student. But you were too smart for your own good." He fired a third shot. Miss.

There was only one pillar left, hence the smile on the master's face. Having run out of potions, Lydia knew she was in a precarious situation. The only possible tool she had on her was the belt around her waist. It might just work.

"Well, it was good to see you, Lydia," the potion master said with closure as he arrived at the final pillar. "But I'm afraid it's time to say goodbye."

Knowing which side her former master would attack from, Lydia grabbed the pillar with both hands on that side and swung herself around from the opposite side, her body parallel with the floor. The gun fired, and the wasted bullet bounced away. Lydia collided, feet first, into the potion master's back. He hit the wall face-first, and any remaining potions in his suit coat were smashed upon impact. Wasting no time, Lydia looped the end of her belt, slipped it around one of the master's wrists, and tightened it as hard as she could. Then she pulled the master away from the wall and swung his back into the pillar. Still holding onto his wrist, she grabbed his other one and yanked them together behind him, around the back of the pillar. The master howled as

Lydia bent his arms way back and tied them with her belt. With amazing speed, she had secured him to the pillar.

The potion master was speechless, partly because of Lydia's swift maneuvers but mostly because he could barely breathe. Plastered against the pillar, his arms were bent so far back that his hands were almost touching. The distortion was pinching his lungs and threatened to dislocate his shoulders, and it was wildly painful.

Having silenced the potion master, Lydia made her next move without haste. She picked up the gun and threw it out the window without so much as a thought of using it. Then she brought out the pair of neuroscopes from her pocket. She placed one on her head and the other on the master's head.

"I have only one thing to say to you," Lydia told him through thought. Stunned by the technology of the neuroscope, a look of surprise seized the master's face, and Lydia knew he was understanding her thoughts. Then his expression turned to fearful anticipation as he waited for what she would do to him. The defenseless potion master was in a state of total submission to his former pupil. After years of untold suffering and misery, Lydia was finally in a position to avenge her injustices. There were acrid tears in her quivering eyes, evidence that she was about to do something that was not easy for her to do.

Lydia looked her curser dead in the eye and thought, *"I forgive you."* She removed his neuroscope and unfastened the belt. The master fell to the floor, gasping for breath.

Lydia turned and began to walk towards the door. Mr. Coy was standing on the other side, an impressed smile on his face. In the thoughts they had shared earlier, he had gotten a small taste of the pain that Lydia had endured for years. Her memories were so agonizing and her emotions so deeply bitter that he was fully expecting Lydia to fight the potion master to the death. But Mr. Coy was happy that she had proven him wrong, and he had just learned for himself that revenge isn't sweet—forgiveness is.

Unfortunately, however, Lydia's magnanimous deed was not enough to change the potion master's wicked heart. Regaining some semblance of strength, he stumbled to his feet and lunged toward the table. Her back turned, Lydia was standing at the double doors, undoing her seal.

"Lydia, look out!" Mr. Coy yelled.

But it was too late. The master picked up the pitcher on the desk, lifted it behind his head, and heaved it at Lydia. It hit the wall above her, showering her with blue liquid. Standing just inches from her, Mr. Coy watched in shock as the extract from the Nile lotus flowers washed over Lydia's body, dissolving her into dust before his very eyes.

Evil laughter filled the air. The potion master cackled with glee at his heinous act. Mr. Coy felt no obligation to inform him that a massive boa constrictor was slithering towards him. Mr. Coy looked away as the snake pounced, wrapping its powerful body around the potion master. The murderer's mirth turned to misery as the hungry boa slid back through the hole in the floor, dragging its prey to his unsightly death.

With the seal now cracked, Mr. Coy kicked open the double doors and fell to his knees at the pile of Lydia's ashes. There was only one thing that hadn't been reduced to dust. He cradled it in his hands and wept.

CHAPTER 22

HEARTS OF GOLD

Conrad and Leo had hardly begun to mourn the loss of Ishmael when they realized he had survived the man CAVE's explosive demise. After the two of them had leapt from the vehicle and while they were rolling down the access road's long hillside, Ishmael had made a similar escape. He put the CAVE on autopilot, which kept it moving at a subdued speed, and then jumped onto a faster-moving truck as it caught up to him from behind. He latched onto the trailer, holding on for dear life, as it surpassed the CAVE, which was blown to bits a few moments later.

Halfway down the hillside, Conrad and Leo watched with relief as Ishmael climbed the side of the truck and into its open-top trailer full of coal. Although the access road had just been sealed shut by a steel gate, they knew their friend would eventually make it out

O 415 O

safely, which was more than they could say for themselves. Dozens of guards were converging on the scene of the explosion, and the helicopters were scanning the area with their searchlights. The two fugitives knew they needed to keep moving or risk being detected.

Leo looked to Conrad for direction. The former slave was much more accustomed to taking orders than giving them. As they scanned the landscape below them for a place to hide, Conrad saw a small figure moving toward the great, golden pyramid. It was Ret.

Conrad placed his massive hand on Leo's head and turned it so that Ret's location fell into Leo's line of vision.

"It's Ret!" Leo cheered. "He must be going to get the element."

Without a word, Conrad started down the hillside toward the pyramid.

"Conrad, sir," Leo called out to him, "where are you going? To help Ret?"

Conrad stopped, turned around, and gave one distinct nod of his head before continuing onward.

"Wait!" Leo petitioned, finding himself alone. "I'll come, too!"

It proved difficult for Leo to keep pace with Conrad, who moved with all the grace and strength of a stallion. With urgency, they flew to the base of the pyramid. When Conrad set foot in the ancient structure, he stopped and stood completely still. A winded Leo arrived at his side a few moments later. Conrad was wholly uninterested in the astounding array of riches before their eyes. Instead of focusing on what there was to see, he seemed more interested in what he could hear. He held his finger to his lips, prompting Leo to hush his heavy breathing. Then Leo heard it, too: voices — very faint voices.

"Lye?" Ret asked incredulously, falling back a few steps in shock. "What are you doing here?"

"Always so surprised to see me," Lye chuckled. "Haven't you realized yet that I know much more about the Oracle and the elements than you do, Ret?"

"But the Guardian?" Ret wondered. "Where — where is he?"

"Oh, you mean Krypto?" Lye shrugged. "He's been dead for centuries."

"Dead?" Ret balked. "He can't be dead. The Earth Guardian, Heliu, told me how the elements give them unnaturally long life — how each Guardian can't die until his element is collected."

"Bah!" Lye spat with contempt. He was obviously perturbed by the conversation, as if talking about the Guardians was one of his least favorite things to do. "All the element does is postpone death; it doesn't make them invincible. Withhold oxygen from someone long enough — even a Guardian — and he will die. Just ask Krypto." Lye grinned.

"You killed him?" Ret winced with sorrow.

"I had to," Lye rationalized without remorse. "He refused to surrender his guardianship. How could I have constructed this magnificent pyramid and amassed my vast fortune with Krypto in my way?" Then, with derision, he pouted, "Humph! Krypto: a *Guardian*. The First Father couldn't have picked a worse steward for the ore element. I never met anyone who cared less about wealth than Krypto."

Ret dropped his head in profound sadness, lamenting his lost opportunity to learn plain and precious wisdom from the mouth of a Guardian. He also remembered the Fire Guardian, Argo, telling him how his First Father had given each of the Guardians a curious object, with the instruction to pass it on to the person with the scars. But now, thanks to Lye the killjoy, there was no way for Ret to receive such a gift from Krypto. No bother, really; Ret didn't know what purpose the trinkets served anyway—and neither could Argo recall such—so it couldn't be very important.

Ret grieved, "I was really looking forward to meeting the Guardian—Krypto."

"Why? So you could tell him all about your trip to the Amazon?"

Ret's head shot up in disbelief. "How do you know about—"

"I know everything, Ret," Lye hissed. "Hope my river dolphins didn't rough you up too much."

"You mean—"

"Yep," Lye nodded with pride. "My pets."

"I should have known," said Ret, shaking his head in disappointment. "So it's you who keeps the golden arches protected. You who makes sure anyone who uncovers them is stopped. You who continues to milk this land for all it's worth while its people suffer— people like Lydia."

"I'm sorry, who?" Lye played dumb.

"It's you—all you," Ret accused.

"Yes, I deserve all the credit," Lye rejoiced.

"All because of your greed—your love of money."

"You can buy anything in this world with money, Ret," Lye told him.

"That's not true."

"Oh, it's not?" Lye challenged. "Tell that to the armies and navies at *my* command. Tell that to the countless judges and lawyers who do *my* bidding. Tell that to the businessmen and women who work for *me.*"

"I don't believe you."

"Believe it, Ret!" Lye threatened. "I have infiltrated every level of society—the corporate, the legal, the civic—you name it, my people are there, running the show. You see, I not only launder money, Ret—I do it with people, too; and the masterful thing is most of them don't even realize it. Money is power, and I control this world with an invisible hand. Create a big enough bureaucracy, ensure no one can see the end from the beginning, run things through enough hands, keep widening the gap between the top and the bottom, and cha-ching! The world of wealth is a pyramid for a reason, Ret."

"You're wrong!" Ret refuted, his voice quivering.

"Then why the tears, Ret?" Lye asked calmly, calling Ret out. As much as Lye's words were getting under his skin, Ret knew there was a lot of truth to them, based on what he had seen of the world and its people. Lye yelled, "I'm right, and you know it!"

"But people can change," Ret said hopefully.

"Don't make me vomit," Lye gagged. "Humans are all hedonists in the end. Love of self will always supersede love of neighbor."

Ret asserted, "We can change our hearts."

"This world will never change," Lye dismissed. "You'd waste your life trying."

"No," Ret countered with growing confidence, "I'd waste my life by *not* trying."

"Fool!"

Suddenly, Lye attacked, swinging his staff at Ret's head. Ret ducked, narrowly missing the blow, and moved quickly to create a fast-growing mountain of earth at Lye's feet, hoping to pin him to the ceiling. Lye slid down the dirt slope and ran back to his dark tunnel to escape the landslide of soil.

Ret knew his first priority was to collect the ore element, not engage in battle with Lye. Turning his attention to the golden nugget floating peacefully in the air, he flew to the edge of the bottomless pit and eagerly reached in his pocket. He cupped his hands together and cradled the Oracle underneath the element. Like before, the Oracle rose a few inches above Ret's palms and aligned its scars with their twins on his hands.

Just as the Oracle was about to open into its six distinct wedges, an untimely and unfortunately familiar sensation washed over Ret. As if a blazing sun had risen behind him, he began to feel very warm, even feverish. Nausea quickly set in. Dizzy and lightheaded, his vision grew blurry, and suddenly he could see multiple versions of the same ore element dancing in front of him. With legs of gelatin, his knees gave out, and he fell to the floor.

The Oracle closed its wedges, having been whisked away from its third element prematurely. It fell out of Ret's limp hands and rolled away, coming to a stop in front of Lye's feet.

"What's the matter, Ret?" Lye wheezed with delight, emerging from the tunnel. "Feeling ill, are we?" He slowly walked towards Ret, stopping a few steps in front of him.

"What's—what's happening—to me?" Ret struggled to say, obviously in great pain. He was drenched in sweat now, writhing prostrate on the ground. He had kept his eyes on the Oracle and yearned to regain it but was powerless to do so.

"I found your weakness, Ret," Lye celebrated, "your one weakness."

Lye was clutching a most peculiar weapon. It was a long and bulky firearm, with a lead shield in front of a thick midsection. If Ishmael had been in the room, he would have recognized it as the same gun Jaret had pointed at him soon after arriving on the South Pacific island of Waters Deep to rescue Lionel.

"Have you ever wondered why you look so strange?" Lye asked, his gun still aimed mercilessly at Ret. "Why your hair is so blonde, your eyes so blue, your skin so pale? It's because you have uranium in your blood—a discovery I attribute to your dear friend, Lionel Zarbock. You see, he told me about your visit to the nuclear power plant some months ago and how your body had a unique reaction when it was exposed to the radiation from the reactor."

"Lionel would—" Ret breathed, gasping for breath, "he would never—never tell you."

"Ah, but he did, Ret," Lye countered, "not willingly though. After I took him prisoner on Fire Island, I brought my old friend back to the Deep, where

I," with a sick smile, *"questioned* him." He laughed in his throat. "It's remarkable what people will tell you once you torture them long enough."

Ret wanted to speak in reply but couldn't find the strength to do so. His skin was speckled with red drops of blood, which were being squeezed out of his pores. Racked with pain, there were long, narrow grooves on the ground where he had dragged his fingers through the dirt.

"Isn't this invention amazing, Ret?" Lye continued to exalt himself. "I call it my fission gun. Within this chamber," he said, pointing to the enclosed rectangular portion above the trigger, "a nuclear fission reaction is taking place, splitting uranium atoms. The radiation is being channeled through the barrel and in your general direction, causing the uranium atoms in your bloodstream to rupture. Supposedly, radiation is harmful, but what do you think?" He threw his head back and emitted a wicked cackle.

"Can you feel it, Ret?—the superiority of nuclear power? It's the greatest known power in the universe! With the Oracle, you may be able to control the elements, but with this weapon, I am able to control *you!* I couldn't just let you waltz right into my Vault and steal my element. This is my personal treasury! It's taken me centuries to amass my vast fortune. Without it, I would hardly be able to fund my secret societies all across the globe. You see, once your lousy First Father scattered the elements, I knew there were two elements that I had to find first if I was ever to have the physical stamina and financial capital to find the other four. It took years, but I found them—both of them—and they'll be the last two elements that you and I return to the Oracle, once I relocate my operations here and at the Deep. That's right: just you and me, Ret. Like I told you before, we have to do this together. And if you won't come willingly, then I'm afraid I'll just have to be a little trigger-happy."

Ret was unconscious by now. He was lying face-down on the dirt floor, his clothes stained with his own blood. With eyes closed, he looked like he was dead, though he was still breathing—faintly.

"Now, you wait here while I go and take care of your friends," Lye said cheerily, finally powering down the fission gun. "I'm sure they're *dying* to see me." He took a few steps back and placed his weapon inside the mouth of the dark tunnel for safe keeping. Then he walked back to the center of the room and crouched down next to Ret. He retrieved a small, glass vial from within his flowing black robes and scooped a sample of Ret's blood before corking it and returning it to his pocket. Then he picked up the Oracle. His eyes lit up with wonder, as if he had just accomplished his fondest dream. The sparkling light of the transparent sphere was reflected in his white pupils. He smiled with elation, exposing his pointed and petrified teeth.

Leaving Ret lifelessly on the ground, Lye marched triumphantly toward the great stone camel where Ret had entered. He had nearly left the shadows and started up the ramp when he bumped into something, which abruptly halted his ascent into the Vault. The obstruction was certainly as tall and impassable as a brick wall, but it wasn't quite as hard as one. Lye stepped back and took a closer look amid the darkness. It was Conrad.

"Whoa!" Lye marveled playfully, sizing up the giant who was standing in his way. "What did your mother feed you?" Though stunned by Conrad's size, Lye was obviously not intimidated. "Here to relieve the camel, are you?"

Without a word, Conrad dealt Lye a bone-crushing backhand, flinging the feeble elder into the air and across the room like a toothpick. The evil lord landed close to Ret, who was still comatose. Dazed, Lye sat up and tried to collect his composure, but Conrad wouldn't allow it. He was already coming towards Lye at a full gallop, shaking the ground with each thundering step. Before Lye could crawl away, Conrad yanked the evil lord by the train of his long robes and swung him into the wall, where he flopped onto the floor.

With the aid of his staff, Lye shakily rose to his feet. One of his eyes was black and blue, and there was a thin stream of blood dribbling from his bottom lip. With a face to scare night into morning, Conrad stomped towards his foe. With uncharacteristic trepidation, Lye turned to a specific section of the wall, which he began to feel with his wrinkled hands like a repairman searching for a wooden stud. Quickly finding some kind of sweet spot, he drove the end of his cane into the clay wall, zapped it with a pulse of electricity, and then yanked the cane out. Like striking oil, water started to squirt into the room. It poured in from some unknown source of immensely pressurized water, as if Lye had punctured a dam.

Just before Conrad could lay his hands on him, Lye spun around and struck the aborigine with a continuous stream of water. It blasted Conrad clear across the room and a few feet into the opposite wall. Then Lye relinquished the geyser and leaned on his cane, gasping for breath.

After a few seconds of stillness, the sounds of movement were heard from the hole in the wall where Conrad had been jettisoned. Lye couldn't see what was going on with so much water and dust in the way. All of a sudden, a massive boulder came hurtling toward Lye. He dove out of its way and watched as it lodged into the water hole, sealing Lye's source. Using what liquid was left in the room, Lye resumed his role as a human fire hydrant, but Conrad met it head-on. With all his weight, he collided with Lye's water spout. It forced him back a few steps, but Conrad dug his feet into the dirt and pushed back. Exerting all his strength, he put one foot in front of the other in his steady trek toward Lye, his hands extended to deflect the water.

As soon as their fingers met, Conrad gripped Lye's hands, which shut off the water, and then headbutted him, forehead to forehead. Conrad heard a snap and was confused when Lye's head did not spring back right away but instead stayed cocked back. Utilizing his opponent's vexation, Lye flung his head back into place, twisted it back into alignment with a pop, and then grasped his cane.

There was a blinding flash of light, and Conrad was repelled by a brilliant bolt of electricity. He flew through the air and landed several yards away but quickly jumped to his feet. From across the room, Lye continued to shoot electrical currents at Conrad, but they merely bounced off his body. The bolts could not penetrate his thick, scarred skin, so they merely flitted atop it before fizzling out. Lye was dumbfounded, wondering to himself, "Who is this guy?"

Conrad knelt on the ground and plunged his fists into the dirt. He wrapped his fingers around one of the metallic veins running along the floor and broke a long piece of it free. With metal pipe in hand, he charged at Lye, deflecting dozens of electrical currents with his pole. When he arrived in front of Lye, he swatted away his cane and wrapped his own around Lye's body, bending the metal with his bare hands. Fear seized Lye's face as Conrad finished the fight with a spinning back kick, launching the evil lord like a hockey puck.

At this point, Lye looked about as close to death as Ret. Breathing with great difficulty and coughing up blood, Lye was badly bruised and internally crushed. More than one of his brittle bones was broken, and his whole body was shaking in shock. He had been hammered by Conrad—pummeled and pulverized—and his ancient body was now on the verge of death.

With his few final breaths, Lye rolled onto his side, his white hair and beard soiled by blood and dirt. With trembling hand, he reached into his robes and pulled out a flask. Gripping it tightly, he took several gulps from it, looking as though his life depended on it. With a sigh, he removed the flask from his lips and returned it to his robes. Within seconds, his wounds were healed, a few wrinkles disappeared, and a splash of color returned to his gaunt face. With supernatural strength, he bent back the bar that Conrad had wrapped around him and discarded it. Then, bearing a smile that spelled trouble, he silently rose to his feet and set out to find his cane.

Meanwhile, Conrad was busy resuming the task of procuring the element. As soon as he had tossed Lye out of the ring, he tracked down the Oracle, which had long since fallen from Lye's grasp. Then he hurried to Ret's side, falling to one knee and inspecting him with great concern. Having watched Ret try and collect the ore element before Lye intervened, Conrad rolled Ret onto his back, brought his hands together, and set them gently on his chest with the palms up. Then he placed the Oracle in Ret's limp hands and waited for the scars to align. When the sphere was beginning to open once again, Conrad slid his large hands under Ret's body and prepared to lift him up so that the Oracle could easily close around the element.

But Lye begged to differ. Just before Conrad elevated Ret's body, Lye appeared from behind and stabbed Conrad in the back with his cane. With renewed strength, Lye pierced the giant's tough skin and wedged the pointed end of his staff into Conrad's spine. With a deafening roar that rattled the earth, Conrad released Ret and shot up in pain, still on his knees and stiff as a board. Then Lye channeled every watt of electrical power possible and electrocuted Conrad to the bone. Conrad's skeletal system lit up like neon. His eye sockets went blank. Smoke began to rise from his body. When Lye at last felt avenged, he dragged Conrad from Ret's side and flung him away. Like dead weight, the fried aborigine crashed onto the floor at the foot of the stone camel and didn't budge.

Without a sound, a small head peeked from behind the backside of the camel. It was Leo. From the relative safety of his hiding place in the shadows behind the statue, he had observed the entire altercation—first the exchange between Ret and Lye, then the showdown between Conrad and Lye. With helplessness, he had watched Lye subdue Ret, wishing he could stop such torturous treatment but knowing there was little he could do. Then, in idle silence, he had also witnessed Conrad fall to Lye's devilish devices, again pained by his inability to help—to do something, anything. Now that his protector was lying before him, facedown and lifeless, Leo was feeling even more guilty, weak, and afraid.

He was somewhat startled when he suddenly saw Conrad move. His flesh still steaming, the massive man brought his chin up until he could see Leo. Then he slowly dragged his arm forward and laid his fist before his small friend, as if presenting a gift. When he relaxed his fingers, Leo saw a neuroscope resting in his palm.

Leo decided to put the device on his head. He glanced at the neuroscope on Conrad's head a few times to make sure he was doing it correctly. When he had done so, he looked into Conrad's deep, brown eyes and felt an external thought enter his brain.

"The mind is stronger than the body," Conrad taught Leo through thought. Conrad removed his neuro-

scope and handed it to Leo. Then he collapsed to the floor, never to move again. Leo waited for Conrad to show the slightest sign of life, but he was dead. The martyr had given his life for Ret and the cause of the Oracle.

Conrad's words (and the miraculous manner in which they were communicated) gave Leo an idea. He may not have had much muscle, but his mind was in as good of shape as was Conrad's body. Leo removed the neuroscope that was on his head, retained it, and put on Conrad's personal one instead. Then he quietly climbed onto the back of the camel.

"Well," said Lye with an air of accomplishment, as if Ret could hear him, "now that Godzilla's history, I'll be on my way." Then, bending down and plucking the Oracle out of Ret's hands, he added, "Not without this, of course." The sphere's wedges had reclosed once again.

Lye began his second jaunt toward the ramp, admiring the Oracle every step of the way. When he arrived at the camel, he stopped and peered over his nose at Conrad. He prodded the electrocuted body with his cane a few times, as if to ensure it was dead. Lye had underestimated Conrad; the brute had certainly given the evil lord a run for his money.

"What a waste of a life," Lye mocked. "Once a slave, always a slave."

Lye's eulogy of enmity provided Leo with just enough time. From his perch atop the camel's hump, he slipped the second neuroscope on Lye's brow. He tried to do it as inconspicuously as Mr. Coy's elevator had done so to him, and it helped that Lye's long white hair covered his temples. As soon as the neuroscope was in place, Leo executed his plan.

"Drop the Oracle."

As if it was his own thought, Lye's nervous system obeyed the internal stimulus, and he released the Oracle.

"What the devil?" Lye said when he saw what he had done.

Leo slid down the camel, picked up the Oracle, and made a beeline for Ret.

"Where did you come from?!" Lye hissed with outrage as Leo ran away with the sphere. "Give me that ball!"

Lye was about to fire a stupefying blast of electricity at Leo from his cane when a different directive entered his mind.

"Shoot the camel."

At the last minute, Lye's hand involuntarily jerked his cane to the side, shooting a bolt at the stone camel. Upon doing so, the camel's upper half exploded, throwing Lye halfway up the ramp. Lye's neuroscope flew off his head, and the camel's detached hump fell onto Lye's robes, immobilizing him.

While Lye continued to squirm, Leo's veins were surging with adrenaline. Now that Lye's neuroscope had been disconnected, he stopped focusing on influencing Lye and instead redirected his thoughts to his own actions. Like a batter sliding into home, he arrived at Ret's side and promptly placed the Oracle in his hands. Then he cupped them tightly together and pulled them up until the Oracle's six wedges were within reach of the ore element.

With hot displeasure, Lye finally managed to blast his way out from underneath the large and jagged stone. He emerged just in time to watch the ore element return to its rightful place within the Oracle.

As it had done twice before, the earth immediately reacted to the collection of the third element. For a moment, the world went mute—all sound was snuffed out. A powerful force, like a mighty wind, pulled everything inward, as if a black hole had emerged in the spot where the element used to be. It was so strong, in fact, that Leo and Ret were pulled over the edge and into the bottomless pit. They would have fallen into oblivion if the powerful, pulling force had not reversed suddenly. Like the secondary wave of an earthquake, this second thrust was much longer and much more potent, pushing everything away from its epicenter. Like vomit, Leo and Ret were expelled out of the bottomless shaft and thrown up onto the floor.

The world was in upheaval now. The ground was shaking continuously. The walls were cracking profusely. Chunks were falling from the ceiling. The Vault was in a state of irreversible meltdown—and, as such, Lye was in a state of pure and utter horror. A truly miserable look of overmastering terror had seized his black heart. He was in disbelief.

It took another tremor to shake him from his incredulity. He ran up the remaining portion of the ramp and into his crumbling pyramid of wealth.

"No," he said with subdued shock. "No, not my Vault—not my money."

He strode from place to place, trying to fill his robes with goods.

"This can't happen—I won't let this happen."

He frantically moved from treasure heap to treasure heap, stuffing his pockets with as much as they could hold. Suddenly, large cracks began to open up in the ground, swallowing entire piles whole.

"No! Stop!" He shot the fissures with bolts of electricity, pointlessly trying to reseal them. Then huge golden pieces of the pyramid's walls started to break away and crash to the floor.

"No! Wait!" Lye gave up trying to fix the ground and focused on holding up the ceiling. Like lightning, he sent great, crackling streaks of electricity at the collapsing walls, desperately trying to keep them up.

Plumes of paper currency filled the air like flocks of birds, with Lye trying to grab hold of every bill.

But it was all to no avail.

Leo knew there was no time to lose. He jammed the Oracle in Ret's pocket and knelt as low to the ground as he could. He flung Ret's arm over his shoulder and staggered to his feet. The load was heavy, and Leo was dragging Ret more than he was carrying him, but he tried not to think about it. He headed for the dark tunnel, on the other side of the room from the ramp and camel. Just when he entered the mouth of the tunnel, he looked back. It killed him to leave Conrad, but the giant hadn't moved a muscle since delivering his neuroscope to Leo.

Another tremor struck. The room reeled. A large slice of the ceiling caved in. Leo saw the fission gun sitting on the ground near his feet, right where Lye had left it. He picked it up and strapped it to his back. Then he pressed on.

Even as he hauled Ret further and further away, Leo could hear Lye in the distance, mourning his losses with great shouts of weeping and wailing that echoed deep into the tunnel.

"NO! NO! NO!"

CHAPTER 23

RAZING THE ROOF

"What's taking them so long?" Ana asked, glaring hopefully at the door through which Mr. Coy and Lydia had entered the nearby building several minutes ago.

"I don't know," Paige said with worry. "I hope they're okay."

The girls had ample cause to be concerned, not only for the adults' safety but also for their own. It didn't take long before the stationary CAVE was spotted by the compound's security cameras. Eventually, a pair of guards sauntered toward the CAVE, sent to investigate the foreign vehicle on the premises.

"This can't be good," Paige observed, noticing the approaching guards in the distance.

"Don't move," Ana said in a hushed tone, crouching down in the backseat. "Maybe we're just parked in a red or something."

Frozen stiff, the girls waited in silence as the guards slowly walked around the CAVE, inspecting its unique features. After a few uneasy moments, one of them tried to open the driver's door but found it locked. One by one, he tried the remaining doors and then the hood and trunk but was denied each time. Finally, his partner began to strike the window on the driver's side with the butt of his gun, hoping to shatter it and gain access.

"Look!" Paige whispered. "The glass is starting to crack!" It was requiring all his strength, but after several repeated hits, the thick glass was beginning to give way.

"I'll handle this," Ana stepped forward with all confidence, climbing into the front seat.

Surprised to find an occupant in the vehicle, the guard recoiled and stopped rapping the window.

Ana rolled the window down halfway and said, "I'll take two cheeseburgers with fries and a large Coke, please."

Confused, the guard replied with a thick Arabic accent, "Coke?"

"Yeah, you know, Coca-Cola?" Ana explained. "And go heavy on the ice—it's a scorcher out here."

The guard, now more annoyed than anything else, demanded, "Do you have the sign?"

"Sign?" Ana questioned.

"Yeah, you know," replied the guard, mocking Ana with her own words, "you give us the sign or else you die."

"Oh, that sign," said Ana. "Hold on, let me check." She quickly turned to Paige, still hiding in the backseat.

Mouthing the words, Paige asked, "What should we do?"

Ana turned back and, while rolling up the window, quickly told the guard, "I'm sorry, but we're not hungry after all. Ciao!"

Thoroughly miffed, the guard recommenced his assault on the window, wreaking havoc on the tempered glass. Then his comrade appeared on the passenger side and wedged a tool into the doorjamb, trying to pry it open.

"Do something!" Ana yelled desperately, as Paige climbed into the front seat. "Anything!"

"I'm trying," Paige told her while randomly pulling the levers and twisting the knobs that covered the control panel. From the horn to the headlights, the CAVE began to make beeping noises and emit flashing lights. Then Paige pressed one button that sent an electrical current across the CAVE's exterior, shocking the guards through their weapons. Stunned, the guards abandoned their design and ran away.

"Serves you right," Ana told them victoriously.

But Ana had spoken too soon. Suddenly, an armored truck appeared around the corner of the building, driving towards the CAVE at full speed.

"Quick—give me the keys!" Ana ordered.

"Use your finger," said Paige.

"What?"

"Your finger acts as the key," Paige explained. "It comes standard on all Coy vehicles."

Ana inserted the tip of her finger into the ignition slot, then quickly pulled it back when she felt a slight shock.

"Ouch!"

Suddenly, a calm computer voice announced, "Access denied."

"Oh, I forgot," said Paige. "It's fingerprint activated. You must not be in the database."

"How rude!" Ana said to the computer voice, massaging her finger.

Paige took her turn. The engine started with a roar.

"Finally," Ana sighed, throwing the transmission into drive.

"You can't drive!" Paige countered. "You don't even have your license!"

"Don't worry, P," said Ana, staring straight ahead at the oncoming truck. "If there's one thing I *can* do, it's hit stuff."

Flooring the gas pedal, the CAVE screeched forward, approaching the truck head-on. Unwilling to play chicken, Paige resumed pressing buttons. She was relieved when the CAVE's metal decal, situated front and center on the hood and in the shape of a koi fish, shot a laser from its mouth at the truck, severing it in half down the middle. Just before the two vehicles were to collide, the truck's two-wheeled halves parted and rolled a little ways before falling over.

"See?" Ana remarked to Paige. "What'd I tell you?" Paige rolled her eyes.

But the struggle was just getting started. As if the compound's entire security force had been alerted, hordes of guards came charging out of the unnamed buildings, driving a wide array of vehicles.

"Alright," said Paige, cracking her knuckles as she surveyed the levers and knobs. "Let's see what this thing can do."

With Ana at the wheel, Paige tested the limits of the CAVE, bringing new meaning to the *extraordinaire* part of its acronym. When a rocket launcher emerged above the roof, Paige drained its arsenal, blowing holes in the walls of nearby buildings and causing trucks to flee for safety. Still randomly pressing buttons, grenades began to shoot out from the CAVE's wheel wells, as if being launched from a skeet thrower. Sticky goo, sharp tacks, some kind of harpoon thing—Paige didn't know what all was being discharged from the CAVE, but it seemed to be doing the job of keeping them safe.

Suddenly, one of the CAVE's front tires popped. The girls weren't sure of the cause, what with so much chaos in the compound, smoke in the air, and debris on the ground. They were relieved when the CAVE fixed itself like a vending machine, releasing the old tire and pushing a new one out from the inner reaches of the axle.

"Heck with a Hummer," Ana cheered. "I've got to get me one of *these!*"

The cheers of celebration quickly turned into shrieks of fright, however, when the girls passed through a blanket of smoke and saw a cement wall only yards in front of them. Ana slammed the brakes but not soon enough. The CAVE plowed through the wall, coming to a halt with half of the vehicle sitting inside the building. As it turned out, it was the same building that Mr. Coy and Lydia had entered.

Amidst all the commotion, neither Paige nor Ana had noticed the reopening of the main gate to the underground access road. A long line of backlogged traffic began to arrive aboveground. There was a steady stream of trucks, one of which was hauling the open-top trailer of coal where Ishmael was concealed. Peering over the top of the trailer, Ishmael saw the smoke rising above the destruction that Paige and Ana had caused. Then he saw the back half of the CAVE protruding from one of the buildings. He leapt from the trailer and ran over to the scene.

Just as Ishmael arrived at the rear of the CAVE, Mr. Coy appeared at the front half inside the building.

"Ishmael!" he rejoiced. "You're okay!"

Ishmael was about to utter a similarly happy salutation when he noticed something shiny in Mr. Coy's hands. Recognizing the familiar object, a sudden horror gripped Ishmael's face.

Mr. Coy fell silent. He had just come from the board room where he had spoken with the masters. He looked down at his hands. He was holding the metal clasp that Lydia had worn around her neck for so many years, having picked it out of the pile of her ashes. It was the one thing that hadn't been dissolved by the lotus flower extract.

"I'm sorry, Ishmael," Coy mourned.

Crushed, Ishmael fell to his knees, put his face in his hands, and groaned a soft but painful, "No."

But there was no time to explain, for suddenly a powerful tremor shook the ground, knocking both Mr. Coy and Ishmael completely to the floor. The shockwave seemed to originate from the nearby pyramid as it shot out across the sands in all directions. Mr. Coy knew it was no common quake—it was the earth's signal that one of its six, original elements had returned to the Oracle.

"That's our cue," Mr. Coy announced, jumping to his feet and rushing to the CAVE.

Ana and Paige seemed to know their joyride was over. They climbed into the backseat just as Mr. Coy slid behind the wheel and Ishmael into the passenger seat.

"Where are we going, Dad?" Paige asked, as her father fired up the CAVE.

"We've got about three minutes to find Conrad and Leo before this place implodes," Mr. Coy explained. "Buckle up!" He put the vehicle in reverse and backed out of the building just before the entire structure collapsed.

The whole landscape was in turmoil now, with buildings buckling left and right. The ground was in a state of continuous agitation. Like a frozen lake thawing in early spring, large swaths of the desert floor were breaking apart. It was a reminder that the whole area aboveground had been unwisely built on the ceiling of the underground basin—a foundation that had suddenly lost its support by the procurement of the ore element. Starting at the pyramid, the brittle ground began to crumble, falling to the riverbed far below.

"What about Ret?" Paige asked in earnest.

"Don't worry, dear; we'll find him, too," Mr. Coy reassured her. "But Ret can hold his own; it's the other two I'm worried about."

Mr. Coy was speeding toward the main gate of the access road. The CAVE was the only vehicle attempting to return underground, as all other drivers were panicked and desperately striving to escape the falling roof. The CAVE was nearing the gate when the access road suddenly disappeared. The CAVE screeched to a halt, and its passengers watched as the access road broke away from the riverbank and crumbled to the floor, taking all of its traffic with it.

Idling on the edge of the riverbed, Mr. Coy and the others witnessed an amazing event taking place before their very eyes. The ceiling of the underground basin was collapsing like a long row of falling dominoes. It had started at the pyramid and was stretching westward continuously, following the natural course of the Great River. The absence of the ore element had sent a global shockwave that was causing the sandy ceiling to crumble like clumps of packed brown sugar. The group marveled as the phenomenon raced out of sight, the brilliant Saharan sun chasing away the shadows that concealed the dried river. After centuries of being hidden, the mystery of the Great River was finally coming to light, destroying the craft of a dark and ancient secret.

"Look!" Paige shouted, more concerned about where Ret was. She was pointing at the base of the crumbling pyramid.

Straining their vision, everyone focused on a small hole from which a familiar figure was emerging. It looked like the opening to just another one of the many mines and tunnels that dotted the sloped sides of the riverbed, although this one was very near the base of the pyramid.

"It's Leo!" Ana beamed with relief.

Then they watched with alarm as Leo stepped out of the tunnel with Ret leaning heavily on his shoulder.

"Oh no, what's wrong with Ret?" Ishmael asked the question that was on everyone's lips.

"He looks hurt," Mr. Coy pointed out.

Though still weak, Ret had bounced back into consciousness, thanks to all of the quaking and shaking. Strength was slowly returning to his exhausted body, but he was still relying substantially on Leo for support.

Terror then seized every heart in the CAVE when they saw the pyramid cave in on itself. The hollow structure had finally succumbed to gravity and was now tumbling to the earth.

"Ret—watch out!" Paige screamed, but it was no use. Catching sight of the wave of bricks falling towards them, Leo pushed Ret back into the tunnel and dove in after him to escape the impending avalanche. Then the tunnel was swallowed from view by the deluge of stone and dust.

Thus was the inglorious end of the mighty pyramid of wealth. What had once been idolized as an icon of ultimate influence now lay in one giant heap of ruins, toppled and flattened by a power far greater than its own. Like a potter to his clay, Ret had turned upside-down the force that, as Lye had claimed, ruled the world with an invisible hand.

When the last of the pyramid's golden bricks had crashed to the ground, a brief moment of profound calm ensued. The earth ceased its terrible shaking. With hardly any breeze in the warm air, the massive plume of dust took its time dissipating. Every pair of eyes in the CAVE was glaring unblinkingly at the place where they had last seen Ret and Leo, praying for some sign that they had survived.

Relief filled the CAVE when they saw the rubble begin to part. Like a clogged rain gutter breaking through its debris, the mess of golden blocks and sandy stone blocking the tunnel was being pushed away, creating a clean path. Ret was standing in the mouth of the tunnel with his hands outstretched. Leo was directly behind him, supporting Ret's back and holding up his arms.

"They're okay!" Ana sang with joy.

Mr. Coy immediately set out to pick up the two stranded young men. With its false ceiling gone, the body of the Great River was fully exposed. Mr. Coy rolled to the edge of the nearest bank and then drove into the dried river. It was a fairly steep descent, one that took their stomachs by surprise. The ground was covered in large clumps of sand—remnants of the roof—that easily broke apart under the CAVE's sturdy wheels. The industrial complex had been completely demolished and was now buried in a thick layer of sand. Only the tallest cranes and highest oil derricks poked above the remains of the fallen ceiling.

Paige was sitting on the edge of the backseat, leaning forward and gripping her father's headrest. She kept a constant eye on Ret. It worried her that he looked so weak. As soon as the CAVE came to a stop, she bolted out the door and rushed to Ret's side. Like a crutch, she slid under his arm, with Leo bracing the other.

"You alright, bro?" Ana asked, arriving next to Leo. "There's blood all over your shirt!"

"Been better," Ret replied with something of a smile. His optimism brought a grin to everyone's face.

"Where's Conrad?" Mr. Coy wondered, gently helping Ret into the CAVE.

There was only one person in the group who knew the answer to that question. Leo stepped forward to Mr. Coy and held out his fist. Mr. Coy extended his hand and a neuroscope fell into it.

The fact that he was holding Conrad's neuroscope was answer enough. Mr. Coy had never seen the aborigine take it off since it was given to him.

Coy looked down and sighed with sadness, "How did it happen?"

"It was Lye, sir," Leo explained. "Conrad died saving Ret."

"He did what?" Ret gasped, having been unconscious during the entire showdown.

"You should've seen him," Leo said with amazement. "He beat up on Lye so bad that I kinda felt sorry for the old guy."

"I would, too," Coy admitted, wincing at the thought of fighting against Conrad. "But how did Lye know we were here? I never saw any signs that he was following us."

Ret spoke up, "He already knew the location of the ore—"

Panic silenced Ret's voice. It suddenly occurred to him that he didn't know who had collected the element. His hand shot into his pocket to check on the Oracle. The distress vanished when he saw a golden wedge.

"Faithful to the end," Mr. Coy beamed in tribute of Conrad.

Leo was glad he was the only one among them who knew what actually happened in the element room with Lye. It wasn't in his nature to exalt himself, so he happily glossed over the essential role he himself had played in the procurement of the element and the rescue of Ret.

With so much to tell each other, the reunion would have lasted much longer had it not been interrupted by a disconcerting noise. It was a sound like the rushing of great waters—a low roar like waves crashing on a shore—and it was getting louder. When the small particles of sand at their feet began to bounce around chaotically, they knew they were not yet in the clear. Rattled to its core, the planet was now reacting to the great change that had just occurred.

Mr. Coy turned around and looked beyond the rubble. Not far behind the foundation of the caved-in pyramid stood a massive, earthen wall. Deep and thick, it stretched from bank to bank and from top to bottom of the Great River. From their low vantage point on the floor of the riverbed, it seemed to the group that the wall was nothing more than the end of the Great River. In reality, however, it was actually a dam, which completely sealed off the nearby Nile River from where it once connected to the Great River. But that was about to change.

Now that the sustaining and stabilizing influences of the element and pyramid were gone, the dam was being washed away like a sandcastle at the beach. Fractured and broken, the dam rapidly burst apart, and the full force of the Nile came charging directly toward the group. Standing in the absolute worst place possible, the six souls craned their necks to stare at the mountainous tsunami, which threatened to send them all to an immediate, watery grave.

METALS OF HONOR

"Everyone get in—now!" Mr. Coy yelled. In panic mode, everyone scrambled into the CAVE. Leo squeezed into the front seat with Ishmael while Paige and the Coopers crammed into the backseat. The wheels started moving even before the last door was shut.

Mr. Coy floored the gas pedal and never eased up. Now that the riverbed had been buried in a thick, uniform layer of sand, there were practically no bumps to avoid or debris to dodge. Like traveling the German autobahns, Mr. Coy threw caution to the wind and drove as fast as the CAVE could go, sending a wild spray of sand in its wake.

In very little time, they arrived at the bend in the basin where, not long before, they had turned and laid their eyes on the city of gold for the first time. On account of his speed, Mr. Coy made a wide turn, even going up on the slope of the riverbank for a bit.

When the CAVE reached its top speed, it became clear that it would be impossible for them to outrun the tidal wave. It was gaining on them, and several drops of water had already splashed on the back window. A literal river was nipping at their wheels, inching closer every second. The floodgates had failed, releasing millions upon millions of gallons of water, now stampeding toward them like legions of hoofed creatures. When the tsunami arrived at the bend, it crashed into the far side of the curve, carving away a significant portion of the riverbank and erupting skyward like a mighty geyser. But, unabated, the water flowed onward, even more tumultuously than before. Overflowing with raw power, it licked the sides of the Great River and heaved itself beyond its banks up onto the desert floor.

"Can we get aboveground somehow?" Ishmael asked.

"Not likely at this speed," Mr. Coy replied.

"Please tell me this thing can fly," Ana importuned the driver.

"Not over long distances," Coy replied, "but it can swim." Paige shot Ret a look of concern.

The water had fallen upon them now. The passengers could feel the wheels lose traction and begin to slide, as if hydroplaning. When the CAVE was at last overtaken, the force of the current made it impossible to steer, and it seemed they were doomed to ride out the storm like a tiny pebble among raging rapids. Fortunately, however, they were riding in a Coy-mobile.

Mr. Coy reached for the control panel and pressed a button called *amphibian mode*. The occupants heard and felt something mechanical going on within the CAVE. The vehicle extraordinaire retracted its wheels and replaced them with submersible pumps, which were something of a cross between the engines of an airplane and the jets of a Jacuzzi. Fully rotational, the pumps drew in water and then forcefully expelled it, and the CAVE was propelled in the opposite direction of the flow of the discharged water. To go up, Mr. Coy turned the pump so that its intake was from the top. To go right, he made sure the discharge was leftward.

In true Coy manner, what had once been a fright-fully dangerous situation was now a pleasantly educa-tional one. The CAVE had been repurposed into a submarine of sorts, and, now that the threat of death had passed, its crew glued their faces to the windows in eager observation.

The tides were changing for the desert, and the wonder was born of one simple ingredient: water. The availability of water was the single most delineating feature between the Amazon Rainforest and the Sahara

Desert, insofar as Ret could tell. Both regions had plenty of sun, sky, and earth, but because the Amazon had water (and lots of it), it was brimming with life while the parched Sahara was barren with death.

Now, however, the desert's imbalance was being undone.

But the roots of such a miracle ran much deeper than water. As monumental as the refilling of the Great River was, there was much more at work than merely grand-scale plumbing. The waves were not only washing away underground schemes that had existed for centuries but also ushering in forfeited dreams that had been postponed for generations. In the flood, the jewels of injustice were drowning while the rights of humanity were dawning. Gone were the years of satiating greed; now were the days of alleviating need.

When the Great River ran dry so long ago, it jaggedly stretched across the continent like an open wound, bringing pain to everything near it. Instead of applying stitches, Lye drained it for its riches. The sore was never doctored up but merely covered up, allowing it to fester and spread. Only when Ret and his brave allies intervened did recovery commence. Now, with sutures secured and ointment poured, the Great River would become a fine scar, a reminder of the impact that even just a few, unskilled hands can have in the effort to cure the world.

Mr. Coy purposely maneuvered the CAVE out of the choppy headwaters, keeping the craft equidistant between both riverbanks but close to the surface where the flow seemed to be the least turbulent. Like a large and lazy fish, the truly all-terrain vehicle floated along with the quick but nonthreatening current. It carried them westward through the desert, back the way they had previously come. They rode the waves for several hours, quite content to sit back and relax after experiencing such an exhilarating and exhausting string of events.

They each took turns explaining the parts they had played in the group effort of collecting the ore element. Ishmael told how he narrowly escaped being blown to bits, becoming a stowaway on a coal truck. Ana and Paige bragged about their rampageous rendezvous through the office buildings. After summarizing his meeting with the masters, Mr. Coy gave the play-by-play of the final minutes of Lydia's life, extolling her heroic deeds and employing ample admiration to soothe Ishmael's sorrow. Ret rehashed as much as he could remember about the pyramid's wealth and Lye's words. Then Leo took over. Mr. Coy was very intrigued by the fission gun and was glad that it was now in their possession.

Near the end of all the recollection, Mr. Coy's attention turned to the gauges and meters on the control panel. He had been keeping an eye on them for a while, but they were now showing greater activity.

"Well that's interesting," he said to himself, reading some of the measurements.

"What is it, Ben?' Ishmael asked.

"The CAVE's sensors are picking up something in the water," Coy said unalarmed. "Salinity, pH, density— they've all been increasing slightly."

Ana whispered to Paige, "Translation?"

"The water's getting saltier," Paige explained.

"There must be a lot of salt along the dried riverbed," Ret hypothesized.

"That's probably true, but I'm not sure mineral salts would dissolve so fast," Mr. Coy stated. "It must be sea salt."

"But the Nile is a freshwater river," Ishmael pointed out.

"Maybe it's from the Mediterranean Sea," Leo said. It was one of those ideas that was so out there that it just might be true—and, oddly enough, it *was* true.

Mr. Coy's hand shot to the GPS on the center console. He changed the screen settings to show a live satellite image of the earth. He adjusted the globe and zoomed in until he could see the Nile delta. The screen flashed every few seconds, updating the live content.

"Incredible!" Mr. Coy gasped. "It would seem you are correct, Swain." By the looks of it, there was obviously something very unusual going on in the region of the Nile delta. The Great River was being backfilled at the expense of the Mediterranean Sea. There was saltwater flowing from the sea, south through the delta, and into the Great River, and there was also freshwater pouring in from the northern flow of the Nile. The angle of the white, frothy waves indicated which way the flow was moving.

"So the Great River is draining the Mediterranean Sea?" Ret deduced.

"Yep," Mr. Coy sighed, massaging his forehead. "We just created an international crisis, folks."

"All that saltwater in the delta is going to devastate the farmlands," Ishmael concluded.

"Not to mention the potable water," Coy added.

"And I wonder where all of this water is going?" said Ishmael. "Will it empty into the Atlantic? Connect with the Niger River? Flow right through Monrovia? Pool up and become a huge lake in the middle of the Sahara?"

Feeling a sense of dismay growing within Ret, Paige quickly inserted, "But the saltwater should be good for the Great River, right? It'll cleanse all the dirt and grime, won't it?"

"Ever an optimist," Coy smiled.

"And if the continents ever rejoin," Leo said, "the Amazon could reverse the flow of the Great River back to normal, couldn't it?"

"One thing is for sure," Mr. Coy said, using a tone of closure to end the speculation. "It's only a matter of time before the world comes knocking on your door, Ret. And I'm willing to bet they won't be happy."

Mr. Coy's sobering words silenced the conversation. Paige could see a blanket of stress fall over Ret. He seemed to sink in his seat under the weight of such a heavy and depressing mantle. She knew how much it pained him to know so much death and destruction had been caused at his hand. She knew how hard he was on himself—how quickly he forgave others but how slowly he forgave himself. She knew what he was thinking about—how both Conrad and Lydia had died for him; how an unknown number of other souls had been swallowed by the sand, whether or not they were innocent; how the cataclysmic changes would impact an entire nation, even the world, for untold years to come. She knew the agonizing irony of it all—that even though filling the Oracle was Ret's most earnest desire and his destiny, it broke his heart to do so. She remembered him asking her once, "Is there no other way?" She knew he was asking himself that very same question now, over and over again.

The one thing Paige *didn't* know was how to ease Ret's burdens. She wished there was some way that she could be of real, significant help to him. Granted, she was arguably his most devoted supporter—a lifelong loyalist, never a naysayer—who had tagged along on all of their exotic and dangerous adventures thus far. But she always had to leave her love at the entrance of the element location—at the foot of a mountain, at the mouth of a volcano, at the door of a pyramid—never accompanying him inside, where his greatest struggles always lurked. When she heard of Conrad and Leo's heroic rescue of Ret, she was displeased—in herself: she felt like she should have been there, too. But she wasn't there, at a time when Lye had brought Ret so close to death's door. She longed to be of real value—to provide substantial assistance instead of merely playing a supporting role—but how? She was willing to do anything to be more equally yoked with Ret.

In her helplessness, Paige couldn't hold back a silent tear. Ana took notice. She watched the teardrop slide noiselessly down her friend's cheek; then she glanced at her brother, his head down and eyes half-closed. She knew Paige was hurting because Ret was, and Ana slipped into similarly somber spirits.

Ever observant, Leo saw Ana lower her head in solemnity. He looked from her to Paige, then from Paige to Ret—finding the same, morose demeanor in triplicate. Leo, the newest member of the team, had yet to truly grasp the global gravity of this Oracle business until, in this instant, he caught sight of Ret's forlorn face. Somehow, in the midst of such a melancholy moment, many hearts became one, knit together in unity and love.

The Great River flowed ever onward, deeper and deeper into the desert. They had recently passed by the ruins, marking the place where they had fallen through the dry quicksand and into the underground basin for the first time. As they neared the remains of Ishmael's village, the Saharan native asked Mr. Coy if they could stop and go ashore. Of course, Mr. Coy obliged.

As the river wasn't quite full yet, Mr. Coy steered the amphibious CAVE to the water's edge and then reengaged the wheels so that he could drive the rest of the way to shore. After Mr. Coy parked, everyone got out and stretched.

Ret strode up to Mr. Coy and asked, "Do you have a shovel?" Without requesting an explanation, Mr. Coy walked to the back of the CAVE and began rummaging through the trunk. He knew he had some tools but didn't know where they had been packed since that had been Conrad's duty. Finally, he found a shovel and presented it to Ret, who promptly set off for the demolished village.

With great curiosity, everyone watched from a distance to see what Ret was up to. He trekked across the sand with a determined pace. Then he stopped at the edge of town and jammed his shovel into the ground—

repeatedly. The others looked at each other. It was obvious to them now. Ret was digging a grave.

Two of them, in fact. It didn't take long before the others joined him, each gripping some kind of tool. Without a word, they dug two graves, side by side—one much larger than the other. It was hard work in the late afternoon sun, the warm wind spraying sand in their faces. In a matter of seconds, Ret easily could have removed the sand with his power over earth. It was a truth that crossed everyone's mind at least once, usually while pausing to wipe the sweat from their forehead. But they all understood why he didn't.

When the holes were dug, Mr. Coy stepped in front of the larger of the two. He pulled Conrad's neuroscope out of his pocket and held it out over the grave. Before he let go, Ret touched it with his finger, coating the device in gold. Then Mr. Coy relinquished his grip.

After a few moments, Ishmael knelt at the foot of the smaller grave. In his hand was the metal clasp that his sister had wrongfully worn for so many years, its silvery finish shining in the waning sunlight. Just before Ishmael placed it in the grave, Ret knelt beside him. With his finger, he touched the clasp, turning it to gold, and broke it in half. Then he put his arm around Ishmael and watched him gently lower the symbol into the earth.

One by one, the others paid their respects, laying blue lotus flowers in the graves, which Mr. Coy had found among Lydia's bag of potions in the back of the CAVE.

"They're free," Ret said, looking down at the body-less graves. Then he laid his shovel over his shoulder and started back toward the CAVE, leaving the task of refilling the holes in the charge of Mother Nature.

Mr. Coy put his arm around his daughter and sighed, "Let's go home." They all turned and followed Ret's tracks.

"I'm afraid I won't be returning to Coy Manor with you," Ishmael announced calmly as they walked back together. "I feel I am needed here—in my homeland. A new day is dawning in the Sahara, with hope on its horizon, and I need to be here to welcome it. There is a great work to be done here, to be done in honor of my sister. She gave her life for the Sahara and its people, and I will give the rest of mine."

"I completely understand," Mr. Coy told him as they arrived at the CAVE.

But Ret wasn't there. Paige searched the area in alarm. She found him close by, sitting on the riverbank. He was gazing out over the expanse of swift-moving water. Paige exchanged smiles with Ana and Leo, all three sharing the same idea.

"What now is six must be one," Paige said with cheer as she walked up to Ret from behind.

"Earth's imbalance to be undone," Ana joined in, copying Paige in sitting down next to Ret.

"Fill the Oracle, pure elements reunite," Leo came next, continuing the recitation of the familiar prophecy.

There was a slight pause. The three supporters all leaned forward and stared at Ret with hopeful faces, waiting for him to finish the prophecy.

Ret couldn't suppress a grin and finally finished, "Cure the world; one line has the rite." His participation earned a playful round of applause, which gladdened his heart and brightened his sagging spirit.

"Three elements down, three to go," Ana summarized. All four of them were looking at the radiant Oracle in Ret's hand, three of its wedges now occupied.

"We're halfway there," Paige said with optimism.

"Any clue where we'll find the next one, Ret?" Leo asked, having loved the adventure of procuring the ore element.

"I have an idea," Ret said with uncertainty, "but Paige, your dad's not going to like it."

So there they sat on the bank of the Great River of ore, now resurrected and refilling. With the sphere's brilliance shining upon their faces and enlightening their minds, they discussed their joint future with the Oracle, each reaffirming his or her unwavering commitment. And, for a moment, Ret felt happy and strengthened, finding himself surrounded by eternal friends (and the spirits of two others), all of whom were as good as gold.

Made in the USA
San Bernardino, CA
23 March 2018